Norse Warrior

Norse Warrior

Book 1 in the Norseman series

By

Griff Hosker

Norse Warrior

Published by Sword Books Ltd 2024

Copyright © Griff Hosker 2024

The author has asserted their moral right under the Copyright, Designs and Patents Act, 1988, to be identified as the author of this work. All Rights reserved. No part of this publication may be reproduced, copied, stored in a retrieval system, or transmitted, in any form or by any means, without the prior written consent of the copyright holder, nor be otherwise circulated in any form of binding or cover other than that in which it is published and without a similar condition being imposed on the subsequent purchaser.

A CIP catalogue record for this title is available from the British Library.

Contents

Norse Warrior i
Prologue 3
Chapter 1 7
Chapter 2 18
Chapter 3 30
Chapter 4 42
Chapter 5 51
Chapter 6 60
Chapter 7 69
Chapter 8 78
Chapter 9 87
Chapter 10 96
Chapter 11 107
Chapter 12 118
Chapter 13 131
Chapter 14 141
Chapter 15 151
Chapter 16 164
Chapter 17 173
Chapter 18 183
Chapter 19 196
Chapter 20 208
Chapter 21 223
Chapter 22 233
Epilogue 245
Glossary 248
Historical Background 250
Other books by Griff Hosker 252

Norse Warrior

Prologue

Detmold – Saxony

Charles the Great or, as he was better known, Charlemagne, King of the Franks, King of the Lombards and Emperor of the Carolingian Empire sat astride his huge horse and viewed the enemy: masses of heathens and barbarians arrayed before him. They were a veritable sea of warriors and stretched as far as the eye could see. Above him fluttered the papal banner given to him by Pope Leo. The stars fluttered on a purple background and seemed to shimmer and shine like silver. It was a sign. He was doing God's work. The income from the Saxons he would rule would not compensate for the cost of maintaining order and building churches but he was building an Empire that was Christian and, thanks to his mighty army, peaceful. He had subdued the land of Pomerania and now would do the same further east in the land of the Saxons and the Frisians. When that was done, he could turn his eye to the north and subdue the barbarians and pagans who lived in the cold inhospitable lands to the north. The northern world would be Christian and it would be a monument to his devotion.

Emperor Charlemagne was a huge man. At more than six feet tall he towered over most men. With short hair and a moustache, he looked a different warrior to his father who wore his hair long. On his head he wore, not a helmet, but a crown. It was a symbol of his power as well as showing the confidence that he would not be threatened. His men would prevail.

The contrast between the two armies could not have been greater. While the barbarians milled around screaming insults and shouting challenges, his mounted warriors and his serried ranks of spearmen stood silently or prayed with the priests who marched along their ranks. The warriors wore well-made helmets, and the front ranks were mailed. They bore long spears, and some had lances. Their shields were not the crudely shaped ones held by the pagans but stoutly made and solid. That the Christians were outnumbered worried some of the emperor's advisors, especially the priests, but Charlemagne had confidence in his generals and his mounted warriors. They had defeated the

Wends, Pomeranians and Saxons in every battle as the papal banner was carried east.

His son, Charles who was also mounted on a magnificent horse, said, "Which one is Widukind, Father?"

Charlemagne pointed his baton at a figure who was also mounted and wearing mail. His mail and the horse marked him out quite clearly, for the rest of the army was made up of foot soldiers. "It is he, my son who leads the Saxons. Mark him for he is wily. I do not doubt that we shall defeat him but he will escape to fight us once more. When you lead your armies in Thuringia you may well face him. Hold firm your resolve and trust in God and our horsemen and you will succeed." Charles nodded. He had the same zeal as his father. The emperor judged the time to be right and said, quietly, "Give the order, my son, and let us go about God's business."

Charles was eager and ready. He turned to the herald next to him, "Sound the order for the advance."

The differences in the two armies became quite clear for every leader in the Frankish army knew what they had to do and, as the mailed men rode forward in a straight line, the barbarians just reacted. The Franks were disciplined and well-trained. The barbarians against whom they fought were not. Arrows were sent by the barbarians without any command being given. Most fell short of the line of advancing horsemen. Those that did strike did no damage. Shields, helmets and mail were too good for the Saxon arrows. As the horses gathered pace the bowmen and slingers fled through the spearmen to take a position behind them. Charlemagne smiled as the ranks of spears and shields were shattered and disordered. The Saxon spearmen had little mail and few helmets, but an unbroken line might have slowed the Frankish horsemen. As it was the thinned line had made places where his lances could sweep through. His horses were as mighty a weapon as the lances carried by his men. Metal found flesh and hooves crushed bones. The sound as the Franks hit the barbarians was like a thousand axes hacking into timber. The cacophony of screams echoed across the field and from his elevated position the ruler of half of the continent smiled as the enemy were broken. The enemy warriors had numbers, but they were like poorly made metal. They were brittle and once they were well struck, they shattered. His orders had been clear. He wanted the Saxon warriors putting to the sword. With their leaders dead he could subjugate the people and then send in the priests to save their souls.

It was almost dark when his son, Charles the Younger, rode in with the weary horsemen. Their armour was bespattered with blood and their swords bloodied and notched, but they were victorious. His son tossed a bloody head to the ground, "It is not Widukind, Emperor, but this man was the leader who tried to rally his people. You have a great victory, and the Saxon nobles lie dead in great numbers."

The emperor shook his head, "This is not a victory. The victory will come when their barbarian altars are thrown down and destroyed. When the heathen priests are slaughtered and when there are churches for those we have baptised and converted, then there will be a victory." He turned and pointed to the north, "And when the Saxons are Christian, then we turn our attention to the Danes, the Norse, the Lapps and the Rus. We will not have a victory until this land, from Rome to the snowy land of the north is Christian."

His warriors were as committed as he was and every one of them who heard the words of the emperor, cheered and banged their shields in acclamation. They were on a crusade and with God on their side would surely succeed.

Norse Warrior

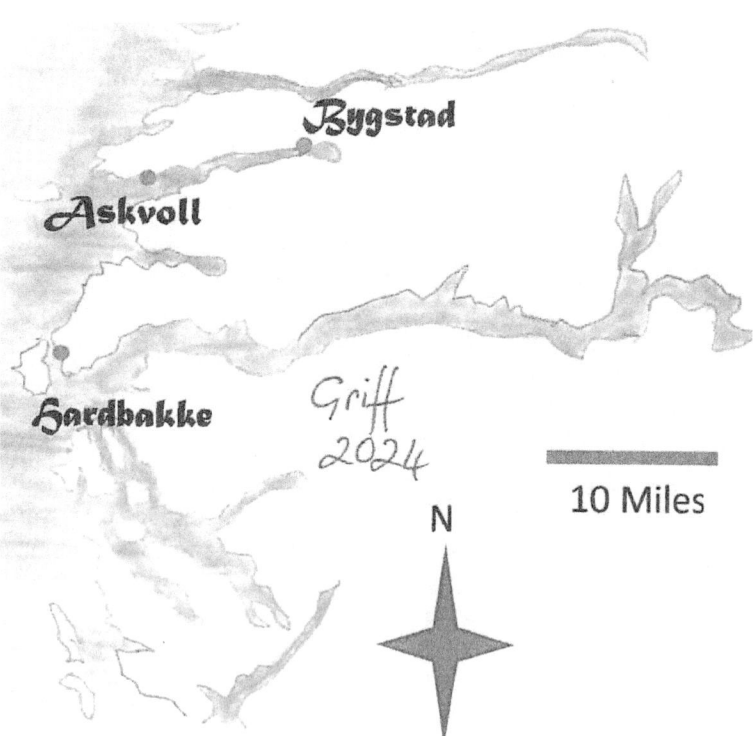

Norse Warrior

Chapter 1

A northern fjord

I held my spear above my shoulder as I climbed through the trees. The ground had no paths and was steep. Carrying the spear helped me to balance but I had to use my left hand to pull me up at times. My father had told me that I had to keep the spear pointed before me but that I should be aware that wolves were cunning and could easily track me. I had to use my nose as well as my eyes and ears to smell for the wily wolf which might hunt me. I was well aware that Arne Arnesson had been found wanting when he had hunted his wolf. Men had found his half-eaten body when they had searched for him after he failed to return from the wolf hunt. The wolf pack had begun to feast on him. I prayed that would not be my fate. When I had been told that a wolf had taken from a farmer, I had volunteered to hunt the animal. I had left the previous evening and I had followed the trail all night. When the sun had risen my task was made easier and I made quicker time. Arne had done the same thing but he had been trapped by the pack. I was wary. To hunt one wolf would give me a chance, but a wolf pack…

It was the smell from ahead that alerted me to the presence of a wolf. The breeze was in my face. I had bathed in the fjord before I had left my home on this hunt for I was ascending the holy mountain Helgafell. Our priests, holy men and volvas told me that to go there unwashed would result in my death but if I bathed in the icy fjord then I would live. Arne had not bathed. I was able to smell more clearly without the assault of a stink from my own body. My mother had given me a freshly washed kyrtle. I could smell the wolf but with the wind coming from the top of Helgafell and my clean body I would be, I hoped, unnoticed by the animal that had taken two of Lars' lambs. I had known where the wolf was for he had taken the lambs from the farm of Lars Greybeard. The blood trail had soon ended but it gave me an indication of where the wolf was to be found. I had promised Lars the wolf's heart as weregeld for his lamb. Lars had promised me his sword. With no sons, a wife who had died and two daughters, he had no one else to give the weapon. I had already planned a wolf hunt, for I wanted the skin and the teeth of a wolf and the promise of a sword was a further inducement.

The smell of wolf became stronger, and I saw that I was reaching the top of the ridge. This close to the exposed ground there were fewer trees and I moved even more slowly. I did not raise my head over the rocks, instead I slowly slid my face close to the rocks and peered over. There was a dell. It was not a den but a sheltered place where an animal could be devoured. Ten paces from me, I saw the female and two cubs feasting on the lambs. The wolf that had hunted the lambs was standing guard. I pulled my head back. There were two cubs with the mother. What would they do when I threw my spear? I could only hit one of them. Once the spear was thrown, I would be defenceless and there were two wolves. It was not a pack, but it was more than one wolf. The cubs might be a problem for while they were young, they had been weaned. In the brief glance I had enjoyed, I had seen them eating the lambs' guts torn by one of the parents. My only other weapon was my knife. It was a prized possession, and it was sharp but was it sharp enough to kill an adult wolf quickly?

I put my hand on the Hammer of Thor that hung around my neck. I was a warrior and Thor had been chosen for me, by my father, as a protector. I had to trust him. I needed the sword from Lars for how else could I become a warrior? That decided me. I moved back to the ridge and peered over. I was too eager. I had not moved as slowly as the first time and, perhaps, my movement had been too sudden. Whatever the reason, as soon as my eyes rose over the top the he-wolf was almost on me. The rocks that lay before me gave the wolf access to me. A lone wolf will rarely attack a man but this one was defending his family. He was on me almost before I knew it. I saw his fierce eyes which seemed to burn red like fire and his teeth which promised a savage death. What had I been thinking? I could not face a wolf. My father's advice saved me. I held the spear halfway along the haft and thrust it up as the wolf leapt at my throat. Perhaps Thor's Hammer also saved me and guided my arm for as I thrust forward and the wolf's forelegs crashed into my chest I began to tumble backwards. I had no time to worry about what rocks might be there to smash into my skull, I had to keep those teeth from me. My spear had found the wolf's chest, but his teeth were still close to me. I thrust my left hand up to hold his lower jaw away from my face. Rowing my father's snekke had given me strong arms. We were both falling, and I would be the one that hit the ground first. I would break the wolf's fall and his teeth would tear out my throat.

It was the hitting of the ground that both hurt and saved me. The spear's butt rammed against the bole of a tree and the wolf's weight drove my spear through its body. The back of my head also hit the tree and just before I blacked out, I saw the light leave the wolf's eyes.

I do not think I was out for long. When my eyes opened the sun was in the same position. I could smell the wolf. I pushed the carcass of the dead beast from me and stood. I put my hand to the back of my head and it came away bloody. Placing my foot on the wolf's body I pulled out the spear and went back to the top of the rocks. The female, the cubs and remains of the lamb were gone. The bloody soil showed where they had been. This would be the last time I came to Helgafell to hunt. The cubs and the female would remember me. They would want vengeance. I had been lucky this time but the next time I might not be so fortunate. The female's instincts to save her cubs had also saved me.

I went back to the wolf and picked it up. It was a little thinner than I had expected. Perhaps hunger had driven it to risk the ire of man. I hefted it across my shoulders and using my spear as a staff made my way down the mountain. Despite the weight of the wolf it was easier going down than it had been ascending. For one thing, I was able to use the path and I was not constantly looking for signs of blood or the wolf. I was heading home to Bygstad. Before I reached my father's house, I would have to call at the farm of Lars Greybeard. The wolf would begin to stink soon. The beast needed to be gutted.

Lars and his daughters, both shepherdesses, were tending their small flock of sheep and goats. They were not kept for their meat, only the young rams were eaten, but for their milk. Lars sold the milk in Bygstad, where Anya Hróolfrsdotter turned it into cheese. Borghildr and Freya were both a little younger than I was and pretty. Another reason I had taken on the commission was to win their approval. Either would make a good wife and the likelihood of inheriting the farm was an attractive prospect.

Lars gave a cry of joy when he spied the wolf, "Well done, Leif Longstride, your first kill."

I nodded and dropped the carcass at his feet, "Aye, Lars, and the last."

"How so?" I told him about the cubs and he clutched at his Hammer of Thor. "Aye, a blood feud with a wolf pack is to be avoided."

I pointed to the wolf, "Take what you will, Lars. I need just the skin and the teeth."

"I will take the heart and the guts. The meat is yours." He took his knife and quickly gutted the dead wolf. His two dogs Snorri and Hrólfr sat up and licked their lips. Lars pulled out the heart and laid it reverently on the ground. That would be a sacrifice, but he and his daughters would make that when they were alone. He took out the rest of the guts and tossed them to the hounds who eagerly tore into them. "Perhaps the taste of wolf will make them more alert. If you have any wolf meat that you do not eat then I would buy it from you. Not for us but for the dogs you understand."

"Of course. My mother likes your milk, she says it makes the best cheese."

He nodded, proudly; he liked to be told such things. He was not a warrior but despite that was well respected, "Aye, this land has good grass and I do not overgraze." He smiled, "And now your payment."

He went into the longhouse he shared with his daughters. Freya came over and said, "Leif, have you not yet chosen a woman?"

Borghildr snapped, "You are brazen, Sister. What a thing to say."

Freya shrugged, "He is the only man we have seen since our first woman's moon. I would not shrivel and waste away."

I smiled, "No, I have not yet taken a wife and you two are as comely a pair as any in Bygstad. When I am ready to make my choice I will come here first."

Their smiles told me I had said the right thing. Of course, I could not take a wife yet. I had neither land nor silver.

Lars returned with the sword in its scabbard. He reverently handed it over, "This was my father's. I have never taken it from its scabbard. I do not even know if it is sharp. You are a warrior and you will use it well."

"Was your father a warrior, Lars Greybeard?"

"When he was young he went a-viking. The Jarl of Askvoll took a ship to raid the Franks. My father took this sword from a Frank he killed, but he suffered a wound to his leg and could not raid anymore. He used the silver he took and the ram and ewe he was given by the jarl and started this farm. It is why I am a farmer. The silver he took was well-used. The flock you see grew from the ram and the ewe." He smiled, "When your father and uncle raided I bought two ewes from them. Their blood made my flock stronger."

Freya said, "Will you go a-viking, Leif Longstride?"

Fitting the scabbard to my belt I said, "Now that I have this then I can. I shall need a shield but as Jarl Bjørn Haraldsson has yet to decide if it is this season or next when we go a-viking then I have time. I am still young; I have seen but sixteen summers." The sword felt good on my belt and after hefting the wolf over my shoulders once more I said, "Farewell, Lars, Freya and Borghildr."

Borghildr said, "Come back whenever you like. I make good cheese too."

Freya snapped, "As do I!"

Lars laughed, "I do not make cheese, Leif, but I would like the company of a man. I live with chattering magpies."

I headed towards the village. It lay just two miles away, but the path wound its way through the trees that flanked the fjord, and with the gutted wolf draped around my shoulders would take time.

The longhouse my father shared with his brother and our family was close to the fjord for Eirik and Brokkr were, like my grandfather Eirik, fishermen. My brothers, Karl, Ivar and Birger, would be on the fjord, or if the wind was right, out at sea. It was another reason to be on the wolf hunt. Two days without having to row the snekke and haul in the nets was a luxury.

People worked outside their homes whenever the weather allowed, and this was late spring. For this part of the world, it was warm. Men mended nets, women prepared vegetables, and some spun while others were salting fish. The smith, Alfr and his son Balder had the hide sides of their workshop raised to allow the breeze to cool them as they hammered and tempered their iron. The result was that I was seen, and a cry went up as they saw the dead wolf. Others had killed a wolf or two, but the last one had been when I was but ten. It was three years since Arne had died. His death had seemed to make men fear to risk hunting.

There were shouts as people saw me, "It is Leif Longstride!"
"He has a wolf."
"Leif has returned, Thor be praised."
"Leif the Wolf Killer."

I would be lying if I said I did not enjoy the praise and the acclamation. I loved it. I raised my spear in acknowledgement and slowed a little. The grin on my face was as wide as the mouth of the fjord. When I neared the longhouse, my mother saw me and wiped her hands on a wet cloth. She had been gutting fish to salt. My aunt Iðunn and my cousin Kára were also salting fish and they also stopped. Kára was but nine years old yet she looked older. Perhaps living in a longhouse with my three brothers and I had made her grow up more quickly.

My mother smiled but I knew there would be no tears. She was a strong woman. Her father had been a great warrior who had died in battle against some Lapps who had raided us. Her own mother was taken in the raid as a slave, and she had raised her brothers and sisters alone. She was like the granite of Helgafell. I knew she cried but it was always when she thought no one was looking. To the village and the clan, she was without tears and fears.

Ever practical, she said, "Is it gutted?"
"Aye, I gave Lars the guts for his dogs."
She snorted, "If Lars had better dogs, then the wolf would not have taken the lambs. There is time before dark to skin it and preserve the skin." She returned to her task. The fish would not salt themselves.

Kára said, "Can I have a wolf tooth, Leif?"
"Just one for I have plans for them."
"I will help you."

Iðunn was a gentle soul, "You were not hurt, Leif? The back of your head is matted with blood."

"I banged my head on a tree."

She shook her head, "I will wash the wound and clean it with vinegar. It would be a shame for the wolf to have vengeance."

I clutched my Hammer of Thor. I had not thought of that. Who knew what poison the wolves had spread on the trees?

She disappeared into the longhouse, and I laid the carcass down and took out my knife. I took the whetstone and honed it. The wolf smelled. It was not a bad smell, but it would be if I did not do something with the skin. Kára helped me by spreading the legs of the wolf so that I could take the skin from the flesh more easily.

Iðunn came out with a pail of water, some soap and a skin of vinegar. "Keep still while I wash the dried blood." The kyrtle, which had been clean was now not only dirty but bloody. The water which she poured on my head soaked it. Kára took the pail and went to the fjord to fill it with clean water.

Iðunn used her fingers to examine the wound. "The skin is broken but it is a graze." The shock of the icy fjord water made me judder and Kára laughed. When the vinegar was applied I felt nothing for my head was still numb from the water. That done I was able to carry on taking the skin from the flesh. When I reached the head, I took my sword and used it for the first time. I hacked the bone that joined the head to the body. It would help me to skin the wolf and use the whole skin, head and all. This would be my trophy. We would boil it and, after removing the teeth, I would place it on a stake outside the longhouse. It would remain there until I left the longhouse to begin my own family. I sheathed the sword and then hammered the skin to the frame we used. Normally it was for a ram we had bought from Lars, but it was big enough to take a wolf. There were no cows in the village but I had been told that some villages had drying frames large enough to take the skin of a cow. I placed the frame on the southwest side of the longhouse. Over the next weeks, the men would make water on the skin and that would tan it. Eventually, I would be able to use it as a cloak.

The boy on the watchtower blew the ram's horn to tell us that the fishing boats were returning. There was still an hour before sunset, but the men had been awake since dawn. My brothers would be weary. Normally my uncle and I did most of the rowing back up the fjord and they took turns to relieve us. These last days would be the first time they would have had to row for longer. My uncle was not tall but he was powerful. I knew that the wind was not with them. The days that it was were a joy but they were few and far between. It would take some time for them to reach us. I hung the carcass of the wolf under the eaves of the longhouse. My mother would butcher it. I had told her that if there was any spare meat then Lars wanted it. I knew there would be. Some of it would be too tough to eat. The bones would be boiled to make soup and then they would be used to make tools and jewellery. I had never eaten wolf and I looked forward to the stew that would be cooked. We ate more fish than meat. The squirrels, hares, foxes and rats we used were really just to give a different flavour to the fish stews that were our staple diet. That done, I washed my hands in a pail of water drawn from the fjord and went inside the longhouse. I pulled the kyrtle from my body and then took the one I had last worn the previous day. I donned it. I strapped on my sword. I knew it was pretentious and that I was striking a pose but I was young and now that I had a sword I could be a warrior.

 As I stepped back outside I saw the first of the fishing boats tie up at the wooden quay. Ours was not the largest and my father had to negotiate the sale of the bigger ones. I went with my mother, aunt and cousin to help them unload. There was a frame that held the fish just aft of the mast fish. I saw the glistening, flickering fins of fish at the top of the frame and knew that it had been a good day. With my wolf and a good catch, the mood in the longhouse would be happy. The fish that were to be sold changed hands and we packed the rest for us.

 As my brothers began to pass the fish to us to place in the baskets we had brought, my father grinned and said, "You have Lars' sword. I am guessing that you have a wolf."

 I pointed to the longhouse, "It is on the frame already and tomorrow we can place the head on the stake."

 My father looked genuinely happy, "Then my son is almost a warrior. Tomorrow, we will go to the sacred grove and show Thor your wolf's head."

My brother, Birger said, "We will not fish tomorrow?" He sounded happy at the prospect. I saw that his hands were red raw from the rowing.

"We have enjoyed a fine day of fishing, and we have wolf meat. We can allow one day to honour the gods and begin work on Leif's shield."

That idea appealed to my brothers. My father and uncle both had a shield. They would have a day with me to make a shield and they would not have to fish. I was the eldest and this was a sign that they too, would, in turn, be soon making their own shields. They would become warriors. At the moment neither even had a real spear. Until they had a metal head for the spear they could only use a fire-hardened stake. My spearhead had been a gift from my uncle when I was taller than he was.

My mother's commanding voice ended the discussion. "This is idle chatter. We have fish to preserve."

We all obeyed her, even my father and uncle. She was the matriarch of the family, and no one would countenance arguing with her. The smaller fish and the shellfish were all taken by my aunt Iðunn and Kára to be placed in a boiling pot of water with vegetables. The larger fish were carried by the rest of us to the large storage pot. Filled with salted water, it would keep the fish fresher until the next day when they would be either salted or cooked. My mother would make that decision.

Darkness had fallen by the time the food was ready. The wolf's skin had already been watered by the men of the house. Few men in the village had a wolf skin and they all wanted this skin to be preserved. Wolves were becoming rarer. The one that had taken Lars' lambs had to have been desperate. We sat around the long table and Iðunn poured the mead and ale. The mead was my favourite drink, but it was precious. Ale was easier to make and more plentiful but Iðunn poured mead into my horn and smiled, "You deserve this, Leif."

My father and Brokkr also had mead and they raised their horns, "Leif Longstride, wolf killer."

I felt myself glowing with pride and that first mouthful of mead tasted as though the gods themselves had made it. The stew tasted better than I could ever remember. I knew that my mother had sliced some of the more tender parts of the animal and that explained the slightly different taste. Most of the wolf's flesh would take longer and slower cooking. It might need all day to make it tender enough to eat. She had placed the meat for Lars in a basket. I would take it to him after the sacrifice.

As we ate, I told the tale of the hunt. This was my first story, and I made the most of it. My uncle and my father normally told the tales at the table, and I had not only listened but watched. I knew how to use my hands to make a point. I raised my voice and lowered it at the appropriate times. I put in pauses at the perfect places. The tale would be retold, and my retelling would only get better. The wolf would become larger and fiercer. The dangers would become more acute. We all enjoyed hearing such stories.

I did not want to go to bed but I was tired. I had gone a night without sleep and drunk more mead than I normally did. My brothers, too, were tired but as we lay beneath the skins and blankets they whispered to me.

"Now you are a warrior, will you go a-viking?"

"That does not depend on me but the hersir and the jarl."

Jarl Bjørn Haraldsson lived at Askvoll, and he was the captain of a drekar. It was not the largest ship, it had only fourteen oars on each side but it was a warship. I could not remember the last time he had called on men from our village, but I hoped he would soon. If we went raiding, then I might get a helmet. I knew that the chances of me winning a mail shirt were so low as to be impossible but if I could begin to gather metal then, in the fullness of time, Alfr could make me a byrnie.

That night I not only slept well but dreamed too. I was a mighty warrior with a fine helmet and wielding a sword to slay enemies and become a hero. In the dream, I even led warriors.

Reality, like the dawn, came the next morning when my mother woke us and set us tasks for the day. My brothers and I were still little more than thralls in the longhouse. Until the tasks were completed then my visit to the sacred grove would have to wait. It was noon when the five of us left the longhouse to walk through the trees to the sacred grove. Thor's tree stood alone. Around it were the various sacrifices offered by others before us. We had the wolf's tail. The head would be placed outside the long house but the tail, flecked with grey, would be a suitable offering to the god. My father was our holy man. The hersir, Erland Brynjarsson, was the one who led the village when making offerings, but he and my father did not get along. I had never been told the reason, but I guessed it had been an incident when they had both been young men and had raided with the jarl. Neither he nor my uncle ever spoke of it. My brothers and I, when we had been younger, had speculated wildly about it.

Now it was my father who reverently placed the tail on the lower branch of the tree.

"Great Thor, take this offering so that my son, Leif, may enjoy your favour when he becomes a warrior." He nodded to me, and I unsheathed the sword and laid it at the bottom of the tree. "Give your blessing and your power to this blade so that he will become a great warrior."

We all stood in silence.

My father nodded to his brother who took my sword and held it vertically. I knew what I had to do, and I gripped the sharpened edges with both hands. The blood flowed down the blade. My uncle handed the sword to me, and I went to the foot of the tree and plunged the bloody blade into the earth. The blood from my hands also dripped to stain the ground. I left it there for a few heartbeats and when I pulled it out the blade was clean. The other four applauded. Thor had taken my blood and it was now mixed with the earth of the sacred grove.

My brothers had brought the vinegar and honey. The vinegar cleaned the blood and the honey sealed the wound. I would have two scars in my palms, and they would remind me of the blood that joined me to our most sacred of places. We headed back to our home, and I was already planning the making of my shield and the design that I would use.

Chapter 2

As we walked back from the grove I asked, "When will the jarl raid, Father?"

"It has not been for some time. His son, Haraldr Bjørnsson is a little older than Birger. Perhaps he will raid to blood his son. The jarl is getting old."

Brokkr snorted, "He has never been a leader in war."

"Yet, little brother, he has kept us safe from raids. He has the mouth of the fjord well protected."

"If a raider came to this fjord what would they find? Lars' sheep and little else. We have no great store of silver and few women and girls to take as slaves. The young men are getting restless. The last time the hersir held a feast in his mead hall to celebrate the marriage of his eldest daughter, I heard the murmurings from young men who wish to go a-viking."

We were nearing the village and my father spread his hand, "And how many young men murmur? If you do not count my son there are less than the fingers on my hand of men who wish to do so."

"And I worry that with few young women, the men of the village might choose to take girls as brides. That can lead to a blood feud and we do not want that, do we?"

He was right. The two girls who were the most attractive brides were Lars' girls. Kára apart there were just four eligible girls in the village. I was not too concerned. I knew that both of Lars' daughters saw me as a man they might like and with the wolf skin I would be the most prized young man in Bygstad. I did not mind that we had not raided. I would need a shield before we could raid. A man could not take an oar without a shield and a chest. I would not go as a ship's boy.

I took the wolf meat and, with bandaged hands, headed back to Lars' farm. I had to step out quickly for I wanted to begin my shield. I handed him the meat and he said, "What payment?"

"Milk, Lars."

"Borghildr, fetch a jug of milk."

Freya saw my hands and her eyes widened, "I will heal them." She went to get the vinegar and after taking the bandages from my hand, she gently washed them. My aunt had washed the back of my head the same way but, somehow, Freya's ministering aroused me. No words were spoken but our eyes talked.

After she had bandaged them, I said, "Thank you, Freya."
She smiled coyly, "No, thank you, Leif Longstride."
Once I was back at the longhouse, I took the wood axe and headed back into the forest. My brothers tagged along behind me. One day they would need a shield. I sought the Linden tree. There were not many of them in the forest. Alder and fir would do but my father's and Brokkr's were made of Linden.

I knew that when I found one I would not need to chop down the tree. The Linden tree had many branches and if I could find one that was thick enough then that would suffice. I would need to find nails and, most difficult of all to find, a boss, but I had a plan. The Linden we found was an old one and someone had taken the main stem, probably to make a shield with. The tree had sprouted many branches. If nothing else the thick branches showed how long it had been since someone had made a shield.

I took the axe in two hands. The fresh cuts on my hands would be aggravated by the cutting of the tree but that was a good thing. Thor had joined me in the bloodletting and the shield would be stronger because of this. I turned to my brothers, "Mark this tree well for one day we shall come here to make your shields." I chose a branch that was relatively straight and came out almost horizontally. It made the cutting easier. I was strong but, even so, it took some time to cut the branch. It was long. I made a second cut halfway along the branch. I wanted to have a big shield. It would need to be longer than my arm. When it was done we carried the branch and the smaller ones that had been cut in the process. They would be dried as kindling. As soon as we got back to our home I took the shaping axes and split the wood. It was not as easy as it was with oak but the sooner I split it the quicker it would season. By the time darkness fell, I had enough planks to begin to make the shield. They were roughly hewn and would need work, but I had done the most important part. I had gathered the wood.

The next day was a work day. We boarded the snekke with ale skins, bread, cheese and dried fish. I wrapped cloth around my hands. The wind would help us head to the sea but that meant we would have to row on the way back. We followed the hersir's fishing boat. He did not go to sea but Erland was precious about his position and we were expected to follow the ship captained by his man. He was not a popular hersir for he appeared to do no work. He was rich for he had three knarr that sailed the seas and brought him the silver gained, not in war, but in trade. Once we reached the fishing grounds we could each choose where we fished but he wanted to show that he was our leader. Our snekke was faster than his and we had to reef the sail to stop us from getting ahead of him. We passed Askvoll and saw that the jarl's ships were already out to sea. The jarl's drekar was on the land, mounted on stands of timber to keep the worm from her. Her name was **'Bylgja'** and she was named after the goddess who was one of the nine daughters of Ægir and Rán. She was a fine-looking ship and the shipwright who had made her had carved a wonderful figurehead that was part woman and part dragon. I had seen the figurehead but once when we had taken my father and Brokkr to attend a Thing held by the jarl. The figurehead was only attached to the ship when it sailed. I knew that it would be safely housed in the jarl's hall and would be beautifully painted before we went a-viking. It was clear that there was little prospect of going a-viking any time soon. The ship would be in the water already if we were going to sail. Her keel would have been painted with pine tar and sails would have been repaired by the volvas who would sew spells into the fabric to ensure our safety.

"Here is as good a spot as any." My father had taken us beyond the last boat from our village. The jarl's boats could be seen further north and close to the coast. Brokkr reefed the sail so that we moved slowly and then I went with my brothers to the larboard side and we dropped the net into the water. We sailed in a lazy circle. The three of us held tightly to the net. Brokkr would help us when we hauled in.

"Haul."

Brokkr came to help us as we pulled up the net. He was not needed. We had a few dozen sild and one larger fish. It was not enough.

"Let us try further out to sea."

Norse Warrior

As usual, my youngest brother Ivar was always fearful of such a test for we would be sailing where we could not see the land, "It is dangerous."

My father laughed. He was a confident sailor, "Once when I was a young man and went a-viking we were blown far to the west. That was when I first saw the land of the Angles. We did not land but we were close enough to touch it. The edge of the world is far to the west of that land. All we need to do is to sail towards the setting sun."

Ivar pointed up at the clouded sky, "Where is the sun?"

Without pause my father pointed and said, "There. I know where it is. On a cloudy night, I would not and I would hove to but here, so close to our home we can venture as far west as I choose."

I think he did it deliberately. He sailed so that we were out of sight of the other ships.

Birger, Karl and I could see that our brother was terrified and we mocked him constantly, "Is that a sea monster I see, Birger? Is it coming to gobble us up?"

"No, Brother, it is Rán herself ready to take us to the depths of the sea."

"Enough! Get the net out and be silent. It does not do to risk the wrath of the gods even one as kindly as Rán."

Rán was anything but kind. My father was appeasing her. He would make a blót when we returned home.

This time when the three of us began to pull on the net it was hard, "Father, Brokkr, the net is full already."

My father threw out the sea anchor as his brother rushed to help us. The sail was down in a heartbeat and then he helped us to haul on the net. Our backs and arms burned with the effort. The net was full and more than that it was full not of sild but huge skrei. We had caught a shoal as they migrated north. We were in danger of capsizing the snekke. Brokkr shouted, "Lower your bodies. Make yourselves a dwarf like me."

My uncle had been born small and he was named after a dwarf from our legends. We obeyed him and the snekke settled back down. We pulled hand over hand to land the mighty bounty. When it was dumped on the deck the snekke sank a little and water came over the side of the boat.

"Spread the catch out and club any that try to escape." We kept clubs for just such an occasion. We rarely had to use them, but I knew that this time we would. My father was laughing as he shouted, "Karl, raise the anchor. Ivar, we shall do as you asked and race for our home but not because we are afraid. We cannot carry more fish." The spreading out of the fish ended the threat of being swamped.

The three of us laughed as we used our clubs to stun any of the skrei that tried to leave our boat. Normally a catch was hidden in the well of a fishing boat but we had a mountain of skrei. I was delighted. We would not need to fish again for some days and I would be able to work on my shield. Sailing home, we had to tack and use the wind but as we passed the rest of the fleet we saw the stares of shock for the fish seemed to glimmer and gleam even under an overcast sky. They would envy us our catch and when the hersir discovered that we had the largest haul he would not be happy.

My father laughed again, "We will have to row again, and it will be hard but they shall not see it." He used the wind to take us south of the fjord and then turned hard to the east, "Now is the time for the oars."

I sat next to Brokkr and my brothers sat before us. As my father lowered the sail, he used one of the clubs to tap out a beat. He chanted as he did so.

We are the clan of the otter
We live where no one else can
We fish the seas and water
We serve the goddess Rán

The simple chant helped us keep an even pace and we all joined my father in the singing of it. Brokkr and I were strong; for the last three seasons, I had rowed with him instead of my father. We had learned each other's ways. We powered up the fjord, bolstered by the fact that we would land the largest catch in the whole fleet. Even the largest boats, those of the hersir, could not hope to match the skrei we had managed to catch.

I laughed when we heard the horn sound. We were back hours before anyone expected. "They will think something terrible has happened to us."

My father nodded, "Today was a good day. My arrogance and desire to teach Ivar that the sea is safe was rewarded by Rán. We will take the largest skrei and use it to make a blót."

We tied up not long after the sun was at its height. The single snekke being rowed up the fjord had brought everyone to watch us. There was an 'ooh' of awe when the catch was seen. Alfr, wiping the sweat from his brow, asked, "Did you sail to the middle of the ocean for such a catch?"

"Further than the hersir's boats, that is true."

"Eirik I would buy a large skrei from you. How about that largest one?"

My father shook his head, "That one is for Rán. How about this?" He held up the second largest and Alfr nodded.

"Have your son bring it to my workshop when you have unloaded. Come, Son, we need to work up a healthy appetite to do that skrei justice."

We sold half the catch to those who waited at the quay for skrei was popular and such large fish were rare. Not every family fished. There were those who worked in wood or metal and others who were too old to fish. My mother, aunt and cousin helped us to put the fish in their baskets. Alfr's was put separately, along with that saved for Rán.

"Let us make the blót now. We are all here and the water will take it back to Rán."

We went to the end of the quay where a stone jutted out into the fjord. It was a flat rock and was used for the swearing of oaths, trysts and the making of a blót.

My father held up the enormous skrei. He could not do so for long. He said the right words and intoned the chant that we used. He turned and handed the skrei to his brother and then took out his gutting knife. It sliced through the belly of the fish and he thrust his hand inside. This was a crucial moment. He had to find the heart the first time. He pulled out the heart along with other organs and held it high in the sky. "Take the heart of the skrei, Mother Rán, and we thank you." He put his hand in the water and the current took the organs. Had he tossed them in the air then the souls of dead sailors, the gulls would have taken them and the blót would have been rendered useless. He then nodded to Brokkr who lowered the skrei into the waters of the fjord,

"And take this king of fish so that you know we honour and thank you." The fish slid into the water and disappeared. The current was strong and the parts that survived the other fish would be taken to the sea.

My mother broke the silence that followed, "This will not get the skrei you have caught, preserved. Leif, take Alfr his purchase."

We all obeyed. I hefted the basket onto my shoulder and headed for the hot workshop of Alfr. The banging, clanging and sparks had made it a frightening place to me when I was a young boy. Now it was a place of fascination, for Alfr was not only the man who made nails and axes for wood, he was also a weaponsmith. In his workshop were sword blanks, spearheads and arrowheads as well as daggers. Alfr made his nails and his hinges but his love was weapons. Until we raided then he would not be able to sell them but Alfr was a philosopher of sorts. He knew that his weapons would be bought.

When I entered he put down his hammer and said, "Thank you, Leif. Balder, take this to your mother and your sisters."

"Yes, Father." As he took the basket I saw that while he was shorter than I was, he was broader and had more muscles. He would be like his father when he was grown.

"And now, the price."

I would have to explain my actions to my father and more worryingly my mother but I had to seize the opportunity. "Alfr, I am making my shield and I need a boss. I would have a boss for my shield."

He stroked his beard, "The skrei is a fine fish but it is not worth a boss. You can have the iron for the boss. The making of the boss will cost you."

I had no silver. Balder returned and his father said, "Work on your hammering skills, Balder, while I speak with Leif."

"Yes, Father."

He began to hammer a spearhead and the idea sprang into my head. "Alfr, your son is your apprentice is he not?" They both looked at me and Alfr nodded. "Balder cannot tend the bellows and learn the skills of a smith. If you will make me the boss and furnish me with the nails for my shield I will tend the bellows." I saw the doubt on Alfr's face and the look of gratitude on

Balder's. "You could let your son make my boss under your eye and it would be part of his training. I trust Balder to make a good one."

That argument worked. Men wanted weapons made by the master and not the apprentice. Alfr could teach his son and have someone work for free.

He nodded, "Agreed. When can you start?"

"Now." I had not told my parents and I knew that I would pay for this when I reached home. My father would understand but my mother…If I was a warrior I would have to endure greater dangers than the wrath of my mother.

I had seen how the leather bellows worked but Alfr was too good a craftsman to take that for granted. I was given a brief lesson and then I spent the rest of the day pumping. It was during a short break in the afternoon when Balder's mother brought us ale that Ivar entered.

"Our mother asks if you have fallen in Alfr's fire, Brother."

I smiled, "Tell her that I have promised Alfr that I will work here for a while. I will explain when I return home."

"I will tell her."

Balder was keen to impress his father and he worked hard on the boss. I was fascinated as I watched the iron ingot be transformed first into a flat piece of iron and then shaped into the dome. When I thought it was finished it was not. It took as long to make the holes in the boss as it had to shape it. I was hot, sweaty and weary by the time it was finished.

Balder looked as though he had made the boss for the jarl himself. He grinned, "Leif, this is the first such object I have made. Father, can I now make knives?"

Alfr looked proud of his son, "Aye, Balder, for this is as good a boss as I might have made." He turned to me, "Are you happy, Leif?"

"I am."

"Balder, fetch the fish basket." He dropped the boss into the basket and then counted out twenty nails. "You have worked hard, Leif. If you need more nails," he smiled, "then you must work the bellows."

I nodded but I would hammer the nails carefully. He was right, I had worked hard, and I was not going to waste a single one.

It was dark when I returned to the longhouse. The other ships had landed their catches and the women were preparing the food. The men were seated around the table with horns of ale.

"Did you see Erland's face when he saw the size of our skrei?"

"Aye, Brother, I am guessing that while we stay at home tomorrow, they will try to find the place we fished this day."

I poured myself a horn of ale and slipped next to Birger. I thought I had done so unnoticed.

"So, where is the payment from Alfr?" My father's voice told me he already knew the answer.

I braced myself, "It is in the basket."

"Oh, he has paid us well then?" He emphasised the word 'us'.

I sighed, "He has made me a boss for my shield and given me nails."

Brokkr nodded, "A good price for the skrei. Some might say too great a price."

"I worked his bellows."

They all looked at my father. He emptied his horn and then smiled, "It is right that one who killed a wolf and is ready to be a warrior should have a shield."

The comment brought smiles. My mother, aunt and cousin entered. As she came in my mother glanced down at the basket. She was a clever woman and she knew, in that single glance, what I had done. They put the skrei and wolf stew on the table. As she ladled it into my wooden bowl she said, "A skrei for a piece of iron and some nails? You clearly know how to bargain, my son, but does this help the family?"

I hung my head, "I am sorry, Mother."

My father's bowl had been filled and he took some of the still-warm bread and broke off a piece, "Had we been raiding, wife, then Brokkr and I might have taken shields from our enemies. Our son will be a warrior and if he is going to raid then he needs a shield. I approve."

She sat down and broke a piece of bread from the same loaf. It was the signal that we could all take a piece. She sighed, "And he has brought us the wolf. You are growing, my son, and this is a sign that I will soon lose you. When a man becomes a warrior, he takes a bride and leaves his mother."

I took the loaf from my uncle and broke off a piece, "I am not a warrior until I have fought an enemy. I am still taking baby steps."

My aunt smiled, "Yes, Leif, but your mother is right. Those steps lead from this longhouse and end, Freya knows where."

I could barely sleep that night for I wanted to begin work on my shield. I knew I had not asked my mother for permission to work on the shield, but I felt I had tacit approval. While the others skinned and gutted skrei, I would take the shaping axes and our hammer to complete as much work on my shield as I could. I would be within sight of them, but my work would be for me. Their work would be for the family.

I rose before dawn. I made water on the wolfskin and then fetched the wood and tools to the front of the longhouse. As the sun rose, I was almost ready to begin. I had taken my father's shield from its place of honour. I would use that as a guide. Karl came from inside the house, "Food is ready, Leif." I nodded, "I envy you. You have a spear, a sword and soon you will have a shield. All that I have is a knife. How will I become a warrior?"

I put my hand on his shoulder, "I promise that when I become a warrior and we raid, I will try to get you and Birger a spear. I intend to be a great warrior. When I faced the wolf, I knew that I had it within me."

Once inside my mother said, "Your father and I will give you this one day. You will have to finish your shield after you have finished your other work."

I nodded. I ate faster that morning than I could ever remember and I was outside again in what seemed like moments. The sun was up and the boats were leaving, I saw the other young men from the village looking enviously at me as I began to use the shaping axes on the wood. While they were fishing their thoughts would be on me.

The first part was relatively simple. I had to make the Linden planks the same thickness. I used the coarsest axe initially and then moved to the more delicate ones to smooth them off. I had a piece of knotted rope to measure, and I made certain that the largest plank, the one that would determine the finished size of the shield, was more than big enough to protect me. I would be able to make it slightly smaller if it proved to be too heavy. By noon, when Ivar fetched me some food and ale, I had the rough shape of the shield.

He looked approvingly at it, "What next, Brother?"

I turned over our father's shield. I pointed to it, "I need to put cross braces on the back to hold the shield and then I make the hole for the boss."

"Will it be finished today?"

I shook my head, "It will be round and the hole for the boss big enough to fit my hand. That will take time to achieve. I will have used some of the nails but it will take a week more if I am to sail with father in a day or two."

He sighed, "I stink of fish, and I am heartily sick of skrei." He sat next to me, "When you, father and our uncle go raiding what will happen to Birger, Karl and me?"

"You will have the chance to come as ship's boys, I think. I was too small the last time the jarl went a-viking. The other boys in our village are too small. Practise each day with your sling."

My words offered hope and he left me in a better frame of mind.

The most frightening part was the making of the hole for the boss. It was necessary to fit my hand. I found that I was shaking by the time I had finished but the wood had not split and as I hammered the precious nails to hold the boss to the shield I was relieved. The shield was not finished when darkness fell; there was no bar for me to hold, there was no strap and it had yet to be painted but I had done the hardest part. When time allowed I would smooth the edges with the smoothing stone and finish the practical side, the part I would hold. Then I would be able to paint the design on the front.

That evening, as we ate, it was not only Birger and Ivar who were keen to know how I would finish it but my father and uncle as well. "What colour do you favour, Leif?"

I knew that what I would say would surprise them. My father had a red shield and Brokkr a green one. Most of the others in the village chose a single colour. The exception was Erland who had red and green, although as he never went raiding it did not matter. "I thought to simply stain the Linden wood so that it remains brown and then use the elderberry stain to put red eyes upon it."

My father frowned, "Why?"

"I want it to look like the wolf I killed."

"And you would wear the wolfskin upon your back?"

"Yes, Uncle."

"You are not thinking of becoming an Ulfheonar, are you?"

I shook my head. That mysterious cult of shapeshifters held no attraction for me, "No, but when we raid, I will have no mail. The wolf's hide upon my back will give me a little protection. Not much but better than a simple kyrtle."

I was pleased that I had surprised my family, but I knew that my design would make me stand out when we raided. I was casting the bones. Where would they lie?

That night, although I was tired, I began to work on the teeth of the wolf. I had given Kára hers. Like me, she would spend time drilling a hole in the tooth so that she could thread cord through it and wear it. I had the rest to do and it would take time. I decided to spend the last hours, each night, before sleep, drilling.

Chapter 3

Although I finished my shield and my necklace of wolf's teeth within seven days of starting it, I had no opportunity to show off the shield. Nor could I flaunt my sword before the other untried warriors of the village. I did, however, wear the teeth. I knew that I was doing it to draw attention to myself. I had killed a wolf, and the teeth told the world of my deed. The main reason I could not show off the shield was because of an important event in the village.

There was to be a marriage. Else Erlandsdotter and Halvard Jørgsson were to be married and the men of the village were tasked with building them a house before their handfasting ceremony at the summer solstice. Else was the second daughter of the hersir. He had sired two girls before fathering Axel and then Galmr. For us, the solstice was the second holiest day of the year. The gods gave us a day where the sun set for but a heartbeat. The winter solstice was more important for that was the day when we saw the end of the world before the next day saw the sun once more. Halvard was a warrior, of sorts. He had a shield and he had gone with Jarl Bjørn Haraldsson, not on a raid, but to visit his cousin in Trondheim. There had been talk of a raid and so Halvard was given the chance to take an oar and put his shield on the side of the drekar. It had come to nothing. The village that had been the subject of the raid sent emissaries with silver to buy off the two jarls and their ships. Halvard had come back with no experience of battle but silver. That had been two years since and although Halvard was only a couple of years older than I was he had accrued enough silver to marry Else, Erland's daughter.

We all laboured, on the days we did not fish, to build a longhouse. If Else had not been the daughter of the hersir then the pair would have lived in the longhouse with Halvard's family. Erland wanted to exercise his authority and show his power. The hersir was not a popular leader for my father and his brother, along with many other men in the village, felt that he did not lead. The house would not be large. It would just be twenty paces long, but it would be built close to the hall of the hersir. It did not take long for the house to take shape but many of those who toiled in its construction resented the work. Erland did no work himself but strutted and commanded. It did not go down well. It was lucky that Else and Halvard were so popular. Else was nothing like her father and Halvard's father, Jørg Halvardsson, was the carver of wood and maker of furniture in the village. He was a master craftsman and it had been he and not the shipwright who had carved the dragon prow of the drekar for Jarl Bjørn Haraldsson. Indeed, we often had visitors from Askvoll who came to commission pieces from Jørg. Sometimes he was hired to carve huge pieces for those with silver. He had spent a month at Askvoll carving two pillars for the jarl. The three were the reason we worked.

Erland did not do any of the work which was supervised by Jørg. His son was a good carver too and this house, whilst plainly built, would be marked by the two posts on either side of the doorway. We did not begrudge the fact that the two men spent all their time with their axes, hammers and chisels intricately carving the beasts on the two trees that were used to help support the roof. We would all be able to admire the carvings every day. We all knew Jørg's work. His carvings were things of beauty and showed a respect for nature and the trees from which they were created. The hall was finished ten days before the handfasting. The turf we laid on the roof would grow and thicken before the winter snows hid it from sight. They would have a dry and comfortable home.

It was when we had finished that my mother began to fuss about the clothes we would wear. She and my aunt had woven us new tunics. Had that been the only demand she had made of us then it might not have been so bad but, especially with me, she had my beard and hair trimmed a week before the ceremony. When I asked why Ivar, Karl and Birger did not have to undergo such attention she told me that this would be the chance for me to show myself off to the eligible girls who would attend. I wanted as little attention drawn to me as possible. I had no battle bands and apart from Thor's scars on my hands and my wolf necklace, nothing to mark me as a warrior. I had wanted to wear my wolfskin but no one, my brothers apart, thought that was a good idea. I would be going to the handfasting as a fisherman!

The jarl arrived on his snekke, the day before the handfasting. He and his hearth-weru, his bodyguards, would stay with the hersir. I had rarely seen him but the wedding of the daughter of the hersir was enough to bring the man we all swore allegiance to. Lars and his daughters would also be coming and they would stay with us. Lars' dead wife and my mother had grown up together. Our longhouse would be crowded for a day or two.

The good part was that I would meet with real warriors. My father and uncle had both fought and participated in raids but the four hearth-weru of Jarl Bjørn Haraldsson were reputed to be real warriors. They had mail byrnies and two of them, so my father told me, had two-handed axes. I would not get to wear my sword, but I was anxious to examine those of the bodyguards. The scabbard I had was old and I wanted a new one. Knowing that there would be a wedding I had waited to make mine. My father's and Brokkr's showed me how to make one, but I wanted to see how other warriors decorated them.

It was impossible to rise before the sun in high summer. The golden orb rarely set. The darkest it became was a sort of dim glow. However, my father and uncle rose and went to the sacred grove. I had not been there since I had made the blood oath. We stood in silence around the sacred tree and, as was usual, the three of us spoke to Thor in our own way. I prayed for the opportunity to become a warrior.

That done we returned to the longhouse and ate before we groomed ourselves and dressed. My uncle and my father each had a single battle band. They wore it with honour. The three of us fastened hlad around our heads. Mine was made of braided leather and I had made it myself. I was proud of it. My mother wore her necklet with a piece of black jet. It had been a gift from my father before they had been married and he had given silver for it. It was mounted on a thin silver necklace that had also been expensive. My mother only wore it for special occasions, and this was clearly one.

We made our way to the mead hall. It was decorated with wildflowers as well as pieces of fir. Our people were connected to the land as well as the sea and this honoured the land in which we lived. The handfasting would take place on the rock where we had made the sacrifice but there would be a procession from the hall to the water. We were not important enough to be close to the jarl and the hersir but we were not at the very back where the poorest of people trudged. All were dressed in their finery but their status was reflected in the clothes that they wore. I saw that the jarl had silver threads in his fine tunic and hat. His bodyguards' mail byrnies had been polished and they shone from the sun in the east. Their battle bands covered their knotted arms. They were warriors.

I saw my mother glancing around at the others. We were all well-presented and dressed in our finest clothes. She was happy. If we raided, then she would be happy for that would mean silver and, if we were lucky, thralls. We would be richer, and she could show that affluence in clothes and jewellery. The well-carved bone combs in her hair and those in my aunt's would be replaced, when we had the silver, by silver ones.

We followed the others down to the stone and the couple stood on the stone. When everyone had arrived the hersir held his hands up for silence. All that could be heard was the lapping of the water on the boats and the quay. Even the souls of dead sailors, the gulls were silent. It felt as though the world we knew was holding its breath. Else did not have as strong a voice as Halvard's and parts of her words were lost. We heard enough and when the hands were tied by Jarl Bjørn Haraldsson himself there was a cheer. The ceremony was over and the part that most young men were eagerly anticipating, the feasting, was about to begin. Not all the guests would stay for the feast. I was a little sad when Lars and his daughters had to leave. Leaving their flock in the day was one thing, their dogs could guard them, but night was a different matter. My father came with me to say goodbye to Lars.

"The sword suits, Leif?"

"It does, Lars."

"My daughters hope that one day you will return to our home." I saw Freya, coyly glancing at me. In the time since she had tended my hands her figure had filled out a little. She no longer looked like a girl, she was almost a woman.

Bearing in mind the nature of the event that struck me as a clear invitation to court one of them. I was quite happy to do so for dressed in their finest, with flowers in their hair and their bodies smelling of herbs they were both an attractive prospect. "Thank you, Lars, and I will avail myself of the opportunity."

The girls' eyes lingered on me, and they left. My father chuckled, "It is not many young men who have the prospect of choosing his bride and both of them so pretty. Lars is the richest man in Bygstad, Leif. If you married either of them those riches would be yours."

"Let me go on a raid and win silver and then I will think about handfasting. I would not go as a pauper to court."

My father bridled at the comment, "We are not poor."

"Nor do we have silver jewellery for mother, do we Father?"

"She has the silver necklace and the jet."

"And Erland's wife has silver around her neck, on her head and even a gold ring."

He sighed, "And that is because he was chosen to raid more times when we were younger men. He benefitted from easy victories and the jarl's father rewarded him. I know not why. He is richer but I am the better fisherman." He put his arm around my shoulders, "Let us hope that the jarl chooses to raid. If nothing else we could do with a thrall to help your mother and your aunt. Once your cousin marries, their workload will increase and neither are getting younger."

There were slaves in the village but few of them. Most belonged to Erland. He had profited well from the raids and used it to begin his trading empire.

I would normally have been as wild as many of the other young warriors but for a number of things. One was the steely glaze of my mother who wished all things to be done properly. The fact that, alone out of the young men who were my age, I was the one who had hunted and killed a wolf but, most importantly, I wanted to be chosen by the jarl as a potential member of any crew he might take to raid. The couple sat in the centre of the table and the hersir sat next to his daughter and the jarl next to him. This was an expense for Erland, and he was going to make as much from it as he could. The food reflected the expense. Naturally, there was fish. It looked to be Erland's whole catch. He had also sent his two hearth-weru to hunt and the meat dish was mainly deer and a side dish of bjórr. The ale and the mead had been made especially for this wedding and the thralls kept it flowing. I drank and enjoyed it but did not become awash with it as did some others. I noticed that the groom Halvard, also drank sparingly.

When the food was finished Erland stood, a little unsteadily to raise his horn to the couple. "I hope for grandsons so that the blood of my family will continue to run through this land." There was a cheer from all and men banged their hands upon the table. My mother frowned for she thought it a little unseemly, even for a wedding. "I wish to thank Jarl Bjørn Haraldsson who has honoured us with his presence today. We are lucky to live in a land that is kept peaceful by such a great warrior." This caused even more acclamation. "I invite him to speak a few words."

The jarl stood and I was able to study him better. He was not as old as I had expected. He was younger than my father and that meant he must have led a raid when he was a very young man. His hearth-weru all had more battle bands. I knew from my father that Haraldr, the jarl's father, had been a belligerent man who had raided far and wide. Perhaps he had made enough so that his son did not need to raid as much. It was clear that he was rich. He had a silver hlad about his head and in the centre were three pieces of well-carved and polished black jet. It was his hearth-weru, sitting not far from him, who were the older men and they were clearly warriors. I deduced that they must have served the old jarl.

"I am honoured to be here. The men of Bygstad are loyal men and I do not visit here as much as I might like. I will make amends. This seems a good time to make an offer to the men of Bygstad. At the start of Tvímánuður, I intend to take *'Bylgja'* and raid the land of the Franks. If there are any young men from Bygstad who would wish to go with me then they should speak to me before I leave on the morrow."

He might have wished to say more but he was drowned out by the outpouring of cheers and cries. He beamed as he sat. Birger turned to me, "I shall ask to go."

My father shook his head, "You cannot. Tvímánuður is the wrong time of year for us. We have winter ahead."

I said, "But what of me?"

My father nodded, "This is your chance, Leif, and I will not stand in your way. The three sisters have spun and your fate is decided. You were given the sword and you have made an oath to Thor. You shall volunteer but you three," he glared at my brothers, "will have to wait."

Birger had drunk as much ale as I had but he could not hold it as well and he boldly continued, "I could be a ship's boy."

My mother leaned over and almost hissed her words out, "You will heed your father. One of our sons is enough for this venture. We will lose you others soon enough. Your father is right, if you wish to prove your valour then while your brother is in Frankia we can see if you can hunt as well as he can. We need meat for the winter and kindling for the fire. This will help you to become men."

Her words cowed Birger but he still mumbled, "This is because Leif is your favourite."

My mother's eyes flared and I intervened to calm the situation, "What say, Birger that if I can, when I raid, I bring you back a weapon? There may be spearheads or Frankish blades."

Birger brightened, "And then when next the jarl raids I could go."

My mother's glare turned to a smile and she patted the back of my hand. I had said the right thing and calmed the mood.

The excited buzz continued around the table as men discussed the raid and if they might be involved. I suspected it would be the younger men. Erland would have to go along with his hearth-weru, as would his son, but the men like my father and Brokkr had been a-viking. Their sons would be the ones taking to the oars.

"Frankia, where is that and is it rich?"

My father nodded, "It is an empire and stretches all the way from Denmark to the land of the Arabs."

"If it is an empire then they will have many warriors to defend it."

Brokkr nodded, "You are wise already, Nephew. They will but from what I have heard they have many rivers that will allow our ships the chance to travel deep into their heartland. It is not like here and ringed by mountains. Besides, their emperor needs to be punished. His warriors destroyed the holy places of our gods in the lands to the south of us, the land of the Danes. It is time he had his holy places taken." He smiled, "It is said that they fill their holy places with gold, silver and fine linens. They do not defend them."

I nodded but I had been working out the distances involved, "It will be a long way for us to sail then?"

"It will." My father was a navigator and the best sailor in the village. He had helped the navigator on *'Bylgja'* to steer in the last raid. He knew the sea, "But the voyage will be along the coast. A raider must cross the open water between the land of the Norse and the land of the Danes but, that apart, it is no more hazardous than what we did when we caught the mountain of skrei. You will not be the navigator but you should know that the land is always to the east, the land where the sun rises. Even on a cloudy day, you know where east and west lie."

As much as I wanted to speak to the jarl I knew that this was not the time. For one thing, he was deep in conversation with the hersir and for another, I would look desperate. I was, of course, but I did not want others to know that. When the jarl grew tired then Erland told us that the feast was over and we could leave. Many had done so already, my mother, aunt and cousin included.

As we left my father said, "And you must have a helmet now. You shall wear mine."

The day had already been the best one ever, but that piece of news elevated it even more. I would look like a warrior. Brokkr added, "And you shall have my cloak clasp. There is a dragon upon it and I believe it will afford protection."

As I rolled into my bed, I was desperate for dawn and the chance to offer my sword. I rose as soon as I needed to make water but when I went outside the village was still asleep. The sun was up but it was still early. When I had done, I went to the holy place and stood on the stone. The fjord was a flat calm. There was barely a ripple. I watched an owl flying back to its nest. It had hunted and I saw a small creature hanging from its claws. It was a predator and we were predators too. When we raided, we would prey on those that could not defend what they had. Brokkr had made it quite clear that what we would be doing was right. The gods wanted us to exact revenge on the people who had desecrated our holy groves. I knew that even without that aspect of the raid I would do all that I could to make myself richer. I would return a warrior with a reputation. A fish suddenly appeared in the fjord and then vanished. Would my dream become a reality? I knew how to use a sword, but I had never used one in combat. I had killed with a spear but that had been a wolf, and a man would be a different prospect.

I turned as I heard a footfall behind me. It was the jarl and his bodyguards. They wore just simple shifts and they had with them their cloaks. The jarl smiled, "I thought I would have the chance to bathe unseen, but you are up early too, I see."

"I am sorry, Jarl, I will return to my home."

He shook his head, "No, it is of no matter. You are Leif Longstride are you not? The youth who slew a wolf."

I nodded, "I am, Jarl, the son of Eirik."

"Your father is a good navigator. Will he go a-viking?"

I shook my head, "He says it is a time for young warriors."

"He is right for young men are fearless and that is what we need when we leave our homes to raid." He smiled, "And you would sail with me?"

"If you would have me, aye."

"Jarl." One of his guards, with a long scar down his left forearm, nodded to the fjord.

"Yes, Haldir." He turned back to me, "We will talk when I have swum."

The holy rock shelved down into the fjord. The jarl took off his shift as did two of his guards and naked, they walked down the sloping rock to the fjord. When it came up to their waists the jarl dived in and disappeared. His head appeared ten paces from where he went in. The two bodyguards kept walking and then they swam to join him. The three swam up and down.

I asked the guard with the scar, "Why does he do this? The water is so cold that it shrivels up a warrior's manhood."

He laughed, "Aye, I know. It is why we take it in turn to accompany him. He believes that if we sail in the sea then we should learn to live in it. For me, I know that if I fell overboard in a battle my byrnie would drag me to the bottom and I would become a gull."

The current took them west to the sea and the three had to swim vigorously to make it back to the slab of rock, where the other four helped them out and then handed them the drying cloths. "Can you swim, Leif?" I nodded. "Then you should try this each morning. It not only hardens the body but it also puts us closer to the gods and goddesses."

We headed back to the village. It was coming awake. The thralls in the hersir's longhouse must have noticed the absence of their guest and had alerted their master. "You said we raid in Frankia, lord…"

"My cousin, Arne Sigurdsson, lives at Hardbakke." That village lay on an island to the south of us. "He has a drekar, but he also owns a knarr. He and his men sailed south and traded along the rivers Sequana and Liger." The names did not sound Norse. "He traded well but he said that there were houses filled with their priests. They were unguarded and filled with silver. I know that our young men need to show their courage and skill in battle. If we do not raid, Leif, then there will be blood shed in our land and that is not good."

I felt honoured to be taken into the confidence of such a leader. He was nothing like Erland.

"I am eager to show my skills, lord." I had the rest of Sólmánuður and almost the whole of Heyannir to prepare. I would learn as much as I could from my father and uncle.

"Good. We meet at my mead hall. Men will be mustering from the last days of Heyannir. Come as soon as you are ready." He stopped and gave me a shrewd look, "I know that here, in this village, there is bad blood between your family and the hersir. I am glad that your family are reasonable men. I would not have dissension amongst my people. When you sail with me on my drekar, there will be more warriors who are not from this village. Do you understand?"

I nodded, "That I will be serving the jarl and not Bygstad."

He beamed, "I was told that you were clever, you will go far. Bring your wolf's skin when you come." My frown told him I did not understand. He said, "The followers of the White Christ think we are the barbarians and not they. Men who wear the skins of wolves will confirm that belief and make them afraid. I want to strike terror into their hearts. They destroyed the holy places of people who are like us. My raid will be a message that if they harm our holy places, we will destroy theirs." I nodded. He leaned in and said, "And make ourselves silver, eh?"

We had reached my home and I said, "Thank you for sharing your thoughts with me, lord. I shall be the best warrior that I can be."

"And that is all that can be asked of any man. For one who does so will be guaranteed to die with a sword in his hand and go to Valhalla."

I entered the hall and was greeted by the smell of fish being fried. Fresh fish was delicious, but it only tasted that good when eaten within a day or two. The wedding and its preparations meant we had no fresh fish, but I loved the taste of smoked fish, especially sild. I was in good humour, and I was grinning from ear to ear as I poured myself some ale and sat at the table. My mother saw my smile but said nothing. It took care to fry the sild and not to burn it.

My father saw the grin and said, "What wakes you so early that you have a smile like a spring dawn?"

I informed him of my chance encounter with the jarl and told him all. He touched his hammer, "The three sisters spin, Leif. I do not say it is a bad thing, but they can be like Loki when they choose. Do not be tempted to think that the jarl has a special place for you. He is a jarl and like all such lords, they have many ways to make men follow them."

"I believed him. His words sounded like they came from his heart. He was not like Erland whose words often sound like they come from within a purse."

My father nodded and poured his own ale, "And from what I saw of him I think he is a man to be followed. All I ask is that you think of yourself. Until you fight in a shield wall then you will not know the strengths that your oar brothers possess. It may be that you are the bravest of them. You are not close to any in the village, are you?" I shook my head. "When Birger, Karl and Ivar become warriors then the three of you can lock shields and protect each other. This raid, from what you say, should not involve fighting in a shield wall but be careful."

My mother brought the hot fish and placed two on each of our platters. The arrival of food ended the conversation, but I knew that some time before I sailed my mother would speak to me. She had that look on her face. She was wise. Some said she was the best volva in the village but all that I knew was that when she spoke, I heeded her words.

Chapter 4

We all gathered to watch the jarl's snekke sail back to Askvoll. As soon as the ship disappeared the hersir turned to address us. Most of the villagers were there. "I would know which men wish to follow the jarl and to raid. Those who intend to do so stay now and the rest can depart."

My father and uncle patted my back as they led my brothers away. The misery on the faces of Birger, Karl and Ivar told me that they would not be happy again until they had the chance to go raiding. The box that had kept the hidden secret was now opened. It could never be closed again.

There were just seven of us who had not been to war before. Oddr led the older men. They had all raided and had been blooded. The oldest was Axel Erlandsson. As the son of the hersir, his clothes and his weapons would be better than the rest of us. I did not like him, and that dislike was mutual. We followed our fathers and the bad blood between them continued with us. The jarl had known this and I now obeyed his words. I did not scowl, as Axel did when he saw me, I smiled. The hersir looked at each of us. Axel's cousin, Brynjar, stood close to his cousin. He was the same age as I was. The others were younger: Dagfinn, Elvind, Gunvald and the youngest Mikkel. I liked Mikkel for he and Birger had often played together when they were younger, and they had remained friends.

The hersir nodded to Oddr. "Thank you, Oddr Gautisson. You warriors know your business, but these young cubs will need to be trained."

I liked Oddr and he smiled as he addressed us, "And I look forward to fighting alongside these cubs, especially as there is a wolf killer amongst them." I grew a handspan as he left but I saw that Axel Erlandsson had a scowl upon his face.

"My son will lead you." Erland's voice was commanding. There would be no discussion about the matter. It was not right but I knew we could do nothing about it. I said nothing. "From now on each Þórsdagr will be reserved for warrior training. We have just six such days before you raid and there are skills you all need. My hearth-weru, Finn and Hallstein will be present to train you. You all need a spear and a shield. If you do not have those then you cannot go a-viking. You seven, along with the older warriors, represent Bygstad. The men of Askvoll will judge us by what you do."

Had that all been said then it would have been well, but Axel decided to exert his authority from the first, "And know that I will judge how well you do. It is me you need to impress."

I hid my smile as I saw the look exchanged between the hearth-weru. They would judge us as warriors and the son of the hersir would have to endure the same training as the rest of us. I felt less annoyed by Axel's attempt to show his power.

The hersir, too, did not like what his son had done. It seemed to diminish his own power. "You have two days to work hard for your families before you return here to learn to become warriors."

We had no time to discuss matters for there was work to be done. The rest of my family were waiting at the snekke for me. We would be leaving an hour or so later than we would normally, but the jarl's departure had to be honoured. I clambered into the snekke as my father sat at the steering board.

"Odin has sent us a good wind. It will bring us back up the fjord." He meant the wind was against us and we would have to row. I did not mind for the current was with us and an easier journey, laden with fish was to be welcomed.

As we rowed, I told the others what the hersir had said. My father nodded, "One day is not too much out of seven days and it will make Ivar, Karl and Birger stronger."

Brokkr said, "Watch out for Axel. From what you told me he will try to hurt you when you train. Finn and Hallstein are good warriors. They will ensure that any injury is not mortal but beware."

"We are all in the same position, Uncle, none of us have trained before. Any weapon skill is that which comes naturally."

Birger said, "When Balder is old enough to become a warrior then he will surely be the best warrior for he works with weapons each day and the fire tempers him much as it does the iron."

Brokkr shook his head as we hauled back on the oars and the snekke slid effortlessly through the water, "Alfr was a sound warrior, Birger, but your father and I were better warriors."

My father smiled, "It helped that we are brothers, Brokkr, and different heights. Between us, we were a formidable weapon. Leif has no one. He will be alone."

"Mikkel knows my brother well."

"And, Birger, he is little older than you. I do not doubt that he will grow into a good warrior, but Leif is closer to being a man than he is." To end the conversation my father said, "Now pull, hard, I will seek the skrei again. If we are to lose Leif for one day in seven, we need to find as much fish as we can in the days when he is with us."

We all knew that the timing of the raid meant we would only have a month or so afterwards to fish. The absence of seven men from such a small village would have an impact. The rest would have to work all that much harder.

We were all easier in the mind as we left the land this time. We did not find the skrei straight away but when we did we had but one cast of the net and we were ready to sail home. So quick had been our journey down the fjord that those who might have wished to follow us and find our secret horde were left to watch us sail by with a gleaming, shimmering, treasure from the sea.

The night before the first day of our training I could barely sleep. Brokkr and my father had done some training with me when we had returned early from the fishing and so I was prepared more than the others. They had tried to prepare me for the raid. They told me not only about how to row but the food or lack of it and the privations we might have to endure. They also told me what I could expect when I stood shield to shield with my shield brothers.

I deliberately left my sword at home. There was no point in taking it as we would not use it to practise and the ones who did not have swords, that was everyone apart from Axel and his cousin, might be resentful. I wore my father's helmet. My mother had made me a woollen protector to go beneath it. It was a good fit. My shield was completely finished and I was inordinately proud of it, especially when my father and uncle commented upon the unique design that I had planned. The leather strap fitted well and I had used some sheepskin to wrap both around the handle and to pad out the boss. Brokkr had told me it would make it easier to use. I had to trust the two of them for I was going into unknown waters.

With a good breakfast inside me, I hefted the shield over my back and rested my spear on my shoulder. Mikkel awaited me outside his house. His shield was his father's. It showed the signs of wear and war. The boss was dented and there were cut marks in it. His spear was also his father's, as was his helmet. Mikkel's head still had some growing and the helmet was looser than it should have been. He looked at my shield and said, "You have done a fine job, Leif. When we return from this raid I will make my own. Would you help me?"

"Of course, although if you covered your father's shield with leather it would both protect it and hide the damage."

He nodded, "Aye, my father fears that an enemy might see the weaknesses and exploit them."

We marched towards the hersir's hall, "I do not think that we shall face such fierce enemies on this raid. I spoke with the jarl, and he says their holy places, the churches of the White Christ, are not guarded by warriors."

The two of us were the first to arrive. Dagfinn, Gunvald and Elvind lived further along the fjord. I had expected Axel and Brynjar to be there but they were not. Finn and Hallstein were. Neither wore mail but their swords hung from their belts.

"Put your war gear down so that we can examine it." I put down my spear and shield. Finn added, "And your knives."

They checked the knives and spearheads first. We had both sharpened them and the two warriors nodded their approval. They picked up my shield and smiled. Hallstein said, "You have made a good shield here, Leif Longstride. Linden is good wood. As you have not yet put a leather covering on it then paint it inside and out with pine tar. It will protect the design and keep out the sea."

"Thank you for the advice, Hallstein."

Finn picked up Mikkel's, "What you warriors do not realise is that your shields have to be as sturdy as a longship." He shook his head and smiled when he picked up Mikkel's, "Your father's?" Mikkel nodded, "These cuts were well earned by

Håkon the Bold. Your father was a fierce warrior." He laid it back on the ground. "It will do for training, but it deserves the honour of resting on your wall. Make a new one."

"I will, Finn, Leif has said that he will help me."

The other three were marching into the village and Finn said, as Hallstein handed me my weapons, "It is good that there are long days for between working for your families, training and making a shield, Mikkel Håkonsson, you will have little time for anything else."

The three who had just arrived did not fare as well as we did. Perhaps our prompt arrival helped, I do not know. Dagfinn had a blunt knife. Elvind's shield was in even worse repair than Mikkel's and Gunvald had a spear whose shaft had clearly broken at some time and would need to be replaced. Hallstein said, "Sharp weapons are vital. Find another spear haft and ensure that the head is fitted well. Elvind, when Leif helps Mikkel to make a shield listen to his advice."

They both looked at the hersir's house and Hallstein snorted, "Take them to the clearing in the woods and I will see what keeps the princelings within."

As we headed away from the prying eyes of the village I felt better already. I had feared that the hersir's hearth-weru would favour Axel and his cousin. It was clear that they would not. I also liked that the two hearth-weru were taking us where we could make mistakes and, I did not doubt, where they could shout at us. The place he took us to had been cleared of the trees to make fishing boats and masts. The stumps had been removed to make pine tar. It was fallow at the moment but once the next stand of trees was cleared then this would be replanted. We worked with the land.

"While we are waiting let me explain how the skjaldborg works. It is a wall of shields. Stand next to each other." We did so. "Leif, Gunvald and Dagfinn you three are the tallest. Stand next to each other. Overlap your shields and place your spears on their rims." We did as we were told. I found myself in the middle. "Mikkel and Elvind, stand behind Gunvald and Dagfinn. Put your shields to press into their backs and poke your spears through the gaps." He seemed pleased with the result, "That is a skjaldborg. Used this way we resist an attack. We will show you later how it is used offensively but this is the way we start. You have to imagine that there will be more than thirty warriors and not just you five."

Just then we heard the rasping voice of Hallstein as he chased Axel and his cousin along the trail to us. We heard his scathing voice as he reprimanded them, "In a raid, we wait for no man and we do not have the luxury of much sleep. Next Þórsdagr, you two had better be the first to arrive for training or there will be punishment."

The two were flushed and red. I did not know if it was the exertion or the embarrassment of the words of the hearth-weru.

Hallstein said, "Good, Finn has begun the training. Axel, you are not as tall as the three at the front. Stand behind Dagfinn and overlap your shield. Poke the head of your spear over the top. Brynjar, you stand next to Elvind." He grinned, "Your training begins now."

It was only then I realised that the two hearth-weru had brought bows. They strung them and moved just thirty paces from us.

Finn took over the training and he nocked an arrow. I saw that it had no arrowhead. "Whoever we are fighting they will either have slings or bows. On a bad day, they will have javelins and darts. We will show you what it is like to endure an attack by missiles. You must use the shield for defence but also watch for men attacking while you wait. There are only two of us and you should be able to see the flight of the arrow."

Hallstein had just nocked his arrow and he said, cheerily, "Of course, while these shafts cannot kill you, they can blind you."

He suddenly released an arrow. I ducked my head and heard the shaft crack into Dagfinn's shield. Finn's arrow struck Mikkel's shield. I hoped that it would hold. Arrows clanked from helmets and struck our shields. After eight arrows I peered over the top and hoped that my helmet's rim would afford me some protection. As I peered, I saw that Hallstein had dropped his bow and taken a hand axe such as the one favoured by Franks and he was running at the shield wall. I did not know what he intended but I knew that we had to do something. I shouted, "Brace!" I put my left leg behind me and used my right to support my shield.

I looked over my rim and saw that he intended to jump at our shields. He landed on the junction of Dagfinn and Axel's shields. Dagfinn had braced but Axel had not. He fell backwards and landed heavily on the rough ground. Hallstein tapped his helmet, none too gently and smiling said, "And you Axel Erlandsson, are dead."

The hersir's son stood and I could see that he was angry, "You said you were using missiles."

"And I also said to keep a watch in case they used the missiles to attack you. Do you think our enemies will tell us what they intend? Will they make it easy for us?" He turned to me, "Quick thinking, Leif. In a real skjaldborg, there would be another line of spearmen behind you and their shields would help you to brace. Now reform and let us try that again."

After an hour we knew how to brace, and the two men were satisfied at the progress we had made.

The next part was less dangerous but harder to master. They taught us to march in a skjaldborg. Of course, the ones in the front marched before the others with their shields before them. The ones behind had their shields in the backs of the front ranks. Had we been marching along the road that ran through the village or the quay then it would have been simplicity itself. Instead, we were marching over ground that had once been a wood. When the stumps had been removed the holes had not been flattened and we found it hard to maintain a cohesive formation. Once more they loosed arrows. We failed and when Axel tripped he brought down Brynjar, Dagfinn and me.

This time Finn came along and rattled our helmets with his sword, "Dead, dead, dead and dead!"

Axel was not liking this at all, "This is impossible. How can we march, keep in line and protect ourselves?"

Hallstein sighed, "Your fathers managed this and your father, Axel, was in the centre of the line and bore the attention of his enemies. Finn and I flanked him. Let me tell you that it is more than possible and you will need to learn the skill."

It said much about our character that, Axel apart, the rest of us took the words of the hearth-weru to heart. We became better. Axel did not. When the sun was at its peak Axel compounded all his actions by asking when we ate and drank.

Hallstein laughed, "Oh, I am sorry, princeling, do you think that men stop a battle when they are hungry to dine and to drink? There will be no food and no drink until we send you back and that time is some hours away. You will learn to do without." He smiled, "And before you ask, there will be no stops for you to piss. If you need to make water, find a way to do it in a skjaldborg."

Brynjar said, "And don't even think about pissing down my legs, Cousin."

For some reason that made us all laugh. Axel did not. I think that was when the bond of warriors was formed. Brynjar had come with his cousin and had all the poor traits of the hersir's son. As the day progressed he realised that he needed to be closer to the rest of us or his body would be left on the battlefield.

By the time we were told the training was over we were all battered and bruised. Elvind had a bloody nose from where he did not react quickly enough to the butt of the spear that was jabbed at him.

Hallstein waved his spear, "Next time, you will train with your weapons. For those of you who need new shields, time is pressing. You need sharp weapons and if you have them, I will bring honey, vinegar and wrappings to bind wounds. In our experience, the next phase of training draws blood. Soon your pretty young bodies will be as scarred as ours, even yours, princeling."

As we trudged back, I wondered if the hearth-weru would get in trouble for their treatment of Axel. I got the impression that he would complain to his father. As we walked back Mikkel said, "Tomorrow, Leif, when we return from fishing I would have you help me to make a start on my shield."

Elvind said, "And if you could help me too, Leif?"

"Of course." One thing the day had taught me was that no man could expect to fight alone. He had to rely on others. Suddenly all the stories about berserkers made sense. They were the men who voluntarily left the shield wall. Biting their shields and sometimes fighting half-naked they would hurl themselves at an enemy. Their actions could result in victory but according to Brokkr more often than not, they simply resulted in death.

When we had parted and I went home I found that despite my hunger, thirst, pain and aching muscles, I was as happy as I had ever been. Life was good. My family were waiting for me as I entered, "Well?"

I smiled, "I think, Father, that I now know what it means to be a warrior. It is not just the helmet, spear and shield, it is more. It is the men alongside whom you fight. You have to put your lives in their hands as they put theirs in yours. It is humbling."

My father and uncle smiled and nodded. Brokkr said, "Those are firm footsteps you have placed on the path to becoming a warrior, Leif. All will be well."

Chapter 5

Fishing seemed easy by comparison with the training. I discovered that I now relished hauling on the nets when the catch was full knowing that it would make me stronger. I was learning about my body and how to use its strengths and eliminate its weaknesses. I was also learning about other strengths I could use and one was the comradeship of those alongside whom I trained. As the weeks passed so the bonds between the five of us grew. The other four all saw me as a sort of leader. As Hallstein had said, I had natural skills. Axel did not improve. His cousin, Brynjar, was still loyal to him, that was family blood, but he did not always agree with him. When we went a-viking I knew that I would have four warriors, untried and untested, but brave, who would be there to back me up. I helped those without shields to make them. That I did so in my own time and after a long and weary day of fishing was also appreciated by them and their families. I had always been popular but now I had more smiles from the families of the other five who saw me helping the young warriors.

As the time drew close for our departure, we worked with the others who would be raiding. Hallstein would be the most experienced warrior we took. He had a mail byrnie. My father deduced, from what I told him, that his father, the hersir, was sending his hearth-weru to watch over his son. The last Þórsdagr before we sailed the other warriors representing our village joined us. All were warriors who had raided before. They had been blooded and had shields, helmets, and spears and one of them, Einarr, even had a battle band. They were all older than I was, but Oddr must have been young when he had raided for he was just five summers older than I was. Sverrir and Ragnavaldr were the other two.

The hersir came to our last training session; he came with his hearth-weru and they were all mailed. He addressed us. There would be eleven of us until Hallstein took his place. He was clearly still training us for he flanked, along with Finn, the hersir who spoke to us.

"In six days, you will all leave our village and join the jarl. You will be led by Hallstein. You will obey his commands as well as those of the jarl. Hallstein is my voice." It seemed to me that his eyes rested upon his son who stood just a short way from me. "Today is your one chance to train together and for me to see if you are worthy to represent our village. Hallstein."

Hallstein said, "Skjaldborg!"

From his smile, I knew that this was a test. We knew those we had trained with but not the four new ones. I also knew, from Hallstein's words, that the front rank were the better warriors and he had made it clear that he considered me the best of the trainees. I went to the left of Oddr. I knew him to be the youngest and the weak part of the skjaldborg would be on the left. When Einarr stood on the right I knew he was right. The others should have stood behind us but Axel, seeing where I stood tried to push between me and Oddr. I was stronger and I did not budge. I saw the flash of anger on Erland Brynjarsson's son's face and wondered if I would be punished for not moving.

Hallstein laughed, "So, Axel Erlandsson, you think you have the skills to stand in the front rank." He nodded, "Let us see. Leif, let him have your place and stand behind Einarr."

I wanted to smack the smirk from Axel's face, but I obeyed. I stood next to Brynjar and locked my shield. I had been given a place of honour. Those on the right had no shield to protect them.

Hallstein nodded and Einarr shouted, "Lock shields." I had already done so and now the rest obeyed the command. I placed my right foot behind my left and the boss of my shield in Einarr's back. The attack from Finn and Hallstein was sudden and, to some, unexpected. They both ran at Axel and Oddr. They did not thrust with their spears but simply locked their shields and barrelled into the three men to the left of our line. Oddr and Sverrir held although Oddr was forced back into Dagfinn and Axel fell to the floor with his arms in a crucifix and Finn pricked the skin at his neck. He drew blood.

"And you, are dead!" He paused, "Again!"

Hallstein said, "Once more, skjaldborg." Giving Axel a contemptuous look he added, "Leif, next to Oddr, and Axel," he paused, "stand between Gunvald and Elvind. There you can do little harm."

I moved along to the left and stood next to Oddr who smiled and nodded. The heath-weru prepared themselves. It was Finn who now gave commands.

"Prepare to be attacked." The two of them advanced to the middle of our line. Both wore mail and so were protected from cuts. I knew that no one would thrust hard enough for a deliberate wound, but accidents could happen and already blood had flowed.

Oddr shouted, "Brace!"

I locked shields with Oddr but the attack this time was on the centre and would be born by Sverri and Ragnavaldr. My young comrades in the second rank were determined to hold and when the two spears were rammed at our shields and the hersir and Finn punched their shields, we held.

Finn was pleased, "Better! Remember the skjaldborg works best when every warrior," he stared at Axel, "plays his part."

The day passed and we endured blows from spears and swords. I realised, as we stopped at noon for ale, that they were not only testing us as warriors but our weapons and shields. I was pleased that our shields, half of which I had helped to make, all held. Axel apart, there was a good feeling amongst us. Even Brynjar was one of us. We seemed to bond together and having Hallstein fight alongside made us, I thought, better. I dared to think, unbeatable.

By the end of the day, weary but feeling like warriors with our shields over our backs and our spears over our shoulders, we made our way back to the village. Hallstein led us in a marching song.

> ***We come from Bygstad, brave and strong***
> ***We stand together as we march along***
> ***Beware our blades for we can slay***
> ***And do so all the battle day***

The song was repeated, and it helped us to march. It made me feel closer to the men with me and I felt hopeful about the raid.

The night before we left my mother cooked a special meal for us, or rather for me. My brother may have been right and I might have been the favourite son. I still had to endure the sharp edge of her tongue, but I knew that, as her firstborn, I was special and

I had been named after her father. She had packed my clothes already in my father's chest and she had made me watch as she did so. She had packed the salve she made to stop my hands chafing when we rowed. Hardened though they were already rowing, perhaps, every day would make them suffer. She had woven my blanket over the last months, and she had ensured that there were pieces of both her hair and my father's in the wool to help protect me. The Hammer of Thor she had added would also ensure that the gods watched over me.

My father had already given me all that I would need but he gave me an extra whetstone. All of those were in the chest along with my spare clothes, my sealskin cape and hat, my bjórr hat and dried, salted fish. It would last months. The last thing I placed in the chest was my wolf skin. Now that it was cured I would wear that when we went to raid. It would give me protection and, with the head over my helmet, might frighten our enemies. The meal was, my mother apart, a merry affair. My brothers were envious of me and even my uncle and father showed that they would enjoy the chance to go a-viking. Kára and her mother were also fond of me and they were happy that I was fulfilling my dream. I was excited and nervous at the same time. Hallstein and Finn had made it clear that while I had the makings of a warrior, the real test would come in battle. I did not want to let anyone down and yet I did not want to die on my first raid.

That night I found it hard to sleep. My father had told me to make the most of the bed for, until the raid was over, the best that I could hope for was a bed of sand if we landed, but more likely it would be a wet deck on the drekar. Despite my racing mind I slept but rose before it was time. I skipped from the bed and went to the fjord and the place where the jarl had bathed. I stripped off my clothes and took the plunge. I did as the jarl had done and jumped in. The icy shock took my breath away. I began to stroke away from the shore and made a loop to return a short while later. When I stepped from the fjord my body tingled. It was as though the waters of my home had infused themselves into my body. Miraculously I did not feel cold but almost warm. I knew that the feeling would not last and so I rubbed myself dry with the old blanket I had brought. It would have until I returned to dry out. That done I returned to the longhouse where my mother, aunt and cousin were preparing food. I would be amongst the first to reach the muster for my father intended to take the snekke to fish out at sea. I would be dropped off at the muster.

I finished my food quickly for I was eager to leave. I dressed in my old sea boots. They were made of sealskin and were comfortable. I left my deer hide boots at home. I strapped my sword over my kyrtle and slipped my cloak around my shoulders. The dragon clasp given to me by my uncle made me look more like a real warrior. The wooden one I used normally was plain by comparison. I looked at my helmet. My father nodded as he chewed the pickled skrei, "Aye, wear your helmet, for you are now a warrior and go to sea. Wear it proudly, my son."

I did so and Kára clapped her hands, "Cousin, you look so handsome. All the girls in the village will wish you to court them!"

My mother snapped, "He is too young!"

I saw my father roll his eyes, "Wife, he will spread his seed on this raid and when he returns he will be ready to take a bride. I did so with you if you remember."

She gave a rare smile, "Aye, I remember."

That softened the mood and Brokkr said, "The fish and the jarl are waiting. Kiss your mother, Leif, and let us be off."

I did as I was asked although first, I took off the helmet. My aunt and cousin also kissed me. I put my helmet on my head and my brothers punched me playfully in the arm.

We headed to the snekke. I carried my own chest. Karl carried my spear and Birger my shield. Poor Ivar looked disconsolate for he had nothing. I smiled, "I will try to fetch you something back, little brother, how is that?"

He brightened, "Thank you, Leif. I will work hard while you are away so that I grow. I would go a-viking with you."

"And that is some time off, but it is good that you prepare."

As we loaded the snekke others came to wish us well. I saw some of the others who were going on the raid heading to their own family boats. Ours was the fastest and we would be there first.

"Sit by the mast, Leif, for today you are a passenger." My father nodded at the pennant on the mast, "The gods smile on us today for we have the wind." It was a good sign.

When we neared the jarl's home I saw that the other drekar was already moored. She looked to be a little longer than *'Bylgja'*. She had a wonderfully carved dragon prow. I wondered why it had been fitted already. We found a place to land and I stepped ashore. My shield, spear and chest were passed to me. There were many people close to the quay for this was an important day for Askvoll. My father just nodded and held out his hand for me to clasp, "May Thor guide your hand. Come home safe, my son." That was all that was said, and I just nodded. We did not show our feelings to others. Uncle Brokkr winked and pushed the snekke off. I stood and watched it as it headed to sea. I marvelled at both its speed and its lines. We had built a fine boat.

Haldir, one of the jarl's hearth-weru was at the steering board of *'Bylgja'*. He shouted down to me, "You are early, Leif Longstride, and that bodes well. Fetch your chest and weapons aboard."

I slung my shield over my back and placed my spear across my sea chest. I could barely contain my excitement as I stepped up the gangplank to my first drekar. There were others aboard and I saw that some chests, along with shields, were already in place.

Haldir nodded to an empty space close to the bows. He told me the number for that was how we would receive our orders when we rowed, "A good place for you and the young men of Bygstad will be here with you." He leaned in, "Of course after Gandalfr the helmsman has seen you row, he may well move you."

I placed the chest where he had indicated. It was on the steerboard side of the ship, "Is that not the jarl's decision?"

He shook his head, "Gandalfr is the navigator, and he makes all decisions about the ship. The raid is commanded by the jarl."

"Where do I put my shield?"

He looked at the shield. Now with a deer hide cover and the red-eyed wolf upon it, it looked magnificent. He nodded his approval, "You have made a good design, Leif Longstride. A

Norse Warrior

warrior who takes such care over minor details will do well. Here, give it to me and I will show you how to fix it." He went to the side and I was able to see how the shield was attached. It was firmly secured and would afford some protection from waves. I had endured many soakings in the snekke.

"And my spear?"

"Place that next to your chest. When your companions arrive, theirs will be placed with yours." I saw that there were pegs in the deck. He pointed to them, "Your spears will be held in place and you can use them for your feet. They will help you to pull harder on the oars."

I saw the sense in that. I had expected to push into the back of the chest before me. I now saw that was foolish as we would be moving other oarsmen.

"Leave your helmet on the bench and then follow me to the hall where the others are meeting." I took off my helmet and he added, "Fetch your horn and your bowl for there will be food later." My horn and bowl were in the chest, and I retrieved them. As I opened the chest he saw the wolf's skin. He nodded, "I heard you had killed a wolf. I have high hopes for you Leif Longstride, but the test of any warrior is when he faces an enemy. Come, I am thirsty and there is a fresh batch of ale to be tried."

Haldir was a true warrior. His scars and battle bands, not to mention the flecks of grey that were appearing in his beard and hair told me he was a veteran, yet he was being kind to a novice. It was a lesson and I learned it.

I saw other ships heading from Bygstad as we stepped ashore. Haldir pointed to them and said to a warrior, "Helgi, we have more oarsmen coming aboard. I leave it to you to assign them."

He nodded and said, "Aye, and it matters not where I place them for grizzly and grumpy Gandalfr will surely move them."

"He will but as he is with the jarl and Arne Sigurdsson, we have to do something. Make your best judgement."

I followed the warrior into the magnificently carved mead hall. The two main posts on each side of the door depicted scenes from the story of Grettir the Strong. I wanted to stay and examine them but I could tell that Haldir was eager for the new ale and I followed him.

Inside the hall was not even a quarter full. I recognised other hearth-weru and I guessed who Gandalfr was. He was an older man with a shock of white hair, a full-plaited beard and eyes that, even across the darkened hall, showed like fire. I deduced that the third man, pointing at the piece of calfskin was Arne Sigurdsson. As Haldir led me past them to the beer barrel I saw that the jarl's cousin was a real warrior. He was huge and he had both battle bands and scars. His beard and his hair were plaited. His skin was a nutty brown and his hands were huge, like human shovels. I was tempted to peer at the calfskin map but knew that would be considered inappropriate for one such as me. I went to the barrel where a man even shorter than my uncle waited with a wonderfully carved wooden ladle.

He grinned at Haldir, "Your nose works as well as ever Haldir. I broached this barrel for the jarl and his guests just moments ago."

Haldir held out his horn, "When Freya makes the ale then I know when it is broached. She is the best of alewives." He nodded to me as his horn was filled, "This is Leif Longstride from Bygstad. Leif this is Snorri. He is of little use when we row for his legs are too short and in the shield wall, he is even more useless, but he knows how to cook and for that, we endure his deficiencies." He smiled. "And, at a pinch, he can navigate. Not as well as his brother but…" He winked at me, and I knew that this was just banter and that Snorri was a good navigator.

Snorri snorted as he poured my ale, "Do not listen to this blowhard, Leif. I am as feisty a fighter as any although he is right. I am of little use in a shield wall, but men of my stature know how to hamstring an enemy and we are often overlooked." He handed me the ale and before I had even taken a mouthful he asked, "Your first voyage?"

"It is."

"I knew your father. He could have been a great navigator had he not met your mother." I took a swig and found it was good ale. The cook had a dreamy look on his face, "Aye, Agnetha was the prettiest of maidens. Your uncle took the other beauty I had my eye on and now I am an old man who lives alone."

"You live alone because you, like your brother Gandalfr, are both grumpy, irascible men who prefer their own company."

I could tell the two got on for they seemed to ignore the insults of the other. He nodded affably, "You may be right, and a raid gives me the chance to enjoy a woman again. From what Lord Arne told us last night they are comely women who do not fight much. When I was younger, I enjoyed such fights but not now."

"Lord Arne's ship, what is it called?"

"The *'Nidhogg'*."

I nodded, "A fine name for a good ship. I admired her figurehead as I passed her."

"Aye, Bolli knew how to carve. That was his last carving before he died. We shall not see his like again."

Haldir shook his head, "You cannot say such things, Snorri, for we do not know. The Norns weave and plot. They took him when *'Nidhogg'* was finished. It seems to me that they will weave and plot a little more and out there, somewhere, perhaps in this fjord, there is another such craftsman."

Perhaps it was the ale speaking, I know not, but I ventured to join in the conversation with these two veterans. "Halvard Jørgsson has just married, and his father Jørg is a master carver, not of ships but he is good with his hands. Perhaps Halvard will sire a son who might become such a man."

They looked at each other, "One thing is sure, Halvard is no warrior. He came on one raid and did little but made enough silver to marry a hersir's daughter. He is better suited to becoming a merchant."

Their words sent a chill through my heart. I had thought that just by going a-viking I would become a warrior. I now saw that it was not as simple as that.

Just then the jarl shouted, "Haldir, come."

He held his horn out for it to be refilled and shouted, "Coming, Jarl." He then nodded towards the open door. "I see three of your fellow warriors are coming."

I looked up and saw Mikkel, Dagfinn and Gunvald. I smiled and waved my horn to them. I did not feel so alone anymore. As they joined me I saw a couple more veterans arrive and, after having their horns filled up, they sat with the jarl. If our hersir had come then he too, would have sat on that table.

Chapter 6

I spent the rest of the day at the table close by the ale barrel. I did not drink heavily but steadily. I was enjoying the sights and sounds of so many warriors. Their battle bands and scars bespoke battles past and I was enthralled. We were all too excited about the voyage. We were close enough to hear snippets of conversation from the table at which the jarl sat and it was clear that there was a discussion going on. It seemed that some warriors, not the jarl nor Arne Sigurdsson, did not want to raid Frankia but sail across the sea to the land of the Angles and the Saxons. They made a good argument saying that it was a shorter voyage and they knew where the holy places with the silver lay. It was the jarl's cousin who argued back although his words were supported by the jarl. He pointed out that the best places in the land of the Angles had already been raided. He also told the others that the weather further south would enable us to raid for longer and that we would have rivers that went deep into their land. The discussions raged.

The last three of our warriors to arrive were Hallstein, Axel and Brynjar. Hallstein was a mighty warrior and the discussion around the table ended when he entered.

The jarl stood to greet him, "Hail Hallstein, now I know that we will enjoy success for your spear and sword alone will sweep our enemies away."

Hallstein gave a half bow and said, "You are too kind, Jarl Bjørn Haraldsson, for I am getting old and these days spend more time training the young."

"Then that bodes well for some of your young warriors were so keen that they arrived before I had finished my breakfast." He chuckled and his eye caught mine, "Any earlier and they would have found me swimming in the fjord."

Everyone laughed and it was clear that the others knew of the jarl's eccentricity.

"This is Axel Erlandsson and his cousin Brynjar."

"You are both welcome and I hope that you are as good a pair of warriors as your father's. Hallstein, get some ale and then join our debate. I would be pleased to hear your words."

Brynjar went to Snorri to have his horn filled and he joined us but Axel gave his horn to Hallstein and sat at the table close to Haldir. That he had made an error was clear to us all and I saw the looks of surprise on the faces of Haldir and Arne. They said nothing but it was clear that they did not like it.

As Brynjar sat he shook his head, "My cousin thinks that he is the hersir already."

Mikkel had been paying the closest attention to the debate and he said, "They will not heed his words and I doubt that he has anything important to say. Only Leif here has sailed beyond the sight of land. What knowledge can the princeling bring?"

We all smiled for since we had begun training we had used the term mockingly.

Dagfinn nodded, "It will make no difference if your father is hersir or not when we have callouses on our hands and our arses and we face the wrath of Rán."

Gunvald said, "My chest and shield were placed next to yours, Leif. We are to be oar brothers."

I held up my right hand and he held up his. We clasped them. "Good, then we shall speed our ship so hard that they will need good men on the larboard side."

Mikkel snorted, "And as that is Dagfinn and I then we have better men."

Boasting about strength was acceptable. Until we had dipped our spears into men's flesh we could not brag about our martial skills and so we bantered. So engrossed in our talk were we that we did not notice Axel sidle up to join us until he spoke.

"It seems that the jarl's cousin has won the day and we sail to Frankia!"

We all turned to look at him. I knew that the days of Brynjar blindly following his cousin were long gone and Axel's words were greeted with silence.

"I agree with the ones who want to sail to the land of the Angles. We could be there and back in a month with silver and slaves. If we go to Frankia we could be away for four months."

Brynjar drained his horn and stood, "Why does that bother you? Have you any plans?"

He went to Snorri for a refill and I said, "If we return within a month then we just endure longer nights at home. We have heard that the land of the Franks keeps the sun longer, even in Mörsugur." The others nodded. That piece of information had been overheard before they arrived.

Axel frowned, "That cannot be right. The world is the same all over. When we lose the sun so does the rest of the world."

"Not so. According to the jarl's cousin, there are places further south where the sun shines for longer and hotter even at Mörsugur."

"He has been there?"

"No, but he has travelled far and traded. He is a good leader."

"My father would be a better one."

Mikkel and Axel did not get on and Mikkel was not afraid of Axel, "Then why is he not here? Our fathers are not the hersir. If your father was a good hersir surely he would wish to lead the men from Bygstad instead of sending a hearth-weru."

Axel had cunning but he was not clever and he lacked both the words and the thoughts to counter Mikkel. He scowled and turned to Brynjar who had just sat opposite him, "Cousin, the best thing about this ill-fated voyage is that we shall meet warriors more akin to us than the dregs we have dragged from our village."

Brynjar shook his head and Mikkel's derisive laugh made Axel's foolish words seem even more ridiculous. He ceased talking and began drinking more heavily.

By the time that food was prepared and the ones who had not had the foresight to bring their bowls, spoons and eating knives had fetched them, he was almost drunk. Hallstein came over and spoke harshly in his ear. I do not know what was said but I saw Hallstein empty Axel's ale into his own horn. The food was good. It would need to be. Hallstein sat with us and told us to make the most of the hot food. "The next time you eat such food we will be in the land of our enemies and we will have fought to take food from them."

"What do we eat then, Hallstein?"

He smiled, "I will tell you, Elvind son of Suni; fish that we have caught but not cooked; dried venison and pickled fish. By the time we land you will crave a blackberry or an old hoary apple. Being a warrior who goes a-viking is not just about standing with locked shields and facing enemies. That is the best of a raid. The rest is the worst. Do you think that there will be no rain when we sail? The sun may shine longer and hotter the further south we go but the rain still falls and we will still be wet." He looked at Axel who had fallen asleep with his face in the stew. "And here is one who will be lucky to survive a week at sea." He nodded to Brynjar, "You know the hersir is relying on you and me to ensure his son returns whole from this raid?"

"Aye, I do, and I wish he had found a different way to make a man of his son." Their words were telling. Those first days of training were long in the past but the shadow remained. Axel was our weakness and we all knew it.

When we finished eating and the men just mopped up the juices with bread the jarl stood. "My friends, this is a great day for me. I will be leading, for the first time, two crews of mighty warriors." Everyone cheered and his cousin smiled. "I say lead but we all know that my cousin, the mighty Arne Sigurdsson is a more experienced sailor than I am. I am happy to defer to him. When this voyage is over who knows what the future will bring? We have many young warriors who have the chance for great deeds and to earn battle bands. We sail on the morning tide." He smiled, "If any wish to join me on my morning swim…"

There were hoots of derision and, as the jarl sat, smiling, the conversation returned to the raid.

I asked, "Hallstein, do we sleep here or on the longship?"

He shrugged, "It is your choice but I will sleep under a roof. I will have one last night where I am dry. From tomorrow on we wake with salt in our hair and the sound of gulls overhead." I looked around and wondered where there was to sleep. He smiled, "Soon the thralls will clear the food and the tables will be moved. You find a place." He chuckled, "It will be cosy." He tapped the sleeping Axel on the head, "I will have to use this one as a pillow, eh?"

It was cosy and noisy. We found a wall where we could sleep. The thralls brought some furs for us to sleep upon but we were all closer than any would have liked. If any of us thought we were in for a night filled with a good sleep we were wrong. The snores, belches and farts rent the air and just when I thought we might be able to get to sleep Axel suddenly rose to race to the door. We heard his vomiting. None went to help him and he was roundly cursed as he staggered back to take his place between his cousin and Hallstein.

I rose early. Something disturbed me but I did not discover what. I found that I had to make water and I went outside. I was about to return to the furs, for it was still early when the jarl and his hearth-weru emerged. He smiled, "Ah, Leif Longstride, you have come to swim with me?"

I had not intended to do so but I felt that I could not refuse. "Aye, Jarl."

He clapped a hand around my shoulders, "Excellent. My hearth-weru are all fine warriors but they do not chatter. I like to chat while I swim. Come."

He led me to a small beach. I could see that it had been tended and the vegetation kept cropped. The jarl stripped off and I joined him. "Here there is no rock from which we can jump. We have to walk."

Somehow it was harder to walk into the icy water than simply jump. For one thing, the rocks hurt my feet and as soon as I could I emulated the jarl and made a flat dive. I swam alongside him and he kept going until we were a hundred paces from the shore. He turned on his back. He said, "You are a good swimmer, Leif, and my hearth-weru must trust you for see, they stand and watch us. Let us swim back and do so on our backs. That way we can talk."

I rolled onto my back and used my legs and arms to keep pace with the jarl.

"I watched you yesterday, as you listened to the words from our table. Unlike the hersir's son, you did not drink to excess. What do you think of our plan?"

"If these people have never endured a raid of men such as us then we have the chance to, indeed, become rich, but what of enemy warriors? We know that the holy places in the land of the Angles and Saxons are not guarded but what of Frankia?"

"A good question and one I asked of my cousin. They have good warriors and some of their horsemen are mailed. It will be a test of our skjaldborg. Lord Arne hopes that we can strike so quickly that none will realise we are there until it is too late and we have gone. Indeed, our greatest fear is that we take so much that we cannot spend as long there as we intend." We had reached the shore and we stood. Haldir and the other hearth-weru had blankets for us to use to dry. "I will confide in you, Leif, for I can see that you are a clever man. We plan, next year, to spend the winter in the land of the Franks. This raid is more in the nature of a scouting expedition to find somewhere we can use to lay up. If we are successful then next year we will take, perhaps, three drekar." He pointed upstream and I saw what I had missed when we had sailed up. There was the skeleton of a drekar. The keel had been laid and the lower strakes had been fitted. "This one will be ready by the time we return and the next time we sail we might have more than one hundred warriors, think of that. With the silver and metal, we take this time we will be stronger." We had dried and dressed as he had been speaking, "Many men wondered why I had not raided before and this is the reason. I want to make my first raid successful. I do not want the leavings of other raiders. I want to be the first and to be the most successful."

I nodded and held the sword and scabbard in the air, "And I will be at your side, Jarl Bjørn Haraldsson."

He laughed, "You are right, Haldir, this is one to watch."

When we entered the hall Haldir banged loudly on the nearest table, "Awake you lazy whoresons. Daylight is here and the tide is with us."

Even as men rose the thralls entered with pots of steaming porridge and platters of freshly cooked fish, loaves and fried salted pork. As the rest of our men went to make water I was able to have the first choice. I found some spring berries and honey and liberally sprinkled them into the porridge. If Hallstein was right then such fare would be rare at sea. By the time they returned, I was eating the fried pork and bread. I would have to eat fish soon enough. I finished first and went to the longship to retrieve my ale skin. It was empty and I went to Snorri's barrel and filled it. I drank two horns of ale. When the ale ran out it would be rainwater or the stale water from the barrel by the mast fish that I would have to endure. Brokkr had given me sound advice before I had left my home. As I returned to the ship I took the opportunity to lift two loaves. The berries had all been eaten as had the pork but the two loaves would give me extra food for the first two days.

Haldir was at the mast fish as I boarded, "Put your sword in your chest, Leif, and your helmet, you will need neither for at least a week. If you have salve and a sealskin cape I would keep those to hand." He pointed to the dragon pennant at the top of the mast, "The wind is against us and while we have the tide we shall still need to row until we reach the open sea."

"Thank you, Haldir and…" I hesitated, "for your kind comments to the jarl."

He shrugged, "I speak the truth. I know Hallstein and he spoke well of you. We may both be wrong and I might have to take back Lars Greybeard's sword to your father and tell him of your death but if that happens then the Norns will have spun. As you will discover, Leif, men can plan and plot but we are playthings when the sisters spin. Now take your place. Gandalfr is a hard taskmaster and woe betide any who are tardy."

I went to my chest and did as he said. I also placed the two loaves inside so that they would not become dampened with salt air. The sky looked clear and so I placed my sealskin cape on top of my chest. I put the pot of salve in the leather pouch I wore around my waist. Inside was the piece of cloth, the spell, my mother and aunt had woven, the spell to keep me safe. I decided to don my beaver cap for if the sun shone it would protect my head and keep some of the spray from me.

Gunvald, Mikkel, Elvind and Dagfinn arrived together. "Haldir said to put your helmets and swords in your chests. Today will be a hard one for we are to row."

They nodded and took my advice. I saw the jarl, Snorri and Gandalfr at the steering board. Haldir and the other hearth-weru were at the foot of the gangplank chivvying aboard the late arrivals.

I saw *'Nidhogg'* edge into the fjord. Her crew was ready and eager. We were still three men short.

It was clear who was in command for Gandalfr shouted, "Rise and take your oars."

I saw that there was a hierarchy to this. The younger ones, like me, were closer to the bows and the experienced rowers chose their oars first. That meant the ones like us had the least choice. I managed to take an oar that was straight but, as I returned to my chest I saw that there were just three oars left and two of them were a little warped. It was then that I realised who had not yet boarded. Hallstein, Axel and Brynjar. It would be Axel who had caused the delay and I saw that Gandalfr was not happy. He shouted, "Haldir, you and the hearth-weru take your places. The tide is on the turn and I would take advantage of it. Ship's boys prepare to haul in the gangplank."

Even as the four boys took the places Hallstein and his charges raced from the hall. I saw the look of anger on the face of Hallstein. He pushed Axel up the gangplank. Brynjar had raced up first and taken an oar. Hallstein would have to make do with a warped one. He would be seated closer to the steering board with the better oarsmen.

"Let us loose from the land." The boys untied the ropes that moored us and then ran up the deck to pull the gangplank up. Even before they had secured the gangplank Gandalfr shouted, "Steerboard oars, push off. Larboard oars, fit your oars."

We stood and Gunvald and I pushed our oar against the jetty. We began to move and the current took us towards the centre of the fjord. *'Nidhogg'* would wait for us. Until we left the mouth of the fjord then the jarl would lead. Once at sea then the more experienced Arne would lead us.

"Steerboard, fit your oars."

Gunvald leaned out to push the oar through the hole and I pulled it through. We were both grinning. We had both rowed, of course, but that had been on a fishing boat or a snekke. We had ten oars on each side and we had two men on each oar. Gunvald and I held our oar at the same angle as those before us. It now made more sense why the younger ones were at the bow. We had the more experienced ones to emulate.

"Oars in the water." We lowered our oar and stopped when we felt the resistance of the fjord. Snorri, standing next to his brother had a spear in his hand and he began to bang rhythmically on the deck. Gandalfr chose his moment and said, "Row."

Gunvald and I pulled. The longship began to move and I heard, from the shore, the cheers of the villagers we were leaving behind. It was, of course, not as smooth as Gandalfr would have liked for he shouted, "Together! Pull."

I heard Brynjar, behind us somewhere, hiss, "Axel, pull and do as the others are doing."

"I still feel sick."

"If you are sick over me then you will find yourself swimming back to Bygstad."

Gunvald and I smiled. We were rowing as one and it was good. Poor Brynjar had the lame duck with him and would have to work twice as hard as we did. I was on my first raid. There were few clouds and the tide was with us. Life was good.

Chapter 7

Hard does not come close to what it was like that first day. Perhaps Gandalfr wanted to punish us all for Axel's tardiness or it may have been he wanted to mould us into a crew quickly. Whatever the reason we rowed, even when we were at sea. We had been told that *'Nidhogg'* would lead but we kept our position and rowed hard even though there was a breeze from the north and west that helped us to go south. My hands were used to rowing but in our snekke Brokkr and I were the strongest and we slowed to help my brothers. Here we were keeping up with men like Haldir and Hallstein. I took solace from the moans from behind as Axel struggled even more than we did. I had known his weaknesses from our training and here they manifested themselves from the start.

The cloudless sky began to fill ominously from the north. The very wind that sped us south now threatened rain. I was grateful for Haldir's advice and, as the first drops fell, I used the backstroke to lift my backside slightly and deftly whip out my cape with my left hand. Gunvald did the same on the next stroke. "Take all the effort while I don my cloak and I will do the same for you."

He nodded, "Now."

I let go of the oar and quickly donned my cape. My hands were on the oar at the forward stroke. When I pulled back, I said, "Now!"

As soon as he let go I felt the strain as I had to pull as hard as the others but I was alone. As soon as Gunvald grabbed the oar again I felt relief and, at that moment the skies decided to deposit a cloud full of rain upon us.

Snorri shouted, "Boys, grab the pails."

Rainwater was too precious to waste and the ship's boys placed the pails close to where the rain would run off the sail and steering board. The shower did not last long but it was so hard that there were puddles on the deck. It was shortly after the rain stopped and the wind veered a little more that Gandalfr relented and said, "Oars in!" When the oars were in, he said, "Stack them on the mast fish."

It felt strange to stand and walk the few paces to the mast fish. I felt like a drunken man. An older warrior, I later learned that his name was Evindr chuckled, "You will get used to it, young 'un. Wait until we land and you have to learn how to walk on the earth once more."

I went to the water barrel but Haldir shook his head, "Drink from the pails first." He smiled, "A gift from the gods."

I nodded and put my horn in the pail. It had a slightly salty taste from the spray from the sea but it refreshed. I returned to my chest. Looking up at the sky I saw that the clouds had blown away. The squall had been but brief. I hung my cape from my shield to dry and went to my chest. I took out one of the loaves and, breaking it in two, offered half to Gunvald.

He shook his head and laughed, "Your first voyage and yet you are like a veteran."

I bit into the loaf and nodded. My mouth half full I said, "I spoke with my father and uncle. They told me to eat as much as I could when I was able and to be like a squirrel and store spare food." I leaned in, "I have a second loaf."

"I am glad that I was seated next to you." He glanced around, "I never thought I would feel sorry for him but poor Brynjar is the worst off of all of us. He has to endure the princeling."

The ship's boys brought around food for us. It was just at the moment when *'Nidhogg'* overtook us to take her place at the fore. Snorri also came around with his barrel of ale and gave us our noon ration of ale. I still had a skin full of ale and I had decided that I would share the bounty of my foresight with Gunvald.

Snorri nodded at Axel and said, quietly, "I watched you young warriors and, with one exception, you did well. I pray that he is better when it comes to fighting for a warband is only as strong as its weakest link." It was clear he was speaking about Axel.

When he had passed us, I said, "He is right. When we fight in the skjaldborg whoever has him beside him or stands before him is in danger."

"Perhaps we will not have to fight. If our leaders are right then the Franks will not be expecting us. We might get in and out so quickly that we do not have to fight."

I shook my head, "I want to fight. If we just raid and take and my spear is not whetted then how will I know if I am a warrior? A man? I might as well have stayed at home if there is to be no fighting."

"You killed a wolf. You are a man."

"But until I blood my spear I am not a warrior and before I take a bride I would be a warrior. Remember what they said about Halvard. He went on a raid but did not kill. He has silver but he is no warrior."

"Aye, you are right." We both turned to look at the hersir's son. Had we brought the weakness that might bring us failure?

Mercifully we did not have to row again that first day. The coast could still be seen on the larboard side of the ship and when it became dark the sails were reefed and a light hung from the stern of *'Nidhogg'*. We would sail slowly at night. I wondered how we would all manage to sleep on the longships for there did not seem enough space. Then I discovered that we would each have a watch. Gandalfr had an hourglass, it was probably the most valuable item on the ship, and it not only helped with the navigation but also ensured that the four-hour watches we had were all the same length. I found myself on watch with Gunvald, Evindr, Haldir, Dagfinn, Mikkel and Elvind. Hallstein might have had something to do with that. He and Brynjar had promised Erland to watch over Axel and as he was proving to be a problem then he would look after the problem himself.

Haldir took charge. The jarl had the steering board and Haldir placed himself there. Gunvald and I were given the task of watching from the prow while poor Mikkel had to climb the mast and watch from there. The others were at the sides and it was Evindr who came around to ensure that we knew what we were doing.

"Keep your eyes on the light. If it disappears then one of you run and tell the jarl." We both nodded, "Don't worry, with a crew this size it means you only have a duty every three days. You can have a full night of rest on the others. Unless," he chuckled, "the seas get up and then it is all hands who will be needed."

"Why?"

"Even with the shields we have a low freeboard. If the sea is rough then everyone has to bail and that is as hard as rowing, believe me." He turned and said, over his shoulder, "Still, it is easier than sailing across the sea to the land of the Angles and Saxons. This close to the coast we should not encounter such big waves."

When we finally finished our duty we rolled in our blankets and the motion of the longship rocked us to sleep.

In such a way we began our voyage south. We grew used to eating the raw fish caught by the boys on the lines they ran out each day. To them, it was a game. Who could catch the most? We found that while we recognised most of the fish, some were new to us. We discovered the delights and joys of hanging with our backsides over the side to empty our bowels. We learned to do so while being held by two oar brothers. The sea ensured that we were cleaned afterwards for we took off our breeks after the first time Elvind was soaked. We had to row for each day the wind varied a little and Gandalfr was keen for us to keep up with **'Nidhogg'**. She had more men at the oars and could always travel faster although, when the wind was right, we flew. Gandalfr had kept a clean, weed-free hull. The salve worked and after a week, as we passed, so we were told, the coast of Jutland, I found that I could touch the oars without wincing.

The Danish coast had been one where we had many eyes watching. The Danes had ships such as we had and they would have been quite happy to take us and make us slaves. As we passed the last of their lairs and entered Frisian waters, we all breathed a sigh of relief. Soon we would reach the land called Flanders, which lay to the north of Frankia. Snorri was our source of all information and when he passed down the ship to give us our daily ration of ale we plied him with questions.

"Once we have passed Flanders then we shall look for targets. There is a river in the north of Frankia. I think the jarl is anxious to raid and to replenish our supplies. This is the last barrel of ale."

Mikkel asked, "Do the men of Flanders have ale?"

Snorri shrugged, "Probably and if not they will have either mead or cider. Raiders cannot be choosy."

Norse Warrior

The river mouths we had passed in Frisia had not looked as though they would yield much but Flanders did. When we sailed past the mouth of the first rivers we were disappointed for we saw no targets. We sailed on and passed many long stretches of beach. They did not look as though they would yield anything. However, when Gandalfr ordered the oars to be run in and the sails were reefed we knew that something was happening. As we laid our oars on the mast fish we could see that Lord Arne was turning his longship towards what looked like a small bay. I glanced to the west. The sun would still be in the sky for an hour or so. We had noticed, as we had sailed south, that the sun set earlier than it did at home.

Haldir came down the longship, "It is time to strap on your swords and don your arming caps."

That was all he said but there was a cheer from all. Even as I went to my chest I was glancing to the shore and I could not see anything that looked like a target worthy of a raid. What I did see was that this was nothing like home. There were no sheer walls of stone rising like fortresses. Here it was soft rounded bumps topped with trees. I strapped on my sword first and took out my boots. I donned the arming cap my mother had knitted for me. I closed my chest and, as Gandalfr followed *'Nidhogg'* into what was now clearly an estuary I put on my socks and then my boots.

Hallstein approached us. He held his byrnie, "Leif, you are almost dressed. Help me with my byrnie."

I was honoured and I took the heavy mail links in my hands. He bowed his head and I put the byrnie over his shoulders. He put his arms through the arm holes and I helped to move the byrnie down.

"Do we raid then, Hallstein?"

He picked up his sword and belt from the deck and said, "This is Frankia and it is a wise warrior who prepares to fight, even if he does not think he will have to. We may well have to row a little more unless this river is straight, deep and rock-free. Just prepare and obey every order quickly." He gave a rare smile at us all, "You have all done well on the voyage south but the real test will come when we pick up our spears."

Snorri shouted as the steering board was turned, "Oars!"

I did not envy those in mail who would have to row encumbered by mail shirts. We would have to contend with our swords. We fitted the oar and arranged our scabbards so that we could row without interference. I had still to make a better scabbard. Snorri began the beat with his spear. I noticed that this time it was slower. When Gandalfr said, "Row," we all pulled on the oars and entered the first river in Frankia. This was not like our fjord where Askvoll guarded the mouth. There was no village at the mouth of this river. I saw a tendril of smoke rising in the distance. There was a farm, or house, perhaps, even a village. We were in the hands of Arne Sigurdsson. He had traded these waters and he knew what he sought.

We could only see the river behind but there was a ship's boy at the prow and he called out instructions to Gandalfr. When he called, "*'Nidhogg'*, is heading to the northern shore," I knew we were about to land. The light had almost left the sky but I could still make out the branches of the trees we passed.

"Larboard oars in."

The beat was now so slow that we were only pulling every few moments.

"Steerboard oars in."

The jarl gave the next command, "Stack your oars and arm yourselves." Gandalfr had done his part and brought us to the land of the Franks. Now it was the turn of the jarl. I went to my chest and took out my helmet. I also took the wolf skin. I slipped the head over my helmet and the skin naturally draped over my shoulders. I retrieved my shield and picked up my spear. There were others who were already splashing into the water as they jumped overboard. Gandalfr, Snorri and the ship's boys would have the task of securing us to the land. For the moment it was the current and the tide that held us.

The water came up to my waist. I waded to the small beach. I spied a rock and, sitting upon it, I lifted my legs so that the water came out of my boots. The others joined me and I vacated the rock so that they could do the same. There would be almost ninety of us but I was not sure that we would all raid. The two ships would need to be guarded. I just hoped that I would not be given that particular duty. I was relieved when I heard Lord Arne order six of his warriors to guard the ships.

Hallstein was our leader and he joined us to inspect us. He seemed satisfied although he gave a contemptuous look at Axel who was the last to wade ashore. He had good weapons, a helmet and a good shield but he did not carry them well.

The two leaders conferred and then Haldir came along to give us our instructions. "We are heading up this trail. There is a monastery and a small village just a mile away. We are to take the village. The jarl and those who have raided before will be at the fore. Hallstein, you and these youngsters will ensure we are not ambushed." Hallstein could not have been happy with the orders but he knew that he was here in place of Hersir Erland. He nodded, "We will do our duty." Haldir nodded and returned to the jarl. "I will lead. Axel, behind me. Leif and Gunvald, guard our rear."

"But..."

Gunvald got no further for Hallstein hissed, "This is not a game played in the village, Gunvald. We all have a part to play and you and Leif Longstride can be relied upon to do your duty. We will watch the rear of the rest but we need your ears and eyes to protect us."

"Yes, Hallstein." He was contrite and I was pleased that I had not voiced the same concerns.

It seemed an age before we left. By the time we did the two longships were tied to the two metal stakes driven into the earth and the ship's boys were gathering kindling for the fire that would cook us our first hot food since we had left our fjord. I had my shield hung over my left shoulder. The others all had them strapped to their backs. The warning I had been given by Snorri was wisely given. I felt like a newborn deer as I wobbled up the slope. I hoped that he had been right and that the feeling would soon pass.

Darkness came as soon as we reached the tree line and headed along what was a well-worn trail. The sounds that could be heard were just the footfall on the ground, the brush of leaves and the sound of heavy breathing. I was aware of our role and I kept glancing to my left and right for signs of danger. I did not think that there could be danger for no one could have known that we had landed. We had seen no watchers and there had been no boats. Any fishermen would have returned to their homes before we arrived.

We travelled the thousand paces or so quite quickly and when we stopped I swung my shield around so that I was ready for danger. Words were not used. I saw the jarl use his spear to organise the men. I could not see the village we were to attack but I could smell it. There was a combination of woodsmoke mixed with animal and human dung. The smell would disguise ours. I also caught a sweeter smell. It was only later I discovered that it was something called incense and came from the monastery. Lord Arne and his men disappeared.

Hallstein pointed his spear and we formed a single line as Jarl Bjørn Haraldsson pointed his spear at our target. The men before us hid the village from view. They surged forward and as they did Hallstein pointed his spear to our left and we followed his lead.

The wail of women and the cries of alarm rent the air. We heard the clash of metal and wood as our warriors struck the hastily organised defences of the village.

"We stand here and watch. Lock your shields."

It was not just Gunvald who wished to complain about our inactivity. Most of us did but none would risk his wrath. He was vindicated when the three men ran out of the dark. They were bareheaded and had small shields and swords but they clearly came from the village.

Hallstein shouted, "Spears!" Our training with him and Finn came to our aid and we thrust our spears at the three surprised men. My spear found flesh in the form of the cheek of one of the villagers. He was a young man, perhaps my age and he screamed. He sounded like a vixen. One of them fell writhing as a spear tore into his middle. Gunvald rammed his spear into the shoulder of the man I had cut and the third turned to run back to the village. Hallstein thrust his spear into the villager's unprotected back. The three were dying. Hallstein stuck his spear into the ground and, taking his sword, ended the three lives. As he wiped his sword on their kyrtles he said, "They did not deserve a slow death. Gunvald and Leif, that villager was slain by you, take what you will. The rest is mine."

We rammed our spears into the ground and knelt. The blood was pooling around his head. I said, "You made the killing blow. His sword should be yours."

He nodded, "It is not a good one but I will take it. His shield has no metal. The rest is yours."

I searched the body. There was no purse but, sticky with blood, there was a cross around his neck. It looked to be silver and I took it and slipped it into my pouch. In his belt I found a short blade. I would take that for my brother. I jammed that in my belt.

"Come, let us join the others."

We trotted along the path the three men had used and found ourselves in a village that had been taken. There were half a dozen women and three children. The men were all dead. I saw that two of our men had been cut and were tending to their own wounds. They would be badges of honour.

Jarl Bjørn Haraldsson said, "We take everything back to the drekar. There we will divide what we have and decide if the women are worthy to be thralls." He nodded to Hallstein, "You and your young warriors did well, Hallstein. Your spears are bloody." That was not quite true. Four of us had bloody spears. The others had struck wood or missed but we all stood taller. I did not think that we were yet warriors but we had been tested and we had passed. It boded well for the future.

Chapter 8

It took time to search the village and Arne Sigurdsson and the men who had raided the monastery passed us on their way back to the ships before we had finished. I saw that while they were laden they had no slaves. The women and children were pushed to the front and we headed back along the trail. The women keened and wept. The children clung to their mothers. I wondered who would take the slaves as their own. In Bygstad there were just a handful of slaves. I had seen more at Askvoll. Some of the Frankish women were old and they kept dropping to their knees. They placed their hands together and looked to the skies. They intoned words I did not understand. Dragged to their feet we continued but they slowed us. It was almost dawn when we reached the river. Snorri and the others left there had water boiling and as food was brought from the village a stew was begun.

The jarl appointed four men to watch the prisoners and he and Lord Arne conferred. I went to the river to wash the blood from my spear. I saw that blood had splashed on my shield and I washed that away too. I was proud of my design and whilst the dark had not allowed my enemies to see it, I still wanted it to be clear. It was a young man's vanity, I suppose.

Inevitably it was Haldir who came to speak to us, "Hallstein, you and your cockerels did well. You and the rest of the men of Bygstad can eat first and then take post half a mile downstream. You can rest but be vigilant. The jarl wants to be warned of any Franks."

"When do we leave?"

"Tonight, when the tide turns."

After he left Hallstein said, "Take off your helmets and stack your spears and shields. We will eat first. I will fetch the others. When the other four joined us we took our bowls and went to Snorri. "Help yourselves to the stew. I did not recognise all that we put in it but as the Franks eat it then it cannot be poisonous. When you have taken your fill come and try some of the local drink. It is fermented apples. It is not as good as ale but it will do."

The stew had fish, meat and vegetables in it. The taste was not unpleasant but it was different. The fermented apples were a little sweeter than the ale we were used to but after stale water it was good. When we finished Hallstein said, "It is time for work." We donned our helmets and with shield and spear we followed him and the other four veterans along the river. He chose a little knoll that overlooked the river. We could see the sea and it also afforded us a view of the ships. He pointed at us as he assigned duties, "Oddr, Einarr, Gunvald and Leif, you have the first watch" he waved a hand from the sea to the ships, "watch both."

Oddr nodded, "Aye, Leif, with me, we watch the sea. Einarr, take Gunvald." We walked a few paces to a gap in the trees. The leaves would give us shade and yet we still had an uninterrupted view to the west. I copied Oddr as he took off his helmet and laid his shield and his spear against a tree. This was still part of my training. He sat with his back against a tree. I took the second tree.

"Well, that was easy."

"Three men tried to escape."

"Aye, you did well to stop them. Had they escaped they might have brought help although I cannot see anywhere close. Still, the jarl is wise to leave in the dark. We came at night and we leave at night," he chuckled. "They will think that we are wraiths. We need these people to fear us."

"Why?"

"We are few in number. We want them cowering behind walls and not seeking us out." He took some dried deer meat from his pouch and offered me a piece. I took it and we sat and chewed as we stared at an empty, dark grey sea. It was not cold but the grey clouds suggested that it might soon be wet.

"Was it a good raid, Oddr?"

He shook his head, "There was not enough silver. By the time our two leaders have taken their share, we will be lucky to be given a silver coin. No, this was to feed us and to give us success. Lord Arne is clever. I was talking, back in Askvoll, to some of his men. He wants to sail much further south. He said there is another river, it is called the Sequana. It is very wide. At its mouth, it is said to be more than two thousand paces wide and goes deep into Frankia. That is our real target."

"But it is far from here?"

"It will take days to reach it, aye, and from what the man told me there are two small ports that are at the entrance. We will need a night passage to avoid detection. I think it will take a good day of sailing to reach the next river." I nodded. "Now do you see why we needed this raid?"

"Aye, the jarl wants us to be able to row at night in an unknown land."

"You will do, Leif Longstride. You pick things up quickly." He stood and dropped his breeks. He began to make water, "What did the princeling do when you fought?"

I shrugged, "I know not. Gunvald and I struck one Frank." I thought back to after the combat. "His spear was unblooded."

"The hersir should have been with us. He wishes to make his firstborn a warrior but, as with Halvard, some men are not born to be warriors. There is no shame in that. Lars Greybeard is well respected and yet he is no warrior." He pulled up his breeks and sat down again. "Unless he thinks that Axel may die. Galmr is younger than his brother but he appears to be made of sterner stuff."

I said nothing for Galmr was a bully. Ivar had suffered at his hands until I had intervened.

His words made me think about Axel. If he died then the next hersir would be Galmr. I did not like that thought. Of course, another could challenge him for the right to be headman. My father had almost opposed Erland but, for the good of the clan, he had stepped back. I thought it would have been better if he had challenged Erland. My father would be a better leader.

I was weary when, after a couple of hours of watching we were relieved. We trudged back to the camp where more hot food awaited us. As I ate, I watched the prisoners. They huddled together. None of us understood a word that they said but it did not matter. I idly wondered if we would take any of them. If we did then the longship would be even more crowded. Treasure, chests and food could be stored beneath the deck but human or animal cargo had to be transported on the deck. The area around the mast fish was the only place I could see that would house them. I put the thought from my mind as I balled the wolf skin to make a pillow and curled up to enjoy some sleep.

I was woken by the noise of movement. There were calls and shouts. I stretched and stood. I needed to make water. As I passed him Snorri shouted, "Get food on your way back, Leif Longstride, for we leave within the hour." I waved an acknowledgement and headed for the bushes. I did not mind my shipmates seeing my manhood but not Franks.

The stew tasted better. It had been bubbling away all day. More salty water had been added and it had all congealed into a messy-looking but very tasty meal. There were some stale loaves and I used one to mop the last of it up. I drank a horn of the fermented apples and then took my shield, helmet and spear back to the ship along with my wolf skin. After I had stored my war gear I took the almost empty ale skin. I drank the last horn of it and then headed back to the barrel to fill up with the fermented apple drink.

Snorri said, "Here, take this empty pot back to the drekar. The sentries have been summoned and we will leave shortly."

I picked up the iron pot and nodded to the prisoners, "And the prisoners?"

He shook his head, "Most are too old and the ones who are suitable have babies. The jarl does not want wailing infants. We will find maidens further south. They make better thralls. If you separate a mother from her child she pines. I have heard of mothers who threw themselves into the sea thanks to their despair. No, we leave them here. They will tell others how terrible we are. Your wolf cloak certainly had them making the sign of their White Christ. They did not know you had blooded your spear but once."

The Franks seemed too petrified to move, even as we boarded our ships and pushed off. When we moved downstream, the current and the oars taking us, they fled back up the trail. I did not envy them their return. It would be to a charnel house. The rats, foxes, magpies and carrion crows would have begun to devour the corpses of the dead. They would have to seek out their families and then bury them. They then faced a future without men or even boys. The women would have to tend the fields. They would remember the first time that the Norsemen came raiding.

We only had to row until we reached the sea and then we stored our oars and curled up to sleep once more. We had done our sentry duty on the land and it would be others who would watch through the night. I saw, as I snuggled into my blanket and covered by my sealskin cape, that we were heading out to sea. It would take a good day of sailing as we wanted to arrive undetected. We would sail out of sight of the land. Our leaders wanted surprise on our side.

When I woke the sun which appeared in an occasional break in the clouds told me that it was noon. I made water. I had ensured that I emptied my bowels after the raid. I still did not enjoy hanging over the side of the longship. I drank some water and peered to larboard. The land was still hidden over the horizon. Most of my fellows were still sleeping and so I wandered down to the steering board, picking my way through the sleeping warriors and careful not to disturb them.

Gandalfr and Snorri were asleep and the jarl was steering. When he saw my approach he said, "Leif, take my horn and fill it from the ale barrel."

"Aye, Jarl."

Snorri had stopped the ale ration when the barrel was half empty. It was reserved now for those who steered the longship. I handed it to him. He said, "Hold the steering board while I drink."

I felt both honoured and terrified. I had steered our snekke but this ship held many men. Surprisingly it felt little different to the snekke. I saw the jarl looking at me out of the corner of his eye. He nodded and hung his horn from his belt. "You seem to have this. I will make water." He turned and after lowering his breeks made water. I had the longship and no one was watching me. I kept the prow directly in line with *'Nidhogg's'* mast. I knew that the steering board was sensitive. A slight movement could make a difference.

On his return he said, "Thank you, Leif. I feel more comfortable now." He took the steering board from me. "Hallstein said you did well during the raid and you and Gunvald accounted for a Frank."

"He was my age and had no skill, Jarl. I will face tougher challenges."

"A man can only fight those who are before him. Any man can kill, even a priest can hurt you."

"Did the priests fight back?"

He laughed, "Aye, one of them swung one of the holy objects, I think they carry the incense, at the head of one of Lord Arne's hearth-weru. He was slain but if the metal had hit Eidel's head he might have been hurt. Always strike to kill even if you think your enemy is weak." He nodded to larboard, "This will be harder. The two settlements on either side of the Sequana river can cause us problems. We might get upstream easily enough and we might even raid successfully, but once the Franks know that we are in the river they can close the door. Still, my cousin believes that this time we shall have the silver we crave." He smiled, "He traded many times in Frankia and chose the places where we could make the most silver."

"Were the Franks not suspicious of him, Jarl?"

"He wore no mail and carried a cross of the White Christ as a disguise. They thought him a barbarian but a tamed one. The cross meant he was allowed into their churches and there he saw the riches that lay within."

Gandalfr rose and stretched, "I will make water, Jarl and take over." He peered towards the land and sniffed, "Another hour and we can make our turn." He went to the hourglass and tapped it. Seemingly satisfied he nodded and then went to the larboard side.

I said, quietly, to the jarl, "How does he know where we are? There are no stars and no landmarks. The sun is hidden. How does he know?"

He shrugged, "Men like Gandalfr the Navigator are special. I do not know how he knows but he does and that is enough for me."

I headed back to my chest. I knew that I could never be a navigator.

The wind was with us and we did not need to row. We ate. We had put our own lines out and mine had caught a sild. I bashed its head against the gunwale and took out my knife. It was very sharp and I slid it along the fish's belly. I took the guts and tossed them overboard. Had we been close to shore then the gulls would have been with us and they would have plucked the tasty morsel from the air. I sat on my chest and ate the fish. You could not eat fish that was fresher and the taste was superior to either salted or pickled fish. I was simply varying what I ate. I still yearned for hot cooked food. We had taken salted pigmeat from the village. We had all shared that bounty out and now there was none left. I wondered if the Franks who lived further south cured their meat the same way. If they did then we were in for a treat.

Gandalfr's call for the crew to tend to the stays and sheets warned us that we were about to turn. I looked ahead and saw that *'Nidhogg'* had already begun her turn eastwards. Glancing to the west I saw the sun was getting lower in the sky. *'Nidhogg'* shortened her sail and a heartbeat later we were ordered to reef our sail. It would slow down our approach and, probably as importantly, it would make us harder to see. We were fortunate that it was cloudy for a bright sunset would have silhouetted us. The gods were smiling at us. I went to the pail of seawater we kept by the bows. It was there for us to wash. I rinsed my hands and shook them dry. Anticipating the opportunity to refill my ale skin I poured a hornful of the fermented apple juice. I was getting used to it and, to be fair, the drink went better with the raw fish than did ale.

The last rays of the sun illuminated white caps and rocks. We had reached the estuary of the Sequana. The jarl shouted, "From now, until we tie up, there will be no shouting. Sound carries at night and while the estuary is wide we dare not alert the Franks to our presence. Use hand signals or whisper."

We had not shouted before. The shouts had been from Gandalfr, Snorri or the jarl but the order was a sound one. The masthead lookout whistled and pointed. I saw, as the sun finally set, a pinprick of light on the steerboard bow. It was evidence of a settlement. We stared at the pinprick which doubled as we drew closer. Then one pinprick disappeared to be replaced by another. Gunvald frowned, "What is happening, Leif?"

"I think it must be the doors of the homes opening and closing. Either that or there is a fire and people pass before it."

Mikkel tugged at my arm and pointed to larboard. There were more pinpricks of light. It was the other settlement. The estuary was indeed wide. As we entered it, I could neither hear nor see the breakers on the shore. At the last river we had. It meant it was wide. I saw that *'Nidhogg'* had run out their oars and, anticipating the order, I tapped Gunvald on the shoulder and pointed to the mast fish. I saw Haldir walk to the mast fish and tap them. We reached them first and I chose the straightest of them. We had learned that they were easier to use. We did not need to be given orders. We knew what we had to do. We had the oar fitted and we were seated on our chests before some of the crew had found their oar. I saw now why we had raided the monastery and village further north. It was to prepare us for this river. I wondered how we would keep the beat for if Snorri banged his staff that would alert the Franks. I saw him stand on the gunwale and gripping the backstay he raised his other hand. We all raised our oars. The voyage down our fjord now paid us back for we all knew what we had to do.

Gandalfr must have hissed an order for the sail was completely reefed. We would make our way upriver with just our oars and the river. Snorri held up three fingers. Then two, then one and finally he lowered his arm. We started to row and we watched his arm as it came up and down. He was giving us the beat for the oars. It was a steady one. I could not see but I knew that he was watching *'Nidhogg'* and matching her speed.

The banks of the river were dark but an occasional pinprick of light that flashed showed us where a dwelling lay. Reassuringly there were no shouts of alarm. Just as we could not make out the houses they could not see the silent shapes sailing up the river. I realised, from the action of the oar, that we had the tide with us. We rowed steadily and I saw the planning of the jarls. That long meeting in the mead hall at Askvoll had not been a wasted time. The charts were studied and the problems were discussed there so that now we could sail as one.

I had no idea how long we had rowed except that my arms ached and my shoulders burned. As I glanced to the side, I saw that the banks were closer. There were no pinpricks of lights and I did not see the shapes of dwellings but I saw the shapes of trees. In the far distance, well away from the river, I heard the tolling of a bell. Snorri had told me that the places where the nuns and monks lived used such bells to announce the times they would worship. It seemed strange to me that they would be summoned in darkness. Was this White Christ a god who liked the night?

I became aware that Snorri's beat was slowing and that we were heading to the northern bank. The jarl, now mailed and with a helmet on his head, strode down the centre of the ship. He hissed orders as he passed the men. Nearing us he said, "On Snorri's command the larboard oars will be raised and then drawn. Stack them and arm yourselves. Steerboard oars will do the same once we have stopped."

I felt the keel grind on the river bed and heard the splash as the boys leapt ashore to tie us to the shore. Gunvald and I took our oar and stacked it. Haldir was there and he said, "Help the others to step the mast."

We obeyed. I was aware that the larboard crew were now armed and were heading ashore. Despite the apparent honour, I did not want to be the rearguard this time. I took comfort from the fact that Hallstein and Haldir were helping with the task. I suppose it made sense to take down the mast. Without our masts, we were so low in the water that the only way we could be seen would be if someone stumbled upon us. The mast stepped, Haldir said, "Now arm yourselves."

I hurried to my chest and took out my knitted head protector and helmet. I donned my boots. I fastened my wolf skin about my helmet and fastened my sword belt around my waist. I took longer to prepare and as I took my spear and shield I saw that only Axel was still preparing. Brynjar and Hallstein were ashore with the others. One advantage of being almost the last was that the gangplank was in place in anticipation of treasure and slaves being loaded at the end of the raid. I would not have soggy feet.

As I joined my shield brothers I was suddenly aware that this land felt warmer and smelled differently even from the land further north. This raid would be different. Haldir signalled to the ones who would be left to guard the ship. His hand passed over me to point at Axel. He was the only one of the men of Bygstad to be selected. I had no time for any other observations as Hallstein said, "Follow me. Oddr, take the rear and make sure these cockerels keep up." We would not be the rearguard and I might, finally, have the real test of warriorhood.

Chapter 9

This time we were not the rearguard but we were behind Lord Arne's men. I heard Lord Arne designate the men who would do as we had done and prevent an escape of any villagers. They did not look happy. Hallstein had taken us close to the jarl and his hearth-weru. We made our way up the bank to the slightly higher ground above the river. It looked to me to be almost man-made as though it was there to stop flooding. I saw a wider trail heading north but we did not take that one. Instead, we took a narrower one that led east. We made our way along it towards what I assumed was our target: a settlement and a church. The wind was in our faces and brought us strange smells. Some of it came from the plants that grew here. I could not see them, in the dark, but their smell was exotic. I also caught the whiff of woodsmoke. There were houses close by. What disturbed me was that we were no longer silent. On that first raid, I had known that Hallstein's mail jingled but it did not matter for we were at the rear. Here I could hear the jarl and his hearth-weru. It sounded too loud. I knew that Lord Arne also had mailed men and they were further ahead of us. If the Franks had sentries surely they would hear us.

Suddenly we stopped. The silence, after the pounding of the feet and the jingling of the mail byrnies, seemed deafening. We listened. It had to have been Lord Arne who commanded the halt. He was not a jarl but this raid was his idea. He would not want failure. When Jarl Bjørn raised his spear and pointed east we moved again. I had learned that the nights were not as long as one might expect and I saw the first hint of dawn in the east. Here there were no mighty mountains to mask the rising of the sun. The river was wide and in a flat plain. We began to descend and I saw ahead the distinctive shapes of houses and what looked, in the dark, like a tower.

Once again we stopped but this time the spears of our leaders directed us to form a line. We were in a tended field. I could not tell what the crop was but our feet had already trampled it. Haldir and the other hearth-weru came along to space us out. We would not be forming a skjaldborg. I swung my shield around and fastened my hand upon the handle. The place I would hold my spear was smooth, I had made it so. It was the best place for balance. The spearhead had been sharpened. That first strike at the young Frank had not blunted it but it had shown me the need for a keen blade. Lars' sword was also whetted and ready for blood.

Hallstein glanced down his line. I was next to Oddr on one side and Gunvald on the other. I did not recognise the warrior next to Oddr for he had a helmet with a mask upon it. The attack, when the order was given, rippled down the line. We moved when Jarl Bjørn pointed forward. Lord Arne's men, closer to the river, moved first. We were heading towards a low line of bushes and, in the first light of dawn, I saw that there were houses. Our line was not straight. The uneven terrain and the low bushes ensured that. Lord Arne and his men looked to have a road of some kind and they were the ones who would reach the houses first. It was they who found the sentry for there was a cry and a shout before I heard the scream of death as a man died.

We were still thirty paces from the first dwelling and as the sun cast a glowing corona over the village, I saw the shape of a tower and heard the bell as it tolled a warning. A flash of light showed a door open and even as we neared the first house I saw armed men pouring from the hall. The glint of light from a sword showed me that these were not just villagers. These were warriors. That had not been anticipated. We had a fight on our hands. The warriors would pose a threat to the jarl and his cousin. We would be fighting the men of the village.

The first men who emerged from the houses were villagers with swords, spears and daggers. The man who ran at me was as big as Alfr our blacksmith and as he wielded a mighty hammer, I took him to be the Frankish smith. He swung the hammer at my head and I held up the shield. Brokkr had told me to slightly angle a shield when defending from a blow and I was glad that I did as the hammer made my arm shiver. His two-handed swing left him open to a thrust and while my left arm felt the power of his strike I was able to thrust with my spear. His belly was large and my spear slid into his left side. He roared at me and lifted the hammer to hit me again. I feared that another blow would either shatter my shield or break my arm. It would be a race as to who could make the next contact. I won after pulling my spear out and thrusting again I drove the spear up under his chin and into his skull. He was a big man but the spear killed him and he fell to the ground.

It was as though someone had lit a lamp for the sun suddenly flared in the east and I was able to see the mayhem all around us. This was not the handful of men we had faced further north. I saw that the warriors who had emerged from the hall were as numerous as the villagers. It was not only the men who were fighting, women were using whatever they had to hand to fight us. The Norns had been spinning.

Hallstein shouted, "Men of Bygstad, push on."

My left arm still felt numb and I dreaded facing another such Frank as the dead smith but I obeyed and Gunvald, Oddr and I moved as quickly as we could over the bodies of those we had already slain. When we reached the houses, Oddr kicked open the door and stepped inside. I followed and as the spear was thrust at Oddr's side I used my body to push the haft away and the head struck not flesh but air. It was a young maiden who had thrust at Oddr but I did not see that until I had swept my spear in an arc. It ripped across her throat and it was then I saw her sex.

I stood, staring, until Oddr shouted, "Thank you, Leif, but we have no time to waste. On. Take the door at the back. Go with him, Gunvald."

Our task was to clear the warriors first and that would allow us to search the village for silver. I stepped out of the other door but did so more warily than Oddr had entered. Ahead of me, I saw mailed Franks. Gunvald and I had managed to get behind them. Lord Arne and Jarl Bjørn, along with their hearth-weru, were fighting for their lives. I saw, even as we neared the Franks, thus far unseen, that one of Lord Arne's hearth-weru had been speared and was falling.

Gunvald and I had trained together and rowed together. It meant that we had an understanding that needed no words and we both thrust together at the backs of the two mailed Franks. In hindsight, we should have struck below the mail shirts but this was all new to us and we both speared the mail. The heads pierced the links but it was not like flesh. The progress of our spears was slowed and the two men, feeling the prick of spear in their backs whipped around. The sword of the warrior I had struck caught my spear so hard that I dropped it. He raised his sword to end the life of the unarmoured youth who had dared to strike him. I drew my sword as my already numb arm tried to block the sword strike. I did but it forced me to my knees. I swashed my sword as I sank and I was rewarded when my sword struck his knee. He tried two things at once as my sword drew blood and ripped flesh. He tried to swing his sword down at me and he attempted to move back and avoid another blow. I did not want to have my shield smashed in two and so I rose, with my shield before me and the rim caught him under the chin. He could not finish his swing and we both toppled to the ground. He hit hard and roared at me. I had no mail shirt and I rose quickly and putting the tip of my sword to his chest leaned heavily on it. This time the combination of Lars' sword and my weight broke the mail links and the sword entered his chest.

Gunvald shouted, "Watch out, Leif!"

A warrior, without mail, was running at me holding his spear in two hands. I brought my shield around and the spear scraped along the leather, tearing a rip in it. I swung my sword at his head. It was not a clean strike but I must have stunned him for he lowered his spear and looked dazed. The battle was still raging and I could not afford to be merciful. I slashed at his head and my sword bit through his cheek. When he fell I knew he was dead.

"Leif!"

I turned and saw that Gunvald had lost his spear and a Frankish warrior had rammed his spear into Gunvald's leg. He was pulling it back for a mortal strike. I just ran roaring, "No!"

He turned and, I think, saw the wolf's head on my helmet. That allied to the wolf painted on my shield, now torn, distracted him sufficiently for me to hit him in the face with the boss of my shield. I struck him a second time and before he could turn his spear at me I had hacked across his side. He wore a simple kyrtle and my blade hacked into his side, scraping off ribs. He was a brave Frank and tried to pull back his spear. It was the sawing action of my sword that ended his life. I must have severed something vital for he gave a shudder and fell.

Norse Warrior

I turned and saw the blood pumping from Gunvald's leg. I could not leave him so exposed. I swung my shield around to my back and sheathed my sword. The men we had attacked were now being forced down to the river by Lord Arne and Jarl Bjørn. I put my hands under Gunvald's arms and dragged him back into the house. As soon as we entered the house the noise of the battle diminished.

I put Gunvald with his back to the door and said, "I will try to find a bandage for you." I was going to rip some of the material from the girl I had slain. As I turned I saw that a man was cradling her head. I was going to slay him and I drew my sword. It was then I saw that he was not armed. He was also an older man. I took him to be Snorri's age but there the similarity ended for this man had a neatly trimmed beard with flecks of grey. I would still have killed him but the necklet that hung around his neck was not a cross but a star. I stayed my hand and our eyes met. I would not kill him. There seemed to be understanding in his eyes and he said something which I did not understand. He reverently laid the girl down and then rose. He said something else. I looked at him blankly. He pointed to Gunvald and mimed bandaging him. I nodded.

Gunvald had lost blood and his eyes were closed. When the man with the star and I approached he opened them and seeing the stranger started, "Peace, Gunvald. I think he comes to help you. I will watch him but I do not think he will harm you." I smiled, "The Norns have been spinning."

The man stood and I watched him warily to see if he tried to flee. He saw my look and, smiling, said something else. He took a bag from behind the door and came over. He took out some vinegar and poured it on the wound. Gunvald cried out but the use of vinegar was reassuring. The man then took out a bone needle and what looked like a type of thread. He lifted Gunvald's knife from his scabbard and I put my sword to his throat. He shook his head and holding it by the blade put the handle in Gunvald's mouth.

I removed the sword, "I think he intends to sew the wound. Bite on the handle. I will take the opportunity to search the house."

"Do not leave me."

"I will not but I do not fear this man. For one thing, he is not a follower of the White Christ."

Outside the sound of combat had faded. I did not know if what I was doing would be sanctioned by the jarl but I had a wounded shield brother and that seemed to me the priority. I studied the interior for the first time. It was a dwelling such as we used but the difference was that there were curtains around the rooms. I took one such curtain down and felt the material. It was well made. The curtains were a treasure, of a sort. I took them all down and folded them on the bed. I saw that the bed linen was well-made. This was the home of someone important. I glanced over at the body of the maiden I had killed. Her dress was also well made and I saw a silver cross around her bloody neck. I would leave that for Gunvald. I reasoned that there had to be treasure here. I looked around the room as the stranger sewed up Gunvald's leg. He was being careful. I saw a chest at the foot of a bed and I went to it.

When I opened it I saw clothes and they were good ones. I took them out and placed them on the bed. I found a good short blade. It was the kind that Saxons used and was called a seax. I stuffed that in my belt. One of my brothers could have that. Then I found the chest. When I opened it I found real treasure. There were not only coins but also pieces of jewellery.

I took it over to Gunvald, "Here, Gunvald, this might ease the pain of your wound. We have treasure." I placed it on the bed next to him and waved an arm around the house, "there are linens and curtains too." The man had finished and he said something. I just said, "Thank you." I pointed to the dead girl, "She has a silver cross. It is yours. I have one already."

Just then the door burst open and Oddr, Mikkel and Dagfinn stood there.

"Hallstein sent us to seek you out." Oddr pointed his sword at the man who had sewed Gunvald's leg, "Why is he not dead?"

"Because, Oddr, he had no weapon, he is not a follower of the White Christ and he has sewn up Gunvald's leg." I saw that Dagfinn and Mikkel were now searching the house for things I had not found.

"He is your slave then?"

I knew that if I said no he would be slain and so I nodded. The Norns were spinning. I waved a hand, "There is treasure here."

He nodded and sheathed his sword, "Have your slave pick up the linens and we will take them to the ship. You take the chest and show it to the jarl. Who knows the two of you may be given a larger share."

Mikkel said, "And the mail shirt and weapons of the Frank you killed are yours. Haldir said no one was to touch them."

I suddenly thought of the others, "We won?"

Dagfinn nodded. He was picking up food from the kitchen and stuffing it into a sack he had found, "Aye, but it was not as easily as Lord Arne said. Words were exchanged. We lost seven men. Lord Arne lost ten."

"Our friends?"

He shook his head as he bit into an apple, "From Bygstad we lost Sverrir and Ragnavaldr. The one who spoke to us, the man from Askvoll, Evindr, died well. I did not know the names of the others. They were from the front oars. Lord Arne lost a hearth-weru and nine others." He pointed the apple at the man, "That is why he is lucky. The rest of the men, boys included, were all beheaded. Both of our leaders are angry because many women and maidens escaped. The men sent by Lord Arne to watch for their flight did not do as well as we did."

Oddr had finished his search, "Come, let us go back."

I nodded and I gestured for the new slave to stand. He had slung his bag around his back and donned a hat and cloak. I deduced that he was a clever man who had worked out his fate and being wise resigned himself to it. I took the curtains and linens and placed them on his arms. I slung my shield and picked up the chest I had found. "Gunvald, can you walk?"

I saw that the cross was gone from the maiden's neck. Gunvald had taken the treasure. He nodded and leaned on his spear, "Aye, I can."

We emerged into the light and it was blinding. I saw men emerging from the other houses. Einarr son of Einarr shouted, "I see you have searched that one. We have mail, weapons and even silver. It has cost us but we go home rich men."

Hallstein appeared and frowned, "A slave?" I sighed and went through the story again. He nodded, "He is the only man. The chest?"

"Treasure."

He opened it and his eyes widened. "This is why we came. Give it to me." My eyes betrayed me and he smiled, "You and Gunvald will be given your share and it will be greater than the others but this is the jarl's to distribute." He nodded to the pile of bodies, "You have warrior treasure there. Haldir told us what you and Gunvald did. The mail shirt, helmet and weapons are yours. No one touched them." He raised his voice, "Back to the longships. The village is to be fired." He nodded to a pyre that had been built. The bodies of our dead were already being burned. We would remember them when we returned home but no one would despoil our dead. They would be in Valhalla now but their ashes would lie here in Frankia, a blackened memory of a raid from the north.

I pointed to my slave and held up my hand. He nodded. He would wait. I saw that all the bodies, save one, had been stripped. The mailed warrior I had slain was now stiffening in death. I rammed my spear into the earth as I first pulled the byrnie from his body. While it was not completely ruined, the short shirt would need to be repaired and that would cost me silver. I folded it and then took the weapons. The sword was at least as good as Lars' and the scabbard was richly decorated. There were silver threads running through it. The helmet, when I took it from his head, was also a good one but it had been badly dented. I did not remember striking the blow that did that but another may have done so. He had a silver cross around his neck and it was a large one. This was mine and would more than pay for the repairs to the mail. He had a purse and there were coins in it. This was an important man I had killed. On his hands were the rings one associated with lords. I took them too and put them in my pouch. He had a dagger, which I took and an eating knife.

I stood. I would struggle to carry all my treasure back to the ship. I looked around and saw a cloak on another of the bodies. It had been left because there was a long cut in it but it would do. I laid it out and put most of my treasure in it. I fastened the four corners and then slung the sword belt and scabbard over my arm.

Norse Warrior

I put my spear through the four corners and heft it across my back. I joined the line of laden warriors who trudged back west, to the two ships.

"Come, healer, let us go." To emphasise my command I nodded down the trail. He walked alongside me. It was then I saw that he was much smaller than me and his skin had a darker hue, it was more olive than even the Franks. He did not look like a Frank.

There looked to be just a handful of women. Only three looked to be worth taking back as slaves. The others were like the ones we had left behind at the other river. I wondered if our leaders would be as generous this time.

I saw the man looking all around him. I did not think he would try to escape but I decided to warn him, "Do not try to run or you will die. I did not expect a slave and I am not sure if my family will welcome you for you seem particularly useless, but the Norns have spun and I will take you."

He said something and I shook my head. I did not understand his words. He sighed and said them so slowly that I made them out. They made no sense to me.

"Jo-seph Ben Yek-ut-iel." He could not use his arms but he nodded down as though he was indicating himself.

I nodded, "Jo-seph? It is your name?"

He smiled and said something else but it sounded like our word for yes.

I said, "Leif Longstride." I had a free hand and I patted my chest. He smiled again.

It was a small thing but the simple exchange of names changed everything. I decided, from that moment, to teach him our language. I hoped that by the time we reached Bygstad, he would understand commands.

Chapter 10

There were men who had not died in the battle but they had been wounded. We had brought no healers with us but there were men who knew how to attend to wounds. They were tending to them. I laid my load down close to our drekar and said, "Jo-seph," and pointed to the ground. He nodded and then, patting his bag pointed to the wounded. I knew what he meant. "Yes, you may go." I waved for him to join the men with the wounded.

I walked with him and he pointed to one who had his face cut to the bone. His eye had been taken. Snorri was tending to him and he looked up and shook his head, "I fear that Steinarr will need a warrior's death." He took out his dagger.

Jo-seph shook his head and opened his bag. I saw Snorri look at him suspiciously. "No, Snorri, this man is a healer, I think. He sewed Gunvald's leg. Let him try to heal the man."

Snorri stood and sheathed his weapon, "I will watch."

My slave knelt and began to work what I saw as magic. He did not seem concerned about the blood and the gore. He spoke soothingly to the wounded man who could clearly not understand him.

Snorri looked at my pile, "You did well as did the rest but this was not the easy fight we expected."

"The Norns, Snorri. I killed a maid."

Snorri was an understanding man and he said, "Tell me." I told him all and when I had finished he nodded, "You could have done nothing else and you saved Oddr from a wound or even death. You have nothing to regret."

The slave said, "Leif." It did not sound exactly the way I had said it but I understood.

"Yes."

He pointed to Snorri and me and gestured for us to hold down the wounded man. I saw that he had stitched up his face but the wound to his eye remained. He pointed to the fire.

Snorri understood, "Aye, I can see that this man is a healer. He wants us to hold down Steinarr so that he can seal the eye. Tell him aye."

I said, "Yes" and nodded.

Norse Warrior

We held down Steinarr and Snorri said, in the man's ear. "There will be pain, Steinarr, but this man will save you." He put the haft of Steinarr's knife in his mouth.

Jo-seph came back and nodding to us put the brand to the eye. There was a hiss and the stink of burning flesh. He held it there for the count of three and then removed it. I saw that Steinarr had passed out.

We stood and Snorri nodded, "Thank you, Jo-seph."

The slave sighed and said his name again. This time he said it quicker and I said, "Joseph?"

He beamed and repeated, "Joseph Ben Yekutiel."

Snorri laughed, "Well there is a mouthful."

Just then Jarl Bjørn Haraldsson and Haldir came over. "What is this?"

Hallstein appeared, "Leif took a slave, Jarl, he healed Gunvald's leg."

Snorri nodded, "And he has saved Steinarr's life. I was about to give him a warrior's death."

Jarl Bjørn Haraldsson looked pleased, "And with the treasure you have taken, Leif Longstride, you have proved that you are a warrior. You may keep the slave." I saw that Joseph had moved on to the next warrior. The jarl smiled, "And, it seems he may be a treasure in himself."

Snorri said, "I will watch him. Put your treasures aboard. Gandalfr has lifted the deck."

I shook my head, "I would not have the mail rust. It is in need of repair already. There will be room in my chest and I will share the other with Gunvald."

The jarl smiled, "You have the makings of a leader, Leif Longstride, for it is a wise warrior who watches out for his shield brother."

I put the weapons and mail in my chest first and then evenly distributed the other items. I examined the helmet and saw that it was cracked. It could not be used as a helmet again. I would sell it to Alfr. He could use the metal again. I descended to the camp.

Haldir, Hallstein and the jarl were still in conversation with Snorri. They were all four watching Joseph. Jarl Bjørn Haraldsson said, "He is a good healer but he is not a Frank. His skin is slightly darker."

"And he wears a star around his neck and not the cross."

"He may be more useful then. It is a pity there were so few maidens."

Just then I heard a shout from behind. It was Oddr, "Leif Longstride, I did not get the chance to thank you properly. That maid would have skewered me but for your quick hands." He held out his arm and I clasped it.

"I did not think, I just reacted."

Haldir nodded, "You have natural skills. Hallstein has taught you well but he cannot teach you that."

Hallstein said, "You asked me once when you would be a warrior. You are now a warrior. That you took Gunvald to safety shows that and the way you and Gunvald took on mailed Franks who were lords, was impressive."

Snorri asked, "There were lords there?"

The jarl said, "Aye, my cousin was not expecting them. The last time he was here there was one lord and four retainers. We had twenty good warriors to face and that is why our losses were so heavy."

Haldir clasped his hammer, "The Norns."

Just then I heard a cry, "Leif!"

I turned and saw that Axel had his sword raised to take the head of Joseph. I reached them in two strides and before Axel could swing the sword I punched him so hard that he fell to the ground as though I had struck him with a hammer. I held up my hand to Joseph and said, "Sorry."

He gave a pale smile and said, slowly, "Thank you, Leif."

It was a start. The others joined me and we stood over Axel. Snorri snorted, "He did not even do a proper duty watching the ships, Jarl Bjørn Haraldsson. We found him sleeping. Had we been attacked he would have been worse than useless."

The hersir's son came to and rubbed his chin. He found blood for I had broken his nose. "Jarl, I demand that Leif Longstride be punished. He hit the son of the hersir."

Hallstein picked him up with one hand, "You are a pathetic piece of goat shit, Axel Erlandsson. You tried to kill the slave of Leif Longstride. Had you done so then it is you who would have been punished. You should thank Leif for saving your life."

The jarl's eyes narrowed, "You have done nothing on this raid yet. Worse than that you did not even do the duty assigned to you. You have lost the right to share in the treasure and when we reach the fjord I will tell the hersir that I do not wish you to raid with me on my ship again. Unless your father builds a drekar then you will never go a-viking again." I did not think that Axel would mind that as a punishment.

The look of hatred from Axel was not directed at the others but at me. I had made an enemy. He sheathed the sword which had fallen to the ground and stormed off. Oddr shook his head, "And he has still to put a drop of blood on that sword."

We had brought food and animals. The most fertile of the animals were kept and distributed between the two ships and the rest were slaughtered and butchered. Sentries were set for the Franks knew we were in their river. When that was done then the spoils were divided. It turned out that the treasure from the church was the greatest but what Gunvald and I had found almost rivalled it. The two leaders took their share. As the owners of the longships, it was half of all that we had taken. Then, to my amazement, Gunvald and I were called forward and given silver from the chest.

Jarl Bjørn Haraldsson waved a hand and said, "These two warriors could have hidden the chest and kept it for themselves. They did not and this is their reward." We took the bounty and then the rest was given out. Every warrior gained silver. Axel was the only exception. Even the warriors who had allowed the maidens, women and children to escape received some. Our crew had three slaves: there was Joseph and two maidens. The two females went to two of Jarl Bjørn Haraldsson's hearth-weru. Lord Arne had four slaves. It was not the bounty we had hoped but it was better than nothing. We ate a hot meal and loaded the cargo beneath the decks.

Our watch was the one before dawn. I did not mind. The wounded were aboard the ship and Snorri, Steinarr and Gunvald were watching Joseph and the two maidens to ensure that they did not run. The rest of our crew slept. Hallstein placed the men of Bygstad on the higher ground above the river. I climbed the lower branch of a large tree and, with Dagfinn, watched. Brynjar had acquitted himself well in the raid and had killed three warriors. He had two fine swords as well as silver crosses he had taken. I found him easier to get on with now that he had seen his cousin's true worth. As he passed me to take his place at the far end of our line, he said, "I know this raid is coming to an end, Leif, but I would raid with you again. I can see that you are like true iron and will not bend."

"And I would share a skjaldborg with you, Brynjar."

Hallstein showed his opinion of Axel by placing him the closest to the longships. Hallstein took the most dangerous place, the one closest to the Frank's village. The men we relieved trudged wearily back. I did not envy them. They would have a couple of hours of sleep. We would simply stay awake.

I do not know if it was our elevated position but it was Dagfinn and I who heard the noise from the north. It was a distant whinny. I whistled. That was the signal for Hallstein. He whistled in reply and then trotted down the path. He looked up and Dagfinn pointed north, "We heard a horse whinny."

"And that may be a solitary animal which has wandered away or it may be horsemen." He looked at the sky, "It is close enough to dawn and I will risk the ire of the jarl. Axel, run to the camp and wake them. Say that Hallstein has heard horses."

I noticed that Hallstein was taking responsibility for the alarm. If it was nothing it would be he who would be reprimanded and not us.

"Yes, Hallstein."

As he ran off, the hearth-weru said, "Come down." As we did so, he said, "At least he cannot mess this task up."

Brynjar asked, in a whisper. "Do we not join the others, too?"

"No, for we are hidden here. We can serve the jarl best by attacking them from a quarter they do not expect. Stay hidden and listen for my command. When we attack we do so without fear or regard for our own safety. Our treasure is on the ships and if we are to die then our families will have security."

I saw that the place we had chosen was off to the side of the trail. It had been chosen so that we could watch the trail from the village but there was another trail, a wide one, that came from the north. The sound of the horses was much clearer now as they drummed. I reasoned that if they came on horses and made such a noise they were confident that they could defeat us. My life as a warrior might turn out to be a brief one. I made my shield more comfortable and ensured that I had a firm grip on my spear. Dagfinn was on one side of me and Mikkel on the other. When I heard the shouts from the ships I knew that Axel had managed to complete one task successfully. He had been looking after his own skin.

In the dark, we could not see numbers but the column of horsemen who rode through the trees looked to be a large warband. The bank tumbled down to the river and the beach. It was not a steep drop but it would aid the horsemen. I tried to picture the hastily formed skjaldborg. In theory, it should have held but we had lost men, good men. Axel would be in the wall and I had no confidence that he would stand. If he fled then others, like him, might run. I was going to move when Hallstein's spear arrested my movement and he shook his head. It was then I heard the jingle of metal. There were more warriors coming, but the lack of hoofbeats told me that it was men.

This time we were able to count them. There were twenty and as they huffed and puffed past us, hidden in the undergrowth, I saw that only the first five were mailed but they had axes and good helmets. The rest had small shields and some had no helmets. They had mustered local men to fight the men from the north. I heard the clash from the ships as the horsemen hit the wall of shields and spears. The men on foot would exploit any weakness.

When the last one had passed Hallstein waved his spear and we ran. Once we reached the wider trail Hallstein said, without a pause, "Form a line and when I shout then roar as if we led an army."

The noise of the battle was such that we would have to shout loudly to be heard above the cacophony of combat.

"Aye, Hallstein."

Hallstein was in the middle and he was flanked by Oddr and Einarr. Mikkel was to the left of Oddr and it was Dagfinn who marked the left of our line. When we reached the top of the bank we saw that the skjaldborg had held. Its edges were bent around the sides. The horses the Franks used were little bigger than ponies and the advantage they gave was not as great as I had expected. It was the twenty reinforcements who would make the difference. I watched them make a wedge as they descended the slight slope. It meant that their mailed warriors with the axes were at the fore and it was pre-arranged for the horsemen parted to allow them to strike and I saw that they would hit the men of Askvoll. It made me angry, I did not know why.

When Hallstein roared, "Bygstad!" We all joined in the shout and each of us screamed our own curse and war cry.

Hallstein's timing was impeccable. Our shout came just as the mailed men were about to hit and the ones behind heard our words and slowed a little. Just by appearing we had weakened the attack. We had practised the wedge ourselves and I knew that it relied upon the weight of numbers. The five men who hit Jarl Bjørn Haraldsson and his hearth-weru were mailed but thanks to the men behind faltering, they would not break the skjaldborg. The fifteen men at the back turned. Some of the horsemen wheeled their animals to attack us. We would be outnumbered and surrounded but we might just save the ships.

The six men at the rear of the Frankish wedge were the ones with the poorest shields. Only three had helmets and two had spears improvised from a dagger and a haft. Pulling back my spear and thrusting I took all of this in and the first six all fell to the ground; my arm was already pulling back to hit the next five as we stepped over the bodies. That was almost my undoing for I slipped a little. The Norns were spinning for that slip meant that the spear thrust at my helmet missed but I did not. I rammed my spear so hard that it not only pierced the man, scraping off his backbone, but it pricked the man behind. As the warrior fell my spear was torn from my grip. Dagfinn was in danger from the horsemen to his left and he had turned slightly to defend himself and our perilously thin line. The two warriors saw their chance as my spear fell. Drawing my sword I ran at them with my head behind my shield. It was a blind attack but I was confident in both my shield and my helmet. I hit them and they reeled.

From ahead I heard the jarl roar, "Men of Askvoll, push!"

The sounds of battle increased in volume. The crescendo coincided with the drawing of my sword. And as I angled my shield to the left I was able to ram my sword into the middle of one of the Franks. The lowering of my shield enabled him, as he died, to rake my cheek with his spear. I knew he had drawn blood. Dagfinn was busy dealing with two horsemen and I punched with my shield's boss at the other man from the wedge. He blocked it with his shield but I knew I had hurt him when he cursed and stepped back. I remembered my shivered arm and I hit again before he could use his spear. My sword meant that we were so close that his spear could not be used effectively. When his arm dropped a little I lunged with the tip of my sword. It hit him in the neck and I tore it to the side.

Dagfinn shouted, "Leif!"

I turned and saw that I had no time to celebrate my victory. There were now three horsemen thrusting spears at my friend. I locked my shield with his and slashed at the head of one of the horses. I hit it and the horse, in trying to turn, crashed into another horse and both riders fell to the ground. Dagfinn's spear was holding the other two at bay but he was not harming them. I had a weapon that would. I dropped to one knee and with my shield above me rose to stab the small horse in the throat. It did not die immediately but reared to get away from the pain of the blade. The rider tried to control it but failed and as he fell backwards and I rose, I saw Dagfinn take advantage and ram his spear under the warrior's arm.

That was the moment I heard the cry from Mikkel, "Hallstein!"

I whipped my head around and saw that one of the mailed men on foot wielding an axe was swinging it into the side of Hallstein. If that was not bad enough I saw Elvind's dead body being trampled by the warrior. Mikkel and Brynjar had to fight three mailed men for Hallstein, although still trying to fight, was mortally wounded.

I shouted, "Dagfinn, to me!"

I turned and as Oddr and Einarr fought back-to-back Dagfinn and I ran to the aid of our shield brothers. Dagfinn did the unexpected. He hurled his spear at the warrior who was raising his axe to finish off Hallstein. It struck him in the shoulder but as he was wearing mail it did not penetrate. It did, however, allow Hallstein with his last blow to ram his sword under the chin of the warrior. They both fell to the ground. Dagfinn drew his sword and the two of us hit one of the two mailed men. It was at that moment that the horn of the Franks sounded and the two men joined the others in retreating up the slope. Had we had archers then our leaders might have been able to order a shower of arrows to hurt them but we had none.

Jarl Bjørn Haraldsson shouted, "Hold!"

The six of us turned and locked our shields. We protected the bodies of Hallstein and Elvind. The sun had risen as we had fought our deadly duel and I saw a field strewn with bodies. Three horses were either dead or dying. I counted, as I surveyed the scene, at least fifteen dead Franks. Hallstein's attack had accounted for at least half of those. He and Elvind, along with the other young warriors of Bygstad, had saved the ships but at the cost of their own lives.

Dagfinn turned to me, "We live and yet the man who trained us now lies dead. How is that, Leif?"

"The Norns have spun. Hallstein is in Valhalla now. He is content for the men he trained did all that could be asked of them."

I turned for it was Oddr who had spoken, "But he has gone, Oddr. I liked him. Who will lead us now?"

He shrugged, "I know not but although Elvind is dead you and Gunvald have shown that Bygstad has warriors who are young but brave. All will be well."

We did not turn but watched the Franks move away. No one had said anything but I knew that they might reform and attack us again. It was only when Haldir came to Dagfinn and me and put his hands on our shoulders that we knew we had won.

"You two did well but do not mourn Hallstein. Instead, celebrate his life. He lived and died a warrior. Elvind did not enjoy a long life but he did die well. I watched him as he died. He did not flinch but faced the Franks like a veteran. He died as a warrior." He sheathed his sword and nodded to the mailed warrior we had slain, "And the two of you have a warrior's mail. Claim your treasures for you have earned them."

I looked at Dagfinn and said, "I have a byrnie. Take this one."

"But yours is damaged."

I nodded. "And it was your spear that enabled Hallstein to kill him. I will take the helmet and his purse. The sword, dagger and mail are yours."

The purse, as I had expected, was full. A mailed warrior would not be a poor man and men such as the dead Frank carried their silver into battle.

Jarl Bjørn Haraldsson shouted, "Bring the wounded aboard **'Bylgja'**. Leif Longstride's slave can heal them."

Lord Arne shouted, "Butcher the horses and cook the meat. Ingi, take ten men and make sure that the Franks have gone." He nodded towards Hallstein and Elvind, "The men of Bygstad have saved us this day. They can rest and we will labour. Make a pyre for our dead and lay the gallant Hallstein on the top. He shall ascend to Valhalla first." I saw that Ingi took Axel with him. As they passed, I saw that Axel's spear had yet to be bloodied.

We put the dead Frank to one side and the last men of Bygstad reverently lifted the two bodies and took them to the small mound of our dead. We had lost too many men. Even as we laid the bodies on the pile of Frankish shields and kindling I realised that we needed more ships. Our crew was too small. I did not think that those who had argued for a raid across to the land of the Angles and the Saxons had been right for the treasure we had collected was, I knew, greater than when my father had raided. It was just that we needed greater numbers or better-protected warriors. It was Jarl Bjørn Haraldsson who lit the brand and tossed it into the pyre. I clutched my hammer as I thanked my shield brothers for their sacrifice. As the flames licked Hallstein's body I reflected that the burning would ruin the mail byrnie. Hallstein would be happy that no other would wear the mail shirt of which he was so proud.

"Back to work. We will leave on the afternoon tide. We need the food to be cooked and all to be secure."

We went back to the men we had slain. They would be burned next and first, they needed to be stripped of all that was useful. That booty included boots. The Frank with the mail shirt and two of the riders we had killed wore fine leather boots and we took them. Even the men who had poor mail had coppers in their purses and daggers. We took them and broke off the spearheads. We would choose better hafts when we reached home. We made sure that we had enough to share with Gunvald. No one, not even Brynjar, thought to include Axel in the distribution of our newfound wealth. Gunvald's wound was the only reason he had not been in the fight. When all had been taken, including the pins and brooches that held their cloaks, we piled the bodies on the larger pyre; we would not waste time in lighting it. The only reason we moved them was to make life easier for us as we loaded the longships. The saddles and leatherwork had been taken from the dead horses and they belonged to us. It was Dagfinn and I who had killed them. We were happy to share the meat with both crews but we had risked all to kill the beasts. The helmets and swords were also taken aboard.

I saw that Joseph was covered in blood. It was not, of course, his. Gunvald was seated on his chest and he said, "You were right to save this slave, Leif. He has saved limbs and lives this day. We should take care of him."

Mikkel nodded, "Aye, the Norns have spun." He dropped Gunvald's share of the loot at his feet. "This is for you."

"I did no fighting. I was a spectator who was desperate to join my shield brothers."

Oddr, who had assumed command following Hallstein's death said, "We are all agreed. We have more than enough. This raid was costly and there are four men of Bygstad who will not return home but the ones who do have been richly rewarded."

Gunvald nodded.

I put my treasures in my chest. I had so much that I had to put the helmets, the saddle and the reins in a sack. I tucked the sack under the newly stacked shields.

The smell of cooking horsemeat reminded me that I had not eaten yet. We would feast before we left and then put the rest of the cooked meat in barrels of salt water to preserve it. We would eat meat all the way home.

It was when I heard distant bells tolling that I wondered if I had tempted the Norns and assumed we would get home. It sounded to me like the land of the Franks was being warned of the presence of Norsemen.

Oddr heard it too, "Come, let us feed while we may. We are not yet in the fjord."

Chapter 11

Ingi and the men returned and reported that the Franks had left but they, too, had not only heard bells but also seen the plumes of fires and smoke that suggested signals. We ate well and drank a whole barrel of the fermented apple juice we had taken from the village we had raided. When the ships were loaded we boarded.

Gandalfr shouted, "We have lost warriors. The eight of you at the bows, you will have to be single-oared." He paused, "Do not make a slip!"

We all looked around at Axel. He was the weakest link.

My slave had eaten, I had ensured that. He had the wounded around the mast fish and main mast where he could tend to them. Gunvald had said that he had learned even more words and while he could not pronounce all the words, he had learned well and it was easier to speak to him.

As I took my oar I said, "Thank you, Joseph."

He smiled and said, "I am a healer."

I said, "We have a long way to go." I had brought a cloak from one of the dead Franks and I dropped it at his feet. "It will be cold."

He clearly had not heard the word and he shook his head and frowned his lack of understanding. I mimed shivering and he nodded. He said, "Thank you, Leif."

As Brynjar and I walked back to our chests he said, "You should have taught him the word, master."

I shook my head, "There will be time and besides, I think it is he who is the master. How many men owe their lives to him now? But for him, Gunvald might be Gunvald One Leg!"

We had slaves and animals, not to mention wounded and Lord Arne decided to sail with some daylight. We knew that once we were close to the estuary we would have sea room but he wanted the luxury of daylight to see obstacles and hindrances where the river was narrower. Before we left we fitted the mast. It would make it easier for us to be seen but, if we had the wind, we could make better speed. I was learning that a raid was not as simple as we had made it sound when we were back in Bygstad.

I had left on my woollen cap and I donned my sealskin cape. My calloused hands were ready for this. While we rowed Snorri led us in a rowing song. He still used his staff to keep the beat but we were able to sing the words as we learned them. It was a song from Askvoll and our handful of men knew the story but not the song. It was a steady, regular beat.

Odin had sons Hermod was one of many
A bright and beautiful god and as valiant as any
He rode with the Valkyrs with his spear Gungnir
He was sent by Allfather Odin upon the steed, Sleipner
With his mail corselet and Gambantein,
He was sent to Rossthiof in the land of the Finns
A horse thief and sorcerer cunning
A mage known for his spinning
With Odin's staff Hermod feard naught
As he rode to the land of night
Rossthiof could not fight the magic wand
And he fell and grovelled upon the land
Commanded by Hermod he obeyed the command
To see the future of Odin's land
His spell revealed a bloody child
And the death of a son of Odin
He told Hermod to see Rinda who dwelt in Ruthene far
And Odin should bed her and heal the scar
Odin had sons Hermod was one of many
A bright and beautiful god and as valiant as any

I think he chose the song, not for its dark message but for its beat but I know that it made me think about the Norns for Hermod was only sent to speak to the Finnish mage, Rossthiof, because the Norns refused to answer him. If the Norns would not obey the Allfather then what chance did a lowly warrior from Bygstad like me stand? Elvind and Hallstein had died and that could so easily have been me. As I chanted with the others and we made our way to the sea I vowed that I would marry, now that I had silver and my seed would live even if I died. Those thoughts filled my head as we headed downstream to the sea. I thought of Odin choosing a maid to bear his seed and, as we rowed I thought of the maidens in the village. The hard work helped me to think and I soon had my decision made. I knew the maiden I would seek as my bride.

The lookout roused me from my reverie, "Ships putting off from the northern bank."

We were looking upstream. I was tempted to look but knew that would be disastrous. When Snorri roared. "Axel Erlandsson!" I knew that at least one of us had given in to temptation. It was only one oar but the missed beat meant we veered slightly to steerboard and we lost a little way.

I heard Brynjar curse his cousin. Oddr would have a word with him when we stopped.

I kept rowing but said, to Mikkel, who now occupied the opposite oar, "Do the Franks have warships?"

I did not turn. "We shall soon find out. I did not think that this raid would have a sea battle too. It seems that we are learning every aspect of becoming a warrior."

"And we have lost many warriors. This will be a severe test."

Dagfinn said, from the oar in front of me, "Gandalfr and Snorri are conferring with the jarl." As soon as the lookout had shouted Snorri had stopped the song but he continued the beat. The jarl was donning his mail as he listened to the two men. They were the ones who would give the jarl the best strategy to survive this encounter and it was all about survival.

"Loose the sail!" As soon as Gandalfr gave the command I knew that a decision had been made. The sail would limit what the three men could see but it would give us extra speed and one thing our longships had was speed. They had sleek lines and unlike the other ships we had seen which were tubbier and slower, we could turn quickly and easily. By the judicious use of our oars, we could outmanoeuvre an enemy vessel. That depended, however, on all the oars working not only together but also obeying every instruction, instantly. We had a weak link: Axel.

It was Snorri who roared out the next order. He began beating his spear haft on the deck as he did so, "Today you will row harder than you have ever done before. There will be no song to help you for you will need all your breath to row." Our oars were already digging into the river as he spoke. "You thought those battles with the Franks were a test for you. They were nothing compared with this for if you fail today then we will be torn apart by these Frankish dogs like a baited bull."

His staff was banging faster now. Thanks to the efforts on the way south I knew how to get into the rhythm of the oars. I had no one to pull on my oar with me and all the effort was my own. I was aware of our speed which was clearly fast. I saw the jarl pick up a bow and nock an arrow. I could see no targets for behind us the river was empty. No one spoke although I could hear, I assumed it was Axel, moaning behind me. When I saw the jarl loose an arrow I knew that there were enemies close by. I glanced to the side and saw the first of the Franks. They were in small boats and I saw at least three. The jarl loosed another arrow. I now saw what Snorri had meant. We could have taken any of the boats I saw but if there were more ahead then they could simply surround us and board us. I gritted my teeth and pulled.

The arrows that fell into our longship were blindly sent and most struck the sea, the sail or hit the deck. I saw one strike Steinarr in the leg. There was no cry but I saw the arrow sticking up. He had lost an eye and now had a second wound. Joseph ran to him and began to tend to him. The staying of my hand in that house in the village was indeed fortunate.

My occasional glances showed me that there were many boats and some looked to be close. The jarl shouted, "Use your slings!"

The command was for the ship's boys. The sail set and the stays taut they were the only ones left to defend the ship. They needed no urging and they, along with the jarl, began to keep away the boats that were closest to us. The side of the longship prevented me from seeing the results but the occasional cheer and 'well done' from the jarl told me that they were enjoying a little success. I was tiring and I wondered how long we could keep this up. It was the motion of the ship that gave me hope and the strength to carry on. We were getting ahead of the smaller boats. The movement was more uneven and that meant the sea was close. We were close to the mouth of the river. Here we would enjoy a better ride than the smaller Frankish ships. They could be swamped. For once I hoped that Rán would send rough seas. I would rather endure a wetting than be slaughtered by Frankish dogs.

The Franks were persistent and even when we left the safety of the river they followed. It was only when one boat was swamped and upturned that they stopped. I saw them picking up the survivors. The jarl raised his bow in celebration and Snorri shouted, after glancing astern, "cease rowing."

We had survived. I leaned on the oar to raise the blade from the sea. I had learned not to slow down the ship. I gulped in great mouthfuls of air. It was like drinking ale. I was soaked in sweat. I used my left hand to sweep the woollen cap from my head.

I glanced to the other side of the longship and saw Mikkel grinning at me. He said, "Snorri is right, now I feel like a warrior."

I nodded and gasped out, "Me too. I will need to strengthen myself when next we sail."

Behind us, we heard Axel say, "I for one will stay in Bygstad. There is nothing I have enjoyed about this raid."

His cousin laughed, "Do you think any would take you to sea, Axel Erlandsson? The barnacles that cling to our keel are of more use than you."

"My father would not agree with you, Brynjar." He sounded sulky and petulant.

"Your father was not here but trust me when this tale is told in his mead hall he will know."

Axel was silenced. There would be a feast after we returned. The dead would be mourned and the stories told. Heroism and bravery would be the main topics but even if Axel was not named his exclusion from the list of deeds would tell all that he had failed.

"Stack the oars. We will use this wind. Now is the time to eat, make water and enjoy the fermented apple juice." The jarl walked down the middle of the drekar to smile at us all. When he reached me he said, "Your thrall, whom I thought an encumbrance, has proved to be the most valuable of treasures. He has saved lives and his efforts mean we shall have more men to man the oars. You and your fellows will be more than welcome when next I raid." He looked ahead at the ship of Lord Arne. It was disappearing into the north.

I stood and stacked my oar. I took a horn of the fermented apple juice and paused near Steinarr. Joseph had bound the wound. Steinarr said, "I think he has saved my leg, Leif Longstride. I am indebted to you and to him."

I smiled, "Thank you, Joseph."

He nodded, "I am a healer." I noticed, as he spoke, that while he had learned only a few words, he had managed to pronounce them better. I hoped, by the time we reached our home that he would have enough for conversations. I was not sure how the volvas would view him but I knew that my mother would make him welcome. Despite her stern demeanour, she had a kind heart as did my aunt.

Mikkel and I stopped, along with Brynjar. Axel had not yet returned his oar and the jarl was speaking to him. I learned that Jarl Bjørn Haraldsson was a good leader. He was not speaking loudly but I could see, from Axel's face, that the son of the hersir was not enjoying the words. I could only guess at them. When he angrily stormed past us to stack his oar I deduced that it had been confirmed that he would not raid with us again. I could not understand it. He did not want to raid and yet he looked angry. Those first lessons with Hallstein when we had learned the skjaldborg came back to me.

The jarl followed him and stopped when he reached us. Brynjar said, "You would raid again, Jarl Bjørn Haraldsson?"

"I would. I know we lost men but the treasure we took was great. My cousin has said that he has lost too many men to raid again next year." I was not sure who he was addressing but we all listened. "I will still raid but it will just be with two ships." He looked down. "I hope that all of you will raid." He smiled, "And your healer, Leif. My cousin told me of a river further south than where we raided, called the Liger. He said there was a town there, Angers, he said they called it." It was not a Norse word and it sounded strange coming from the jarl. "There the sun is hotter and the land was raided by men from the south; men with skin as black as a whale's back. My cousin said the treasures there are greater than on the Sequana. We thought to use this raid to test our warriors. I am happy that most have passed the test."

Gunvald had joined us, limping down the longship and using his spear as a walking stick, "But if they have fought men from the south then two ships would not be enough, Jarl Bjørn Haraldsson."

He nodded, "We would need more ships and men." He sat on Gunvald's chest and we squatted around him. "When we reach home it will soon be winter. What will we do?"

Dagfinn said, "Sit in our longhouses and wait for winter to pass. We will carve and tell tales until the sun returns."

He nodded, "And what if I were to tell you that further south, along the Liger, the sun still shines for ten hours each day, even in midwinter, and there is neither snow nor ice."

I saw his idea immediately, "We could stay for the winter along the Liger. If we made a camp we could raid and feed while, at home, our families would have more food and we would not be needed."

The others looked at me as though I was a mage or a seer for the jarl clapped me on the back and laughed, "You are as sharp as your sword, Leif Longstride. You are right. Instead of raiding at Tvímánuður, we spend from Ýlir to Gói on the Liger."

Gunvald was eager to show that his mind had not been dulled by his wound, "And that gives us one year to build another drekar."

"Perhaps two and it also means we can train more men. You and the other young warriors from Bygstad have shown me the worth of youth. At least two of you will have mail byrnies and your skills mean that you can train others."

There was silence as we all took in his words. "Jarl Bjørn, there are youths at home who, while they cannot row, could use slings and bows to defend the ship. From what you say we would be raiding away from our winter camp. We would need men to guard the camp. The handful of boys we brought did well but they are not enough."

"Aye, you are right." Axel had still to rejoin us and he lowered his voice as he said, "I hope that your hersir will build a drekar and sail with us but, even if he does, I would have you five with me."

I knew that I would say yes but Brynjar was the hersir's nephew. I looked at him. He beamed, "There are ties, Jarl, that go beyond the blood of birth. I feel closer to these four young warriors than my relatives in Bygstad. If they will sail with you then so will I."

I nodded, "I would sail with you." The others quickly nodded their agreement.

The jarl said, "And if you can teach your slave our words then I would have him as a member of my crew. Snorri was our healer but he is in awe of this olive-skinned slave." He stood and put his hand out. "Your loyalty will be rewarded."

We all put our hands on his. No oath was sworn but, in our heads we all did. I could see it in our eyes.

By the time night had fallen and we headed north with a reefed sail, the weather had changed. Gunvald and I rigged a couple of Frankish cloaks to make a shelter. We waved for Joseph to join us. The poor man was shivering. I took out the wolf's skin and draped it around his shoulders. He said, "Thank you. I am so cold."

The two of us then began his lessons in Norse. As we huddled beneath the cloaks we taught him words and told him of our home. He was far cleverer than we were and he picked things up much more quickly.

The next morning, when the rains had stopped and we peered east we saw that first river where we had raided. It was a measure of the journey ahead. Of Lord Arne, there was no sign. He had abandoned us. The jarl explained it away by saying that he had lost more men and did not have a healer like ours but I could tell that he was disappointed. Joseph tended to the wounded and we brought food and drink to our chests to eat. We continued our lessons. The weather was as varied as the land we passed as we headed north. We had showers and we had sun. We had strong winds that carried us quickly and others that were so slow that we had to take to the oars. We also saw more ships as we headed closer to the land of the Angles and the Saxons. They recognised our sleek lines and avoided us. They did not know that we were not raiding. By the time we were passing Frisia Joseph's words had improved to the point that we could have conversations. The problem came when he tried to tell us about his life. He did not know the words for they were not our words and when he spoke his own we gave him blank looks. No matter how many gestures and mimes were used we found that there were some words we could not find. It was frustrating.

The wounded all healed sufficiently so that we had every oar manned as we neared Hardbakke. We hove to closer to the port of Lord Arne. His ship had arrived not long before ours. We deduced that it had been damaged on the river. The two cousins shouted to one another and it was agreed that the two leaders would meet again at Askvoll in the middle of Harpa. They rowed to their port and we turned to head up the coast to Askvoll. The jarl honoured us by telling us that he would sail, first to Bygstad so that our treasure could be unloaded and he could speak to the hersir. We knew as we pulled on the oars, that would be an interesting conversation.

We were comfortable rowing. The flight down the Sequana had done that and Gunvald and I were able to talk as we rowed.

"What will happen to Hallstein's chest?"

"What?" I had not even thought of that.

"The chests of the other dead can be returned to their families with their share of the treasure. Hallstein has no treasure but in the chest are what is left of his life."

I had not thought of that, "He was hearth-weru. Perhaps Finn will take it."

"If I die on a raid, Leif, I want my chest to be shared between my shield brothers." He grinned, "Unless I am wed."

"Aye." The thought of wedding a maiden had, increasingly, filled my dreams. I had silver and I wanted to have heirs. Hallstein had none, at least none who would mourn him. He had told us that he had taken women and might have fathered children but they would not mourn him. Rather, they would curse him. I wanted to be mourned.

It was the start of Haustmánuður when we reached the fjord. Our masthead was seen before we reached the village and I heard the horn sound as the lookout spotted us. The shields of the dead had been removed from the side. It was a kindness. That way loved ones would not search for their men when we disembarked. The many gaps showed that we had paid a heavy price for our silver. We rowed in silence to honour our dead. We tied up and, as was his right, Jarl Bjørn was the first one ashore.

We slung our shields upon our backs and hefted our spears and chests as we waited at the gunwale.

The hersir greeted him and they clasped arms. We waited while the jarl spoke to Erland. I knew he would be telling him of the deaths of the men of Bygstad. Finn had already noted the missing shield and his head was hung. They had been shield brothers as well as hearth-weru. Hallstein had told us that they had sworn a blood oath when they were young men. His loss would be as hard as that of Elvind's parents, and the wives and children of Sverrir and Ragnalvadr. The difference was that Hallstein would have no treasure to give.

Jarl Bjørn turned and waved a hand. He said loudly, "Bygstad, welcome home your warriors who have brought treasure and honour back to your village. I am proud of all of them and would sail with them again. For those whose men have died, their share of the treasure and their weapons are in their chests. They all died well." He took out his sword and raised it, "The warriors of Bygstad."

We had arranged our own order. Oddr and Einarr were at the fore and then the others insisted that I be next and then the wounded Gunvald. Axel, of course, was last and that would be noted by all. I had told Joseph to follow with the two other thralls. He had been able to translate for them and had helped to teach them words. They would serve Oddr and Einarr. We allowed a pause between each man leaving the ship so that they could be welcomed and cheered by all. As I stepped off the ship I felt like a giant and the cheers rang around.

My mother put her arms around me and, for the first time that I could remember, she wept. I saw my father and uncle looking proud. I said, to my brothers, "Take my shield, spear and chest. I would embrace our mother." When they took them, I was able to put my arms around my weeping mother and lift her from the ground.

She hissed in my ear, "I have missed my brave boy and I am happy that you are whole."

I put her down and clasped my father's hand and then Brokkr's. Finally, I picked my aunt and cousin up as one. Kára squealed with delight. The others had all left the ship and Axel had a muted cheer from his mother, brother, sister and father. I turned and waved over to Joseph, "And this is my thrall, Joseph Ben Yekutiel. He is a healer from a land half a year to the south." He had managed to convey the distance to his home which he had told me lay beyond the sea we had sailed and another one he called the Blue Sea.

My mother frowned, "A healer? A labourer would be of more use."

I sighed. The sentimental mother had not lasted long, "Mother, he saved the lives of many warriors. Gunvald would have lost his leg but for Joseph. Steinarr One Eye was saved by his ministerings. Besides, he is mine."

She frowned, "But you share our longhouse and he is another mouth to feed."

I decided this was the moment for my news, "As I now have enough silver I shall marry and leave the house, Mother. Joseph can be my servant."

There was stunned silence from everyone.

Joseph's word skills had improved and he had understood what I had said. Both he and Gunvald knew of my plans. He shook his head and said, quietly, "You choose your moments a little unwisely, Lord Leif."

I smiled. He had taken to calling me lord as he felt I acted more like a lord than a simple master.

Chapter 12

My words stunned everyone into silence. My father broke it, "Come, let us go home."

My brothers did not care for my statement. They wanted presents and they wished to hear my stories.

Once we were in the hall they badgered me to open the chest and give my treasure. I gave them each a dagger in a scabbard. I would have been delighted to have been given such gifts when I was their age. I also had two swords I had taken. I held the lesser of the two and said, "Birger, when you train to be a warrior, here is your sword." I smiled at the other two, "You will have to wait until our next raid until I can win swords for you."

They seemed satisfied. Everyone was staring at me but for my brothers. They wandered off clutching their gifts and I said, "Joseph, that is where I sleep. You will share the space with me."

"Yes, my lord."

He went to the bed I had indicated.

Brokkr had heard my words and said, "Raiding again?"

I nodded, "Before I speak of this and, other matters, it has been a long time since I had enjoyed an ale."

Taking the horn from my belt, Kára said, "I will get it for you, Leif."

I sat at the table and they sat around. "First, the raid. Jarl Bjørn intends to spend the winter after next raiding the land around the Liger."

My father frowned, "That is in the southern part of Frankia." I saw his navigator's mind working out where that was. "It is north of Aquitaine." I nodded, "He intends to spend the winter there?"

"Aye, he will build another drekar and he has asked, or will ask the hersir to build one for the men of Bygstad."

My father nodded, "Bold and dangerous."

"We fought the Franks three times, four if you count our escape from their river. I do not fear them. I have a mail byrnie. It needs work but when I go to raid I will have protection."

My mother said, "That did not help Hallstein."

"He was unlucky." I took out the silver and the treasure from the bottom of the chest where I had hidden it and spread it on the table. "Next time I will bring back more."

All were impressed at the sight.

Kára brought me my ale and I took out the copper brooch with the jet upon it, "This is for you. I thought it would suit."

The frown on her face was replaced by a look of joy. She kissed my cheek, "Thank you, Leif."

Aunt Iðunn nodded, "And this is why you would wed."

I nodded, "I want to leave my mark upon this earth. Elvind died. He died well but his line is ended. I want my children to mourn my death when I die."

I could see that most of them understood but not my mother, "But you have shown no interest in the girls of the village."

I smiled, "You have not seen into my heart, Mother, but it is true, I had not selected a bride before I left. I had girls in mind but I had not chosen. Now I have."

I stunned them all and they were desperate to know who it was. It was my mother who boldly asked the question.

"I will not embarrass myself by telling you her name only to have her father reject my offer. When I have spoken to her father and she has agreed, then I will tell you."

My mother's eyes filled with tears, "I thought that I might lose you when you went a-viking but I thought it would be to a sword and not to a woman."

I put my hand on hers, "You would have me stay at home and live a life without a woman?"

She did not answer at first but finally, she nodded and stood, "Aye, I would."

Iðunn followed her to the cooking area and said, over her shoulder, "Kára, let the men talk."

My uncle and father filled their horns with ale and my father said, "She will come around. I thought you were mad when you spoke but I can see that the raid has changed you and this is well thought out. Now tell us of the raid and leave nothing out. This treasure trove speaks well of the raid."

I went through it all and told them of Axel and the problems he had caused. When I spoke of the girl I had killed their hands went to their hammers. As I spoke of Joseph I saw them looking over to him. He had buried himself beneath the animal skins on my bed and was asleep.

My father said, quietly, "Your mother and the volvas will not be happy that a healer who is a man has come into their world."

I sighed, "Uncle, I did not choose him as a slave. The Norns spun. My sword was ready to kill him when I realised he was the only one who could save Gunvald. We all know that we cannot fight the Norns. Even the Allfather knows that they are a force unto themselves. Besides, when I am wed he will just be my problem. I may not need a healer but I believe he has other skills we can use, and when we raid the jarl would have him aboard our ship."

"You will raid with the jarl and not the hersir?"

"He asked for us, the young warriors for whom this was our first raid, and we all agreed. Do you really think that Erland Haraldsson will raid?" I saw the answer on their faces. "He will send another in his place." I paused to emphasise the words, "Father, he will send you. Snorri and Gandalfr spoke highly of your skills as a navigator. He will find some way to stay at home and let you take the risks."

My father drank more of the ale and Brokkr studied him. "He is right. Erland will not risk his life. If he builds the ship then the profits are his. He reaps the reward without the risks. He is now a merchant and makes more silver by sending his knarr to Frisia and Frankia to trade. His captains wear the crosses of the White Christ to fool the Franks into thinking they are tame barbarians."

My father smiled, "I confess that the thought of spending months under the sun rather than living like a troll beneath a hill does appeal." He picked up the silver and let it run through his hands, "And this treasure is greater than we took in many raids. We brought back iron, animals and some copper. This is a real treasure." He used his fingers to make it into piles as he spoke. "That is a year or more away. We have you home for now, my son, and I shall be interested in whom you choose as a bride."

I had made my choice when we had rowed down the Sequana and I was confident that my offer would be accepted.

My Mother's voice was commanding, "Food is ready, move your treasure, Leif." As I collected up the treasure my mother fetched in the bowl of stew and looked over at Joseph. "We have no thrall quarters."

"Let him eat with us, Mother. He is civilised and we have room."

She was about to reject the idea out of hand when my father asserted his authority, "He deserves the opportunity for he saved Leif's shield brothers."

She rolled her eyes but said nothing. My father had a rare victory and he looked pleased with himself, perhaps the thought of sailing a drekar had rekindled his martial spirit.

I went to my bed and roused Joseph. "Food." He stood and I placed the treasure close to my bed. I realised my brothers had not returned and I went to the door, "Birger, fetch your brothers. There is food."

From the woods, I heard a cry of, "We come." I smiled as I re-entered the hall. They had been using the daggers and pretending to be warriors.

Joseph stood while the rest were seated. I took my usual place and patted the bench next to me for Joseph. Birger would have to sit on the other side of him. Joseph had his own eating spoon and I had given him one of the eating knives I had taken on the raid. He looked nervously at my mother who glared at him. I smiled and said, "Inside that stony face beats a warm heart." He did not understand *stony* and I repeated the word and passed my hand over my face. I made it serious. He nodded.

He had become used to our food when we had eaten on the Sequana and then on the longship but my mother and aunt were the best of cooks and the food was like a feast for the gods. I saw him beam and he ventured, "This is good. Thank you, my lady."

I had taught him as many words as I could and he chose the right ones for my mother allowed the briefest of smiles and she said, "Eat for tomorrow you work."

I did not argue. There was no point but he was my slave and I had plans for him. I would take him with me when I made my two visits the next day.

The meal over I took Joseph to show him where we made water and so on. When we returned to the hall I pointed to the bottom of my bed, "This, for the moment, will be your bed. I do not need the furs but I can see that you do."

His face showed his gratitude, "Thank you, Lord Leif. You have a good family."

As he made himself a nest at the bottom of the bed I asked, "Do you have a family?"

"I did but they were slain when I was taken."

"Taken?"

"Moors," I frowned for I did not know the word he said. He explained, "Fierce warriors from the land where the sun always shines." Words to do with the weather had been the first ones I had taught him. "They made my wife and children slaves and I was put to work. The men you slew took me after a battle."

I realised I had not asked him enough about the village when we had sailed back. It was as though the battle had not taken place. "Tell me, Joseph, why were there so many warriors in the village?"

He gave a sad smile, "The maiden you slew was due to be married. The warriors were there to take her and her husband to their new home."

I grabbed my hammer. The Norns had spun. A week either side and we would not have had to deal with so many warriors. Hallstein and the others would be alive.

I rose early and, leaving a sleeping Joseph, went to the fjord and swam. I knew that I was copying the jarl but he seemed a good man to emulate. I felt much better when I emerged. Joseph was waiting at the side with a cloak and a drying blanket. He shook his head, "You are a brave man to enter such an icy place."

"I feel good when I have done so."

Back in the hall, the women were cooking breakfast. Joseph said, "I had better make myself useful." He went outside and I heard him chopping wood for kindling.

My mother brought over a horn of ale, "He seems to have a good heart and I can see that there is no chance for him to flee."

I nodded and told her of his family. Her face softened. "Then he has been made a slave twice. He has soft hands. He must have had a good life before he was taken."

I realised that I had not spoken to him about his life before he was a slave.

Norse Warrior

When we had eaten I went to the chest and took out the damaged byrnie and the helmets. Birger and my brothers were most impressed with the shirt.

"Come, Joseph, we will visit with Alfr and it will be a chance for me to introduce you to the others in Bygstad."

I handed the shirt and other pieces of metal I had brought back to him and smiled for he could barely carry it. My mother was right, he had enjoyed a soft life.

The return of the drekar and the warriors meant more people were up and about. As we made our way to the smith's workshop, where I could see the smoke rising from the forge, I was greeted and welcomed back. From their words, I knew that the story of our fight had been spread and, as with all such stories, exaggeration had begun. I also noticed that they were staring at Joseph, His size, skin and the fact that he was shivering made him unique. I could see that he was struggling with the weight so I made my apologies and hurried to the forge. He smiled when we entered the smithy for it was not just warm, it was hot.

Alfr and Balder were dressed for work and they beamed when I entered, "You did well, we hear, Leif Longstride. It seems that you can kill Franks as well as you kill wolves."

"I was lucky." I took the byrnie from Joseph. "This is damaged. I would have it repaired."

Alfr took it as though it was a piece of parchment and held it up. He shook his head, "It will be neither quick nor cheap."

I handed him the helmets and a damaged sword I had taken at the Sequana, "I would use these for payment and, if they are not enough I have silver."

He examined the metal and nodded, "These will do. It will not be ready until Einmánuður."

"That is not a problem," I told him of the plans the jarl had made. Balder became quite excited, "And I will go on that raid, Father. Think of the iron and silver I could bring back."

"Aye, it would be a good thing." He held his arm out and I clasped it, "and as part of the payment, Leif Longstride, I want you to teach my son to be a warrior. He has the strength but from what Dagfinn and Brynjar told us you have the skill."

We stepped from the forge and Joseph shivered. I laughed, "The first thing we must do is to make you a cloak that is lined with fur. I cannot have you shivering when we step from our home."

Brynjar, Oddr and Mikkel were talking outside and there was a group of young men listening to all their words. Oddr saw me and said, "And here is the hero who saved my life. It was not a warrior who almost took it, but a maiden. Leif Longstride has fast hands."

With Joseph shivering, the four of us told the story of the two raids. I saw the eyes of the youths widen. They would be old enough to sail when next we went.

We were interrupted by the voice of the hersir, "Hold Leif Longstride. He is to be punished."

We all turned and saw the hersir flanked by his sons, Galmr and Axel striding towards us. Finn followed.

Oddr said, "What? Why what has he done?"

Axel pointed an accusing finger at me, "He struck me."

The other three all burst out laughing, "You were lucky, Cousin, that he did not slay you."

Oddr pointed at the son of the hersir, "Hersir, he was about as much use as a barnacle on the keel of a drekar. Hallstein also struck him. He deserved to be hit for he was going to take the life of this slave, the one who saved Gunvald's leg. He saved the life of more than one warrior."

I saw that Finn was uncomfortable with this. He shared our opinion and Hallstein's of Axel. Galmr just smirked. The hersir said, "He will be punished."

My three shield brothers stepped before me and put their bodies between me and the hersir. Oddr said, darkly, "Hersir, no one will lay a hand on this warrior. Do not make men choose between you and Leif Longstride."

Many others had come from their homes. Gunvald limped over using a walking stick. He was accompanied by Dagfinn. Dagfinn had heard the words and said, loudly, "Aye, there is but one we would choose and it is not Axel the Useless' father."

I could see that this was getting out of hand. This was a rebellion against the hersir. I stepped forward, "There is an easy way to settle this, Hersir. I have done no wrong but I would not have dissention. Let this be decided by the gods. I will face Axel in a circle of spears and first blood will determine who is right and who is wrong."

Axel shrank back.

Finn grinned, "Aye, that is the right way to do this."

Erland did not know how weak his son was and I saw him look at his son for the right response. Axel shook his head, "Punish him, Father!"

Brynjar laughed, "He will not kill you, Cousin. Who knows, a scar may be the making of you."

"I will not fight."

Silence fell. Even the hersir looked shocked. I said slowly and calmly, "Then there is no charge for me to face?"

The hersir looked confused and Finn came to me and clasped my arm, "There is no charge for you to face."

Erland said, "I am hersir."

Oddr said, "Then act like one."

The faces of the whole village save Erland's and his sons told a story and he snapped, "There is no charge."

He turned around and stormed off followed by his sons who looked like chastened puppies.

I said, "Thank you, Finn, but you are hearth-weru."

He shook his head, "I was hearth-weru, I swore an oath to Hallstein long before Erland Haraldsson. I will train two warriors to take my place and the next time the men of Bygstad raid I will regain my honour and join the jarl on his raid." He turned to follow the hersir.

I could almost hear the Norns spinning. The killing of the maiden had set the stones tumbling down the rock face.

I turned to the others, "Thank you but was this wisely done?"

Oddr shrugged, "A leader keeps men loyal by rewarding them. Erland did not come with us on the raid. He gave us no silver but the jarl did. I did not like the way Axel behaved on the raid. He shamed the men of Bygstad. Perhaps it is time for a Thing where we can decide if we wish to have Erland as our hersir."

The others nodded. Brynjar added, "And I, for one, would like to make the blood oath."

That was a serious matter. The swearing of such an oath bound shield brothers so that they were closer than family.

Oddr nodded, "Then we will speak of this again in seven days. That will give us the chance to speak to the others, the warriors of the Sequana, to decide."

I said, "And now I must go. Joseph and I still have much to do."

As we turned Joseph said, quietly, "What is a blood oath?"

"We cut open a sod and place a spear haft in the ground. We each grasp the spearhead so that the blood drops into the ground and then we replace the sods."

He shook his head, "As a healer I have to say that I find that... what is the word? Wrong."

"It is what we do." I showed him the scar on my palm. "I have one oath I swore before we raided. That bound me to the gods. The next one will bind me to the men with whom I fight."

We returned to the hall and I went to my chest. I took a fur for Joseph, "Put this around your shoulders." He did so. I gave him my beaver skin hat, "And this upon your head."

As he dressed himself for the walk I intended to make, I took out the silver crosses I had found. One was bigger than the other. I also took out one of the silver brooches I had taken. They were fitting to give to the father of my intended. I strapped on my sword and shouted to my mother and my aunt. "I will be back later this afternoon."

They both came into the hall to look at me, "You have decided?"

"Yes, Mother. I made my choice when I rowed on the Sequana. I will now see if my choice was a good one."

Leaving the hall, we turned to head up to Lars Greybeard's farm. His daughters had given me enough encouragement to think that they would listen to my offer. It was Freya who had stirred my loins but her sister, whilst younger, was just as attractive a proposition.

As we walked Joseph showed that he had been listening, "You go to buy a bride, Lord Leif?"

"Not buy. The silver is a gift, but yes, I am going to choose a bride. How did you choose your wife?"

"Our parents made the arrangement. We are of the same…" I saw him struggle for the word, "I think you say clan but that is different from us."

"Do your people make war and take slaves, as we do?"

"We have warriors but not like you. We also have slaves." He gave a wry smile, "I never thought that I would be a slave."

"How did that happen?"

"The Moors came from the sea and we had no walls. I heal and I had no weapons."

"You should have defended your family."

I saw that my words had hurt him and I regretted them immediately. He nodded, "I know that now but what good would have come of it? I would be dead and my family would still be slaves. You, I can see, might have been able to slay your enemies, but me? I heal."

"Then the lord who ruled you should have defended you."

"My people left our homeland long ago. We are Ashkenazi."

I tried to say it and failed.

He laughed, "It is the name of our…clan. We live in the lands ruled by others for they value our skills."

"Not well enough."

I heard the barking of Lars' dogs, Snorri and Hrólfr. They had smelled us. As we ascended the low ridge before the farm and the flock, they bounded up to us. They recognised me but bared their teeth and growled at Joseph. He sheltered behind me. I held up my hand, "Down!" They obeyed. "Joseph, hold out your hand and let them smell you. While I am here, they will not bite."

"You are sure?"

"I am sure." He obeyed but I saw that his hand was shaking. "Now stroke their heads." He looked terrified but he had been a slave long enough to obey. When the dogs licked his hand rather than biting it he looked relieved.

Lars and his daughters came to the door of the farm and I waved. We made our way down to meet them. The dogs returned to their duty of watching the flock.

Joseph said, quietly, "One of these is the woman?"

"She is."

"They are both pretty."

"And will bear strong warriors."

Lars beamed, "Leif Longstride returned from the raid, alive, with a visitor and, I think, a tale to tell. Come within. Daughters, ale and food."

They had both been staring at Joseph. He looked different to every man they had ever seen. With his dark hair and olive skin he looked like no one they had encountered. They obeyed and scurried within.

We entered the hall and I saw the smile on Joseph's face. The hall was warm.

"Sit."

As we sat, I said, "Joseph, take off your hat and cloak. You will need them when we go out again."

He shed his outer layers and looked even smaller than he had. I could see curiosity etched all over Lars' face but he waited until the two maidens had brought ale, bread and the cheese that I so enjoyed. I had learned, whilst talking to Joseph on the way north that bread and cheese were more familiar to him than the food he had eaten on the longship. When the girls were seated, I started my story. As much as I did not want to relive the moment I had slain the girl I had to include it each time I told the story. That was the spinning of the Norns. If I did not speak of it then they might spin another and I wanted to be forgotten by the three sisters. I shocked the girls and I wondered if Freya might reject my advances. When I told them of Joseph and the healing of the warriors their faces became animated and, I hoped, they had forgotten the death of the maid. I told them of Axel and the consequences.

Lars interrupted me at that point, "Hallstein was a good warrior and a sound advisor. Finn is the same. If Finn leaves the hersir then I fear for Bygstad. Erland should never have been hersir. His father was a good man but Erland…he does not lead."

I nodded, "I fear you are right, and it will divide the clan." I concluded with the flight down the river and our arrival home.

Lars banged the table, "A good tale and while brave warriors died, from what you say, this man you have with you kept alive others who might have died."

I nodded, "We were lucky, that I know. The jarl wishes to take at least two longships in the winter after this to raid the land of Aquitaine and beyond." I took out the treasure and pushed it over to him. "This is for you and your daughters. The sword you gave me saved my life and this is payment."

He took the treasure and put the two crosses to one side. "Thank you, Leif. I will let my daughters share their prize later. You have more than a year at home then." He gave a sly smile, "And what really brings you here, Leif Longstride, the Wolf Killer and slayer of Franks? I do not think it was just to give me silver."

I had faced men in battle and never baulked but looking at Lars, whom I viewed as a friend and his daughters, staring intently at me, I almost faltered. Then I thought of Hallstein who had never married and Elvind who had not enjoyed the opportunity to marry. Lars' words had struck a chord, I had a year and then my life would be in danger once more.

"I wish to marry Freya if you will allow it and if she will have me."

I saw the look of joy on Freya's face and the one of disappointment on that of Borghildr. Lars nodded, "The first is easy. You are an admirable young man and I would be proud to have you marry my daughter. As for the second that is even easier, for since you killed the wolf and following the wedding at Bygstad the two have bickered and argued over who would be the better wife for Leif Longstride. Let us set the day for Ýlir. When I have culled the flock for winter and while there is still some daylight would be a good time."

"Good."

"There is one thing more."

"Yes?"

"I would have you live here and not in Bygstad. I will make part of the hall separate. You, Freya and the slave can be apart when you need privacy."

"I will need to be with the other warriors when we train and, if a ship is to be built then I will have to join them."

He nodded, "But both of those things will not take place until Gói. It is a healthy walk to Bygstad. I have but two children, Leif, and I would keep them both close if I can. If you go raiding it will be a comfort for Freya to be at home."

I could see the sense in that. I also realised it would ease the situation at Bygstad. I was not afraid of a confrontation and Axel struck me as one who would avoid a direct attack but I wanted peace for my home and my absence might heal the wounds I had unwittingly created.

Lars stood, "You will need to tell your mother and father." It was the signal for me to leave. Freya stood and came before me. I was in strange waters and I did not know what to do. Lars smiled, "I think that an embrace and a kiss will seal the pact."

I nodded and put my arms around her. She put her hands around my neck and, pulling herself up, kissed me hard on the mouth, her tongue darting around mine like a butterfly dancing amongst the summer flowers. I was taken aback but when I felt a stirring in my loins I knew I had made the right choice. When I lowered her to the ground I saw that her eyes were wide.

"Leif, I have dreamed of your embrace and we will make fine warriors. I cannot wait for Ýlir. I shall make myself as beautiful as I can."

As Lars shepherded us from the hall he said, "I am the father of the bride and the wedding feast will be here. You and Freya will determine the guests." He looked me in the eyes, "I do not like the hersir and he will not be invited."

I sighed. That would do nothing to ease the tension in the village. I nodded, "Aye, I will let my family know." As Joseph and I walked back down the trail to the village I could hear the Norns spinning. There was no need for Lars to invite the hersir but Erland and his family would take it as an insult and the divide in the clan would only grow.

Chapter 13

As we walked back Joseph spoke to me. His words told me that he had listened and understood much of what Lars had said. I suppose having been a slave in one part of the world and having to learn a new language had made it easier for him to pick up a new one. That allied to his clever mind made him more astute than any man I had ever met.

"We will live on that farm?"

"We will."

"I hoped that I could use my skills in the village."

I smiled, "Joseph, what you do not know is that when it is the middle of winter you will see the sun for no more than an hour a day. The land will be covered in ice and snow. There will be no need for your skills. In the winter it is not disease that kills but old age and even a healer cannot stop time."

He was a clever man but my words had shocked him. We walked in silence and he nodded, "I had noticed that the sun shines longer here in your land than that of my birth. God has made your world different to mine."

I learned that his people, like those of the White Christ, had but one God. I was not sure if it was the same God but his god, from what he had said, was nothing like Odin. Certainly, he did not regard the two as the same. His God was more like a strict father than the Allfather.

My mother was shocked at the haste but my father nodded his approval. When I spoke of living at Lars' hall, my mother broke down and wept. My father put his arm around her and shook his head, "Agnetha, it is time for him to go. We knew this day would come and I am happy for our son."

"But it is so sudden."

"And is that not the way? I knew that when he went a-viking it would change him and it has. He is a better man now than when he left and I thought him a good man then. It will be the same when he marries for Freya is a fine and healthy young woman. She will bear him sons and you shall have grandchildren."

His words did nothing to assuage my mother's tears and my father shrugged. He was more interested in the fact that the hersir would not be invited.

"There has always been bad blood between Lars and Erland. It is why Lars farms where he does. Erland is walking a dangerous path. The men in the village are less than happy with him and his son has done little to endear them to him. Even his nephew now sides with Oddr and the men who confronted him this morning."

Brokkr nodded, "We need a Thing. This will tear the clan apart if we do not. Finn has told the hersir that he will train two more hearth-weru and then he will sail with the jarl. The hersir is not happy."

I nodded and then added slowly, "And the hersir blames me." Their silence told me that I was right. "Then perhaps my marriage and absence from the village might be the best thing for all, eh?"

"Perhaps, but this has been brewing for a long time. A leader who does not fight and fails to reward his warriors is asking for trouble. You can get away with it if you are a powerful warrior. Erland is not a powerful warrior."

Word spread around the village about the wedding. At first, it was gossip spread like an early morning mist; patches here and there but unsubstantiated by fact. When Lars came into the village with his dogs and daughters to announce it and invite the village then the gossip became fact and took form. He did not tell the hersir he was not invited. Instead, he went around every house in the village except for the hersir's to ask if they would attend. It was clever for he knew that the hersir would avoid confrontation. He stayed within his hall but sent servants to listen. By the time Lars and his daughters left, after a long meeting with my mother and father, then the hersir knew.

My mother knew how to behave before guests and there were no tears. She smiled at Freya and commented on her beauty. It was not a false face for she had nothing personally against my bride-to-be. It was any woman who took me from her that she objected to. Lars told them that he expected nothing from them as, in his words, he had the best of the bargain as he was gaining a son-in-law he saw as the finest warrior who lived along the fjord. He promised a lamb a week during the lambing season. That was a most generous offer. It meant my family could either raise the lamb or eat it. Food was as valuable as silver.

Ýlir was far enough away for us to forget about it as we had much to do to prepare for winter. Lars and his daughters would be busy but my part would be to simply show up. Ýlir would be when the days were becoming so short that a man could blink and miss them. I think that was another reason why Lars had chosen that date. The long nights were a time to be indoors and celebrate.

The first task that the men of the village had to do was to lift the drekar, '*Bylgja*', from the fjord and clean the hull. It was not our drekar and lay at the jarl's port but the men who had sailed her were expected to maintain her. The jarl's knarr came down the fjord one late afternoon and tied up. Gandalfr and Snorri stepped from her. We had seen her approach and made our way to the quay. When I was named I felt myself rise a head above the others, "Leif Longstride, it is good to see you again."

"And you, Snorri. What brings you here?"

Gandalfr spoke, "We have a ship to lift from the fjord. All those who sailed on her are invited by the jarl to Askvoll for two days of hard work."

Snorri grinned, "And some serious drinking."

My father nodded, "We can do without you for two days, Leif, and it is our duty to the jarl."

The hersir and his son strode imperiously towards us. Erland waved aside those who barred his way, "What is this, Gandalfr?"

Gandalfr sighed, "The jarl needs the men who sailed the drekar on the raid to come and help to clean it."

Erland frowned, "Are there not enough men in Askvoll for that task?"

Oddr said, angrily, "You know this is expected of us, Erland, why do you ask such questions?"

"Because I am the hersir of this place."

Oddr said, "For the moment."

"You challenge me?"

Brokkr was a peacemaker and he said, reasonably, "No one said a challenge, Hersir, but Oddr is right. When we sailed with the jarl and his father, we cleaned the drekar."

While the conversation had been going on the ones who had raided, me included, had moved behind Oddr. I saw the hersir's eyes taking it in. This was not the time for a confrontation. He waved an irritated arm and said, "Go then but remember that by Gormánuður I will expect the work to be completed on the new hall." We did not need a new hall but Erland had held a Thing months before we had raided and gained the grudging permission from the men of the village to raise a new hall. It was unnecessary but would be a measure of his power. We had the bones erected already but we had not yet added the walls and the roof. He did not give anyone the chance to object for he and his son turned on their heels and headed back to his home.

Gandalfr said, "He is not a pleasant man. Is he a good hersir?" He knew the answer when no one replied.

My father said, "If you and your brother would stay with us we would be honoured."

It should have been the hersir who made the offer but that was not going to happen and Gandalfr smiled, "It would be an honour."

My mother fussed when we arrived but she would make the best of it. That was her way. While the three women, aided by Joseph, prepared the food, we sat and spoke of the jarl. "He was pleased with the service he had from the men of this village." Gandalfr nodded towards me, "He was especially pleased with Leif here." Once more I grew inside.

"And he is to be married."

Snorri slapped a huge hand on my back, "Good! You can sire warriors."

Gandalfr nodded appreciatively at the quality of the ale, "The jarl has his new drekar almost completed. It is why he asked for all the men who sailed on the raid. He is keen to return south of where we raided last time."

Joseph had come in with platters of sliced meat and cheese. I saw his eyes widen when he heard the word south. He said nothing but I knew what he was thinking.

Snorri added, "Aye, he has a mind to spend the winter in the sun, raiding."

My mother had brought in a jug of ale and she said, "You mean that the men would not be here for the winter solstice?"

My father sighed, "Agnetha, what happens at that time of year? We squat inside our longhouses while outside it snows and the land is frozen. I, for one, wish that I was younger and could also spend the time raiding."

Brokkr laughed, "But you are too old, eh?"

Gandalfr shook his head, "You are no older than I am. You are a good navigator, and we need two."

My father took one look at my mother's face and shook his head, "No, I will leave that to another."

"You could teach Leif."

"I could try, Snorri, but you know that such skills are best taught at sea. He can navigate in the fjord but out of sight of land? Your brother could teach him."

Gandalfr nodded, "Aye, I could. We shall see. That is some way off. We have a ship to clean."

Birger asked, "What is it that you will do?"

"We will haul her from the water and once the weed and wildlife have been removed we will paint pine tar on her keel." He smiled, "That stinking concoction will stop the weed and the worms, at least for a while."

"That does not sound so bad."

Snorri emptied his horn, "It is not but it is hard work to lift the ship and turn her over. It is why we need the men we do."

That night, as I snuggled under my fur Joseph spoke in my ear, "Master, if you are to raid south of Frankia, can I come?"

I turned to look at him. His eyes were wide and I could tell that he was excited, "So that you could run?"

I could not see his eyes in the dark and he kept his voice even. "I could help. If we meet other ships my language skills would be useful, and although I am no sailor I know the customs of the people who live far from here. You do not."

His suggestion was a reasonable one and I still had to get used to the idea of owning a slave. I said, "Perhaps but that is half a year away and the world can change in that time. Now is the time for sleep."

Axel did not turn up the next day. We waited a short time but when it became clear that he would not be coming we left. We had not wanted him to come for he was unpopular but we felt that he ought to share the burden of labour. As the knarr headed down the fjord Oddr said, "I will ask for a Thing when we return. We need a new hersir."

Einarr said, "But who?"

Oddr shrugged, "Anyone would be better than Erland. What does he do for our people? He does not bring food to the village. He does not lead us in raids. He squats like a toad and reaps the reward of his fleet of knarr. He does not even command that but lets his men sail them for him."

Snorri said, darkly, "But he is a cunning man, Oddr. Do not underestimate him. Once he knows that there will be a Thing he will plot and plan."

Gandalfr said, "That is not our concern, Snorri." He pointed, "That is." We saw the drekar looking sad without her prow and her mast. The others who had raided with us were gathered on the quay, along with the jarl. All were stripped for work and were just awaiting us. I saw the fires that were burning beneath the pots that contained, I assumed, pine tar. We made our own pine tar but the snekke did not need the vast quantities that the drekar would.

When we had tied up, we went to join the others. We had bonded on the raid and they felt like family. We greeted each other while Gandalfr and Snorri spoke with the jarl. We quickly exchanged news. Steinarr came over to thank me for Joseph saving his life. Mikkel could not help but blurt out that I was to be married and that brought slaps on my back. I did not like the attention and I was glad when the jarl shouted, "Welcome. There will be time for chatter this evening when we have finished our work. For now, we need bare backs and strong arms."

We all stripped to the waist and obeyed the waved arm of Gandalfr. We marched down to the drekar. He waved us aboard and we took our places. There were no chests for us and we copied the older warriors and knelt. Once we were untied we rowed the drekar to the small patch of beach. It had been cleared of rocks and was obviously the place they always used.

The jarl and his hearth-weru leapt into the water. They pulled the ropes that were attached to the drekar. We sculled our oars to aid them and when we felt the keel grind on the sand we stopped.

"Everyone over the side and take your oars with you."

I watched Gandalfr and Snorri as they removed the steering board. The water was icy when we jumped in. We stacked our oars and then joined the others to haul on the ropes. Only Gandalfr was not involved. He supervised and shouted orders. Even the jarl obeyed. It showed me the difference between a real leader and Erland. The critical moment was when the ship was balanced on one gunwale. Gandalfr ordered the fifteen strongest men, the jarl included, to stand close to the ship.

"The rest of you pull but do so slowly." We obeyed and the ship began to move. The men caught the gunwale and Gandalfr shouted, "Let go of the ropes and help the others." We did so and took the weight of the ship. With so many men it was easy to gently lower her to the sand.

Gandalfr looked pleased, "The sand has taken some of the worst of the weed from her." He pointed to a pile of flint scrapers. I had not seen them. "Choose your scraper and find your own section of the keel. We have until noon to clean her and then we begin to paint her."

By the time the afternoon was becoming evening, we were done and we stank of weed and dead crustaceans. I stripped off my breeks and joined the jarl and some of the others who swam in the fjord. The sweat and the stink disappeared and I felt much better after I had dried and donned my boots and kyrtle once more.

"And now the reward. We hunted last week and you shall all dine well. We have ale and mead. You have all earned it."

As we had been the ones who had swum it was natural that I walked back with the jarl and his hearth-weru. I think his men tolerated me but the jarl seemed genuinely fond of me. "How is the thrall you took?"

"He now speaks our language well and my mother has become accustomed to him."

"He will go with you when you are married?"

I stopped, "You know of this?"

He laughed, "Gandalfr and Snorri told me all."

"Aye, he will." I hesitated and then went on, "Joseph, that is the thrall, said he could be useful when we raid south of Frankia for he knows the land and the people."

137

He nodded, thoughtfully, "He would and he is a healer but," he stopped and looked at me, "he may wish to run."

"I know, Jarl, but if he helped us before he ran it could not hurt."

"And you would not mind losing a thrall?"

"We have not yet become used to him and if it helped the raid…"

He nodded, "You are a thoughtful warrior, Leif, and I am pleased that you are one of my crew. I think it is a good idea to bring him. We need someone who knows the land of Frankia."

It was a great compliment and I walked into the mead hall feeling like a giant.

I took my place among the younger ones from Bygstad. I could have sat with Oddr and the others for I had been accepted by them, but having trained with the younger ones I felt tied to them. I held my horn out for the thrall to pour, "Ale! I am thirsty!"

When it was filled the others held theirs up. Brynjar said, "The wolves of Bygstad!"

"The wolves of Bygstad!"

When we had drunk Mikkel asked, "Are we the wolves?"

Brynjar shrugged, "When we fought, we fought as ferociously as wolves and Leif here has his wolf cloak. It is as good a name as any and when we battle the Franks it will be a rallying call for our little band."

We all nodded. Brynjar had changed since he had shed the mantle of Axel's cousin. Axel was now isolated in the village and he had become his father's shadow. Part of that was fear of violence from one of us. We would never harm him, he was not worthy of it, but he seemed to feel that he was in danger. Brynjar had told us that a week or so after our return. We chatted, while we waited for the food, about the work we had done and the new ship. We had seen the ship when we had docked. She was more than a skeleton now. She had her strakes fitted and her keel had been painted with pine tar already. The mast was ready to be fitted and the last thing would be her dragon prow. Snorri had said that she would not be launched until the end of Gói. I hoped that we would be invited as I wanted to see a drekar's birth.

There was a mighty cheer when the steaming pile of meat was brought in. The beasts that had been hunted had been mighty ones for the platters were laden.

The jarl was between his wife and their two sons. He stood and raised his horn, "Eat for you have earned the food this day and when you are all done I have words I would say. For the moment, eat, drink and enjoy yourselves."

We obeyed his order and the mountain of food gradually disappeared. I had eaten enough but there was a bone with some meat attached. I knew that the meat from the bone was the tastiest so I picked the bone and gnawed the meat from it.

When it became clear that men had eaten the jarl stood again and his hearth-weru left their places to stand behind him. "Warriors, when we raided Frankia with my cousin it opened a chest that was filled with treasure but the hint of greater treasure still waiting draws my eye there. Know that when the new drekar is launched and we have made a blót, we will ask the warriors of Bygstad and Askvoll to come with us and spend half a year filling our chests with treasure."

He still had more to say but we all cheered and banged our hands on the table.

He held his hands up and we fell silent, "You all did well on the raid and took home treasure. I wish to mark you as my men." He waved his arms and his hearth-weru began to move towards us, "I have had my weaponsmith make each of you a herkumbl. It is a silver dragon and will be a measure of how much I value each of you."

He sat for all of us were too interested in the gift to hear any more words. I took mine and marvelled at the intricacy of the detail. Looking at Mikkel's next to me I saw that they were identical and had been cast. Each was as long as my thumb and had a spike at the back to fix it to a helmet. I ran my fingers over the silver. It was smooth and polished. This was a worthy gift for a warrior. Its value was more than the silver it was made from. It was a measure of our value to the jarl.

When his men returned and took their seats he stood once more, "Tomorrow the men of Bygstad will return to their homes and we shall not see them until our drekar, both of them, sail up the fjord to pick them up for a half year of raiding. The silver dragon will be a reminder of our bond." He sat and we cheered. He paused, "One more thing. My cousin has confirmed that he has lost too many men to come with us. As Bygstad does not have a drekar, yet, we will just take two ships. It means we cannot raid Angers but there will be other prizes for us; of that I am sure."

After we had all examined the dragons in detail Brynjar slipped the one he had been given into the pouch attached to his belt. He drank some mead and then said, "Erland, my uncle, will not like this."

Dagfinn said, "He cannot object for this is a gift from the jarl."

Gunvald shook his head, "Brynjar is right. It marks us not as the men who follow the hersir but those who follow the jarl." He nodded to the older warriors, "Oddr and the others are seen as the heart of the clan. Our fathers were the past and they are the future. It is the marks that they carry which will cause trouble."

Silence fell amongst our group while a buzz of conversation filled the rest of the room. I nodded, "Then the sooner we hold a Thing the better."

Brynjar said, "Aye, but the first act we must make is a blood oath." He waved an arm around the hall, "This day has shown me that we are bound and I would make that binding stronger with an oath of blood."

Chapter 14

The herkumbl we had been given were not displayed as we left the knarr. Any problems caused by them would arise later when word reached Erland. That would be when Alfr began to attach them to helmets. On the way back upstream we had mentioned to Oddr our fears and he had nodded his agreement.

"I will speak to the other older warriors, men like your father and uncle, Leif, and we will organise a Thing as soon as we can. It would not do to let gossip fester in men's hearts."

I told my father and uncle after they had returned from fishing and we had eaten. We had enjoyed a good meal for the fishing had been good when I brought out the herkumbl and told them of my fears. My brothers were impressed by the silver herkumbl. Uncle Brokkr nodded, "Aye, the hersir will not like this. He has never rewarded warriors. This is what a good leader does. He ties his men to him with silver." We then spoke of leaders my father and uncle had known.

That night, as I lay in bed, Joseph at my feet, he asked, "Master, I did not understand all that was said. I heard the words but not the meaning beneath."

I spoke quietly in the dark and explained it as best as I could, "The hersir is our leader. He is the head man in the village. We owe allegiance to the jarl as does the hersir but our land does not have a king and men can choose who they wish to follow. The silver dragon tells Erland that we will follow the jarl and not him."

He was silent as he took it all in then he said, so quietly, that I almost did not hear him, "You will still raid the land south of the Liger?"

I knew then why he was so interested.

"We will, and before you ask the jarl may allow you to come with us." In the dark, I could not see his features but I knew that he was smiling. He saw a chance to get back to his homeland.

The next day, after we had all returned from the sea Brynjar gathered us, the ones he called the wolves. "Let us go now before we do anything else. We need to swear an oath. We will meet at the sacred grove."

I hurried to the hall and told my father that I would be back later for the food. He cocked an eye but nodded.

When we reached the grove I saw that Brynjar had a spear with him. He used the spearhead to cut the turf and he laid the sod to one side. He stood and said, "This was Hallstein's spear. Finn gave it to me for he said that if we sacrificed this and made the blood oath then the oath would be stronger."

We all nodded for we could see that was true.

He unfastened the head and laid the haft on the ground. "I will give the haft back to Finn. We do not need it." He put his hand on the long head. I put mine next to his and the others joined. We did not grip tightly but I could feel the sharp edge of the spearhead.

Brynjar said, "Great Thor, we make an oath to be brothers to the end of time. We swear to fight as one. We are the Wolves of Bygstad." He paused and then nodded. I had done this before and knew what it would feel like. The others did not and as they gripped the sharp head I saw their eyes widen. It was not just the pain and the sensation of blood, it was the sense that the god was with us, or, perhaps, the spirit of Hallstein. The blood flowed and Brynjar nodded. He took the spearhead and placed it on the blood. I knelt and replaced the sod. We both stood and held our palms out. The blood mingled. When everyone had done the same then it was over. We were oath sworn and it was with blood. There was no greater bond.

Oddr visited us two days later and he had Finn with him, Erland's hearth-weru. Finn had been training two warriors to take his place and I wondered at his presence. It reeked of conspiracy. The women and Joseph moved away so that we could talk and my brothers were sent to fetch wood. They were not happy.

"I agree with you, Oddr, we need a Thing. The hersir is not a good leader but Finn's presence here makes me concerned."

Finn nodded, "I know what you are saying, Eirik, I should be Erland's man but I swore an oath not to Erland but to Hallstein. He was the one oathsworn to the hersir. I was hearth-weru but not oath-bound. The hersir knows that." He paused and gave a grim smile, "He is not happy and asked me to make a blood oath when I told him I was leaving. I refused." He shrugged, "I am made to sleep across the threshold of the house. The hersir seeks to punish me. I have almost trained Egil and Sven. When the Thing is held then I can leave Erland's service."

Egil and Sven were two warriors who had come to the village when the hersir's ship had picked them up in the land of the Frisians. They had worked on his ship. Neither were sailors but they had been warriors. It made sense for them to become hearth-weru.

Oddr said, "I have spoken with most of the older warriors and we wish to approach Erland to ask to hold a Thing on Óðinsdagr."

Brokkr nodded, "A good choice."

"Then the two of you will support the idea?"

"We will but Erland is cunning. He may try to influence others to support him as hersir. He likes the power."

I said, "We should ask Lars to come for the Thing."

My father shook his head, "That would be like pouring oil onto a fire, my son. The two hate each other and as he has made it clear the hersir is not invited to the wedding it might provoke bloodshed. Besides, Lars chose to leave the village. He will not mind being excluded. He is just happy to have you coming into his life."

After they left my brothers and the others returned. My father told them what had been said. It was Brokkr who said what I had been thinking. "It is one thing to get rid of a the hersir but who will replace him?"

My father smiled, "The Norns are spinning, Brokkr, and the Thing will decide that. You know better than any that the three sisters have decided who that shall be, even as we sit here and discuss the matter."

The next day, when the fishing boats had all returned with another good catch, the senior men went to the hersir's hall. He had to have known something was afoot and he wore, as he stood in the doorway, not only his sword but also the small silver crown he had been given by his father. It was a trophy of a raid. His father had been a good warrior and Erland had been made hersir in the hope that he would be a leader like his father.

Oddr was the spokesman, "Hersir, we would have a Thing and we would like it on Óðinsdagr."

His eyes took in the assembled men. He nodded, "So, you plot behind my back."

Oddr sighed, "No, Hersir. We have not held a Thing since you asked for one to build your new hall. This is more important than a hall. There are matters that need to be discussed."

"You mean like the treachery of wearing the mark of the jarl rather than your hersir?"

"That is not treachery. It was a reward for a raid." He smiled, "Had you offered us one we might have worn it but you did not."

"It is treachery for my son was on the raid and he was not rewarded." We all knew that was because he had not come to work on the drekar but we said nothing. Suddenly the hersir jabbed an accusing finger at Finn, "And you have betrayed your oath. You are part of this plot."

Finn was wearing his sword and his hand went instinctively to the hilt. I saw him close his eyes to compose himself and then he said, quietly, "You and I know, Hersir, that the oath I took was to Hallstein. He was your man."

The hersir's voice hissed as he said, "Then as I now have two men who have sworn an oath you are no longer needed in my hall. Egil."

This had to have been planned for Egil disappeared into the hall and, when he returned, brought out Finn's belongings. They were hurled to the ground. There was a murmur of anger from all the others at the clear insult but Finn nodded, "At least I know where I stand." He was calm and bloodshed would be avoided.

Oddr said, "There is room for you in my home, Finn."

Erland gave a thin smile, "Then in two days' time we hold a Thing at the place by the fjord."

He turned and he and his sons entered their hall. The two new hearth-weru glowered and glared at us and then went within. Oddr helped Finn to gather his belongings and the two went off to Oddr's home. I walked back to our home with my family and our catch.

Brokkr shook his head, "That was not the way to treat Finn."

My father nodded and I said, "What will Finn do now?"

We reached our hall and the women and Joseph came out to begin to prepare the fish we had caught. We helped them and spoke while we worked.

"He is a warrior. He and Hallstein were the two in the village who had no other skills except that of being a warrior. Oddr's home will suffice for a while but once the winter is over then he will have to make a decision. Hallstein's death was like the throwing of a stone into a pond. The ripples are still making their way to the shore."

"I do not think that Hallstein was happy with the hersir. He certainly did not like Axel."

Brokkr was a thoughtful man, "And that is the problem. It would have been better if Axel had died on the raid and not Elvind."

My father nodded, "The Norns, Brother."

We did not fish every day and the next day we cleaned the snekke and repaired our nets. We would fish the following day. Other fishermen were of the same mind and there was a buzz of conversation on the wooden quay. I noticed Erland and Axel, followed by their two guards, as they visited the homes of the men the hersir thought would support them. He had to know that the village wished to rid itself of his rule. He was garnering support.

We dressed in our finest clothes for the Thing. I had my Hammer of Thor, my wolf's teeth and my hlad. There would be no weapons except for the two bodyguards. We gathered by the fjord and waited for the hersir. He wore the crown and had a silver necklet with a green emerald hanging around his neck.

He was still the hersir and it was incumbent upon him to begin the proceedings. He first invoked Odin and his guidance. I touched my Hammer of Thor and asked him for his help.

"Oddr Gautisson, this Thing came at your request. Why did you ask for it?" The hersir might not like the Thing being called but he knew the protocol.

Poor Oddr had organised it but the opinion of the warriors, especially those who had raided, had guided him, "Hersir, when we raided you did not lead us. There are many of us in the clan who think that we need a leader who will lead."

"You wish for a new hersir?" There was a murmur from most of us. He nodded, "I am your leader and my leadership has seen prosperity in this village. The jarl took you to war and four of the men from the village died. None died because of me."

Einarr spoke, "We are warriors, Hersir, and warriors sometimes die. You are a merchant."

"And you wish a warrior as a hersir? You want someone to lead you into battle and to raid?"

My father spoke, "Perhaps, or it may be that we want a leader who leads and does not hide behind well-carved pillars and demands a new hall that no one needs."

Erland's eyes narrowed, "And you would be that man, Eirik Eiriksson?"

"I have no desire to be hersir. I just want a different one."

I saw a look of triumph crease the hersir's face, "Then until there is a man who can replace me, I shall still be hersir. Is there one that you wish to be hersir?"

Oddr's plan was unravelling like an old spell. The hersir was a clever man and had known that he could defeat us by using our own customs. It was my father's voice which broke the silence, "I would have my brother Brokkr as hersir."

That it had not been discussed was clear from my uncle's face. Before he could say anything there was a loud acclamation from the other men. The majority approved.

Erland's face darkened, "You would have a dwarf as a hersir?"

I think my uncle might have declined the offer but for Erland's insult. He nodded, "Better a dwarf than a counter of coins. If it is the will of the whole clan then I would accept the honour."

It was Finn who shouted, "Brokkr Eiriksson!" The wall of noise showed the approval of the majority.

I had never attended such a Thing, indeed this was my first Thing for the last one had been before I had killed the wolf, but it became clear what the procedure was. Men moved behind their choice of candidate. A couple of older men moved behind Erland but the majority came towards Brokkr. Even Brynjar came to stand by me but his father, Brynjar stood in the middle. He would not support his brother, nor would he oppose him.

Brokkr nodded, "It is decided then." He strode over to Erland and held out his hand. It was not for the old hersir to take but it was to take the necklet with the emerald. It was passed from hersir to hersir. There was hatred in Erland's eyes as he took it off and almost slammed it into Brokkr's open palm. My uncle nodded and, when he had placed it around his neck said, "We will finish the new hall that you began, Erland Brynjarsson, soon. Until then I will move into the mead hall."

By rights, he should have been able to move into Erland's existing hall but my uncle was clever enough to realise that would cause further problems. The mead hall was not Erland's, it belonged to all the clan. The new hall we were building would belong to the hersir.

Finn strode forward and dropped to one knee, "And if you would have me, Hersir," he emphasised the word, "then I would be your hearth-weru."

My uncle beamed, "I would be honoured, Finn. We will go to the sacred grove and make the blood oath."

Erland, his son and his bodyguards stormed off. He had lost and we had a new leader. How would it all turn out?

My aunt and my mother did not know what to make of it. They were happy that we had a new hersir, but the domestic arrangements meant that they would no longer share a longhouse. It would take a month to build a new home for them and, until then, while they would sleep in the mead hall and eat there, the food would be prepared in our home. By the time the house was ready, it was almost time for my handfasting. It had almost been forgotten in the drama of the Thing but as the days grew shorter and the nights longer even my mother knew that we had preparations to make. When the new house was built we had a fine meal with a huge fish that we had caught. Then Brokkr and his family left us to live closer to the heart of the village. There were tears and the embraces were long. Their departure seemed to hasten the time of my handfasting.

The men in the village, the hersir and his sons apart, worked hard to finish the new hall for Brokkr and it was ready before my wedding day.

The night before the wedding Brokkr held a feast in the mead hall. All the men were invited for it was a custom in the village to do so. Erland pointedly stayed away. Brynjar came but said his father did not wish to offend his brother and would not attend. That night was, for the first time in my life, all about me and I was a little embarrassed about it. I was praised as was my choice of bride. There was also a great deal of talk about the old and the new hersir. I think, for the first time, I realised what marriage would mean. My old life would change irrevocably. I would be living with Lars and not my family. My uncle would be the hersir and nothing would ever be the same again. I do not think that it all started with Hallstein's death but that had contributed to it.

I did not drink as much as many of the others. My father and my uncle also drank in moderation. When some of the younger men, the ones yet to be blooded, raced outside to vomit the ale, men like Oddr laughed. It was a rite of passage. Many young men endured the humiliation and changed their behaviour. As the one who was to be wed, I was the first to leave and my father accompanied me home. Joseph had come to help serve the ale and mead. He walked with us and was slightly bemused.

"I have seen such feasts before but they had more food and less ale than this one."

My father nodded, "We like our ale and our mead, Joseph, and such feasts are not as common as our enemies think." We walked in silence and then he said, "And tonight will be your last night in our home, Leif."

"I will return from Lars' hall when we train and when the time comes to sail away, I will sleep in my old bed then."

"But you will be a married man and your home will be elsewhere." He put his arm around my shoulder, "I am telling you this for your mother may well be upset both tonight and tomorrow. Now that she is the only woman in the house she feels, well, lonely." My aunt and cousin now lived, until we finished the hall, in the mead hall.

Joseph said, "Your father is right, Master. I have seen and heard her weeping often since the new hersir left to live in the mead hall."

He was right. Her upset manifested itself in anger directed towards my father and Joseph. Even though we returned quietly and in a relatively sober manner she still snapped and carped like one of Lars' hounds. My brothers were asleep and she had been waiting for our return. I saw my father becoming angry at her stern face and I went to my mother and just put my arm around her. I said nothing.

My father said, "Come, Joseph, we will soak the oats for the morning porridge."

They headed for the far end of the hall and left me with my mother. "This is not like you, Mother, I am going and it cannot be helped. A man must have his own family and I know that you wish me to live here with you but Lars has asked for me to live with him and then he can care for his daughter while I am a-viking. This time next year I shall be with the jarl and you would not see me for half a year."

"And that is why I am so upset. I know that you will go to sea and I want to see as much of you as I can."

"When the days begin to become longer I will be in the village for one day every week while Finn trains the men for the raid. It is not much but I shall make a point of spending as much time on that day close to you."

She put her arms around me and hugged me, "It is not enough."

I sighed, "The Norns have spun, Mother. You know we cannot fight them."

She nodded, salt tears streaking her lined face, "I know." She kissed me.

"Tomorrow, I would like my mother to smile while I am handfasted." She nodded but said nothing.

I had made peace and I slept as well as could have been expected for a man whose life was to change so much.

My bride looked radiant as did her sister. I saw many of my younger oar brothers casting admiring glances in her direction. Living this far from the village meant the two sisters had grown up almost in isolation. I had known the girls because I frequently visited with Lars.

The handfasting over we feasted. Lars was clever; he had chosen the date for a number of reasons, not least that it was the time when he culled his older sheep and the surplus meat was put to good use. There was ale and mead and plentiful food. My mother smiled but I knew it was not a genuine one although the presence of Brokkr and his family helped to make it a happier time. Not all the guests stayed all night, some braved the almost freezing temperatures to head back to the village. As was expected Freya and I went to our bed, on a raised platform at the end of the hall and hidden from the rest, relatively early. There were cheers, especially from the young warriors and my brothers as we ascended the ladder. As we cuddled in the bed, we heard the singing and the laughter. The noise seemed to make a wall that protected us and we kissed and then, both learning, coupled. My father and Brokkr had both told me what to expect but it surprised and pleased me. Freya seemed happy too and when we both nodded off to sleep it was in each other's arms.

The women who had stayed rose early and Lars' home was clean and food was ready when we rose. I saw that just half a dozen families had remained. Mikkel had also stayed and when I watched him and Borghildr laughing together I knew why my friend had not returned to the village with his family. It was almost noon when my mother, father and brothers finally left. Mikkel waited to leave with them using the excuse that he would be of help. He fooled no one. Mother wept but the tears were understandable. My father just clasped my arm and said, quietly, "Come and see us when you can."

"I will."

The hall seemed empty when they had all gone. Joseph waited for he was unsure of his position. Lars just smiled at his lost look, "Well, Joseph, welcome to my home. I look forward to speaking to one who has travelled far. I have rarely left my home and when you have time I would sit and talk. Winter is the time for talking and reflecting on matters we have little time for in summer."

Joseph seemed relieved. He beamed, "It would be an honour."

It was Borghildr who was at a loss. My courtship of her sister had been brief and Mikkel could not be expected to visit during the winter. When the first blizzard of the winter struck us, it was like the closing of a curtain. Lars' tiny fiefdom became cut off from the world. With his sheep in the barn, guarded from the wolves by his dogs, we hunkered down to a life cut off from the world.

Chapter 15

It was Þorri when Freya found that she was with child. How she knew I did not know but she did. Our world was still covered in snow but Lars' ram had done his work and Lars took me to inspect the ewes, "Winter does that. The lambs will be born sooner than my first grandchild and that will help you understand what Freya will go through while you sail south."

"I may be here for the birth. The jarl said that it might not be until Tvímánuður that we sail."

"Good, but babies can be unpredictable. Make the most of the time that you have here. My life is not hard. When the snows have gone I will take my sheep to their pastures and watch them. Freya and Borghildr used to help me. Now that will be your task for Freya will keep to the hall."

And my life soon fell into a routine. It was not the work I was used to. I was not rowing a snekke down an icy fjord but I was working from the moment the sun rose until the moment it set. I was able to do that which Lars' daughters could not. I hunted. I sought signs of danger and food for the pot. The result was that I became a better bowman. I had always enjoyed using a bow. Rowing a snekke gave a warrior strong arms and I was able to send an arrow a long way. By itself, that was of little use but I seemed to have a natural eye and I hit more than I missed. I tasted a greater variety of animals and birds than I had. I found myself, however, yearning for fish. In my father's hall, I had eaten fish every day.

It was Einmánuður when I was summoned to the village. Inevitably it was Mikkel who arrived early one morning. He had to have left the village while it was still dark. The days were becoming longer and the snow had disappeared from the lower part of the farm. Soon it would retreat and disappear. Lars always rose before the sun was up and he was out with his dogs. Freya, being married, now took charge and it was she who went to fetch ale and food for our guest. Borghildr remained close to us.

Mikkel spoke to me but his eyes flickered towards Borghildr and her eyes responded. "Your uncle, the hersir, has asked for men to come to the village to train each Þórsdagr. Finn will command the Bóndi." He smiled, "He will join us. The days of Erland are long gone."

"How is the old hersir taking the change?"

"Not well. He has argued with all of his neighbours and his handful of allies has shrunk to a few. It is rumoured that he is seeking to move his home."

That surprised me. "That is unexpected."

Mikkel said, "He has a third knarr now. It was begun before you were married and he seeks a home that is further south. He sent one of his captains, Baldor, to find a new place he could use that lay to the south of Jæren at Oddernes."

I frowned, "There is little at Oddernes as I recall from speaking to Snorri and Gandalfr."

"There is a port but it is close to the land of the Danes and the Østersjøen, he can trade with the Wends as well as the Rus. It also means he can send ships to the land of the Mercians."

"That is a mighty move."

"He can no longer charge what he likes for the goods he sells. Your uncle stopped it. He has to accept what Brokkr deems to be a fair price and his profits have shrunk."

It suddenly made sense to me. He had been like a fat spider and we had been his flies. He did not have to go to war to gain treasure. He did it by making money from people who could not argue with him.

"Thank you for telling me." It was Sunnudagr and that meant I had Mánadagr to prepare. My weapons were still in my father's hall and my byrnie was with Alfr. Lars was out with his sheep.

Freya brought in the ale and food. She had clearly heard the last part of the conversation, "When do you leave, Husband?"

She now had a noticeable bump. Slight at the moment, it presaged the birth of what I hoped would be my son. As Borghildr poured ale into his horn I said, "I will leave tomorrow morning, early. I have much to prepare but I will return before the sun has set on Þórsdagr."

She smiled, "Come the day after. Your mother would like you to be home for two nights." She put her hand on her tummy. "I know that when our child is born I shall want as much time with him as possible."

Mikkel said, "And if you wish, Leif, I can stay for the day and go with you tomorrow." I cocked an eye and he added hurriedly, "I could help you on the farm and I am not needed today. We are not fishing."

Freya knew what was going on and she smiled, "That would be kind, Mikkel Håkonsson, I am sure my father would appreciate the help."

Borghildr beamed, "And I will make up a bed."

Joseph had been busy kneading dough. He had proved to be a good baker. He wiped the flour from his hands and said, "I shall do that, Borghildr. I will make one close to me for he is a man and a guest."

The faces of both Mikkel and Borghildr fell a little. Joseph was a wise man.

Freya said, "Thank you, Joseph. I do not know what we would do without you."

"It is my pleasure, Mistress. Master, will you wish me to come with you when you visit Bygstad?"

"No, Joseph. As my wife said, you are too invaluable to lose for even a day."

I waited until Mikkel had finished and then said, "Let us go and join Lars. He works hard and if we are to be of any use to him then we should go now."

As we headed out to the pastures where Lars was examining his sheep to see if any were ready for birthing, I spoke to Mikkel about the muster, "Do we have new warriors or those who would be warriors?"

"Aye, your brother Birger is one and Dagfinn's younger brother, Fritjof, joins us. There are others too who are older but did not come the last time." He smiled, "Our success and the encouragement of your uncle means that there are more men who see the opportunity of adventure and treasure."

"Yet that will leave the village vulnerable to an attack."

He shook his head, "The hersir is not worried for he says that there are enough strong men left to guard it. There is my father, your father, the hersir, Finn, Brynjar Brynjarsson and at least four more older men who can wield a sword. It will not just be the younger warriors who will practise, all the men will be there."

I suddenly stopped, "Including Erland and his sons?"

He smiled, "It is another reason why Erland Brynjarsson is leaving Bygstad. He does not want to but he cannot avoid it as it was decided by a Thing. He argued against it but even his brother did not support him. He will ensure that he and his sons are not in Bygstad on Þórsdagr." He smiled, "The new drekar is launched. I saw her in the fjord when we went to the fishing grounds. There is no prow yet and the mast has to be fitted but apart from that the drekar is ready for the sea."

Lars was pleased to see us. Some of the ewes had taken themselves off to give birth away from the flock and while Lars attended to those who remained we were tasked with taking the hounds and finding them. The search took us many miles away but we found all four of them. Mikkel and I carried the four lambs while the dogs chivvied and chased the mothers. Noon had come and gone when we reached the farm and we were ready for food.

Borghildr was keen to impress Mikkel and she had made honey cakes filled with the last of the dried blackberries from autumn. She gave the two largest ones to Mikkel. I saw Lars as his eyes twinkled. He knew that soon he would have his other daughter married and another labourer for his farm. He was a clever man. They had shown signs that they desired each other at the wedding and Mikkel's eagerness to please Lars was the final confirmation.

We ate well that night and as I lay with Freya she said, "Mikkel is good for Borghildr. After we were wed she spoke of him for he is handsome and she makes him laugh."

"Is that important?"

In the dark, she said, "To Borghildr it is."

We rose early the next morning but ate before we set off for Bygstad. I had my sword but all else was in my father's hall. Joseph seemed pleased to be staying with Lars, my wife and her sister. They did not treat him as a slave. He had worked hard since the wedding and endeared himself to all three. I felt a pang of regret as I left my wife. I would only be gone for a couple of nights. What would it be like when I left for half a year? Was it a wise thing to do? I donned my wolf cloak and beaver skin hat. The air was still what one might call, fresh.

Norse Warrior

Mikkel said, as we tramped towards Bygstad, "Would Lars have me as a husband to Borghildr do you think?"

I waited for a few moments. I knew that I was teasing Mikkel but that was what warriors did.

"Come, Leif, we are oar brothers and I need an answer."

I laughed, "Aye, he would. Remember though, the jarl wants us ready to sail his new ship. You must either be swift or wait until we return and that may not be until this time next year."

"Then when you return to Lars, I will come with you and ask him. I want to be as happy as you are."

I looked at him in surprise, "Me, happy?"

"Of course. You were never what one might call grumpy but you smile more and you seem at ease. That is Freya, is it not?"

I had not thought about it but perhaps he was right.

It felt strange to walk into my old home. It was familiar and yet it felt strange. Mother, of course, made a huge fuss over me. I think she was looking for a fault but I had eaten well and the exercise had made me fill out.

"I will cook a good meal for you this night."

I kissed her, "Good, for I have missed your cooking." It was the right thing to say and she beamed.

My father and brothers were fishing, and so I went to my chest and took out my helmet. I took my shield and spear from the wall and examined them. The herkumbl looked splendid and I polished it with my arm. When I went to war it would impress an enemy. I laid my gear on the bed and then shouted, "I will go to speak to Alfr and then the hersir. The smith said my byrnie would be ready."

"There will be many who will speak as you pass them, Leif. You have been missed."

I wondered why people would miss me. I was nothing special.

The clanging from the smithy and the sparks flying from the open side told me that he was working. I entered and saw that he and his sons had been making swords and axe heads. The axes could be used for any manner of activity but the swords were for war. I also spied four new helmets. Each one had a nasal and as there was no herkumbl I knew that they were for warriors who had yet to raid.

They stopped when I entered and Balder said, with a grin as wide as the moon, "How does married life suit you, Leif Longstride?"

I smiled back, "Well enough and Freya is with child. It will be born at harvest time."

Alfr nodded, "A propitious time. Odin favours those born under the harvest moon."

"I have come to see if my byrnie is ready."

He nodded, "Aye, we did that the week after the wedding. It has been in a sack with sand waiting for you. Falco, fetch it."

Falco had grown since I had last seen him. Balder too was almost as big as his father. I wondered if they would be going on the raid. Falco was stronger but even he struggled with the weight. He took it out and held it up for me. Sand fell from the links. He tried to shake it but it was too heavy. I took it and shook the last of the sand from it.

"Examine it, Leif, and I will guarantee you will not find where the links were broken."

I knew where they had been but he was right and I could not see where the damage had been. "Thank you, Alfr. It is a fine job."

"Aye, well, you deserve it. Men have spoken of your actions when you raided with the jarl and all see you as a warrior who will be a great one. Balder will be training with you but he will not be raiding this time."

I looked at Balder who shook his head, "As much as I want to go I know that I will not be ready in time. I would not wish to be another Axel Erlandsson."

I shook my head, "That you could never be."

"Nor would I wish to be an Elvind and die in my first raid. No, I will spend a year honing my skills and by then Falco can take my place here."

I said, "Falco, help me to put my byrnie on."

It took the two of us to do so and it hung a little loosely on me. It did not look like our byrnies for it had come from the Frank I had killed. It was shorter than the ones Hallstein and Finn wore. Even so, it hung down and felt loose. Alfr said, "You need a padded undershirt. It will make it easier to wear and afford you more protection. It will be like the head protector you wear under your helmet."

It made sense and I remembered that when I had taken it from the body of the dead Frank he had such a garment. The cut and the blood had rendered it useless and it remained on his body. We took the byrnie from me and replaced it in the sack.

"Keep it in the sack as long as you can. The sand will stop it from gathering rust."

"Thank you, Alfr." I slung the sack over my shoulder, "I will see you tomorrow, Balder."

He nodded, "I hope to learn much from the warrior who managed to kill a mailed enemy on his first raid."

When I returned to my former home it was well past noon for my mother was right. Many people wished to speak to me and having heard about Freya and the baby they talked for longer than I wished. Mother had food for me and when she saw the sack she said, "Is that mail?" I nodded, my mouth full of food already for I was starving. "Then I have something for you." She went to my father's chest and brought out a padded undershirt. "This was your father's." She smiled, "I made it for him when we were first married and there is a spell sewn into it. I will make one for you before you go. That way I know that you will be protected."

I could not help but smile. She was tying me to her. I did not mind. Freya could make a second spell for me and then I would have twice the protection.

I enjoyed talking to my father and brothers when they returned from the day of fishing. The time apart had made me change for I was married and lived away from the longhouse and yet the relationships were still good. It felt easier to talk to my father than I had when I had been his son working the snekke. He was more than happy that Erland had decided to move. "He left two days ago on his knarr. He took his sons with him so that they would not have to endure the humiliation of training. The sooner he leaves the better."

"And what about his hall, when he does, eventually, leave?"

"It might be that your uncle will use it as a warrior hall for the unmarried warriors. He seems to think it might bond them."

"Would he not want it? It is a better hall than his."

"My brother does not think like that. His home is more than adequate. He does not need to use it to impress as Erland tried."

Birger was excited to be training with us. He had made a shield and our father had helped him to make a spear. He had the dagger I had given him but no sword. "I wanted to buy one from Alfr but I do not have enough silver."

"If Lars had not given his sword to me then I would not have had a sword. If you are skilled enough with a spear you can always take one from an enemy." He looked doubtful, "Listen, Birger, this raid of the jarls is to far-off places and I believe that we will find silver and gold. We were unlucky last time to find a large number of warriors. This time I hope to enjoy better luck."

My father gave a sad shake of the head, "Luck is a double-edged sword, Leif. I would rather have no luck for often the luck that might appear to be good can be bad. It is better to rely on skill."

He was right. "Snorri said that I might be able to be a navigator like you. Is he right?"

"You navigate a snekke well, that is true, but sailing where there is no land is harder. You need the sun or the stars."

"We believe that in the land where we will raid the sun shines more than it is cloudy."

"Then you need," he tapped his head, "to keep a map up here." He dipped his finger into his ale and drew a cross on the table. "These are the four points. You will be sailing towards this one." He made the southern line wetter. "That means to get back home you sail in this direction." He made the northern one wetter. "As the land will always be in this direction," he made the one to the east stand out, "then the one to avoid is this one, to the west, for there it is an empty ocean."

"How do you know?"

"There was a captain I met when I was young and he told me that a storm blew him far to the west and all he saw was empty ocean. There was not even a hint of land. He believed that the word ended there."

I nodded, "So to reach home I would need to sail north and keep the coast close to the steerboard side?"

"Aye. For the rest, it comes with experience. When you row watch the sky and feel the sea. See what Gandalfr and his brother are doing. You know how to sail a ship. A drekar is just a big snekke but navigating is something different."

We talked about the village and the training we would all be enjoying. When I had returned with my mail I had oiled my shield and sharpened my spear. I would be ready. Birger was so excited that I feared he would never get to sleep. It was my father who sent us to bed. The instructions were aimed at Birger. He tossed and turned for a while and then I drifted off to sleep.

Brokkr had decided that the training would not be out of the way and hidden as it had been the last time. He used the open space before the mead hall. He and my father, along with the other veteran warriors wore all their war gear. In some cases that meant a byrnie and so I wore mine. It was shorter than the rest but I was just grateful to have some protection for my upper body. I had been in battle and knew the effect of weapons on bodies that had no protection. I stood with Brokkr, my father and Birger as we waited for those who lived a walk away to arrive. With every man in the village present, we were a large number. Finn stood apart. I knew that he would be thinking of his blood brother, Hallstein. They had trained us the last time. I saw my shield brothers. They no longer looked like novices. Their shields were well made and bore their sign. Each of them now had a good sword. The raid had brought us weapons. I saw Gunvald still limping a little when he arrived but he assured us that it would not impede him. The younger warriors, like Birger, were marked by the paucity of their arms. That was what we would have looked like to Oddr and the others. As the last men arrived Finn ordered us to listen. His commanding voice made us silent.

It became clear that he knew our training would have to be different this time. The novices, all seven of them, would not enjoy the personal attention we had been given. He ordered them to one side. "Hersir, you and the older warriors who did not raid last time, stand over here, if you would." He directed them to one side and I saw that they were the largest group of men. "Those who have never fought, stand there." He moved them to the opposite side. That left just the handful who had raided with the jarl the last time. There were seven of us. He nodded to my uncle, "Hersir, you wished to address the warriors." Even as my uncle nodded and walked towards his hearth-weru I saw the novices almost grow as they were named, for the first time, warriors.

"Men of Bygstad, today is the start of a new way of living. We had forgotten that we were warriors. This handful of men who sailed with me the last time," he pointed to the seven of us, "was an embarrassment. That the jarl did not say anything shows him in a better light than us. When he raids again he will need more men for he has two ships. Over the next months, we will become one. I will train with you. I am the hersir but Finn is the one who will mould you into a band of brothers. I will not sail on this raid but I know that the men of Bygstad will represent a greater proportion of the warriors who do. Finn." He stepped down.

Finn nodded, "We have seven new warriors and they will need to work even harder. Leif Longstride and Mikkel Håkonsson, take these seven and show them how to run. You have until noon to teach them the rules of the skjaldborg. When you return we will make a Bygstad skjaldborg."

Mikkel and I raised our spears and shouted, as one, "Aye, Finn."

I knew that this would be a test for me as well as my brother and the others. I was wearing my mail. I was also wearing my father's padded shirt as my mother had yet to make mine. I turned to Mikkel, "I will lead." He nodded. I said to the new warriors, "Mikkel will prod those who cannot keep up."

I slung my shield over my back and, raising my spear, led them towards the grove where we had learned our first skills. My mail meant I could not run as fast as I would normally and that was good. It gave a better pace. I saw the method behind Finn. He would not have to worry about untried warriors who did not know how to stand in a skjaldborg. When we returned, they would be placed at the rear. The mail jingled. I realised, in a detached sort of way, that if this was a raid then the jingling mail would be a problem. Our prey would hear us. Then I heard the pounding of feet. That too was louder than I had expected. When we raided we would not run but walk. We would be like a pack of wolves and move silently but as one. I did not turn around but I knew that our feet were moving at the same time. It was the start of the moulding of the novices into one. When we rowed the drekar this running would help. I kept my breathing steady. Behind me, I heard Balder huffing and puffing already. The son of the smith was a strong man but his strength lay in his arms and not his legs. I did not lead us directly to the grove but took a mile-and-a-half detour. When I saw the grove, I was feeling the effects of the mail. I raised my spear, stopped and turned.

Balder dropped his spear and stood gulping in air. The others were little better. Karsten Egilsson shook his head, "My shoulders are red raw from this shield, Leif Longstride. This is impossible."

I smiled, "You can talk, good. That gives me hope. As for the rawness then you need to make your shield more comfortable. When we stand in the skjaldborg it is the shield that protects not only you but the men next to you. Now, take your shields and spears. Stand in a line." I took my shield off and laid it down. I also took off my helmet and placed it on the shield's boss. Mikkel did the same.

My friend smiled at me, "It does not seem that long ago since we did this."

I nodded, "And now we have to be the smiths of men and forge them into one weapon, *wyrd*."

The seven novices were standing in a loose line. I took the spear and held it before me. I walked to the end of the line and held the spear out. "Put your shields together and press against the spear." They managed to push the spear. I smiled, "Good. Now stand so that your shoulders are touching and hold your spears above the shields."

I had not spoken to Mikkel, but I knew that he would know what to do. As I stepped away, I nodded and Mikkel suddenly ran at them and leaping in the air crashed into Balder and Birger who were in the middle. As they fell back, they took the others with them and I walked over and touched the tip of my spear to Birger's chest. "And you, Birger Eiriksson, are dead."

"But we did not know what you intended."

Mikkel said, "And do you think that the Franks will let you know what they plan? Leif and I have shown you what one man can do. Imagine twenty like us."

I said, "Skjaldborg." This time they braced themselves. Mikkel and I picked up our shields and without speaking ran at them. They braced their legs and locked their shields but, even though there were just two of us we managed to push them back a step. None fell. We spent the next part of the training with us standing behind the seven of them so that they could get used to a shield's boss pressing into their backs. The last session was the scariest for them. Mikkel and I hurled our spears at them. They were terrified. The seven shields were a huge target and we knew that they were in no danger. We hit the shields for we aimed at them. That the shields would suffer damage would become clear only later.

I shaded my eyes and looked at the sky. It was almost noon. I slung my shield, "Now we run back. Balder, stand behind me. You will need to run every morning. Can you swim?" He shook his head. "A pity because if you swam each day it would help your breathing and make your legs stronger. Your arms will help your shield brothers when we fight but your legs will be your weakness."

He nodded, "Aye, Leif Longstride."

We ran back and arrived just as the others were enjoying ale and food brought by my aunt and cousin. I took off my shield and helmet and joined Finn, my father and the hersir. "Well?" It was the training master who spoke.

I smiled, "They were as raw as we were but there is no Axel. Balder needs to work on his legs but they can all stand at the rear of the skjaldborg."

"Good, for we are ready to use all the men."

My father said, quietly, "Birger?"

"He coped but like all of them he thought it would be easier than it was."

By the end of the day, we had become used to a three-line skjaldborg. I was surprised to find myself in the front rank but when I looked down the second line I saw that none of those had a mail byrnie. We also tried a wedge formation. I was in the fourth rank and behind me were the younger warriors who had been on the first raid and had no mail.

Finn seemed pleased with the progress, "The next time we will try the boar's tusks." We all wondered what that would entail but none asked. "You have all seen what needs to be done and you have six days to make your shields better and your legs and arms stronger."

As we headed back Birger shook his head, "I am bruised all over, Brother."

I laughed, "When we raid bruises will be the least of your worries. You will not have to stand at the fore when we fight. There will be no enemy to hurl himself at your shield but, standing at the rear you will have to give the strength to the skjaldborg that will defeat our enemies."

That night, after we had bathed and changed into comfortable clothes, he sat and spoke quietly to me, "I know we cannot train for this but what does it feel like when you plunge your spear into a man's flesh?"

I shook my head, "It is better not to think of him as a man. If you do, then you think of his family and you may weaken and not push home. He is an enemy who is trying to kill you and you must kill him first." I nodded at our father who was sitting and talking to Karl and Ivar. They had not been at the training and my father was telling them what we had done. "Ask our father to take you hunting. That will give you an idea of what to expect." He looked at my father and I added, "There is no disgrace in not wanting to raid."

"There is for no one wishes to be an Axel Erlandsson. I will have to steel myself." He gave a wry smile, "It might help if I did not have a brother who was so admired by even seasoned warriors."

"Birger, you are who you are and not me. Do not try to be someone else. We were all made differently. Joseph has taught me that. He is not our father, but I admire him as much. Look at Lars. He does not fight in a shield wall, but no one thinks less of him. It is his choice, and you must make yours."

Chapter 16

It was Einmánuður and the day was Þórsdagr, our training day, when the drekar sailed up the fjord. We had all trained hard and now we looked and acted as one. We stopped for this was not '*Bylgja.*' It was the new drekar and it looked fast. The sail had the image of a fierce god sewn upon it. The prow, however, was not a dragon. Instead, it had the face of a fierce warrior with a white beard. It stood out but I knew that after months at sea, it would not look as good. We all stopped what we were doing and moved towards the water. I saw that there were just ten oars on each side but there were ports for more. It was Gandalfr at the steering board and he brought her skilfully around to the quay and, as the sail was lowered and the oars were withdrawn, he bumped the new ship gently into the wood. The ship's boys leapt ashore to secure the drekar to the quay. The warship dwarfed the handful of snekke that were tied up.

The jarl leapt ashore. He wore no mail but his hair was longer and he looked as though he and his hearth-weru had been training hard. They were muscled and fit. Brokkr walked to him, his arm held out. It was a warrior's handclasp.

"I have come on a good day, Brokkr Eiriksson. I see keen and sharp warriors who are ready to raid."

Brokkr nodded proudly, "The men of Bygstad are now prepared."

The jarl glanced up at the hall vacated by Erland. It had been a month since his men had returned and emptied the hall of everything. All that remained were the walls and roof. Brokkr had taken the snekke to Askvoll to tell the jarl of his departure. "And the old hersir's hall?"

"Will be used by the young men who have yet to wed. It will tie them together."

"Good," he turned and waved to his new ship, "What do you think of my new vessel? We fitted her mast and prow last week, and this is her first voyage."

"A good ship."

My father asked, "How does she handle?"

Gandalfr had joined us as the crew disembarked, "She is lithe and quick. *'Ægir'* is a good ship."

I saw the surprise on Brokkr's face, "You have named the drekar after the king of the sea?"

I studied the figurehead and saw that it had the claws associated with the giant who was one of the Aesir.

The jarl smiled, "It is not an insult to the gods. Rather it honours them for this drekar will sail further than any other ship of the Norse. I think Ægir will approve."

Brokkr nodded but I could see that it disturbed him, "And when do you need a crew?"

"The first day of Sólmánuður. That will give men the chance to plant crops that the women can harvest."

Brokkr nodded. "How many men will come from Bygstad?"

"I have not asked them. Now might be a good time as they are all here." He strode back to the drekar and, climbing to the gunwale held the forestay for balance, "Men of Bygstad, I am here to ask which of you would go a-viking? We sail on the first day of Sólmánuður and we will not return until the middle of Gói."

Men looked at one another and the jarl was wise enough not to push the matter. He wanted volunteers and not men who felt obligated to come. It was a commitment.

Oddr raised his hand, "I will come with you, Jarl." It was like a stone beginning an avalanche. Mikkel and I, along with the others who had sailed before, raised our arms and then there were others, men who had not sailed as well as some of the younger warriors. Balder did not and I understood his reasons. He had improved since the first day but he was still the one who huffed and puffed as we ran. Birger, of course, raised his hand when I did. In all, there were twenty men from Bygstad. I could see that the jarl was pleased, "Then you shall sail in my new drekar. Gandalfr will be the helmsman and Haldir, of my hearth-weru, will command the ship."

That evoked a huge cheer. Brokkr nodded for he was not losing as many men as he might have expected. The longer time away from home had deterred some. The jarl looked pleased. "Then Gandalfr will return on the last day of Skerpla."

Brokkr leaned in. I was close enough, as was Birger, to hear their words, "Just two ships, Jarl? My nephew thought that you wanted three ships."

"I had hoped that my cousin might come but he suffered too many losses last year and he has not enough men ready to sail. He will come next time." I saw the jarl smile, "We cannot sail as far as we had planned but we can still winter where there is no snow and we do not lose the sun. This means that the men of Askvoll and Bygstad will have all the riches."

He and the hersir clasped arms. We watched as Gandalfr had the sail hoisted and the elegant ship's fierce god took the new ship down the fjord. The men stood by the gunwale. The current would take the new drekar and they could enjoy the short voyage home.

When the ship disappeared Brokkr addressed us all. "Now that we know the time our work must increase. We will still spend each Þórsdagr training with weapons but there will be no more time off. The village will need as much food as can be gathered. The ones who remain will have many months to endure. We must all work as one."

That evening, as we headed back to my father's hall, we were weary but it was an excited weariness. I said to my father, "Erland would not have inspired the men with words as Brokkr did nor would he have worried about food for all. It was a good day when we rid ourselves of Erland."

My father clutched his Hammer of Thor, "Leif, you may be right but it does not do to speak of such things. The Norns are spinning and I know Erland. He is a vindictive man. He may have gone but he will remember the insult he and his sons suffered."

Birger said, "What can he do?"

My father said, "If we knew that then we could prepare but we do not know anything. I, for one, will be vigilant."

I left not long after dawn the next day. I found I had missed Freya. My bed had felt empty. I even missed Joseph for, when I was in Lars' hall, he would hover close by to attend to any of my needs. Joseph would be with me on the voyage but I would have many months without my wife and now, it seemed, I would not be there for the birth of my first child. I began to understand why my father and Brokkr had stopped raiding. Having what they needed, they stayed with their families.

The two dogs bounded towards me as I neared my new home. I had a slobbery welcome from both of them and when Freya appeared she beamed radiantly at me and, after throwing her arms around me, kissed me hard. She had missed me too.

I spent the day doing the work I should have done on the previous two days. That night as we ate, I had the full attention of the other three as I described the new drekar and then told them of the planned raid. There was silence when I spoke of the time I would be away. Freya was calculating if I would see the birth of my son and Borghildr was wondering if Mikkel would return to marry her before the raid. I caught the glint of excitement in Joseph's eyes. For him, it would be a step closer to home.

Lars looked concerned, "You and the other warriors will be away for a long time. Bygstad will be vulnerable."

I shook my head, "The length of the raid meant that many men chose not to come."

"But why endure the length of the voyage that is planned?"

I sighed, "Lars, I can understand the plan. Ask Joseph here about the length of the day in the middle of winter further south. The jarl is taking a long voyage so that, in winter, instead of warriors hunkering down in their furs and making new warriors, they can spend long days raiding. He plans on finding an island which we will fortify and then using that to raid Frankia." I smiled, "It may be that one raid will make us all so rich that we never need to raid again."

"Or it may make men wish to raid more often."

I nodded, "Perhaps, Lars. What will be, will be. It is dangerous to try to see too far into the future."

While I had been at Lars' hall, I had not stopped the regular swims I had taken at Bygstad. They were not every day but I would often rise before dawn and walk the thousand or so paces to the fjord. I knew it made my body stronger and seemed to invigorate me for the day. Lars' hall was further up the fjord and it was both narrower and somehow, colder. I found that I could swim to the other side and back. The first time I did it I felt as though I had achieved something mighty. Now I took it for granted.

When I rose the next day and sneaked out of the hall I found Joseph waiting for me. "Joseph?"

He gave an apologetic smile, "I have watched you leave the hall and I know that you go to bathe in the fjord. I thought I might come, Master."

"Of course."

As we walked, he said, "The bathing seems to do you good, Master."

"It makes my arms stronger and stops my belly from getting too big."

He laughed, "Could I learn?"

I stopped and studied him. His face looked innocent enough but he had not shown any inclination to involve himself in extra physical activity before. "Of course, it is easy but why?"

He tapped his head, "My hair is thinning and becoming white. I am a healer and know that my body is getting old. It seems to me that your bathing makes you healthier and I wish to live as long as I can."

It seemed a reasonable request and so I nodded. As we walked the last paces to the fjord, I told him the basic technique he would need. "If you stay close to the shore the bottom is always there for you to stand. Do not follow me but stay where you are able to stop swimming and walk on the bottom. Do not be afraid if your head goes beneath the water. Just keep your mouth closed."

He looked thin when he stripped to enter the water. I dived in and swam straight away. When my head broke surface I saw him still edging in. The water was barely over his knees. Sculling the water behind me with my hands I shouted, "Just get in and get it over with. Move both your arms and your legs."

He obeyed and while it was not a dive, it was more of a falling forward, he entered the water and his arms flailed.

I shouted, "The water will hold you. Calm yourself." I swam back. I would not be able to swim across the fjord. I swam at his side, and it seemed to give him confidence. By the time he was beginning to turn blue, he could move forward in the water, and I deemed we had swum enough. As we dried ourselves, I said, "Do you still wish to swim with me?"

He nodded, "I feel as though my skin is glowing. It is strange, Master, but I feel warm. I would not like to swim where the water was deep but knowing I could stand made it easier."

"Then you may join me again but next time I will not be at your side."

He nodded. When we were dressed and while I pulled on my boots he said, "If it will help me to gain a place on the ship, I have some information that may be of use to you."

I looked at him. I had learned to see a lie in a man's eyes, and I watched for it with Joseph. "Go on."

"A few miles upstream from the place you took me is a holy place. It is a place of monks. There is an abbey at Jumièges. It is undefended and richly endowed."

I saw no lie in his eyes. "Tell me again, why are you giving me this golden nugget?"

"I have no love for the Christians. Thanks to my religion I was treated badly. The monks and priests of the abbey were the worst. Besides, as it is on the way south the jarl may think more kindly of me and let me sail."

I was still suspicious, "You might run and return home."

He laughed, "Do you think, Master, that I would exchange this for a return to that life?" he sighed, "Master, I was taken from the Blue Sea. It is far to the south of the Liger. It is beyond the land of Andalusia, it is past the Pillars of Hercules. It is so far to the east that it might take as much time to reach it as the time that you will raid. Trust me, my lord. I will not return to the land from which you took me. I shall stay aboard the drekar and pray that you are successful."

As we walked back to the farm, I stored that information. If he was right then it would be a good prize to take.

Harpa and Skerpla seemed to fly by. A combination of the normal demands of those fertile months allied to the need to prepare for the voyage contributed. Joseph learned to swim and, at the end of the first week of Harpa, Mikkel returned to the hall. He had some silver which he presented to Lars as he asked to wed Borghildr. Lars was happy but told Mikkel to keep the silver. He needed none. The wedding was arranged for the first week of Skerpla. This time he agreed that the wedding could take place in Bygstad. It suited everyone as Brokkr made the mead hall available. I was also delighted as it meant I could spend two days at my home where I hoped that my mother would warm to Freya.

My mother was waiting at the door when we arrived. She smiled but I looked for the smile in her eyes and it was not there, at first. The new life within my wife's womb was the deciding factor. My mother's maternal instincts took over and within an hour of our arrival, the two were sitting together and talking as though they were old friends reunited.

The wedding was better than mine, mainly because people did not have to leave early to travel home. Lars stayed with us and got on well with my father who had missed both Brokkr and me since we had moved out.

When we returned to Lars' hall, I realised that Lars, who was a clever man, had gained two labourers for his farm. As Joseph also helped in the hall, he was much better off than in the days before I had married Freya.

When the day we were supposed to leave approached, so I became concerned about Freya and my unborn child. "Will you give birth before I leave?"

She was a calm woman and she smiled and patted her bulging belly, "When I was speaking with your mother she said it would not be until the end of Sólmánuður."

I frowned, "How did she know? She wasn't there when the baby was conceived."

"She is a volva and a mother. Your aunt concurred. When the baby becomes lower inside me then it will be close to the time of the birth. Fear not, Leif, my sister and I have attended enough birthings here on the farm so that it will not be a problem. Now that Borghildr is married soon she will have Mikkel's child within her. When you come back there will be another birth that may be imminent and you shall have a son."

"A son?" I was excited. "How do you know?"

"Your mother and your aunt listened to the baby in my womb and said that the heartbeat was that of a warrior." She shrugged, "I do not know how they know these things, but I believe your mother."

I was excited beyond words and, for the first time, regretted my decision to go on the raid.

Freya and Borghildr came with us when Mikkel and I went to Bygstad. Joseph carried the new clothes I would need but everything else was in my chest at my father's hall. Lars bade me farewell and stayed at the farm. I had not wanted Freya, in her condition, to walk to and from Bygstad but she was adamant she would see me off and that the walking would help her to give birth. We suspected that Borghildr was with child, but did not know. Freya thought that the volvas of Bygstad would know.

The drekar had not arrived when we reached the hall. The first thing I did was to ensure that Karl and Ivar would escort my wife back to the farm. They were honoured. That done, and while my mother and my wife spun a spell, I went to sort out my chest. I first inspected the shield, spear, mail and helmet. They had lain in my chest since I had last visited but I wanted, nay, I needed them to be perfect. I took my bow and unstrung it. I placed it and my arrow bag in the chest. I had spare strings and they were tucked away in my beaver skin hat. That done, I repacked them and then sharpened my weapons. The warrior part completed, Joseph and I packed my chest. I would have Joseph's belongings with me. He now had more than when he had come to me. He had a sheepskin-lined sealskin cloak that would keep him warm. He also had a beaver skin hat as well as sealskin boots. Before I had married we had managed to slay a stray seal while we were fishing and Joseph benefitted. We also had dried and preserved mutton with us and that was packed. It could be soaked in seawater and cooked once we reached the place in Frankia where we would raid. The last thing I put in the chest was the wolf cloak. It took longer to complete than we expected.

When we had finished Joseph took the chest to place it by the door of the hall with my shield and spear. My wife and mother came over to me. My mother handed me the piece of wool they had spun. I saw that they had woven the head of a wolf in the centre. It felt damp.

My mother said, "This is a powerful spell, my son. There is, within this my hair and your wife's. There are also some hairs from your wolf skin. Your wife's water will soon dry but it means that part of your unborn son is also within it." She took my knife from my belt and pricked her finger. The blood dripped onto the wool. Freya held her hand out and her finger was pricked. The two blood spots were symmetrical and were pleasing to look at. My mother took Freya's hand and I saw that the two wounds touched so that their blood mixed. My mother intoned, "Frigga, hear the words of your handmaidens and watch over this warrior. Guide his thoughts and bring him home safely to us."

It was strange for I felt a shiver up my spine and the hairs on the back of my neck seemed to stand up. My mother had changed. She and Freya held hands and looked as close as mother and daughter. Their smiles were for me and I was content. I placed the damp spell inside my tunic. There it would remain until I returned home. Once home we would burn it.

My aunt, uncle and cousin came to eat with us and it was a wonderful evening. The imminent birth seemed to bond all four women and I saw, for the first time, that my cousin was a woman. Soon she would be wed. As the daughter of the hersir, she would be much sought after. When we returned, some warrior, laden down with Frankish riches, would wed her. While the four chattered like magpies Birger and I were given sage advice from my uncle and father. I think it was aimed more at Birger than me but I listened.

That night as I lay in the hall, filled for the first time since Erland's fall, Freya in my arms, I reflected that this voyage, as long as it was, might be the last one I made. I think I consoled myself with that fact for I was now torn. My unborn child, within the womb, seemed so close that I wished we were not leaving when we did. When I returned, I would have a child, a boy, whom I could mould into a man. I could not wait. I decided that the voyage was meant to be, it was not just my wife and mother who had spun it was also the Norns and this raid was pre-ordained. Whatever befell me I would make the best of it and get back home.

Chapter 17

'*Ægir*' came up the fjord with the sail furled. The wind was against her and the twelve men who rowed were having a hard time pulling against both the current and the wind. When our twenty men joined her then every oar would be manned and we would have six spare oarsmen. That was useful as it meant we could row for longer and the men could be rotated. We had, in addition to the twenty men from Bygstad, three ship's boys. Karl and Ivar had wished to come but my father was adamant that they remain at home. He needed them for the snekke. They were disappointed but understood. One of the boys was Falco, the son of the smith. He was a strong boy and with his older brother still to join the ship, could be spared. There were three boys from Askvoll aboard the ship. This time there was no hearth-weru leading the oarsmen. Gandalfr was in command and he stepped ashore. He beamed but his voice was commanding, "Fetch your chests. We sail on the morrow and the jarl wishes to speak to both crews before we sail."

Nodding we all turned and hurried back to our homes. Birger's chest was much lighter than mine. Joseph carried my spear and shield. Karl carried Birger's shield and Ivar, his spear. The whole family came to see us off and with so many men from the village sailing, it seemed everyone was heading for the quay. We had all known the day was coming but it still seemed sudden.

When we reached the ship Gandalfr assigned us our places. Gandalfr used numbers to make it easier for us. It began at the prow and began larboard one and steerboard one. There were younger warriors now and they were at the prow end of the drekar, the ones with the lower numbers. I had sailed already and I was nearer to the middle. Gandalfr placed me across from Mikkel. As we were single-oared, we had more room. I placed my chest on the deck and fixed my spear under the gunwale. Then I fitted my shield. I saw Birger looking hesitant. I walked to him and moved his chest to the best position. I showed him how to fasten his spear and then his shield. I smiled, "It will get easier and this is your place for the next months. Here you will row and sleep. You make this into your home, your nest." I turned to Joseph, "Your bed will be at the prow, Joseph. Make yourself comfortable now. Take what you need from the chest."

He looked happy and excited, "Yes, Master, thank you."

I went ashore for some of those who lived further away had still to arrive. I knew that Gandalfr would use the trip down to Askvoll to ensure that the new men understood how to row. The three boys were being shown what to do by Gandalfr. This was his ship.

I put my arms around Freya. She pressed against me and smiled as she looked up at me and the baby kicked. She laughed when I widened my eyes, "Your son says goodbye too, my husband, in his own way." She stood on tiptoe, "Say goodbye to your mother, eh?"

I nodded and released her. I turned to my mother, "Come give your son an embrace and then you can say farewell to Birger."

The hug was firm and loving. She stood to kiss me on the cheek and I kissed her forehead. She put her mouth to my ear, "I am proud of you and I am sorry for how I behaved before you were married. Freya is all that I could have wished for." She stepped back and said, "Watch over Birger for me, too."

"I will." As Birger hurried to her, I clasped my father's arm.

"Have a safe voyage, Leif. I confess I envy you the voyage. To see new places and to enjoy the sun whilst we shiver under a blanket of snow is almost magical. Come home safe. I would rather have a living son than a dead hero."

"I will."

He went to speak to Birger and I grabbed Freya and kissed her hard, "This is more difficult than I thought it would be. The last time I sailed I knew that I would be back soon. This time I will return to a different world."

"You will return to a home with a family and you will come back with silver and treasure not to mention tales for our son."

"The jarl awaits. Goodbyes are over!" Gandalfr was our captain and from now until we returned it was his voice that we would obey.

I nodded and turned. Birger looked both excited and fearful. Had I looked like that when I had first sailed?

"Choose your oars."

Norse Warrior

This time I knew to pick a good one but, as a new ship, they were all straight. Birger followed me and copied everything I did. I slid the oar through the oar-port, I was able to do so as I was on the fjord side, and I sat on my bench. Birger was a couple of oars behind me and was able to copy me. I made myself as comfortable as I could. Once we left Askvoll I would use the wolf skin as a covering for my bench but the short voyage down the fjord would not need it.

The ship and those watching fell silent as Brokkr brought a cock to the quay. He was making a blót. As he slit the fowl's neck he said, "Rán, watch over these warriors and bring them home safe to Bygstad." There was a cheer from those on the quay when the blood spurted onto the side of the drekar. It was a good omen and the ship had been blooded.

Gandalfr nodded and shouted, "Larboard oars, prepare to push us off. Steerboard oars, ready." I held the oar horizontally ensuring that the blade was at an angle. I hoped Birger was still emulating me. "Cast off!"

The ship's boys untied the ropes and leapt aboard before the current moved us too far from the quay.

"Larboard oars, push us off." As we were pushed away from the shore the current took us and Gandalfr said, "Steerboard oars, in." We obeyed, "Pull!" As soon as we pulled, we began to turn. I knew that we could have used the sail to voyage down the fjord but I also knew that Gandalfr was too good a sailor to miss the opportunity of seeing his crew row. "Larboard oars, ready." I heard the sound of oars slipping through the oar-ports. "Raise steerboard oars." Now that we were facing towards the sea and were in the middle of the channel it was time for us all to row. He nodded to one of the ship's boys who had a staff. He began to bang rhythmically. "Oars!" I lowered my oar and felt the water pushing against it. "Row!" He timed the command to coincide with the sound of the staff. I pulled and felt the power of twenty-six oars all pulling together. I say twenty-six but it was not for Gandalfr shouted, "Larboard, close to the prow use your oar." Someone had made a mistake. I was glad it was not Birger. Gandalfr would have a word when we reached Askvoll and give advice. The next time the oarsman made a mistake there would be punishment. We were all allowed one mistake.

With a favourable wind and a current that took us seaward, it was as easy a row as I could remember. I knew that the new oarsmen would have hands that were red raw but the older hands had palms that were calloused and hoary. I am not sure that the voyage was long enough for Gandalfr for we reached Askvoll in a very short time. He did not look unhappy and apart from the one mistake it had all been flawless. We took in the steerboard oars and he pushed us to the quay using just the larboard oars. I saw that *'Bylgja'* apart, there was a knarr tied up.

He shouted, as the boys tied us up, "You have done well on a fjord. Tomorrow, we sail in the open sea and with a sail, let us see if you are as successful there." It was a compliment but with enough of a threat to ensure that we would all do our best.

I stood and turned, "Birger, remember your blanket and drinking horn." I watched as he opened his chest. Joseph joined me and took out our blankets. I had my horn attached to my belt.

Mikkel slung his blanket over his shoulder. He shook his head, "It was hard leaving Borghildr."

I nodded as we headed towards the newly fitted gangplank. "Aye, it was and when we are out on the ocean and there are waves breaking over the prow and we are rowing with scarred hands then it will be even harder. We must be like our swords, Mikkel, and become metal; hard and unyielding."

We were not the first ashore and Oddr was waiting for us on the quay. He waited until the last of us had left the ship. "As I am the senior warrior I will give orders for the men of Bygstad. Does anyone disagree?"

No one did and he nodded.

"I want no one to drink so much this night that they are unwell. Tomorrow, we row. The jarl has given us the honour of sailing his new drekar and I do not intend to let him down." I saw in that moment that Oddr had aspirations. When Brokkr died would he try to become the hersir? He nodded and led us towards the jarl's hall. Joseph followed Birger and me.

The hall was filled already. The other men who had come from the outlying farms had been coming all day and now that the last boatload had arrived our muster was complete. I did not see the jarl, but I did see Snorri and I led Birger to him. He looked pleased to see me, "Leif Longstride, I am happy to see you."

"This is Birger, my brother."

Snorri held out a mighty fist and clasped Birger's arm, "Good to see another of Eirik's sons here. I see great deeds in your future."

I clasped the Hammer of Thor. It did not do to risk the wrath of the Norns. I said, quickly, "And I hear that you are to be the navigator with the jarl."

"Aye. I think that the jarl hoped your father would choose to go a-viking but…"

"Our father gave up the sea. Tell me, why did the jarl not choose to sail in *'Ægir'*? It is a fine ship and new. There will be no weed on her hull and she will fly."

"She is smaller than *'Bylgja'* and he does not wish to lose the luck we had. *'Ægir'* will be his son's ship. His eldest, Haraldr, sails as a ship's boy this time. He is big enough to sail as a warrior but he is not yet skilled enough. This voyage will teach him much."

I looked around and still could not see the jarl. "Where is the jarl? I expected to see him when we arrived. The last time he greeted us all." I also saw that Gandalfr had not entered the hall.

Snorri said, conspiratorially, "He is speaking with a sea captain who knows the waters around the Liger. Since Erland Brynjarsson left we have not had much news from beyond our land and we also lacked goods that came from the land of the Angles, Franks and Frisians. Gunther is a Frisian and this is his second visit here. The jarl asked him for information about the land close to the Liger and he is extracting it now." He emptied his horn and smiled, "Come let us get some ale. This is a special brew and we shall not be able to take enough to last for six months. Let us enjoy it while we may."

I turned to Joseph, "Take our blankets and make us a good bed."

"Yes, Master."

As he wandered off Snorri said, "It is good that you brought him, not least for his healing and language skills but are you not afraid that when we reach the Liger he might run?"

I shrugged as he filled our horns, "The Norns spun and I found him. Either he will not run or the Norns will spin and plan. We had no thrall before and if we have none in the future then it will be no different to the past."

Some of the jarl's hearth-weru came over and I introduced Birger. For some reason, they seemed to like me and spoke to me, if not as an equal, then certainly a warrior that they respected. I felt Birger's eyes on me. The jarl's steward came over and spoke in Haldir's ear. He nodded, "The jarl's guest is leaving. We are summoned to give an honour guard as he leaves. I will see you later."

Snorri nodded and, draining his horn said, "And I should go. There may be nautical information for Gandalfr and me."

Mikkel, Dagfinn and Brynjar came over to me. Mikkel said, "One of the jarl's inner circle, eh, Leif?"

I shook my head, "I was speaking to Snorri and they came over."

Brynjar shook his head, "Leif, do not be so modest. When we first trained you were the most skilled. On the raid, you were the most successful. Thor has marked you. The killing of the wolf made you special. The gods like the courage that you showed. I, for one, will make sure that when we fight, I shall be close to you."

I could smell the food and by the time the jarl, his navigators and hearth-weru returned, the thralls and servants were bringing in the platters.

"Sit, friends and my apologies for keeping you waiting. As you will learn the wait will prove to be worthwhile and beneficial to our enterprise."

Birger and I sat with my friends. Joseph helped the servants and meant that we were served food as quickly as the jarl. It was good food and there was plenty of it. It marked the jarl as a clever man who knew how to get the best from his men. We were giving up six months of our lives and there would be hunger and thirst. He was satiating our appetites before we left. By the time the platters were empty, we were replete and could not eat another thing. I had ensured that Birger did not drink to excess so that when the jarl rose to speak the two of us were still alert enough to hear and understand all that was said.

"The reason for my delay was that I was speaking to a Frisian sea captain. He told me of two islands that lie to the west of the Liger: Nervouster and Guidel. The latter is an island defended by warriors and while larger than Nervouster is not a place we could use as a base. He told me that the water between Nervouster and the coast is shallow but a drekar could navigate it. Any Frank could not use it. I have decided to make it our home. I have been told that there are no men on the island and we will be able to raid the Liger when we want."

There was a cheer. That was what we wanted to hear. We had no glory hunters with us. We sought treasure and if we could do so without fighting too many enemies then so much the better.

"Enjoy your food. We leave on the morning tide. Know that I am pleased to be leading so many warriors on this raid. This time it is the men of our fjord alone who will reap the reward of our efforts." Did I detect some bitterness that his grand plan was now modified thanks to his cousin?

I knew that the feast would soon end but the jarl would have to leave first for we would be sleeping in the hall. As he left I saw Haldir pointing to me and as he waved to other warriors he and his hearth-weru made their way to our table. "Leif, it is good that you are here." He nodded to the others, "And your shield brothers. This bodes well and your servant too will be useful." Joseph had cleared the last of the platters and had gone outside, presumably to make water.

I nodded and then blurted out, "A few months ago he gave me some useful information, Jarl. I thought to pass it on to you."

"Go on."

Those around us were silent, intrigued no doubt about the conversation. "Joseph told me of an abbey upstream from where we raided last. It is richly endowed and undefended."

"It is on the Sequana?" I nodded. "But we planned on raiding the Liger."

I smiled, "If we raided this abbey at Jumièges, and the Franks followed us, Jarl, which direction would they take?"

"North, back to our home, as we did the last time."
Realisation dawned and he beamed, "But we would be heading south. I like that idea. Can your man speak our words?"

"He can."

"Then rise before dawn and meet me and my navigators by the drekar." He patted my shoulder, "You are a lucky warrior, Leif, and I shall keep you close."

As we snuggled into our blankets, surrounded by the warm fug of men who had eaten and drunk well I told Joseph of the meeting and he seemed pleased.

When we rose, alerted by Haldir's arm, the rest of the hall snored, farted and rustled beneath their blankets. We stepped out into a chill night with the moon just setting. We went aboard **'Bylgja'** and I saw the jarl, Snorri and Gandalfr standing at the steering board where a light burned and they studied a sheepskin map. Birger had stayed in the hall, at Haldir's request, and so just Joseph and I approached.

The jarl pointed at the map. I could see our home and then a long and jagged line. Marked in blue were two lines that looked parallel. I guessed they were the rivers. "Thrall, you say there is an abbey close to the place we took you. Point to it."

He shook his head, "I am sorry, lord, I do not know this drawing. Mark where you took me and I will show you."

Gandalfr jabbed a finger close to the end of the northernmost blue line. Joseph put his finger a short distance away. "The Sequana twists and turns. The abbey lies less than a dozen miles, as the crow flies, from my home. It nestles in a loop of the river."

The navigators and the jarl looked at each other. Gandalfr said, "Then we could do this. If we sail at night we know that we can pass upstream unseen and we have a better idea of the channel. We will be guided by the bells and the smell of their incense."

Snorri nodded his agreement, "We could do as we did the last time and use the current and our oars to take us to the sea. If we headed west, beyond the coast and the watchers there, we could then turn south. Leif is right. The Franks would assume we were heading home. There is no way that they could know we planned on wintering there."

The jarl looked at Joseph, "Thank you, Thrall." Joseph, realising he had been dismissed, moved away. The jarl looked at me, "I see the threads of the Norns in this, Leif. Keep this man close. You understand?"

"I do, Jarl." Like me, he knew that Joseph might flee. I knew that there was a possibility he might do so but we would have to be beyond the place he called the Pillars of Hercules before he did so.

"We will raid this abbey first."

We were the first to eat and by the time most had risen, made water and had food Birger, Joseph and I were aboard the drekar. While we waited for the crew as the sun rose, thralls brought on board the supplies for the voyage. There were ale and water barrels. Part of the deck was lifted and barrels of salted meat and fish were placed there. When the deck was replaced barrels of fresh food were secured to the gunwales at the prow. Joseph would have to reorganise his home but it would be a cosier one.

Askvoll turned out to wave us away. These were not our families and so we were able to concentrate on the oars and the ship. Our mother had given us a salve for our hands. I did not use it but I advised Birger to put that on before we rowed. I also told him to wear his hat. He wondered why. I explained that the further south we went, then the hotter the sun would burn and the hat would make him cooler. He did not understand that and I sighed, "I am giving you the lessons I learned when last I raided."

Mikkel nodded, "Your brother is right, Birger. Heed his advice and ours. That way you may survive."

We followed the jarl. Gandalfr was the better navigator but the jarl was leading us. We sailed two lengths behind *'Bylgja'*. What I noticed, especially once we reached the sea and we had stacked our oars, was that Gandalfr seemed to react to the wind quicker than his brother and the jarl. Our passage was smoother and I had the impression that had we wanted to we could easily have overtaken the jarl. Our ship was the faster. As noon approached and Gandalfr used the compass to mark our position I joined him, "Gandalfr, my father was a navigator and I would learn the skill. Might I watch you when I am not rowing?"

"Of course." He glanced down the ship, "And your brother?"

I smiled. Birger was throwing dice. I shook my head, "I am the one who wishes this."

"Good, then this is timely. I will need a watchkeeper and a sailor. The jarl intends to sail at night and that means I must sleep sometimes during the day. Stand with me and I shall teach you."

After watching him for a short time and heeding his words he gave me the chance to steer the drekar. It was easier than I had expected. Being a new ship she had no weed and responded well to the slightest of touches on the steering board.

"All you have to do when you steer is to match *'Bylgja'*. Our sails and course should be identical."

I looked up and frowning said, "We have slightly less sail."

He laughed, "I thought to test you. Aye, you are right. We have a little to spare for our keel is clean of weed and we are smaller and faster than the jarl's ship. This bodes well. Give another hour and if you manage not to ram us up *'Bylgja's'* arse I will let you steer and I will steal an hour or two of sleep."

I did not think I would and a short time later, not even an hour of the hourglass, he nodded and lay down close to me beneath his cloak. His voice said, "Wake me if anything happens. Rouse me when the sun is a handspan above the horizon."

I found it testing. Mikkel joined me. He spoke quietly so as not to disturb Gandalfr, "An honour, Leif."

"My father thinks I have natural skills and, who knows, one day my uncle might build a drekar and might need a navigator."

Until we passed the land of the Danes we would be in waters that were relatively friendly. The Franks were hostile and the Frisians, whose land lay to the north of Frankia, were unpredictable. I hoped that we would pass their land at night.

I had to order the sails trimmed just once and it was a testing time but the boys obeyed my commands and we stayed two lengths behind the jarl.

I held my hand against the western sky and, deciding it was time, coughed and said, "Gandalfr, it is dusk."

Either he was able to wake instantly or had been awake already for he rose like a wraith and, seeing that we were in exactly the same position behind the jarl, nodded his approval. "You'll do, Leif Longstride."

Chapter 18

The ships that headed from the blackened line that marked the coast were not drekars. They were the shallow-bottomed, fatter boats favoured by Frisians. I had risen to make water and was there as Gandalfr spied them. With the wind from the land I was standing to the steerboard side facing out to sea and I heard Gandalfr shout, "Awake!"

His voice must have carried to *'Bylgja'* for I heard a call from that ship too. I pulled up my breeks and ran to the steering board. "Is there danger?"

Gandalfr nodded as he laughed, "Three Frisians heading out to the west? I think so. These are not traders, these are pirates." He rubbed his beard and said, "What I wonder is how they knew to wait here?"

"I do not understand."

"Those ships had to have been waiting offshore until they saw our sails. They were expecting us. How did they know?" I had no answer. Gandalfr said, "That is a question to ask when we land. For now, rouse the warriors and arm them."

"Do we not take to the oars?"

He shook his head, "As fast as we are they will have more men and more oars." He smiled, "The jarl has also seen them and he is heading out to sea. That may help us. Go. Rouse the warriors."

I ran down the drekar. Men were awake but knew not the danger. As I ran, I shouted, "Pirates. Arm yourselves."

Reaching my chest, I took out the helmet and wolf cloak. I did not remove the shield for that would afford us protection from their arrows. I took out my bow and arrow bag. I strung the bow. I might be able to hit a couple of the pirates as they closed with us.

Birger, spear in hand, joined me. "Will you not wear your mail?"

I shook my head, "Not today."

As the light from the rising sun began to illuminate the eastern sky, I was able to make out the boats. They were low in the water but not as narrow as ours. Their sails were filled for the

Norse Warrior

wind was behind them. They still had men rowing. I wondered if Gandalfr and the jarl had miscalculated. Perhaps we should row.

Suddenly Gandalfr shouted, "Prepare to change course. Boys, to the sheets. Leif Longstride, stand by me." As the boys hurried to attend to the sheets and stays, I went, bow in hand, to Gandalfr. He nodded to the *'Bylgja'*, "The jarl sent a signal and we are about to turn. It is time, if you wish to be a navigator, for another lesson."

I saw the jarl at the stern of his ship. Snorri had the board but the jarl was looking at the Frisian ships. I glanced up at the fluttering pennant. The wind was still blowing due west. "If we turn, will they not begin to catch up to us for they will have the wind astern of them."

The old sailor smiled, "That is why this is a lesson. When you sail with the wind at an angle you can travel faster and when the Frisians try to turn, unless they are a very well-drilled crew, they risk running foul of one another or catching oars. That is why you are here. Put down your bow and when I give the command help me to put the steering board over to head south and west."

I did as I was commanded and, like Gandalfr, watched the other drekar. As soon as the jarl put his arm down Gandalfr said, "Now! Ship's boys, make secure the sheets and stays as we turn." I felt the ship fighting us as we pushed over the board. As the sheets on one side were loosened the ones on the other side were tightened so that we did not lose one gust of wind and the sail stayed taut. I risked glancing at the Frisians. They were still heading west. Their lookouts had not done their job and the billowing sail had hidden us from their view.

Gandalfr chuckled, "If we needed to we could gain a couple of extra knots and overtake the jarl but this is good. We will tire them out and then, when the jarl commands we will use our own oars. The Frisian commander is not a good one."

"Why not?"

"This is like the game we play on the hnefatafl board where the pieces try to catch the king. They are following in a fan and that fan should be wider to ensure we cannot escape. That is how you win at hnefatafl, by outwitting your opponent. The coast of the land of the Angles is to the north and west of us and, if they were cleverer, they would drive us there." He suddenly laughed and said, "See, they are too close and one has fouled another."

I looked up and saw that the leading Frisian and the one to its larboard side had collided oars. They had slowed dramatically and the third had to sail closer to the land to avoid a collision. That one little mistake had cost them their prey for within a few moments we started to pull away and it became clear, not long after, that they had given up. Our men cheered. The jarl kept us on the same course for another hour. I knew that for Gandalfr had me turn the hourglass. He then turned to sail south and east. It was slower progress but we had to get back so that the coast was on our larboard beam.

When it became clear that we were back on our original course, Gandalf said, "Take over, Leif, and I will sleep. That excitement will make for a dream-filled sleep." He went to the larboard side of the stern and buried himself in his furs.

I felt more confident now, as I held the steering board. I had been worried that it would be vastly different to a snekke. The drekar was just larger and as I was just copying the jarl and Snorri, who knew how to sail, I would not make moves that would be too large and threaten to swamp us.

Mikkel and Birger joined me. I said, "Birger, unstring my bow and put my weapons back in the chest."

Mikkel smiled as Birger struggled to take the string from the bow. He had to help him. When Birger hurried off Mikkel said, "I thought we would have to fight, Leif."

I nodded but said nothing. My mind was working away.

When Birger returned Mikkel said, "What is wrong, Leif, you are quiet. I would have thought you were excited to have escaped the trap."

"You are right, Mikkel, it was a trap and but for the skill of Gandalfr, his brother and the jarl, we would have been caught." I saw that neither of them understood what I had said. I explained it, "How did they know we would be sailing down their coast? We were fast and no ships passed us. They were waiting and I cannot believe that they would use three ships to take a knarr. They knew that there would be two ships and that they would be filled with warriors. I say again, who set the trap?"

Birger still did not understand but Mikkel did. "Then there may be more danger further south."

I nodded. "The jarl made no secret of his plans. The knarr that sailed when we arrived was Frisian. Who knows what mischief might be caused?"

"You should tell Gandalfr and the jarl."

"As we are not going to stop until we reach the Sequana then it will have to be Gandalfr and by then we will be deep in Frankish-controlled territory and dangerous waters. Here we had sea room but there?"

When Gandalfr awoke, at noon, it was clear that he, too, had been thinking along the same lines as me. As he drank ale I told him my thoughts and he nodded, "Aye, the Frisian could be the one who set off the trap but there have been many knarr visiting Askvoll over the past months. Any of them could have warned whoever set this trap."

"But who would do that?"

He shrugged, "The Franks have an empire and they have power. They might have employed the Frisians." He frowned, "They may well be waiting close to the Liger for us." I leaned against the gunwale as the ship's boys threw lines out to catch some fish. Gandalfr finished eating and said, "My watch." I sat with my back to the gunwale. Gandalfr kept glancing from the masthead to the jarl's drekar and back. It was almost as though his body was doing the actions but his mind was elsewhere. He suddenly smiled, "By the Allfather the Norns are spinning."

"What?"

"We are not going to the Liger first, Leif. Thanks to you we are going to the Sequana to raid an abbey. That was only decided after the Frisian knarr left Askvoll. Only we know that. Your thrall's information might have just thwarted our enemies' attempts to trap us."

The weather changed, as we headed into Frankish waters. The winds came from the west and they were always wet ones. Gandalfr told me that there would also be larger seas and we spent three days wearing sealskins and fighting the weather. I spent more time at the steering board than before for often I had to help Gandalfr to hold the steering board and keep us in the wake of *'Bylgja'*. Joseph kept the two of us fed.

By the end of the third day, the storm had blown itself out and we could inspect the ship for damage. We were luckier than the jarl for our newer drekar had fared better than the older vessel he commanded. We spied land to the west and Gandalfr identified them as islands. He knew one of them but knew it was inhabited. He pointed to a smaller one that lay to the north of the larger island we could see. "Leif, go to the prow and signal the jarl to head to the smaller island."

I ran to the prow and stood with my hands on the giant's head and my feet braced on the gunwale. I waved my right arm until one of the boys who was fishing drew the jarl's attention to me. I pointed to the smaller island and when the jarl repeated my gesture I knew that I had been seen. We headed for the island and I saw that it was largely rocks but there was a low green part that would hide us from the inhabited island. We reefed the sails and, using oars gently nudged our way into the shallows. There were rocky islets that afforded protection from the north and the water was much calmer. The jarl anchored just ten feet from the shore and Gandalfr put us next to him so that we could tie the two ships together.

Our sterns were touching and I was privy to the conversation. "You have found us a good place to repair, Gandalfr."

He nodded, "I had heard of this island although until we saw it, I did not know where it was. I hear there are animals to be hunted here. Have you much damage, Jarl?"

It was Snorri who answered, "The sail needs to be stitched and we have to replace the forestay. It has not yet sheared but another good blow and it could."

The jarl said, "We will land and light fires. Hot fresh food is welcome."

Gandalfr nodded, "I will make my ship secure. Oddr, take the men ashore. Leif, you stay with me."

I watched the men jump over the side. The water was shallow at the prow. It came up to the men's chests. Hersir Brokkr would have been up to his neck and Snorri might have to swim. I shouted, "Birger, take my bow and arrows ashore as well as your sling."

"Aye, Brother."

I went with Gandalfr and his boys as we examined the sheets and stays for damage. They were all new and had fared well. "Lift the deck." We removed the opening to the hold and he peered inside. He nodded to the smallest boy, Karl, "Climb inside and see if it is dry."

He slipped into the dark and we heard him scurrying around like a rat on a roof. When he emerged, he held up a palm and grinned, "Dry as a bone, Gandalfr."

"Good, then we can go ashore. After you have eaten you will each take a turn at watching the ship. Falco, I leave you in charge of the boys. Leif and I will go ashore."

By the time we were ashore the fires were lit and pots of sea water bubbled away. Already a couple of rabbits had been taken and having been skinned were tossed into the pot along with wild greens, wild herbs and some seaweed that cooked well. Pieces of dried ham and some pickled fish were added. It would be an interesting taste.

Joseph had already laid out a bed for me next to Mikkel and Birger. I had taken off my boots before I jumped into the sea and now I took off my breeks to let them dry. The storm having passed the sun shone and it was warm. Others were cooking. They had enjoyed a relatively leisurely voyage with little need to row while I had stood long watches at the steering board. I lay on the wolf skin and quickly fell asleep. It seemed moments later that I was shaken awake but, looking at the sun I saw that it was past noon and I had slept for at least an hour.

Mikkel said, "The jarl wishes to speak to you and Joseph."

I donned my breeks which were damp rather than wet and walked across the close-cropped grass to the fire and the jarl. Joseph had brought my bowl and he filled it with the stew. It smelled delicious and after raw fish and dried food, it would be like a feast.

"Gandalfr tells me that you have your suspicions about the trap laid by the Frisians."

I nodded, "You are right, Jarl, I think it was a trap and might have worked but for Gandalfr's keen eyes."

"Then our plan to raid the abbey is a good one. You are right, Leif Longstride, it will catch the Franks unawares. If they are waiting for us at the Liger, then they will wait in vain." He looked up at Joseph, "When we sail along the Sequana then it will be *'Ægir'* that leads and you shall be at the prow. We need the eyes of your thrall to steer us to the abbey."

"Yes, Jarl, I will be honoured." Joseph gave a bow.

"And there will be a reward."

Joseph's eyes did not smile along with his mouth as he said, "Thank you, Jarl."

I knew that Joseph's reward, in his mind, would be that we might get to the Blue Sea where he could run.

We spent two days on the island. The repairs were completed in less than a day but the animals and sea birds on the island were a source of food and we hunted them. We cooked them before we sailed for the Sequana. They would feed us for four days. They might be cold, but they would have a different taste.

We had to row as well as use the sail as we sailed south. Our course was to the estuary of the Sequana and Gandalfr, now leading, timed our arrival so that it was dark as we neared the wide estuary. The sail was reefed but we did not step the mast. We still had memories of the flight down the river the last time. The sail might make all the difference. We were at the oars and Falco stood by Joseph to pass on the signals. They would not be needed until we neared the abbey but there was no harm in keeping the two of them there. Joseph had told the jarl that it was forty miles or so up the river. That necessitated finding a place to hide during the day.

I suppose that our first raid had come as a shock to those who lived along this river. It was a peaceful river. As we rowed upstream all that we heard was the swish of the keel and the soft sound of the oars' blades slicing through the water. There was no other sound. The struggles of the night ceased as we passed. The occasional whiff of woodsmoke came to us and once the stink of some animal dung but other than that we could have been in an empty land.

Gandalfr was relying on Joseph and Falco for our course, but he had a seaman's eye and when he spotted, looming up in the light from early dawn, the stand of willows he put the steering board over and hissed, "Larboard oars in. Steerboard, slow your oars."

He was a master seaman and he nudged us close to the bank. The flexible willow branches did not break when they were fouled by our mast but bent and parted.

"Stack oars. Tie us off."

By the time the jarl's drekar had reached the trees, Gandalfr had the boys cutting willows to disguise our steerboard side. Before we had left the island of the rabbits, we had been told that there would be no fires when we stopped and we would have to sleep aboard the drekar. The row up the river had been the longest one we had endured and Birger's hands showed the effect. I knew others would be suffering too but Birger was my brother.

When Joseph came aft, he examined the hands and I handed him my mother's salve. He sniffed it and nodded. He did not apply it immediately but took his vinegar skin. He whispered, "Brace yourself, Master Birger. I need to clean the wounds." He poured the vinegar onto the open skin and massaged it gently in. Birger winced but bore it stoically. He smiled when the soothing salve was applied.

"Your home is nearby." We were all speaking in hushed and whispered tones.

He nodded, "We could be there within an hour of walking." He looked into my eyes. "I have a home here and I am happy."

I nodded but I did not truly believe him. We were in a safe place until we reached the Blue Sea and then he would think about running.

We made water or emptied our bowels. We ate and drank and then, after Gandalfr had assigned sentries, we slept. I buried my head in the wolf's skin. It was not for warmth but darkness. Perhaps it was the spirit of the wolf but that day I dreamt of the hunt once more and the search for the killer of lambs. I could almost smell the scent of the animal and, in my dream, I relived the sinking of the spear into its flesh.

Joseph shook me awake. He handed me a horn of water. "Soon it will be dark, Master."

I rose. To the west, the sky was turning pink and blue. It had been a sunny day and I had slept through it.

We set off when it was dark. This time we knew that we would find the abbey and soon. While I had slept Gandalfr had interrogated Joseph. He had us row harder for he intended to reach the abbey as close to Matins as we could. Joseph had explained how the monks of the abbey rang bells to call the monks to prayer. He had told us their times. Gandalfr and the jarl had decided that as the first call to prayers was in the dark of night we would launch our attack just after that bell. Joseph had assured us that we would hear the bell.

What I noticed, before we heard the bell, was the smell. It was not the smell of night flowers but of perfume, the incense used by the monks and carried on the night breeze. When the bell sounded I realised we were close to the abbey and as a cloud passed from before the moon, we saw, bathed in moonlight, the monastery standing on a piece of land in a loop in the river. The bell ceased and, as we slowed our oars we heard a murmur from the church. They were singing their prayers.

Joseph and Falco pointed to the larboard and I felt the drekar shift as Gandalfr took us towards the landing place that they had seen. As with the first landing the larboard oars came in first and then we sculled the drekar to the shore. Gandalfr's skill was awesome and he ground onto the sand and shingle shore softly. It seemed to me as though the drekar sighed. I was beginning to realise that this drekar was a living thing.

We worked quickly for we had all been told what to do. After stacking my oar I opened my chest and took out my arming cap and helmet. I would not need my mail byrnie for these were monks. If we found warriors then we would be in trouble. I strapped on my sword and then placed the wolf's skin so that the head was on my helmet and hung down my shoulders. Along with the wolf's teeth necklace it made me look fierce. It might not intimidate a warrior but a monk might be terrified. I left my spear where it was but took my shield. Joseph had said that there was a wall that ran around the monastery and we might need shields to climb it.

Leaving Joseph with the ship's boys and Gandalfr to watch the ship we followed the jarl, running in single file. Birger ran between Mikkel and I. Neither of us wanted my brother to suffer Elvind's fate and die on his first raid. There were houses that lay in the settlement nestling below the place of the monks but all was silent as we padded through. The service must have been over and the monks returned to their beds. Like me the others had decided not to wear mail and there was just the creak of leather to disturb the night. I saw the jarl wave his sword and Ansgar, one of the warriors from Askvoll peeled off with eight warriors. When I saw them stand close to the doors of the dwellings, I knew that they were there to silence any who tried to give warning and to attack once they heard noise from within the place of the monks.

The gates were barred but the wall was just the height of a very tall man. We spread out and Mikkel and I held my shield between us. With his shield slung over his back and his spear in his hand, Birger was boosted over the wall. Other young warriors followed him, and we hurried to the gate. This was a monastery and the monks did not have men watching the gates. I suspected that after this raid they would.

As soon as we ran through the gates, I paused for the buildings were enormous and dwarfed the jarl's mead hall. The jarl pointed at Oddr and the man whose life I had saved from this river hissed, "Bygstad, with me."

We ran, not to the main church but to the wooden building that lay close to it. The door was not locked and Dagfinn opened it and, with a shield protecting his body and his sword before him, stepped inside. This was not a warrior hall with warriors sleeping together, this was a monastery with cells and we saw a long corridor with doors leading from it. There were tallow candles in sconces on the walls and Oddr waved us left and right to move down the corridor.

Perhaps one of the monks needed to make water or he might have heard a noise. I do not know but when a door opened and the monk saw Brynjar he opened his mouth to shout out. Brynjar rammed his sword under the monk's chin and any cry died with the man. His falling body made a loud crack as it hit, first the door jamb and then the floor. I had placed myself close to a door and when the monk who was inside opened it I was ready. I used the flat of my blade to smack him on the head. I hoped it would not kill him but I needed him to be silenced. He fell. Further down the place of the sleeping monks, men died and not all of them did so silently. Cries rent the night and within moments the air was filled with the sound of death as men were slain. I hurried down the corridor, but the monks had all been dealt with.

Oddr shouted, "Search for treasure."

I did not think there would be any. Joseph had told us that the treasure would all be found in the church. I obeyed the command. The flames from the candles threw a soft golden light in the cell. I saw a holy book. That, to me, was not treasure. The silver cross which hung above the bed was and I grabbed it and dropped it into the pouch around my waist. I found another three metal crosses although the first was the only silver one.

"Outside. Search the other buildings."

The moon was a full one and the monastery was bathed in silvery light. I could hear, from the settlement, the sound of cries as Ansgar and his warriors slew the men and collected from the houses. The jarl was in the church and we hurried to join him. There were bodies scattered at the entrance and, inside, it was already being ransacked. Candlesticks, platters and incense burners from the altar were all being placed on the white sheets that must have had a purpose but I could not divine what it was.

The jarl pointed his sword at me, "Leif Longstride, take your young warriors and see what lies in the lesser buildings."

"Aye, Jarl."

I doubted that we would find treasure but I knew that we would all get to share in whatever the jarl found. He was an honourable man.

"Follow me."

We headed to the smaller buildings that lay on the far side of the church. I opened the first door and peered in. It was dark and I did not detect any movement. "Birger, fetch a light. Brynjar, take Gunvald and search the next building." I could smell food and when Birger arrived with the burning brand it illuminated a larder and it was stacked. The monks, or some of them at least, ate well and there were rounds of cheese as well as hams hanging from hooks.

Mikkel laughed, "It may not be gold or silver but this is truly treasure."

We sheathed our weapons and with our shields upon our backs began to carry the food to the drekar. As we passed through the monastery grounds I saw monks who had not been slain weeping. The same was true as we headed through the village although here it was women and children who wept. They feared that they would be taken as slaves. I knew that they would not for we were not going home and the jarl would not want men to take female slaves as bed mates, it would cause dissension.

By the time dawn came the two drekars were laden with gold, silver, food, wine and even some animals we had found. The gold and silver were placed beneath the decks and the animals spread between the two ships. It was noon when we left. We set fire to as many wooden buildings as we could. It was not a vindictive act. We wanted any warriors who lived close by to be drawn to the monastery and not the river. The jarl intended to race for the sea and to make it in one day. The women, children and monks would douse most of the flames but we hoped to be well down the river by then.

I told Joseph about the holy books and he shook his head, "Master, they are worth gold. Men will buy them."

I cursed myself. I had held treasure in my hands and discarded it.

The sails were raised and we took to our oars. We would fly down the river. We had edged our way up and sneaked into the heartland of the Franks but we would use the wind, the current and men's backs to reach the sea before they even knew where we were. We passed into the open sea an hour after sunset. We stacked our oars for we were weary beyond words. We had not eaten for a whole day but all I wanted was ale and to sleep. The sleep was a dreamless one. Neither wolf nor monk haunted me.

Norse Warrior

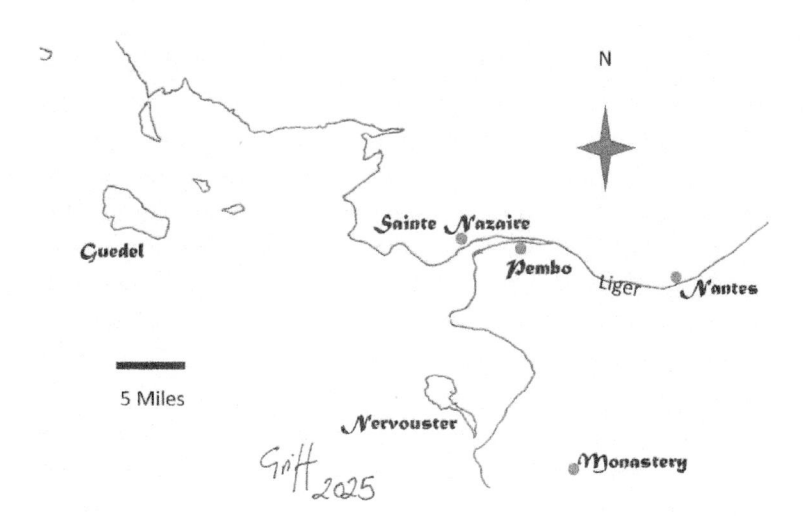

Chapter 19

When I woke it was getting close to dark and I headed for the steering board. Gandalfr looked tired. He had not raided but he had sailed the drekar down the river and continued to do so while I slept. I smiled, "You should have woken me."

"I will sleep now." Not having drunk much or eaten I did not need to make water. I went to take the steering board. He said, "You should eat."

"I will eat while I steer." I looked ahead and saw that the jarl was now leading. "We hold the same course?"

He nodded, "We are standing well off from the coast for this is where the rocks are savage and will tear out a keel. Watch for the turn. Soon we will head south and the lookouts will need to watch for Guedel. We will pass that island to larboard. If there is danger, then wake me." He yawned, "By my reckoning, we should reach Nervouster before dark but if we have not then wake me when the sun starts to set. You are not yet ready for a night watch."

He went to make water and Joseph approached. He had fresh food taken from Jumièges and a horn of ale. We had liberated some barrels. The seas were coming from our steerboard quarter and it was hard to keep the ship straight. I said, "Treat me as a child, Joseph. Hold the horn to let me drink ale and then feed me food for my stomach thinks that my throat has been cut."

"Yes, Master."

He judged my capacity well and I did not choke on the ale. I bit into the bread that was slightly stale but smeared with Frankish butter and topped with cured ham it was a delicious meal. When I was done, I said, "More ale."

"And more food?"

I shook my head, "Make sure my little brother eats."

He nodded, "Of course." He said it as though I had insulted him. He was a good thrall yet he did not feel like one. I felt that he was a friend.

I could have called Gandalfr when it came time for the turn but I knew that it was not fair on him and I had watched him do it often enough. As **'Bylgja'** came about I set the ship's boys to stand by the lines. I eased over the steering board and the boys, well-practised now, did the rest. I kept a critical eye on the sail but it just slackened slightly and then filled and firmed. It was all good. I was glad that there was no weed. *'Ægir'* was a responsive ship. The next turn was easier for me and when the jarl turned to head south and east I did not feel my stomach knot up as much. The wind was now from the west and when the ship heeled a little Gandalfr woke. He stood and looked first ahead and then to larboard. Seemingly satisfied he said, "Give me until the hourglass needs to be turned and I will relieve you. You have done well and have the makings of a navigator. Your father taught you well." I thought back to the times he had let me sail the snekke out to sea. Had he known that one day I would steer a drekar?

My arms and back were aching when I returned to my chest. Joseph brought me more ale and food. I looked towards Frankia and saw Guedel to larboard. It was far enough away so that it was just a smudge on the horizon but it meant that our temporary home was not far away.

We approached the island that would be our temporary home from the west and the blót that Brokkr had made was a good one. The sea was calm, and the rays of the setting sun pointed shafts of sunlight across a bluer sea than at home to a sandy beach nestled beneath a crown of green. The jarl nudged us in, and we slid the drekar up onto the beach. This time we secured our ships well. We would not be sailing for a day or so and who knew when a storm could blow in from the west? Men were sent, while there was still light, to the island of Nervouster. It was larger than the one we had used on our way south. It was dark when they returned and we had fires that were cooking our hot meal. I was close enough to the navigators to hear their words.

"We saw no signs of men. There were pits where fires had been lit but grass grows on them. The main island is about five thousand paces by three thousand but there is a narrow spit of land that goes towards the coast of Frankia. We saw a sea passage between the island and the coast. We saw no sign of any lights on the mainland. We could not smell woodsmoke."

"Water?"

"Aye, Jarl, there are pools, and they are fresh. We could not tell if they were springs. There are trees and we saw signs of rabbits."

"You have done well. Eat." He turned to Gandalfr and Snorri. "We will rest for a day and share the treasure from the monks. The day after we will take *'Ægir'* and explore the island and the passage to the coast of Frankia. Step the mast and use the oars. Have the shields taken from the sides of the drekar." Gandalfr nodded. While you do that we will take *'Bylgja'* and find the Liger. We, too, will step the mast. It may confuse the Franks if they just see low ships with no shields. If the Franks have been warned of raiders from the north then let us keep them guessing a little while longer. The more treasure we can accumulate before they know that the fox is in their henhouse the better."

We had our own little camp. Oddr and the older warriors were close by but we younger ones had our own and Joseph acted as a servant for all of us. When we raided, he would stay on the island. We were excited to be so far south and in weather that was so warm we did not need blankets and furs at night.

The next morning the decks were lifted and the treasure spread out. It was divided. Four portions were larger than the rest. The jarl had the biggest pile. Brokkr had the next, even though he was not with us, and Gandalfr and Snorri had two piles that were smaller than those but larger than the rest. We did not mind for we all had some treasure and for most it was more than we had taken on the last raid. What disappointed the younger warriors, the ones like Birger, was that we had not taken weapons and they had hoped for swords. The men in the village we had attacked were ill-armed and the weapons we took were fit for melting down only. Having Falco with us provided the jarl with an expert. He took the best of the swords and even he could bend it. He had shaken his head and tossed the weapon aside in disgust. We placed our treasures in our chests. Mine nestled in the bottom. Birger had more space in his and if we took a great deal of treasure, he could store mine with his.

We took *'Ægir'* off the beach on the first high tide. With the mast removed and no shields, it looked like a totally different ship. Even the prow did not look like a dragon. While *'Bylgja'* headed north we sailed south. Our scouts had been right. There were no settlements close to the coast. We saw no tell-tale tendril of smoke and there were no fishing boats. No one stood on the beaches casting nets or sought shellfish in the rocks. When we neared the narrow passage Gandalfr ordered us to stop rowing. He commanded that just four men were at the oars as he wanted as little way on the drekar as possible.

"Leif, steer her and watch for my signals. Keep her straight unless I command otherwise. I will investigate the channel."

With Oddr and three other experienced warriors rowing, we headed through the narrow piece of water that separated the island from the mainland. The scouts were right, it was a narrow spit of land. The tide was on its way out by the time we reached it, but I could see that there was weed showing that at high tide it would be an even smaller piece of earth. We had to make but one course correction as we headed through it and when Gandalfr came striding back to the stern I knew that all was well.

He nodded to me as he took over the steering board, "Even at low tide we could pass through under sail and with oars. A larger ship might tear out her keel." He shouted, "Man the oars, let us continue our voyage."

By noon we were back at the camp. There was a place on the eastern side that could have been made into a landing place, but Gandalfr was happy with our site. We were hidden from the mainland and with open water to the west we had many ways to escape if we were discovered.

'Bylgja' did not return until after dark. Oddr was summoned to the jarl along with Gandalfr while they ate the food we had prepared. It was a stew. Rabbits, shellfish, fish and some dried meat added to the greens we found made a tasty meal although we all yearned for bread. The loaves we had taken from Jumièges had long gone. While the jarl and the crew of *'Bylgja'* ate, Gandalfr and Oddr told us what they had found.

"The river is twenty miles to the north of us. There is a small fishing village on the north bank but no defences that could be seen. There is a church. Tomorrow, we sail north. The jarl said that as it is twenty miles we will use the sails, but we will sail in the afternoon. The river looks to be wide and although he did not explore the river, he is confident that we can sail up it."

I had steered the drekar and knew the problems, "But does he know for certain, Gandalfr?"

"The knarr captain said that the river was navigable even for a Frankish ship for many miles. He said that there is a mighty city called Tours and it is many leagues from the sea."

I said, "Is this the same captain who may have told the Frisians of our voyage?"

He chuckled, "You have a suspicious mind, Leif Longstride, but you are right to question the motives of the Frisian. However, Lord Arne, the jarl's cousin, also spoke of this river and Tours. The jarl intends to raid the river close to the sea. If we are not disturbed we may sail further east to this fabled city."

Brynjar said, "He is going to poke the bear until it does something."

Oddr shook his head, "No, we will see what we can take while the bear sleeps and be ready to run when he awakes."

As we lay on our furs and looked at the stars I said, "We came here to raid, Brynjar, and we all know that may involve us fighting the Franks. I am not afraid of their ships. *'Ægir'* is fast, and she can outsail any lumbering Frank. This island is a haven. We have a narrow passage we can use as well as the open sea. So long as a good watch is kept then we are safe."

The jarl showed that he was also planning for danger. He left four men to construct a small tower that could be manned to keep watch on the east. Joseph also remained on the island. He would act as a cook. The dried beans we had brought needed long cooking and someone to stir the stew constantly. When we returned, whenever that was, we would have a fine meal. Joseph and the others we left would begin to cook them in a couple of days.

"We will be away for, perhaps, three days. Keep a good watch."

This time, with mast and sail fitted, not to mention the shields along the side, the jarl was announcing to Frankia and the land of Aquitaine that there were raiders in their lands. Knowing that we were there and doing something about it were two entirely different things. We reached the mouth an hour or so before dusk and we turned to head upstream. We reefed the sails a little. We would still need to row but we had some help from the wind. The current was strong and we had to work hard. Falco was at the prow and he signalled, just a few miles up the river, that the jarl had reefed his sail and was heading to shore. The sun was just beginning to set in the west but there was enough light to see the land.

The boys scampered up the mast to reef our sail as Gandalfr put the steering board over. We ran in our oars while the larboard ones pushed us to the shore. Snorri had found us a beach on the southern side of the river and we slid sideways onto it, our keel scraping over sand. The sand would not harm us and would clear some of the sea life which might have begun to attach itself to our keel.

We were raiding once more and we would need to be armed. After stacking my oar, I opened my chest and took out the helmet, sword and wolf's skin. I also took my spear as well as my shield. There might be warriors this time. As I stepped ashore the breeze brought the smell not only of woodsmoke but also dung, both animal and human. We were close to a settlement.

The jarl wore his mail and with a full-face helmet looked like a god. He pointed his spear and his scouts hurried off down the clearly marked path. We all knew that it would lead to a village. We trotted behind in pairs. I was next to Mikkel. Birger was my brother, but he would fight alongside the other new men. This time we knew we would have to fight. The men we were going to attack would protect their families.

It was relatively early, and we knew that the men in the village that lay ahead of us would not be asleep. Like the men who were still in Bygstad, they would have worked all day and were now enjoying food. There might be those in the village who would see us. In the end, it proved to be a watchdog who barked a warning as the scouts approached. The shouts of alarm made us run faster to follow the jarl. The scream that rent the night was the start of our first real battle in this foreign land.

The jarl was right to attack quickly but what he could not have known was that this was a large village. It had a wall around the southern side but was open to the river. That gave us entry but the men of the village, we later learned it was called Pembo, were used to fighting the men of Aquitaine and they were armed. I heard the clash of metal on metal and as we neared the village saw the chaos and confusion as the men of the village fought this new and, hitherto, unknown terror. I saw at least two dead villagers but I also saw one of the jarl's men, Bjarni, binding a wound to his leg. I was flanked by Mikkel and Dagfinn and we ran at three warriors who had helmets, small shields and swords. They emerged from a long hut, and I later deduced they must have sought weapons before joining the fray. I lunged at the one in the middle and he blocked the strike with his shield. Even so, I put effort into the blow, and he reeled. I took advantage and punched hard with the boss of my shield. I caught him on the chin and his reel became a fall. I did not hesitate when he sprawled on the ground. I plunged my spear into his chest. This was not the time to collect swords and I ran to where I saw Oddr and Asbjørn fighting off three warriors and a boy. My spear struck the unprotected side of a warrior and it made him turn allowing Asbjørn to attack another of the men with even more vigour. The man I had wounded had a wood axe and he swung it at my head. I ducked beneath the blow and struck blindly towards him with my spear. I felt it sink into his flesh. The spear that struck my wolf cloak was fire-hardened. Had it been made of metal then I might have been hurt. As it was I turned and saw the boy, fourteen summers or so, pulling back for a second strike. Birger did not hesitate and his spear drove through the boy's back. My little brother had been blooded. Those deaths, allied to the success the jarl was enjoying, turned the tide of the fight. I heard a command from our enemies. I did not understand the words. Had Joseph been with us then we might. I knew it was a Frankish sort of word but not one that Joseph had used. The women and children fled. Some better-armed warriors formed a shield wall to slow us down. Jarl Bjørn Haraldsson and his hearth-weru were all mailed and they formed a wedge and ran at the line of men. The defenders fought well but it was an uneven contest and they were soon slain.

 Seeing that there was no more opposition the jarl raised his face mask and shouted, "Secure that gate and search for treasure."

 One of the men who had not raided before, Frode, shouted, "What about the women and children?"

"We do not need slaves. Search the dead and the houses. Look for chests buried beneath the houses."

I rammed my spear into the ground, placed my helmet on the spear and slung my shield on my back. I hurried back to the two warriors I had slain. I took their swords and daggers and then their purses. There were just a couple of coppers in them. I spied Birger and shouted, "There are two swords. Choose the one you want."

"But I did not slay them."

"You saved me from the young warrior, and this is your reward." He eagerly examined the two weapons.

By the time dawn broke, we had searched the village. The two drekars had been pulled to the landing stage next to the village and we loaded the food we had found, the wine, ale and animals. We had all taken our own treasure. We would only share in the horde that we might take from a church or the hall of a lord. I had found a small chest with a handful of silver within it as well as another silver cross. I was happy. We loaded the drekar and then ate in the village. The four men who had been wounded were tended to. None were serious wounds and did not require limbs to be amputated. Snorri was handy with a needle and he stitched them up.

I heard Haldir ask the jarl, "Do we burn the village?"

"What and tell the land that there are raiders? I think not. Word will have spread to the south, and Aquitaine might be alerted. We will head along the river and raid the northern bank."

I said to Mikkel, "And the next time I will wear my mail. If that boy who struck me had been using a proper spear, then I would have been hurt."

"Aye, none of these wore mail and they had few helmets. Still, we are eating well and the animals we have can be taken back to the island."

We had three goats, four sheep and a dozen fowl. We would keep them alive and that way we would have milk and, when we left this land, meat.

I donned my mail. It would be uncomfortable to row in it but I would be safer. We left the empty village, the corpses of their dead still littering the ground, not long after the sun was high in the sky. We rowed as the wind was against us. It meant we moved more slowly but we were harder to see. Five miles after we had left the first village when we heard monastery bells south of the river peeling what we assumed was Nones, we came around a bend and saw another village on the north bank. While we had eaten the jarl had explained what we would do when we came upon another target. *'Bylgja'* swung her bows and the drekar slid next to the beach. The jarl and his warriors swarmed over the side. Gandalfr took us beyond the drekar to another beach fifty paces upstream. I had my mail already and donning my helmet I grabbed my sword and shield to be the first one ashore. I landed in the water but it only came to my knees. I hurried up the bank and turned along the path to head to the village. I could hear the screams and shouts as the jarl fell upon the unsuspecting Frankish village. As I ran down the path, I saw women and children fleeing towards me. They screamed when they saw me and ran away to their left, away from the river. I heard feet pounding behind me and knew, without even looking that it would be Mikkel and my shield brothers along with my brother, Birger.

The next women and children who saw me let out such a wail and shouted out a word I recognised, "Barbarians!" Joseph had taught me the word. That made some men in the village turn and, seeing me, five of them ran at me. These had spears and shields. None wore mail but they had all donned helmets. I could have halted and waited for the others but I knew from my talks with Hallstein that if you gave an enemy the chance to make the decision you were doomed. You used your speed and skill to surprise them.

I shouted, "Bygstad! Leif Wolf Killer is coming for you!" The words would mean nothing to them but when I heard a cheer and a roar from behind me, I knew that it had an effect on my friends and brother. They would run all the harder.

I pulled my shield up to cover the lower half of my face and I pulled back my spear. The five men had stopped to make an improvised shield wall but we had practised destroying such shield walls. I would not jump at the skjaldborg. Instead, like a wild pig charging a hunter I lowered my head and bowled into them. Spears struck my shield and I angled it to deflect them. One scraped and gouged along my helmet but the boss of my shield struck a Frank in the face and he fell. His falling was nearly the undoing of me for I began to trip but by lengthening my stride I managed to keep my feet and when my right foot inadvertently smashed down on his face then the warrior was rendered unconscious. I had no time to think about the other four for more men were coming. I stood and faced them. I would rely on Mikkel and the others guarding my back. I heard the clash of weapons and screams from behind me. I hoped that Birger would not be hurt but I had no time to think of that for two Franks came at me. This time one wore a short byrnie. It looked similar in design to mine but not as well made. In that first glance, I took in that it had larger links than the one I wore. I took a decision. Hallstein had taught me that using your instincts could often save your life and I hurled the spear at the mailed warrior. Had I thrown it at my mail it would have done no harm but Thor must have guided the head for it found a gap and at a range of less than four paces drove through the links, the undershirt and into the flesh. I saw the look of surprise as his eyes widened. He dropped his spear and clutched at mine, I drew my sword and was just able to deflect the second Frank's sword. As he raised his sword to strike down at me, I tried something I had seen Hallstein do in training; I whirled around so that the Frank struck fresh air while my sword hacked into his back. The first warrior had removed my spear and was trying to take his sword from his scabbard. The wound had weakened him, I saw the pool of blood at his feet and I gave him a warrior's death by slicing through his neck.

Mikkel and Brynjar joined me. I saw that their spears were bloody. After sheathing my sword, I retrieved my spear and said, "Mikkel, I give this byrnie to you."

"I am honoured but I do not deserve it."

I shrugged, "I do not need it and Birger needs experience. I would give you protection for Borghildr's sake." Our marriages had made us brothers.

"Then I take it."

The Franks had all been slain and I raised my spear, hearing the rest of the crew of *'Ægir'* joining us. "Bygstad!" The others joined in my shout, and we ran.

By the time we reached the centre of the village, it was over. This time the jarl had lost two warriors. It meant that he had suffered six casualties but our drekar none. He nodded, "Thank you. You drew off enough warriors for us to win. Search the village."

This was a more prosperous village and we found some silver buried. There was a church and we found vestments, candlesticks, platters and holy books. They were about to be discarded when I spoke, "Joseph says such things are worth silver. They can be sold to the followers of the White Christ."

The jarl nodded, "Thank you, Leif." He turned to his hearth-weru, "Take them."

It was dark by the time we had finished. The jarl knew we could not tie the two drekars together and he sent our crew back to cook further upstream. We stored our treasure. The two spears and swords, along with the helmets I had taken, were placed in the hold. Mikkel stored his byrnie. It would need to be repaired. Falco said that if he had time on the island then he could effect a temporary one that would hold.

We kept a good watch and ate hot food. We slept on the drekar and, at dawn the message came from the jarl. We would raid a little further upstream and then return to the island. This time we would lead. We were told to sail immediately. Taking to the oars we headed around a bend and saw another village. This one was just coming to life and we saw boats in the river, fishing. Gandalfr did not hesitate. He aimed our drekar at the nearest boat and we rammed it. We hit and sank three before he turned to the quay where another two fishing boats were tied up. Our hull crushed them to kindling and we tied up. I had not had time to don my byrnie and I just ran ashore with helmet, shield and spear. This time everyone ran away from us, including the men. I guess that we had drowned and crushed too many warriors in the river for them to fight us. We had no losses and an empty village. We emptied it of everything and this time we found a pair of pigs. They could be fattened and eaten although one of the warriors thought that the sow was about to give birth.

We did set fire to the village. The jarl had a simple explanation. "The fire will draw any warriors here and by the time they reach it we will be downstream."

The two ships were laden and with the animals would stink by the time we reached our island. It would be worth it for fresh meat and milk. We happily rowed and with the current and the wind we made swift progress down the river. We were seen by four warriors who were mounted. It was close to the mouth of the river and I guessed that there must be a stronghold further north. They were too far away to identify but they were clearly warriors who wore helmets and carried spears, one of which had a banner on it. As a result of the sighting, the jarl turned his ship north and west when we left the mouth of the river. He held that course until we could not see the coast of Frankia. Only then did he head, first west and then southeast. We reached our island after dark. The animals complained for most of the latter part of the journey.

The tower that had been built stood out against the eastern sky. Our men had done as we had asked and the fire that burned beneath the pot was a beacon that led us to our anchorage. Our first raid had been more than successful. It boded well for the future.

Chapter 20

We built pens for the animals and milked the goats immediately. We would use their milk to make cheese. We had taken flour from all three villages as well as bread. Once the stale bread had been used we could make flatbreads on hot stones. The ships' boys were set to work cleaning the decks.

The next day Joseph used the daylight to ensure that the wounds incurred by the warriors had been tended properly. It was good that he did for Gudmund's showed signs of badness. Joseph tut-tutted and cut away the stitches. Rather than using vinegar and honey as we might have done he found some maggots and placed them next to the wound. He bandaged them and then wagged a finger at Gudmund. "Do not try to remove the bandage and if the wound itches do not scratch. I will examine it every day. I will tell you when you are healed." To the others, Joseph was almost like a galdramenn and Gudmund obeyed.

We spent the next days repairing damaged weapons and recovering from the raid. Falco managed to repair the byrnie by taking a couple of links from the bottom, where they would not be missed, and fixing them in the hole my spear had made. As he told Mikkel, it was not perfect but it would last until his father could repair it.

Birger was more than happy with his new sword not least because there was a good scabbard and baldric. He strutted around as though he was Thor himself. Falco put a good edge on the sword. A weaponsmith could make even the sharpest blade sharper. I sharpened my other spare sword but I would not need it. The damage to my helmet was slight and it was not cracked. As Falco said, knocking out the dent would risk making it weaker.

After two days I was summoned, along with Oddr and Gandalfr, to the shelter that had been made for the jarl. Snorri was there already and they had the map that I had last seen in Askvoll. Haldir joined us and we sat around the map.

"The raid is going better than I had hoped." We all nodded, "I have called you all together so that you can hear my plans and offer suggestions."

I said, "Jarl, I can understand why the others are here but why me?"

He smiled, "Firstly, because it is thanks to your thrall that we have been as successful as we have. He found Jumièges. Secondly, you have shown that you are a thoughtful warrior and thirdly, because Gandalfr thinks you have the makings of a navigator."

The others smiled, even Haldir, and I nodded.

"I think that, as we were seen, the Franks will be watching for us north of the river. It is the start of the harvest season and they will be wary. I have decided that we will sail south. I know not what lies ahead of us but as no one knows what we intend," he looked at me, "not even the Frisian captain, then we should be safer there. Besides, I think that this coast will yield us great treasure. They will guard their monasteries on the river from now on. Our advantage is that they do not know where we will strike next. We will sail tomorrow after the sun has been at its zenith. Wherever we find south of us, we will raid. Snorri has this map. I intend to make a copy as soon as we have killed a sheep. We will use its skin and that map will go on *'Ægir'*. By the time we return to Bygstad, we will have a map which is worth its weight in gold."

I joined Gandalfr and Snorri to study the map.

Haldir said, "We lost men, Jarl, do we need to transfer some from *'Ægir'*?"

I glanced up and saw the jarl shake his head, "We had more men to begin with. I would not harm the bonds that have grown up on Gandalfr's ship."

The navigator looked up, "It is your ship, Jarl. I am just the ship's master."

"No, Gandalfr, I have watched you sailing behind me. You get more out of the drekar than I could. I own the ship but the heart belongs to you and Leif."

We slaughtered one sheep that night. I suspect the villagers would have killed it for a harvest feast as it was old. We would hang it and it would be cooked slowly. When we returned from the south that would be our feast. After removing the wool, we stretched the skin and pegged it out. When it dried, we would use it for a map.

Joseph said, "Will I be coming with you, Master?"

I shook my head, "Gudmund and the other wounded men will stay here as camp guards and you can continue their healing."

"You know that I will not run."

"I know that you will not run until we reach the Blue Sea but this is not a punishment. By healing the men, you are improving our chances of success."

He nodded and looked south, "The land of Aquitaine is rich, Master. You will find more gold there. They are also reputed to have the finest of wines."

"Aye, but we prefer ale or mead, still, if it is richer and we can find another island such as this one then there is no reason why we cannot spend longer further south." I smiled, "I for one enjoy this warm climate."

I had taken to swimming each morning, along with the jarl, and the water was almost warm. It was as we swam that we spoke and I learned more about this warrior who led us. I liked him. I saw that he cared about those who followed him. He was obviously keen to take treasure and become richer, we all were, but he was not reckless about his men. He was concerned about the men who had been wounded and the two who had died. He told me that the dead men's families would be given an equal share of the treasure we collected. I was biased I knew but I preferred Brokkr as a hersir than Erland. I knew that if I had to choose between the jarl and my uncle as a man to follow it would be a hard decision.

One day, as we dressed, he said, "You are the wolf killer and you are like the leader of your pack. The young warriors from Bygstad follow you as though you were born to it."

I shrugged, "I do not see myself as a leader."

He smiled, enigmatically, "And that is the mark of a true leader for it is others who see you as a leader. They will follow you. Do not be afraid to command, Leif Longstride."

With plentiful food and no need to hasten we spent many days on the island. In fact, as Gandalfr said, the longer we remained hidden the more likely it was that the Franks and Aquitanians alike would think that we had returned home. Our sentries on the tower were able to see the coast and we saw no ships there. We did see sails towards the west as an occasional vessel plied the seas further away from the rocky teeth of the coast. Our masts were stepped and the jarl was confident we would not be seen. We were encouraged that there were few ships and that they kept well out to sea. We had a home that was safe.

As Joseph was the one constant at the camp he almost became the steward of our temporary home. The wounded men we were leaving naturally deferred to the man who was looking after them. He would make the decisions about the food that was eaten and the care of the animals. The shelters we had built looked natural but were relatively comfortable. Joseph would use the one my brother and I had built. With our furs and blankets, he would enjoy a comfortable sleep.

We left an hour after the sun had risen. It took time to fit the mast and then we sailed south. We kept the coast a smudge on the larboard horizon. The jarl planned to sail south until not long before dusk and then head into the coast and find a coastal settlement. It was a simple plan and while it would not guarantee great treasure we could ask questions. I had learned enough of the words of the Franks to be able to ask questions. We knew that the people of Aquitaine spoke a slightly different language from that of those who lived north of the Liger but the jarl hoped to learn more about the lands to the south.

We did not need to row and I spent my time with Gandalfr, occasionally taking a turn at the steering board while he ate or made water. What I noticed was that the air was much warmer here than at our home. It was now the middle of Tvímánuður and we had days so hot that many of the men lay naked on the deck. We also had more darkness than we would at home. In a couple of months when the nights at home would grow shorter and colder we would, so Joseph told us, enjoy days and nights that were little different to those we enjoyed now.

"You know, Gandalfr, I wonder why we stay in our fjord. I have noticed that further south, even in Frisia, there is more land to farm than we have at home. The flour we took was wheat. Even the thralls eat the finest of bread."

He nodded, "Yet that is our home, Leif."

"It is not yours, Gandalfr."

He said, "What do you mean?"

"You have no family save Snorri and no ties."

He chuckled, "You are right. When the jarl suggested this extended raid Snorri and I were pleased beyond words. We are happiest at sea and this long voyage is a dream for us. These are new seas and I am learning more about the realm of the sea gods each day. See how the birds and fish are different. We see some that we know but others…I hope that this is the start of something new. I know that men like you and Mikkel who have families will want to spend some time in Bygstad but when we return with riches from the south then more men will want to sail. Who knows, if you remain at home your father might come. He is a good navigator."

I wondered about that. If I stayed in our home then with Birger more experienced, he could leave me to sail the snekke. As I thought about that I knew it would mean taking my family from Lars's farm to Bygstad. My decision to marry had made my life complicated.

When the jarl turned his ship we had to take to the oars. The naked men dressed. Some of them would suffer as their skin was burning red already. We rowed towards the distant line of land. As the sun set behind us, I knew that we would be silhouetted. The jarl seemed to see that problem too and our sails were ordered to be lowered. To anyone watching from the land, it would be as though we had turned or disappeared. We turned to sail a diagonal course. With no flapping, snapping sail the only sounds were the birds above us and the oars as they cut into the water. When the sun had set we sailed in darkness and the young eyes of the lookouts sought the flicker of firelights while older noses sniffed for the smells of wood smoke. The jarl's ship would hear, see and smell a settlement before we did and when the light from the stern of **'Bylgja'** flashed as it was covered and uncovered, we knew that something had been seen. We followed the jarl as he turned his ship towards the land and soon one of our lookouts called, "A light to larboard." We could see nothing for we faced the open sea and so we rowed. It was not a hard pull. The wind was from the north and did not hinder us.

"Slow oars. Odd numbers stack your oars." I was an odd number and Mikkel and I stacked our oars and then returned to our chests. Oddr was an even number and on the steerboard side.

We did not need to be told to prepare to go ashore. I donned my arming cap, helmet, and wolf cloak. After fixing the head to my helmet I slung my shield on my back. It was as I turned that I saw the flickering lights at the shore. There was darkness on either side but ahead and to larboard there were houses. I did not take my spear. The darkness, while it hid us could be a dangerous place for a man armed with a long weapon. I needed a shorter one, a sword and then I could live on my reactions.

When Gandalfr said, "Larboard side, stack your oars," then I knew we would edge in like a crab sideways. I knew how to steer but I had not learned the skill that would enable me to use the steering board to counter the current and the steerboard oars.

'Bylgja' touched first and I heard the splash as the jarl and his warriors leapt ashore. I stood on the gunwale holding the stays. When I saw the flash of white sand and felt *'Ægir'* back a little from the shore I jumped. The water came to my waist but was surprisingly warm. I waded ashore. The jarl and his men had not shouted and I hissed to those who had followed me, "No noise and no shouting. The jarl wants silence." I knew that Oddr would still be aboard the drekar. Someone had to lead. Hallstein had taught me that. As I stepped onto the sand, I saw that there were fishing boats drawn up on the beach and, ahead of us, I saw houses. They looked to be wattle and daub and had been painted white. The shadows of the jarl and his men stood out. I also saw the stone tower. That was unexpected.

The shout that came from above us was from the tower. There was a watch there but he had either been asleep or inattentive or else he would have seen us. I hurried to join the jarl, swinging my shield around as I did so. The arrows that fell from above were poorly loosed. I knew that if I had my bow with me then the archers in the tower would soon die. I did not and so I raised my shield. The arrow that slammed into the leather cover was blindly sent but if had I not raised the shield then it would have hit my left shoulder. It was a warning.

The jarl shouted, "Bygstad, take the tower."

I did not hesitate, "Bygstad with me!"

I turned to run towards the tower which I saw had been built on a spit of rock that jutted out into the sea. It was a large tower and I saw the door facing the land. Our shields protected us and we made the door. Holding our shields above us I tried the door. They might have not been good sentries but the men in the tower had barred it.

Oddr arrived and I saw that he had an axe. He grinned, "Thank you, Leif, I will now take command. Protect me with your shields and I will break it down."

As he began to hack at the door, I heard the screams and shouts from the village as the jarl and his men fell upon the unsuspecting villagers. I guessed that the tower would be used as a refuge but our unexpected arrival had negated that function. Soon not only arrows fell but stones too. They cracked and crashed on our shields but the roof of wood, iron and leather held. With a triumphant cry from Oddr, the door broke open and he shouted, "Leif, lead them within."

With my shield before me, I entered and saw the ladder that led to the upper floors. I would need my right hand to climb and I left my sword in its sheath. With my shield above me, I climbed to the opening above me. I heard Mikkel say, "I am behind you." It was comforting.

The floor above was empty and there was another ladder. The size of the floor confirmed my view that this was a refuge. The whole village could have sheltered within. I headed to the next ladder and said, "This one may be contested."

As I climbed I saw that Dagfinn and Brynjar were close behind Mikkel. When I reached the top of the ladder something cracked hard on my shield. A warrior had hit it with some weapon. I was holding the top of the hatch and although it shook me it did not shake me from my perch. I saw a leg and I took a chance. Grabbing the leg with my right hand I punched the edge of my shield at where I thought the warrior's knee was. I was lucky on both counts. My shield struck him and he toppled. I launched myself through the hatch and landed on him. My body pinned his limbs. He was a big man with a full black beard. He spat at me and tried to push me off. I reached down and tried to draw my seax. As I did, I saw Mikkel and Dagfinn rise through the hatch. I was not alone. My hand found my blade and as the warrior's mouth opened to try to bite off my nose I rammed my dagger under his ribs. I saw his eyes widen and he wriggled to escape the pain. I felt his blood ooze over my hand and I twisted and pushed harder. I felt his severed flesh as my hand entered the gaping wound I had caused. I must have struck something vital for I saw the light leave his eyes. I jumped to my feet and looked around. There were three men dead.

Oddr appeared through the hatch and nodded, "Nils, follow me. Leif, ensure that all here are dead." As the two warriors climbed up it was clear to me that we had killed all the defenders. We searched their bodies and took their weapons and coins. Above us, we heard combat and then Oddr descended. "There were just two archers. You young warriors defeated their warriors. Well done. Now let us join the jarl."

We left the tower and hurried across to the village but there was no need for haste. We had the village. The jarl looked up and smiled, "You took the tower. Good. When I saw that I wondered if we had made a mistake but the men of Bygstad do not disappoint."

Haldir came over, "Jarl, we have found a slave. He is not a Frank and he is one of us, from the north."

He led us to what can only be described as a cell. It was barely big enough for a pig yet a man had been tethered there. Galmr was helping to remove the yoke from around his neck and I saw that he had a stump where his left hand should have been. He was thin, emaciated and his hair seemed to move. His body and head were covered with nits and lice. The jarl said, kindly, "Who are you?"

Haldir said, "Fetch ale, food and a seat."

Oddr shouted, "Secure the village and make sure no one leaves."

The man seemed disorientated and he looked at us as though we were wraiths or ghosts. He smiled and I saw that his mouth had half of his teeth missing. It looked like the graveyard we had seen at Jumièges. He said, "Am I dreaming? Have I entered the Otherworld and see men from my homeland?"

Some of the jarl's crew had obeyed Haldir's command and the jarl helped the one-handed man to the chair they had found. "Drink." He handed the beaker to the man and continued, "I am Jarl Bjørn Haraldsson and we have come from Askvoll. We have come a-viking."

I saw the relief on the man's face as he emptied the beaker. He smiled and held it out. Galmr filled it again. "I am Palle Orlasson, and I was on a Danish knarr that sailed these waters. Our captain, Peder Pedersson, heard of great treasure in the Blue Sea. He was told that he could buy spices for coppers and sell them for silver in Mercia and Wessex." He shook his head and emptied half of the beaker. "That may have been true but all we found were fierce Moors who took our ship and killed half of our crew. We were sold at a slave market." His eyes closed.

"And the others?"

He opened his eyes and shook his head, "I know not. I was sold to a sea captain who traded with the men of Aquitaine. I rowed one of their galleys with other slaves. We were worked hard and many others died but I determined to stay alive, if only to warn others from my homeland that the treasure of the east was too highly-priced to risk taking."

He emptied the beaker and the jarl asked, "Then how do you end up here?"

"We were shipwrecked in a storm. All were drowned but me." He smiled, "I could swim. I found a spar and held on to it and kicked for the coast. I was at sea for two days and almost died but the gods smiled on me and I found myself on the shore. When I landed I hoped that I was saved but I was not. The Moors were hard men but they fed me and ensured I lived. The men of Aquitaine treated me like a beast of burden. When I tried to escape, they chopped off my hand. Had you not come then I do not think I would have survived another month."

The jarl's face hardened, "These people will pay for their cruelty. Is there anything else you can tell us for we can continue to raid?"

He nodded, "Each town and village on this coast has a tower such as the one I think that you must have taken." The jarl nodded. "They are there to guard against the Moors and Saracens. Their ships come to look for slaves. The slavers normally come during the day and people are taken into the tower. You will need to take the towers before you can take their towns. They normally have a night watch of three or four men."

"This one had six."

He frowned, "That is unusual." He shrugged, "I was kept in my pen and there is much I do not know. You do not tell the ass what it is that you do."

"Haldir, take him to my ship."

"Aye, Jarl Bjørn Haraldsson."

"The rest of you take everything from these people and drive them hence. Then we will burn their homes and their boats."

The jarl was not a cruel man by nature but their treatment of a man saved from the sea angered him. It was dawn when we returned to our ships and the pall of smoke from the burning village rose high in the sky.

We headed west, out to sea. There were watchers on the shore and the jarl wanted them to think we were heading home. We used the sails and rested on the deck, enjoying the warm sun. I must have fallen asleep for I was shaken awake by Falco, "Leif, Gandalfr would speak to you."

I rose and made my way astern. He pointed to *'Bylgja'* which lay under reefed sails. "The jarl wishes us to speak. I need you on the steering board while I do so." He smiled, "I will take us close. All you need to do is to hold us against the current." I nodded nervously. I did not wish to damage either drekar. Gandalfr had great skill. I knew that no matter how long I sailed I could not match him as a sailor. We barely touched the side of the other ship. I could feel the current from the sea and I held the board to keep us pressed close.

"I have spoken with Palle, he is sleeping now. He says that there is a bigger town just down from the one we raided. It is called Allionis. I intend to raid it and then return to our island. It is due east of us. We will use the same method we did the last time." Oddr had joined Gandalfr and the jarl continued, "Palle says that they have a tower. I want you to land north of the town. Palle says that there is a headland. Land warriors to take the tower so that it cannot alert the villagers. The last time the men in the tower were lax. We cannot rely on such luck a second time." Oddr nodded and the jarl pointed at me, "Send Leif Longstride and his wolves. They have skill and luck."

Oddr nodded, "Aye, Jarl, and then what do we do?"

"Follow me. We will head back out to sea and approach the town from the west. Snorri has the course set. We will lead you. Reef the sail and row in. Let Leif and his men prepare."

I gathered the others around me. There would be just five of us. I saw Birger looking enviously at me but I could not risk my little brother. The jarl had said to lead and now he had commanded me to do so.

"There are few of us but we know, from the first tower, that they do not have a large number of men. I will take my bow and we need an axe in case they have barred the door."

Dagfinn said, "I will take an axe in case we have to break down a door."

Gunvald snorted, "They would be fools to leave open the door to a tower."

"You heard what Palle said, the raiders normally come in daylight or at dawn. If they have not been raided for a while then they will grow lax."

We prepared. I would not wear my byrnie, and neither would Mikkel. We needed silence and speed. Mail would slow us and the jingling alert the men in the tower. The men we might fight would not be mailed. Guided by Palle's knowledge we edged towards the coast, and we landed at a secluded piece of sand. We were close enough to the first place we had raided to see the tendrils of smoke still lingering in the sky. The jarl had said that he would land us three miles from the tower and as soon as we landed I led the five of us up the dunes to take shelter there. I strung my bow and slung it over my back. I had left my shield on the drekar. I pointed south. "I will lead, Brynjar, stay at the rear. You have sharp ears and a quick mind." He nodded, "Gunvald, will your leg hold?"

He snorted, "Do not worry about me, Leif Longstride. I will keep pace with you."

"Then do so." I set off and headed to the east. The sand sucked at our feet and would tire us. I sought and found a sort of road or track that ran parallel to the sea. It was easier going and less tiring. We loped along at a steady pace. The whistle from behind made me stop and turn. Brynjar was frantically signalling. He was signing that we had men coming along the track. There was a low wall on one side of the track and I waved for us all to take shelter. I walked through the willow gate and the others jumped over. We saw pasture and a small flock of sheep. The sheep moved to the far side of the field. The wall was there to give them shelter from the sea.

Brynjar said, breathlessly, when he joined us, "There are riders coming from the north. I heard their horses."

"Did they see you?"

"I think not."

I thought quickly, "There were no horses in the place we burned. My guess is that these men were sent to investigate. They must be on their way back. We have to stop them or else the next place we raid will be warned."

They nodded and, as we heard the sound of hooves, they drew their swords and, in Dagfinn's case, an axe. I nocked an arrow. Timing was all. I heard the hooves and the conversation from the men as they approached. Their words were a mumble but a mumble that grew as they neared us. I had no idea of the numbers, but I had the bow. I hurried to the willow gate and, pulling it open, stepped out. I was raising my bow as I did so. I saw four men on small horses. They had helmets and spears but no shields. At a range of twenty paces, I could not miss but, seeing me, and no doubt forewarned by the survivors from the north, they galloped towards us. Even as I pulled back, I took in that they had no stirrups. The warrior I hit was less than ten paces from me when my arrow slammed into his chest. As he fell backward his dead hand clutched the reins and his horse fell. They effectively blocked the track and my four companions had the easiest of tasks to slay the other three.

The Norns had been spinning. "Mikkel, secure the horses. The rest of you take their helmets and weapons. We will pretend to be these men returning from the north."

Gunvald said, "We do not look like them. We are bigger and there are five of us."

Brynjar sighed and began to strip one of the dead, "Leif is right. One of us can dismount and if we ride in from the dark then the deception will work."

I had already decided that I would be the one who would dismount. I had my bow. I used my knife to dig out the arrow. The shaft was whole and who knew when I might need an arrow.

"I will ride behind Mikkel. Keep a steady pace and," I smiled, "try not to fall off." I did not wear one of the helmets taken from the riders. I retained mine.

The delay we had incurred in the ambush was soon made up by the speed of the small horses. It was not comfortable but we only had a couple of thousand paces or so to go. We stopped when I saw the smoke from the village and we dismounted to walk until we could see the tower. The sun was setting in the west but there was no sign of our ships. They would wait until dark before approaching. We had time.

"I will get closer to the tower. Wait until the sun has dropped below the horizon and then ride in."

"What if we are challenged?"

"Just wave. I will be there to end the threat. We need to get into the tower."

Mikkel said, "We will not let you down, Leif Longstride."

"I know."

I held my bow and an arrow, a fresh one, as I made my way, using whatever cover I could find, towards the distant tower. I was less than a thousand paces away and as the sun had yet to set I had time. The town was much larger than the village we had raided. There was a jetty and not only were fishing boats drawn up but a small trading vessel much like a knarr, fat-bellied and short. I saw a rock which would afford me cover. It was less than fifty paces from the tower and, more importantly, was close to the door. I saw two men on the top. One looked north and I waited. As soon as he turned to look west, to the setting sun, I ran. I made the rock and slid behind its bulk. I did not peer around straightaway. There was no point. Instead, I looked west. I had an unobstructed view of the sea. At home the sun set slowly, often taking almost an hour to disappear. Here I noticed that once the sun began to set, its movement was visible. As soon as the sun was poised on the horizon I risked peering over the rock. The men were looking west. I nocked an arrow. When the sun did set it was as though someone had doused a candle. It was then I heard the hooves. I did not raise my head again. They would be looking in my direction. I heard a shouted challenge. I could not be certain, but I think it was something like *'who goes there?'*

An unintelligible reply came from Mikkel. It was made up of Frankish words but it was nonsense. I slowly stood and drew back my bow. I saw one of the sentries drawing back on his bow. I loosed and even while the arrow was in the air, nocked another. I hit the man in the shoulder and my arrow drew the eye of the second sentry. He shouted the alarm. We had known that was inevitable and everything depended on the speed of my four companions. My second arrow was seen and the archer ducked. The arrow flew over the top of the tower. Nocking a third arrow I ran to the door. Mikkel made it first and he threw himself from the back of his horse and entered. Brynjar had the wit to slap the rumps of the horses which raced towards the nearest houses. The others quickly followed Mikkel. I heard the clash of steel. I ran to the door and peered at the horses. A man with a sword led a band of men towards the tower. I sent an arrow at him and struck him in the shoulder. I entered the tower and barred it. I hurried up the ladder. When I reached the top it was over. The four sentries were dead. I had incapacitated one and the others had not been able to withstand the four fierce Norsemen who suddenly appeared.

Dagfinn pointed out to the sea, "I see the drekars!"

I then heard the sound of axes from below. "Gunvald, pull up the last ladder. There are two bows here and rocks, let us use them."

I took the arrow from the dead man and nocked it. I went to the side of the tower near to the door and sent my arrow into the mass of men who were trying to hack through the door. Unlike the rest of our men, they were not using shields and I was rewarded by a cry. The hammering stopped as they scrambled for shields. Dagfinn and Brynjar had the two bows they had found in the tower and they joined me in sending arrows at the men below.

The jarl had not planned it this way and I knew that the Norns had been spinning. Mikkel shouted, "The jarl has landed. Our men are ashore."

The warriors attacking the tower could not see what we could see and when Jarl Bjørn Haraldsson led the men of Askvoll and Bygstad to fall upon the rear of the men attacking their own tower then the battle was over in minutes.

Mikkel bowed, "Leif Longstride, you are a leader and we will follow you anywhere." The other three clapped me on the back too. It was a victory. A surprising one but a victory nonetheless.

Chapter 21

The five of us were lauded as heroes. Despite the size of the town, we learned it was called Allionis, our men had taken it without a loss. As the jarl said, when we ate in the large house of the warrior who had led the men to attack the tower, "Had we lost a man I would have been surprised as we attacked men in the rear. Thanks to you five their attention was on the tower. You shall all receive the same share from this raid as Snorri and Gandalfr."

I was not sure we deserved it and we had not been in much danger but we smiled and accepted the reward. It was the richest place that we had raided outside of Jumièges and there was treasure in abundance. The church was richly endowed. It was said that the Duke of Aquitaine often visited. The house of the luedes, we learned the title from Palle, also yielded silver and even a little gold. There was a fine mail byrnie and good weapons. We were given our choice of weapons and I took a sword. It was better than the one Lars had given me but I would continue to use Lars'; it would be unlucky not to do so. The sword of Aquitaine would be kept for when I wished to look my best. We had animals too. As much as the horses would be useful we did not take them but freed them. We butchered the bull and two cows that we found and put their meat in barrels of brine. We took the bones to use on our island. We also took the small trading vessel. Crewed by Haldir and four men it helped to carry some of our treasure.

This time, when we left, we headed down the coast. The jarl was a clever man. Sailing down the coast would give us the chance to see further targets whilst also duping the men of Aquitaine. We passed between the mainland and the island of Oléron. Palle knew all the names of the places and they were added to our map. Men watched us impotently from both the island and the mainland but all they could do was watch. We were too far from bows. We took it slowly so that the jarl and his navigators could inspect the channel. We headed south to another mighty estuary. We were not privy to the conversation but we watched the jarl, Snorri and Palle as they pointed and gesticulated at the estuary. When the jarl turned and pointed to the west Gandalfr and I knew that we would be heading back to our island sanctuary. We had seen dwellings on both the island and the mainland. The estuary promised much. We sailed much further west than we had before. Perhaps Palle had told the jarl that it was safe to do so. Whatever the reason it was pitch black and we were hidden from view as we turned north and followed the light hanging from *'Bylgja's'* stern.

We did not sail as fast north as we had south. We had a small trader with us and the winds did not cooperate. We had to row frequently. Added to that we saw a more unpleasant side to the climate and a storm blew in from the west. A sheep was lost overboard as well as four fowl. When we finally reached our home all three ships would need repairs. There was nothing major but before we headed south again to raid the lands we had seen we would need to make our ships seaworthy and ready to face Ran's wrath once more.

Our wounded had been healed and both Joseph and our men were happy to see us. Once ashore the jarl asked Joseph to tend to Palle. He had improved much since he had been with us but Joseph tut-tutted and spent half a day examining the former slave and tending to his hurts. It was then I learned the names of the islands and the estuary. There were two rivers, the Dordogne and Garonne. They fed into the estuary of the Gironde. Palle said it was like a small sea. There was a large port on the south bank of the river. It was in Vasconian land and was called Bordèu. Palle had never been there but he had heard stories of its riches and I knew that the jarl would want to raid.

I also learned that there were no real winters in this part of the world. That confirmed what Joseph had told us but coming from a sailor was more reassuring. Brynjar said, "Then why do we need to sail home at Gormánuður? We could spend a year here."

Mikkel shook his head, "Leif and I have wives. Leif has a child he has never seen and I hope that I have fathered one."

Brynjar shrugged, "This raid should be for those without families."

I smiled, "And if that was the case then we would only have one ship. Speaking to Palle I know that Bordèu might be too big a morsel for just two ships. He says we would need a fleet."

Dagfinn liked his food and we had just enjoyed some of the beef we had taken in the raid. He was licking his fingers and said, "When we return home, Brynjar, then we will have captains clamouring to accompany us."

Brynjar nodded, "I suppose."

We spent another week repairing our ships. As we worked on the hull, painting pine tar on a seam that had split, Dagfinn said, "By my reckoning, it is Haustmánuður and yet it does not feel like that. It is so hot it feels like Heyannir. Perhaps Brynjar is right and we could stay longer."

I shook my head, "Even with the trader we have holds that are almost full. It might be that we should leave now."

Gandalfr was supervising the work and he gave me a sad smile, "The jarl wants to raid for six months and six months it will be. Even if we do not raid we will explore the seas so that when we return we have a better idea of what we can take. The earliest that we will leave will be Ýlir."

As Palle's health improved so did his conversations with Gandalfr, the jarl and Snorri. As another of the navigators, I was privy to those conversations. He asked if he could sail the trader. That made sense to us all and gave the jarl an idea. "We could send the trader back with the animals we do not need and some of the treasure. It would give our people news and hope. He could also visit Lord Arne. I am sure that my cousin would like to have some of this honey pot we have discovered. Even with a depleted crew his ship could help us."

Snorri said, "A good idea but you would need to send someone back with Palle who could speak to Lord Arne."

The jarl nodded, "One of my hearth-weru."

"And," I added, "a crew."

They looked at me, "You, perhaps, Leif?"

I shook my head, "As much as I wish to see my wife and child I promised to stay until the end but there are others, Mikkel, perhaps, who might choose to go home. The trader and Palle would need to be protected."

Palle grinned. His half-empty mouth made me smile back, "I have been taken once, my friend and it will not happen again. This trader is not as capacious as a knarr but it is fast. I want to get back to the north. I am beholden to all of you and if I can help you by sailing your ship to Askvoll then I swear I will do so."

Gandalfr asked, "And then what?"

"I have had enough of warm seas and inhospitable Franks. I will sail the seas of home and spend my winters in a longhouse."

"Then you can sail this trader for me and have a home in Askvoll." With that decided the jarl offered four berths in the trader. He commanded Bjarni to be one, Mikkel was a second, Gudmund a third and Sigurd, who came from Askvoll and whose wife was also due to give birth was the fourth. The jarl sent some of his treasure as well as the two pigs. The sow had given birth and the eight piglets who had been born were now weaned and we could raise or eat them. The three men also took their treasure and Birger and I gave some of our treasure for Mikkel to give to our families. They left just as we were preparing to head south to raid once more. We waved the trader off and I saw that Palle was a good sailor for he almost made the trader skip the waves.

We would head, not to Bordèu, for we needed more ships to take that juicy plum, but further south, to explore the coast where Palle had told us there lay prizes worth taking. We now had two maps that had considerably more detail than before. Poor Joseph did not want to be left alone but we were now getting short of men and until Lord Arne joined us, he would have to care for the animals.

This time, when we left, Gandalfr kept me by the steering board. Mikkel had returned home and rather than having an unbalanced feel to the drekar, I would act as helmsman under the supervision of the navigator. It suited me and as we had discovered we did not have to use the oars too often. It also allowed Gandalfr to study the new map and to add his own marks upon it. As I was there when he made them I would also know what they meant.

Palle had told us of a port that lay to the south. It was, he said, a large one and there were old Roman walls that afforded protection. The jarl believed the sailor but wanted to see for himself. Gandalfr confided in me that the jarl preferred to believe his own eyes. Bayonne lay in the small kingdom of Labourd and lay at the mouth of a river. A river was always tempting although Palle had said that there was a bridge across it.

Before we reached the port and a day or so after we had passed the Gironde estuary, we came upon a huge bay with the largest sand dune I have ever seen. The forests that bordered the bay excited Gandalfr. "See how straight the trees are, Leif. If we needed to build a drekar or to repair one then there is the place to come. You have younger eyes, are there people there?"

He took the steering board and I climbed up to stand on the gunwale and grab a backstay. I shaded my eyes, "There are boats drawn up on the beaches but just a handful of houses. It does not look to be worth raiding."

When we reached Bayonne, Palle was proved to be correct. The Roman bridge across the river just beyond the port prevented passage upstream and they not only had a watch tower but stone walls on a citadel. We could raid it but not without Lord Arne. We continued south. Gandalfr made many marks on the map.

When the coast turned to head west then we knew where we were. Palle had told us that this was the land of Vasconia. It was part of Charlemagne's empire and ruled by a Duke. That made it a place worth raiding. We sailed slowly along the coast identifying features and places. We raided but once.

After a week of sailing, we found a secluded beach. We had not passed any settlement for half a day. There was a fine pine forest that rose just beyond the beach and the jarl chose to land there. While the ship's boys and younger warriors sought shellfish, Oddr led the older warriors to hew down some of the pine trees. They could be taken to our island home and seasoned. They would make good masts. The jarl gathered his hearth-weru and his navigators, along with me, to study the maps.

"This looks to be a coastline that is worth raiding."

Haldir said, "But not without a third ship, Jarl."

The jarl smiled, "You are right, not without a third ship. There was one place we passed through." He pointed a finger, "Just twelve or so miles from Bayonne."

Gandalfr nodded, "A fishing port as I recall. We passed between the fishing fleet and the port."

The jarl nodded, "And that is why I thought to raid. I do not think that the people of this part of the world have seen ships such as ours. In Frankia they know what the dragon prow means but here? We did not harm them when we sailed through. I propose that we approach at dusk and follow the fishing boats in. They will be laden and the fishermen tired. We have almost exhausted our supplies. Whatever we find today will augment what we have but it is more than a week back to our island."

The other three all nodded their agreement.

The jarl said, "Leif, what do you think?"

I was taken aback, "I did not think you wished for my opinion, Jarl."

"Of course, I do. You are becoming a navigator and everyone can see that you have the skills of a leader. Men follow you. Your father could have been the hersir instead of Erland."

I had learned that the jarl had a very low opinion of Erland and had been more than happy that he had been ousted.

"Then I think it is a juicy target. We can fill our hold with food and there may be treasure." I smiled, "Who knows we may find another Palle or Joseph. Those two have proved to be as valuable as gold or silver."

The others nodded and the jarl said, "And you have wisdom beyond your years. When you slew the wolf its spirit must have entered yours."

I found myself clutching my Hammer of Thor. He was right. The slaying of the wolf had been the start of my life as a warrior. Before my spear had taken the wolf I had been no different from my brothers or any other young man in the village, but after that I had shown skills that I did not know I possessed.

We spent two days in the bay and collected not only timber and shellfish but also animals hunted in the forest. The four long pieces of timber were stacked in the middle of the two ships and secured. The smaller branches were taken too as kindling for our island home. Summer was almost passed and if we had to spend longer in these waters then we would need fuel for fires.

When we left to sail back to the island then everyone knew what they had to do. As I took a watch on the steering board and while Gandalfr slept I watched Birger as he rowed. His back was already a little broader and his hands were calloused and hard. The voyage had changed my little brother. He had killed men and he had fought. He had proved that he was no Axel Erlandsson. Like me, he could never go back to a mundane life in Bygstad. I knew that the sea and the lure of raiding would always draw me away from my home. My father and Brokkr had done the same when they were young men. Their rewards had not been as great as ours. I knew that when we returned all of us would be rich and others would envy us. It was one thing to envy and quite another to emulate. As Axel had shown, not every man was born to be a warrior.

Gandalfr knew exactly where we were and when the jarl had his sails reefed, he nodded, "We are close to where we should find the fishing fleet. Oddr, oars."

"Find your oars and take your places."

Every man on the ship now had a favourite oar and they each took the one they liked. I do not think that there was a great deal of difference in any of them but I knew that a man pulled harder with an oar he liked. When the jarl completely reefed his sail so did we. The ship's boys perched precariously on the yard would be able to spot the fishing fleet and with our sails reefed we would be almost invisible.

It was Falco who shouted down, "I see the fishing boats."

I said, "The jarl has stopped rowing."

Gandalfr shouted, "Raise oars."

We bobbed uncomfortably on the water. *'Ægir'* was a restless beast and liked to keep moving. We had to wait until *'Bylgja'* moved again before we could row. I glanced to the west. The sun was setting. The days were marginally shorter but not by much. Soon it would be the end of Haustmánuður and at Bygstad that meant everyone would be preparing for winter. Once Gormánuður was over then the frosts, snows and shorter days would be upon us.

I turned and saw the oars of *'Bylgja'* dip into the sea. Gandalfr shouted, "Oars in the water. A steady pace, Oddr."

We were stalking the fishing fleet. The fishermen would not be watching the west. They would be doing what my father and two brothers would be doing on the fjord. They would anticipate reaching home and a freshly cooked meal. They would be almost tasting the ale that would take away the taste of salt and the sea. They would not know that a pair of wolves from the sea was stalking them. The sun had almost dipped below the horizon when we saw the two beacons burning at the entrance to the harbour. Stones had been used to make a breakwater and two fires were burning having been lit on the arms. We had not seen that on our outward voyage but now I saw that it helped us enormously. If there were men watching the sea then they would have their night vision ruined by the two fires.

Gandalfr said, "I can steer this part. Arm yourself, Leif."

I went to my chest. My routine was familiar now and I was ready for the raid within moments. I did not need mail and the spear would be an encumbrance. We would not need a shield wall. I slung my shield across my back but I doubted that I would need it. I went to the prow and stood holding a forestay and the figurehead. I hoped that mighty Ægir would bring me luck and keep me safe.

As soon as we passed through the two breakwaters we were seen and there was a shout. The twang of an arrow and a scream silenced the voice but the hens knew we were in the henhouse and a cacophony of noise rose from the small village. I heard the crunch of crushed timbers as **'*Bylgja*'** smashed over a fishing boat and its crew. The Norns were spinning for that one accident allowed us to be the first into the harbour. Gandalfr laid us next to three fishing boats. They must have been the first to land for they were empty.

I jumped down and landed on the catch that still remained in the bottom of the boat. The jarl and the others saw me as a leader, and I led. I jumped from the boat to the quay and waited for others to join me. They had to arm themselves. Four fishermen ran at me. They must have hurried to collect weapons. Others would be following. They had spears, swords and axes. I swung my shield around and drew my sword.

Behind me, I heard Brynjar shout, "Hurry, Leif is alone."

Oddr added, "Bygstad, on me!"

I concentrated on the four fishermen. I was under no illusions. They might not be warriors but they would be strong and intent on defending their homes. The axe could hurt me more than the other weapons but it would be the spear that would strike me first. I held my shield at an angle and as the spear struck it turned the shield and then slashed at the man with the axe. My sword was sharp and I hacked through the fingers of his right hand. The weapon fell to the ground as he tried to staunch the bleeding with his left. The two men with the swords swung them simultaneously at my head. Taking in that the man with the spear was pulling back for another strike I did what they did not expect. I dropped my knee, slashing sideways with my sword as I did so. I was rewarded when I struck flesh. The two swords clashed and then caught my helmet while the spear pushed against my shield. Dagfinn's sword hacked into the arm of the spearman while Brynjar and Gunvald slew the two swordsmen. The axeman ran off, clutching his maimed hand.

Oddr shouted, "Wedge!"

The men with spears went to the fore and my shield brothers and I filled the middle. Oddr pointed his spear and led us down the quay to the village. The handful of men who stood before us stood no chance. Oddr and the ones at the fore simply bowled into them. When we reached the houses we found that the villagers had fled.

The jarl shouted orders and the village was secured. "Search the houses and then load the drekars."

By the time the sun rose we had taken all the fish that the fishermen had caught and emptied the houses of bread, food and coins. There were few coins and no animals. The men who had stood before Oddr had ensured that the bulk of the village could escape. Many had gone to the tower where they stood and cursed us. They could not harm us and the jarl chose not to reduce the tower. There was no need. By noon we had the ships loaded and with the tide in our favour left to sail back to the island. This time it did not matter if they saw the direction that we took and we sailed due north, taken by a wind that blew from the south and west. It was a fresh wind and the clouds that followed it promised rain.

It took a week to reach the island. Joseph looked mightily relieved to see us. He had to have been busy as, in our absence, he had to care for the animals we had taken. We emptied the ships and took ashore the timbers to season. We enjoyed a hot meal and the wine we had taken from the fishing village.

Norse Warrior

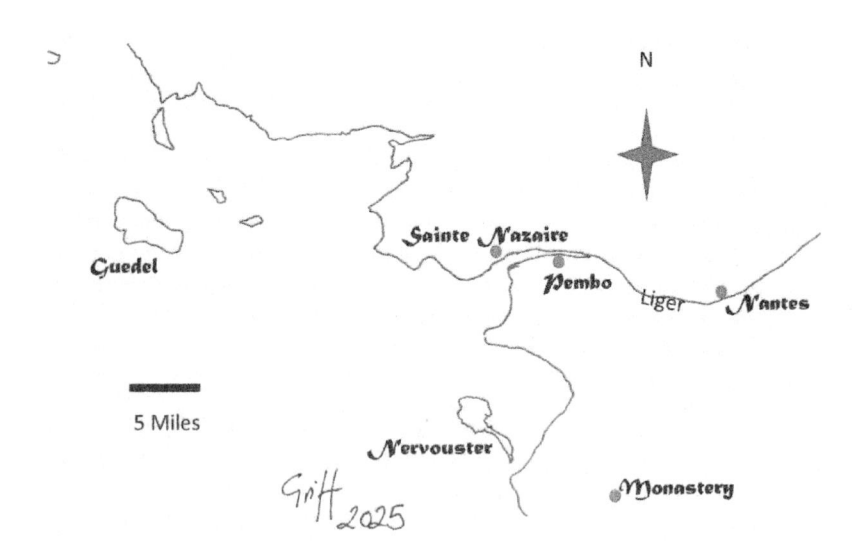

5 Miles

Guedel · Sainte Nazaire · Pembo · Liger · Nantes · Nervouster · Monastery

Chapter 22

A week after we had returned to the island the jarl held a Thing. He did so because there had been grumbling from some of the men of Askvoll. They wondered why, as our holds were full, we did not return to the fjord. The jarl wanted the Thing to decide in his favour and before we spoke, he gave a feast. Two of the pigs were slaughtered and he had the last of the captured catch cooked too. Joseph had become adept, in our absence, at cooking flatbread on hot stones and there was more than enough thanks to the sacks of flour we had captured at the fishing village.

We drank the last of the wine and the jarl began. "I have called this Thing because I have heard murmurings." He shrugged, "I do not know why this is so. When we planned this voyage, I said we would be away for six months and thus far it has been but three or four months. Why do we need to run home? Do you relish snow and ice?"

Jens Folkesson spoke. He was from Askvoll and was an older warrior with three young children, "No, Jarl, but our holds are full and we are just enjoying life here. Our families need us."

"You know that our people at home will not see any family suffering and, true, we have full holds but there is still silver to be had. That silver will not be put in the hold but in your chests."

Kåre Karlsson shook his head, "But we do not have enough men yet to take places that have churches. Men have returned home, and we have lost warriors. Perhaps we can come back next year with more ships."

There were nods and murmurs of approval from many men. I noticed that the men of Bygstad appeared to be undecided. I would happily return home but being one who might be needed to navigate I would abide by the wishes of the majority.

The jarl said, "The trader that we sent home should have reached there a couple of weeks ago. If Lord Arne is to return, he cannot be here for another two weeks. Will you wait until then?"

This caused some debate. Joseph sidled next to me. He did not want us to return home, I knew that and I wondered what he would say. He whispered in my ear. He knew he had no right to speak at the Thing for he was a slave, a valued one but a slave nonetheless.

"Master, one night when the sea was silent and the wind came from the east I heard the sound of a bell tolling. I believe it was for Lauds."

"A church?"

"A monastery, Master. Why else would a bell toll in the middle of the night and then suddenly stop?"

I spoke loudly, above the murmurings, "Jarl, Joseph thinks that there is a monastery on the mainland. He heard it in the night."

Ketill Madsson said, "When I stood a watch, I thought I heard a bell in the night. I told myself I was overtired, but the healer may be right."

There might be a doubt about the word of a thrall but a warrior was a different matter.

The jarl seized upon the words much like a hungry hawk grabs a fat pigeon. "Then let us raid this church and see what it yields."

The clamour of approval made the jarl smile. He nodded to me and mouthed, *'Thank you.'*

I was, of course, involved in the planning; neither Joseph nor Ketill could be specific about the direction of the bells except that it came from the east. Haldir was the practical one. "It is simple, Jarl, we land before sunset and head east. We know that the churches of the White Christ ring every few hours. If we are on the mainland and do not have the sound of the surf between us and the church, then we will hear it."

This time the jarl left warriors at the camp. He was worried that men on the mainland might become suspicious about the two strange ships and investigate. Joseph could not stop them and so four men were selected by lot to deter any fisherman who might choose to investigate the smoke coming from a deserted island.

We sailed around the island to approach the land from the north. We rowed and the mast was stepped. Oddr joked that we could have walked across the channel. I doubted that but he made us laugh. He was a good leader. We landed as the sun set behind our island and, as with the camp we had left, we had two warriors who would stay behind with the boys and the two navigators to watch our ships. We had not seen any people on the shore of the mainland but this was no time to be careless. This was a land of pine trees and small streams. The streams did not slow us but until we could find a way through it would be slow going. We found a path that headed east and followed it, slowly. No one, not even the jarl, wore mail. We wanted nothing to jingle. We stopped frequently. We had only a rough idea of when a church would ring its bells but the further east we were the better chance we had of finding it.

Suddenly, we heard the sound of bells. It seemed close but we knew that was an illusion. It was slightly south of the path and we backtracked half a mile to the place where we had passed another path heading south. The bells had stopped but as the path we were taking appeared to lead in the direction we had heard them we continued. Haldir was leading and when he stopped and held up his hand we knew that he had found something. The jarl went forward and the two of them disappeared through the trees.

They came back and the jarl drew Oddr and me to one side, "There is a monastery ahead. The wall is not high but there may be another entrance. Take the men of Bygstad and find the other side. We will count to two hundred and then we will attack."

"Aye, Jarl."

Oddr waved at the men and, with shields slung over our backs, we ran off through the trees. It was dark but our eyes were accustomed to it and when we saw the trees becoming lighter to our right we moved towards them. We saw the walls of the monastery. They were made of wood but we could spy a stone tower beyond it. The tower would be a church of the White Christ. Encouraged we moved through the eaves of the trees and turned around the end of the building. Oddr pointed and I nodded. There was another gate. Oddr signalled for us to prepare and we drew swords. As soon as we heard a scream in the night we ran at the gate. Two of our men had axes and they made short work of the bar that held it closed. Oddr signalled for two young warriors, Birger was one of them, to watch the gate and we hurried inside.

Chaos and mayhem ruled. The monks had no idea that a warband of Norsemen was raiding. They fled from the swords and that meant they ran into us. I had never felt good about slaying men who could not fight back and I used the flat of my sword to render them unconscious. I estimate that there were no more than twenty or so monks for, within a very short space of time there was no movement. The monks were either dead or unconscious. We stripped the buildings of everything, including the bells which represented huge pieces of metal that Alfr could use again. There were silver and gold platters and candlesticks. This was not a poor order. We also found fine food and spices as well as wine. As we left the monastery, with some of the monks awaking from their enforced sleep, we were all laden.

As we trekked back Birger complained, "I had no opportunity to fight. Next time I wish to fight."

Brynjar laughed, "Fight? The servants of the White Christ have no weapons and they simply implore us to let them live. I do not like the work but I appreciate the rewards."

Dagfinn said, "Once more, Leif, we are in the debt of Joseph. But for his sharp ears…"

We reached our camp an hour or so after dawn. The monastery had been no more than ten miles from the coast. The monks had not expected to be raided. At the back of my mind was a nagging thought that if this Frankish Emperor and his lords hated we barbarians so much then they might do something to rid their land of us. We were the infestation in their clothes and there was just one way to rid themselves of us. I expected retribution.

The raid, the sharing of the treasure and a spell of very pleasant weather assuaged the mood of the camp. Chests needed to be rearranged to accommodate that which we had found. I spoke to the jarl of my fears, that the Franks would seek to rid themselves of us and, remarkably, he heeded my words. He sent the ships' boys to collect shellfish from the mainland side of the island and had the men on the tower be even more vigilant.

Two weeks after the raid we were discovered or, rather, the Franks sent ships to look for us. It was the boys collecting shellfish who ran back to tell us that there were three small Frankish ships sailing from the north. The tower was hidden from the mainland. We knew that for when we had returned from the raid we had not seen it.

The jarl acted quickly and commanded both ships to be manned and launched. While men hurried there he said to Snorri, Gandalfr and me, "We need to keep this camp a secret. When my cousin comes then it will not matter for we will sail south and raid, but for now we must remain hidden from view.

The jarl took us north and west. The inhabited island, Guedel, we had first seen lay to the north of us. We had avoided passing close by it. When Palle had left for home he had been commanded to sail as far to the west as he could to avoid being seen. Now the jarl chose to take the mainland passage and sail close to the island of Guedel. He wanted them to sound the alarm and, perhaps, follow us north. He was trying to make the men of this area think that we had raided and were returning home. We had enjoyed a week of leisure and now we would put our efforts into outsailing those who hunted us. Our lookouts watched ahead, behind and to the land. The sails were full and billowing. They would be seen. The peeling bells on the large island told us that we had been identified as raiders. The jarl was hoping that the sound would carry across the sea to the three small ships that were hunting us. We had no oars out and I stood at the steering board.

"I know that Erd has good eyes, but you are a navigator, Leif, watch to the south and let me know when you see a sail. This is a fine idea that the jarl has but we have put our head perilously close to the bear's mouth. If this channel is closed to us then we could be trapped. I do not fear these small Frankish ships but if they trap us then their numbers could overwhelm us."

I nodded and turned. Erd was at the larboard side of the stern and I went to the steerboard side. I steadied myself and concentrated on seeking a flash of white above the southern horizon. It was as we neared the mouth of the Liger that I saw the flash of white. I waited until I could confirm it was a sail before I said, "I see them, Gandalfr."

At the same time the masthead lookout called, "Two ships to steerboard. They are leaving the mouth of the river."

The channel between the mainland and the island was wide. Gandalfr thought it was more than twenty miles but we had not sailed it. We had skirted the island by sailing to the west on our passage south. We had no idea if there were rocks. We knew there were two small islands but they were uninhabited. We knew that from our first raid with Lord Arne.

Gandalfr looked at the masthead pennant. We had the wind. He rubbed his salt-rimmed beard, "If the wind holds then we will outrun them. When we pass the island the jarl can head north and west. The winds will take us from these ships and then we can return to our camp." He chuckled, "I hope Joseph is preparing a feast for after a day at sea we shall be hungry."

I kept my eyes astern and I said, "There are three of them."

Gandalfr grunted. They would also have the wind, but Frankish ships were wider in the beam than we were. Lean and hungry like hunting dogs, we could outrun anything in these waters.

"Three ships coming from the river."

The rest of the crew were standing to steerboard to watch the ships approaching from the river. Gandalfr just said, "Six, eh?" He looked at the sail. "We could get more speed out of her. I do not think the jarl would mind if we began to overtake him, eh?" He winked and shouted, "Take the last reef out."

He eased the steering board over as the ship's boys ceased their lookout duties and took the last reef from the sail. We had never yet used the full power of *'Ægir'* as we had followed in the wake of *'Bylgja'*. Now we began, slowly, to overhaul the older ship. The landings on shingle beaches had scoured the drekar of any weed that had tried to cling to our bottom and the keel was almost as clean as when the drekar was launched. By the time we reached the southern tip of the inhabited island, we were almost level with *'Bylgja'*.

"Leif, take the steering board." I did so and he went to the steerboard gunwale and, cupping his hands said, "There are three astern and three to steerboard."

The jarl's voice drifted over to us, "Aye, you take the lead. When we are clear of the island take us north and west."

"Aye, Jarl." Gandalfr was a good sailor. I was honoured to be learning from him. Relieved of any guilt about his decision he took the steering board and said, "Let us make this giant fly, eh?" He had told me that he felt the ship living beneath his feet. He almost sniffed the air and while I detected nothing, he did and he put the steering board over a touch. I do not know how he sensed it but he must have found an extra gust for we almost leapt forward and, within a few moments, we were half a length ahead of *'Bylgja'*. The crew cheered. It was almost like a game.

Falco's voice came like a dose of icy water from the fjord, "Three ships to larboard. They are leaving a small harbour."

Gandalfr frowned. Hounds were hunting us. Just as I had hunted the wolf so they had finally acted to stop us. In many ways, Gandalfr's decision to speed up had paid off. We had seen the three ships before the jarl. He said, "Leif, tell the jarl."

This was no time for the apprentice to take the helm. Gandalfr needed to concentrate. I went to the steerboard side and, cupping my hands shouted, "Three ships coming from the island!" I pointed to emphasise my words. The jarl waved his acknowledgement.

Oddr shouted, "Arm yourselves." He had seen that with ships coming from the west we would have to sail close to the unknown rocks and islands to the east. The dogs were closing on us.

Gandalfr said, "Arm yourself, Leif. We may have to fight yet."

"Do you want your helmet?"

He laughed, "I have older eyes and need to see everything. Go. I am the helmsman and you are a warrior."

I hurried to my chest and took out my helmet and sword. I also took and strung my bow. Even as I did so I heard Falco cry out, "Two more ships from the north."

The trap was being closed and we were surrounded. That was a potential disaster. The ones from the island did not have the wind but our slight change in course had slowed us slightly. The six who were chasing us would be gaining and the ones ahead just had to make a barrier.

Brynjar said to Birger, "Now you may have a fight on your hands, Birger Eiriksson."

I grabbed my shield and slung it over my back. I smiled at my brother whose face showed his fear, "Do not worry, Birger, Gandalfr is the greatest navigator. He will get us from this trap."

As I hurried to the steering board, I saw that *'Bylgja'* was also prepared. There were no shields along the sides. Her warriors were preparing to fight.

Gandalfr shouted, "Falco, can you see rocks ahead?"

He had the best view for he was straddling the yard. He shouted down, "No, Gandalfr, but the ships ahead are beam on and they have lowered their sails."

I said, "Lowered their sails?"

Gandalfr knew what that meant, "These are their waters and they know them better than we do. They are making a barrier to stop us."

Just then Erd, who was on the larboard side, shouted, "Fishing boats putting off from the island."

"How many?" I called.

"At least a dozen."

Gandalfr gave a wry shake of his white-haired head, "Now we will pay the price for burning the fishing boats."

"But they are small."

"And they can make a barrier too. We are being channelled and soon the nine ships will close with us. Those two ships want us to avoid them and that means they are trying to send us to rip out our keel on hidden rocks. We will steer between them. There it will be a clear channel. Tell Oddr to prepare to fight."

I nodded and hurried to the waiting warriors, "Oddr, Gandalfr will sail between the two ships that block our passage. He says to prepare to fight."

He nodded at my bow, "You were wise to bring your bow, Leif. We only have slings. Until they close with us, we might as well just spit at them." He shook his head, "Brynjar take half of the men to larboard. The rest with me." He held out his arm to me, "May the Allfather be with you."

I clasped it, "And with you."

As much as I wanted to be with the warriors my place was with the navigator. I could protect him. I shouted, "Ship's boys, arm yourselves and defend, *'Ægir'*."

They chorused, "Aye, Leif."

When I reached the steering board I saw that the jarl was now following us. Our stern would be protected. The six ships following us would have to get past the jarl to reach us. The danger came from the ships to larboard. The three small ships alone were not a danger but the fishing boats had given them more of a chance. They could close with us and there were too many for us to fend off. It was, however, the two ships ahead that represented the greatest danger. There was enough space to get between them but it was their position, as Gandalfr had said, that was the real threat. They were making us go in a direction they had chosen. They had stopped for a reason and wished us to go either to the east or the west of them. If we chose the west then we risked being caught by the other ships and they were tempting us to the east and the mainland.

It was then that Dagfinn, who was at the prow, shouted, "White water astern of the steerboard ship that is waiting for us." That was the ship to the east.

Gandalfr nodded, "As I thought. They plan on making us rip out our keel on those rocks. We plough on!" He was laughing. We were in great danger but to Gandalfr this was a test of his skill as a sailor. He did not fight with a sword but he had a warrior's heart and he would fight the Franks with his ship. "Have your shield ready. If I am any judge, they will make the passage between the ships perilous."

I put my bow to the deck and took my shield from my back. I rested it against the gunwale and then took my bow and an arrow from my arrow bag. The two ships were much closer and Gandalfr was taking us to the one that lay closer to the west. He was not risking the rocks. I went to the larboard side and loosely nocked the arrow. I could see light glinting off metal. They had helmets and swords. I also saw archers and when a handful of arrows landed a length before us I knew that we would have to endure an arrow storm. Their arrows were sent into the wind and I realised that ours had the wind with them. I nocked an arrow and sent it high in the sky. The ship at which I aimed was not moving and I was aiming in the middle, close to the mast.

When there was a cry from the Frank, Gandalfr shouted, "Well done, Leif, now try for the helmsman."

I was encouraged and, nocking a second arrow, I shifted my aim to the stern. My first arrow had caused consternation and there were fewer arrows coming in our direction as shields were raised. My arrow slammed into a shield. We were now less than two lengths away and Gandalfr had aimed *'Ægir'* directly between the two boats. I heard a cry from the steerboard side, "Shields!" The second ship was now loosing arrows. Our ship was moving quickly and we were abeam the two ships. Soon we would pass through. I saw some flesh appear on the western ship and sent an arrow to slam into the careless warrior. My cheer and the cheers from the men on our larboard side were short-lived as *'Ægir'* dramatically lurched to steerboard. Had we hit something? I looked aft and saw the fletch of an arrow sticking from Gandalfr. He still held the steering board but his life blood was pumping away as he fought to steer the ship despite a mortal wound. I hurled my bow to the deck and ran back.

He was slipping down the gunwale. He had one hand on the steering board but his other held the hilt of his sword. I could not remember the last time he had drawn it. He looked up weakly and said, "Take the helm, Navigator." Even as I grabbed it, I saw the life leave his eyes as the pool of blood spread across the deck, marking forever the place where Gandalfr died. Now was not the time for mourning. The ship's fate now lay in my hands and I had to make the decisions that, until moments before, had been Gandalfr's. The Norns had spun once more.

"Oddr!"

I put the steering board over and it was not a moment too soon. We were about to hit the eastern boat. Gandalfr, even in his dying had tried to save his ship. As it was our wake caused a wave that threw three of the crew of the Frankish ship overboard. It was cold comfort to know that *'Ægir'* might have killed the man who had slain Gandalfr.

Oddr joined me and looked at Gandalfr. He knelt and closed his eyes, "He is dead, and we are in your hands, Leif Longstride."

I nodded grimly and said, "I will not let Gandalfr down."

The slight change in course had enabled the fishing boats and three ships from the mainland to close with us. Although the jarl was in more danger, the Franks seemed to become encouraged that we were hurt for they pursued us. I put the board over to take us north and west. Gandalfr had been right; this was the fastest ship afloat. Perhaps his spirit was still guiding my hand for we were soon clear of the trap. I looked astern and saw that the Franks were now closing in on the jarl. They were like dogs around a baited bull.

I made my decision quickly. "Oddr, I am going to come about and go to the aid of the jarl. Ship's boys stand by the sail."

Oddr could have commanded me to do something else but he nodded, "You are the navigator."

Brynjar ran to my bow and, picking it up, said, "I will try to account for some of them."

The drekar responded well to my touch on the board. Gandalfr had trained the boys well and the sail remained firm as we turned. Gandalfr was dead but his lessons had been well learned. Our move took the Franks by surprise. They must have thought that they had lost one prize and were closing like hunting dogs on *'Bylgja'*. The nearest Frankish ship, one of those that had sailed from Guedel did not see us as we headed towards them. It was not a warship but a tubby ship like the one Palle had sailed home. I aimed the drekar for it. We had slowed, for we did not have the wind but the ship was still moving faster than the Frank. As Brynjar sent an arrow to slam into the back of a warrior whose attention was on *'Bylgja'* I shouted, "Brace!"

I saw the terrified Franks as the prow of *'Ægir'* rose and crashed down to shatter the boat into kindling. I had caught her abeam. The effect was astounding. The other two turned to head south and as I put the steering board over we smashed into two more fishing boats. The sinking of three ships must have filled the other captains with terror and they used the wind to get out of our way. The bull they had baited had now turned and its horns were sharp. They were fleeing as quickly as they could. *'Ægir'* the giant hunted them. Even the two barrier boats hoisted sail and tried to get out of the way. I turned the drekar to take the wind and resume our course north and west. There were no ships to bar our way. Perhaps they thought we were a berserker or a bull maddened and gone wild. Whatever the reason *'Bylgja'* fought her way clear of the ships that had tried to board her and was soon sailing in our wake. Our men cheered but, to me, they were hollow cheers. Gandalfr was dead.

Brynjar and Birger came aft. They moved the body of Gandalf to the side and laid a cloak over it. I had no time to mourn for I had a ship to steer. Once we had open sea behind us, I had a couple of reefs put in the sail and *'Bylgja'* joined us. I saw that they had lost men too. There was damage from arrows and stones.

I had no one I could hand the steering board to and I had to speak while steering, "Gandalfr is dead, Jarl. I am sorry, Snorri, I was not here to defend your brother."

Snorri's voice drifted over, "The Norns have spun, Leif." He pointed to the keel, "And your courage has cost you. There are sprung strakes. We had best get back to our island camp as quickly as we can."

The jarl said, "You did well, and your skill saved this ship and crew. Follow in our wake and we will head back to the camp. There we will bury Gandalfr the Navigator."

Epilogue

The crushing of the three Frankish ships had come at a price. The saving of the jarl's drekar had sprung strakes and we had to bail all the way back to the island. We beached her and then attended to Gandalfr. We needed to honour the great man. We dug a deep grave and laid his body at the bottom with his hands on his sword. He had no shield but we placed his helmet by his head. We covered his body with a cloak and then stones from the beach upon the cloak. It would tie the navigator to the sea. With his body buried deeply, we said goodbye to him.

Snorri, the jarl and I were the last to leave the grave. Both men knew that I blamed myself for not being there to protect him with my shield. The jarl put his arm around me as Snorri said, "It was the Norns, Leif. Gandalfr wanted you to use your bow and your arrows were well sent. You cannot look ahead and looking back only shows the mistakes that were made. We are men and men make mistakes. This was meant to be. My brother said that you were a better navigator than either your father or me." He nodded, "He is right. If you had been ready earlier then it would have been you who sailed, *'Bylgja'*."

The jarl nodded, "And now you are the navigator of *'Ægir'*."

"But I am a warrior." I shook my head, "When we get home, I would spend time with my wife and family. I may choose not to raid."

The jarl sighed, "Sometimes, Leif Longstride, those decisions are not made by us but by others. We have a ship to repair. Until *'Ægir'* is seaworthy we are vulnerable. Tomorrow we will sail to the mainland and find the stand of pines that Gandalfr so admired when we first saw them. We will return here with the roots and make pine tar. You will need to haul her from the sea. Can you do that?"

I smiled, "I will have to."

When they left, I had our crew take down the mast and empty the hold. We found all the shaping axes and tools that Gandalfr had placed in a chest. The chest was marked with his rune. I would see that they went to Snorri when we had used them. We would need many of them for we had much damage. The deck was placed high above the waterline. I decided that we would take the opportunity of having her out of the water to use pine tar on the decks and the inside of the keel. It would not hurt. While we waited for the **'*Bylgja*'** to return we used the shaping axes to smooth off the worst of the damage from the prow. There was less than I had expected for the drekar had been well built. We had to replace a piece of wood that was badly damaged for we had to shape and then fit the new wood so that the joint could barely be seen. At the prow, the giant Ægir, had a new scar but we left it there. I would simply add the juice of elderberries and paint it with pine tar. It would look like a scar carved by a shipwright. We had enough trenails for us to hammer back the sprung strakes. Luckily none needed to be replaced. There was damage on the gunwale but that was the easiest to repair. We also built the ovens that would be needed to make the pine tar. This was normally a rushed job but, with the ship beached and **'*Bylgja*'** not yet returned, we had time to place it where we needed it, close to the keel. We lined the channel with sand, pebbles and rocks. We used flat ones for the tops and sides to guide the tar into the containers we would use. We used some pots we had captured from the Franks and emptied them as receptacles for the pine tar. When **'*Bylgja*'** returned, everyone was needed to build the fires and load the roots into the three ovens.

    Once that was done it was a case of waiting for the tar to seep from the ovens. In my case it was also a time of brooding as I went over the fight in my mind. Even when I slept it was still there and made me wake. Joseph was astute and recognised that my sudden wakings and wild eyes came as a result of the death of Gandalfr. After searching for herbs and roots on the island he made potions to help me sleep. When I woke the nightmare returned as I looked at the drekar and the tools arrayed on the beach. They were Gandalfr's and a reminder that he was gone. I threw myself into work and as soon as the first of the pungent pine tar was ready, I was there to use the brushes made from squirrel's tails to cover the keel. Although we began where the strakes had sprung, I would not waste one brushful of the tar. We used every drop of the precious pine tar. Of course, one problem was that we could not leave until the tar dried completely and if the Franks had attacked then we would have been trapped. They did not and, at the end of Gormánuður, we hauled the ship back to the water. *'Bylgja'* helped. Ropes were attached to the older drekar and while we used logs beneath her keel she was pulled back to the sea. When the ship floated, I checked the hull for leaks and I found that there were none. We pulled the ship inshore and fitted the decks and mast. We would be ready to sail when the jarl decided. *'Ægir'* was now healed. We could go home.

Most of the two crews wanted to go home. Gandalfr's death was seen as bad luck. The jarl procrastinated and found tasks to do that would enable a safe voyage home. On the second day of Ýlir, we slaughtered the young pigs and had a fine feast. Songs were sung and Gandalfr's name resounded. Songs were sung but I found them painful for they reminded me of the man who was gone forever. Snorri seemed to be able to hear it without becoming upset. I wanted to tear myself away and hide. It was Snorri and Joseph who comforted me and used words to bring me from my pit of melancholy.

It was the start of Ýlir when Lord Arne's ship, *'Nidhogg'* hove into view. I saw Bjarni at the stern, directing the jarl's cousin, but I could not see Mikkel. It was the day after the feast that *'Nidhogg'* arrived. Lord Arne brought more men and with it a sentence of an even longer time spent in this land of riches and, for me, painful memories. I should have sailed home with Mikkel.

The End

Glossary

Allionis - Châtelaillon
Bóndi - Freemen who were allowed to use weapons
Bordèu - Bordeaux
Blót - a Norse sacrifice
Bjórr - Beaver
Frilla - a concubine
Guedel - Belle Île
Hnefatafl - Viking board games. Skáktafl is chess
Herkumbl - a piece of metal fixed to a helmet to identify the allegiance of the warrior
Hlad - a ribbon or headband of leather tied around the hair
Luedes - lord
Liger - River Loire
Nervouster - Île de Noirmoutier,
Østersjøen - The Baltic Sea
Sanctus Nazarius de Sinuario - St Nazaire
Sequana - River Seine
Sild - Norse for herring
Skjaldborg - Shield wall
Skrei - Norwegian cod
Volva - a Norse witch, a spinner of spells (quite literally)

Norse Calendar

Gormánuður - October 14th – November 13th
Ýlir - November 14th – December 13th
Mörsugur - December 14th – January 12th
Þorri - January 13th – February 11th
Gói - February 12th – March 13th
Einmánuður - March 14th – April 13th
Harpa - April 14th – May 13th
Skerpla - May 14th – June 12th
Sólmánuður - June 13th – July 12th
Heyannir - July 13th – August 14th
Tvímánuður - August 15th – September 14th
Haustmánuður - September 15th - October 13th

Days of the week

Sunnudagr – Sunday
Mánadagr – Monday
Tysdagr – Tuesday

Óðinsdagr - Wednesday
þórsdagr – Thursday
Frjádagr – Friday
Laugardagr – Saturday

Canonical Hours

- Matins (nighttime)
- Lauds (early morning)
- Prime (first hour of daylight)
- Terce (third hour)
- Sext (noon)
- Nones (ninth hour)
- Vespers (sunset evening)
- Compline (end of the day)

Historical Background

There is a school of thought that argues the attack on Lindisfarne and the other religious houses was not just prompted by the love of silver and gold but as retribution for Charlemagne destroying the pagan holy places in Pomerania, Saxony and Denmark. It makes sense for how would the Norsemen who raided Lindisfarne know how rich they were? It could have been that the land in Norway and Sweden did not support the number of people who wished to live there. Whatever the reason the fact remains that in the late eighth and early ninth century seafarers from Norway, Sweden, Denmark and Frisia began to raid the east coast of England. They took religious artefacts, gold and silver as well as slaves. Apart from the odd Romano-Saxon shore fort, there was nothing to stop them. Din Guardi or Bebbeanburgh and then Bamburgh as it came to be known was just a rocky outcrop with a wooden wall, mead hall and harbour. It was not a castle with a rapid response force of horsemen to deter the raiders. The result was that the people we now refer to as Vikings had no reason to stop their plundering. It was highly profitable, and the greatest danger came not from the Saxons and their warriors but from the sea. For the Norsemen, it was a mighty undertaking.

Nidhogg (roughly translated to The Corpse Gnawer or Corpse Sucker) is the dragon said to live under the great tree Yggdrasill. This tree nourishes all life in the Norse worlds, and the dark dragon Nidhogg munches on its roots in the meantime, feeding from both the tree and the corpses that make their way down there.

Noirmoutier was the location of an early Viking raid when raiders attacked the monastery of Saint Philibert of Jumièges that same year. The Vikings established a permanent base on the island around 824, from which they could control southeast Brittany by the 840s.

The island where they repair the drekar is Burhou north of Alderney. It was, from ancient times, a place of refuge for fishermen and somewhere they could hunt rabbits.

The monasteries at this time were largely built of wood. The stone ones that remain to this day were begun after the time of the Normans and when the Franks became the French.

The coastline of Gascony, Anjou and Aquitaine was not as populated then as now. The towers that I mention are still visible in Italy and Southern France but there were slave traders who attacked little isolated villages. Eventually they would be repopulated, but this was a dark time for any who lived close to a coast or a river. The Vikings were not the only ones who raided.

Noirmoutier was an island at this time. Nowadays a road connects it to the land and the island is bigger now that it once was.

Griff Hosker
July 2024

Books used
Charlemagne – Roger Collins
The Age of Charlemagne – Nicolle and McBride
Norse Myths and Legends – Schorn
Vikings Life and Legend – British Museum
Saxon, Viking and Norman – Wise and Embleton
The Vikings – Heath and McBride
Viking Hersir – Harrison and Embleton

Other books by Griff Hosker

If you enjoyed reading this book, then why not read another one by the author?

Ancient History

The Sword of Cartimandua Series
(Germania and Britannia 50 A.D. – 128 A.D.)
Ulpius Felix- Roman Warrior (prequel)
The Sword of Cartimandua
The Horse Warriors
Invasion Caledonia
Roman Retreat
Revolt of the Red Witch
Druid's Gold
Trajan's Hunters
The Last Frontier
Hero of Rome
Roman Hawk
Roman Treachery
Roman Wall
Roman Courage

The Wolf Brethren series
(Britain in the late 6th Century)
Saxon Dawn
Saxon Revenge
Saxon England
Saxon Blood
Saxon Slayer
Saxon Slaughter
Saxon Bane
Saxon Fall: Rise of the Warlord

Norse Warrior

Saxon Throne
Saxon Sword

Medieval History

The Dragon Heart Series
Viking Slave *
Viking Warrior *
Viking Jarl *
Viking Kingdom *
Viking Wolf *
Viking War*
Viking Sword
Viking Wrath
Viking Raid
Viking Legend
Viking Vengeance
Viking Dragon
Viking Treasure
Viking Enemy
Viking Witch
Viking Blood
Viking Weregeld
Viking Storm
Viking Warband
Viking Shadow
Viking Legacy
Viking Clan
Viking Bravery

Norseman
Norse Warrior

The Norman Genesis Series
Hrolf the Viking *

253

Norse Warrior

Horseman *
The Battle for a Home *
Revenge of the Franks *
The Land of the Northmen
Ragnvald Hrolfsson
Brothers in Blood
Lord of Rouen
Drekar in the Seine
Duke of Normandy
The Duke and the King

Danelaw
(England and Denmark in the 11th Century)
Dragon Sword *
Oathsword *
Bloodsword *
Danish Sword*
The Sword of Cnut*

New World Series
Blood on the Blade *
Across the Seas *
The Savage Wilderness *
The Bear and the Wolf *
Erik The Navigator *
Erik's Clan *
The Last Viking*

The Vengeance Trail *

The Conquest Series
(Normandy and England 1050-1100)
Hastings*
Conquest*

The Aelfraed Series

Norse Warrior

(Britain and Byzantium 1050 A.D. - 1085 A.D.)
Housecarl *
Outlaw *
Varangian *

The Reconquista Chronicles
Castilian Knight *
El Campeador *
The Lord of Valencia *

The Anarchy Series England
1120-1180
English Knight *
Knight of the Empress *
Northern Knight *
Baron of the North *
Earl *
King Henry's Champion *
The King is Dead *
Warlord of the North*
Enemy at the Gate*
The Fallen Crown*
Warlord's War*
Kingmaker*
Henry II
Crusader
The Welsh Marches
Irish War
Poisonous Plots
The Princes' Revolt
Earl Marshal
The Perfect Knight

Border Knight
1182-1300
Sword for Hire *

255

Norse Warrior

Return of the Knight *
Baron's War *
Magna Carta *
Welsh Wars *
Henry III *
The Bloody Border *
Baron's Crusade*
Sentinel of the North*
War in the West*
Debt of Honour
The Blood of the Warlord
The Fettered King
de Montfort's Crown
Ripples of Rebellion

Sir John Hawkwood Series
France and Italy 1339- 1387
Crécy: The Age of the Archer *
Man At Arms *
The White Company *
Leader of Men *
Tuscan Warlord *
Condottiere*
Legacy

Lord Edward's Archer
Lord Edward's Archer *
King in Waiting *
An Archer's Crusade *
Targets of Treachery *
The Great Cause *
Wallace's War *
The Hunt*
The Prince and the Archer

Struggle for a Crown

Norse Warrior

1360- 1485
Blood on the Crown *
To Murder a King *
The Throne *
King Henry IV *
The Road to Agincourt *
St Crispin's Day *
The Battle for France *
The Last Knight *
Queen's Knight *
The Knight's Tale

Tales from the Sword I
(Short stories from the Medieval period)

Tudor Warrior series
England and Scotland in the late 15th and early 16th century
Tudor Warrior *
Tudor Spy *
Flodden*

Conquistador
England and America in the 16th Century
Conquistador *
The English Adventurer *

English Mercenary
The 30 Years War and the English Civil War
Horse and Pistol*

Modern History

The Napoleonic Horseman Series
Chasseur à Cheval
Napoleon's Guard
British Light Dragoon

257

Norse Warrior

Soldier Spy
1808: The Road to Coruña
Talavera
The Lines of Torres Vedras
Bloody Badajoz
The Road to France
Waterloo

The Lucky Jack American Civil War series
Rebel Raiders
Confederate Rangers
The Road to Gettysburg

Soldier of the Queen series
Soldier of the Queen*
Redcoat's Rifle*
Omdurman*
Desert War

The British Ace Series
1914
1915 Fokker Scourge
1916 Angels over the Somme
1917 Eagles Fall
1918 We will remember them
From Arctic Snow to Desert Sand
Wings over Persia

Combined Operations series
1940-1951

Commando *
Raider *
Behind Enemy Lines
Dieppe
Toehold in Europe

258

Norse Warrior

Sword Beach
Breakout
The Battle for Antwerp
King Tiger
Beyond the Rhine
Korea
Korean Winter

Tales from the Sword II
(Short stories from the Modern period)

Books marked thus *, are also available in the audio format.
For more information on all of the books then please visit the author's website at www.griffhosker.com where there is a link to contact him or visit his Facebook page: GriffHosker at Sword Books or follow him on Twitter: @HoskerGriff or Sword (@swordbooksltd)
If you wish to be on the mailing list then contact the author through his website.